A
MADE IN TEXAS

A MATCH MADE IN TEXAS

A NOVELLA COLLECTION

A Cowboy Unmatched
✳ BY KAREN WITEMEYER ✳

An Unforeseen Match
✳ BY REGINA JENNINGS ✳

No Match for Love
✳ BY CAROL COX ✳

Meeting Her Match
✳ BY MARY CONNEALY ✳

BETHANYHOUSE

a division of Baker Publishing Group
Minneapolis, Minnesota

A Cowboy Unmatched © 2014 by Karen Witemeyer
An Unforeseen Match © 2014 by Regina Jennings
No Match for Love © 2014 by Carol Cox
Meeting Her Match © 2014 by Mary Connealy

Published by Bethany House Publishers
11400 Hampshire Avenue South
Bloomington, Minnesota 55438
www.bethanyhouse.com

Bethany House Publishers is a division of
Baker Publishing Group, Grand Rapids, Michigan

Printed in the United States of America

Library of Congress Cataloging-in-Publication Data
A match made in Texas : a novella collection / Karen Witemeyer, Mary
Connealy, Regina Jennings, Carol Cox.
    pages cm
    ISBN 978-0-7642-1176-8 (pbk.)
    1. Love stories, American. 2. Western stories. I. Witemeyer, Karen. Cowboy
unmatched. II. Jennings, Regina (Regina Lea). Unforeseen match. III. Cox,
Carol. No match for love. IV. Connealy, Mary. Meeting her match.
PS648.L6M38 2014
813'.0850806—dc23   2013032379

Scripture quotations are from the King James Version of the Bible.

Karen Witemeyer, Regina Jennings, and Carol Cox represented by Books & Such Literary Agency. Mary Connealy represented by Natasha Kern Literary Agency.

Cover design by Dan Thornberg, Design Source Creative Services

13 14 15 16 17 18 19   7 6 5 4 3 2 1

Contents

A Cowboy
Unmatched

Karen Witemeyer

✳ Chapter 1 ✳

TEXAS PANHANDLE
SUMMER 1893

Neill Archer sighed and slouched a bit in the saddle when he caught his first glimpse of Dry Gulch. Another dusty, dirt-colored town in the middle of nowhere. And to think when he first left his family's ranch two years ago, he'd hungered for wide-open spaces. What he wouldn't give to be hemmed in by those big, beautiful Archer pines right about now. But he hadn't earned his right to return to them. Not yet.

Straightening his spine, he clicked his tongue and urged his sturdy roan forward. A new town—no matter how dusty—meant new opportunities and the possibility of work. He'd left home with a goal, and he'd not falter in his pursuit of it—not when he was so close to his target.

The deep *bong* of a church bell reverberated through the crisp morning air, drawing Neill down Dry Gulch's main street. Townsfolk trudged along boardwalks on either side of him, past a general store, a bank, and even a diner. Maybe Dry Gulch had more to offer than he'd first thought.

A wagon, its bed overflowing with a passel of young'uns

spit shined and Sunday ready, rolled ahead of him. The oldest girl smiled shyly up at him as he came alongside. Neill tipped his hat in response, which set the boys to hootin' and hollerin' and the younger girls to gigglin'. The poor gal turned apple red and tried to hide beneath the brim of her bonnet. Yet she managed a bit of well-aimed retribution when the toe of her shoe collided rather squarely with the length of the loudest boy's thigh.

Neill hid his grin and nudged Mo into a trot, taking him past the wagon before the squabble escalated to a level that required parental interference. He and his brothers used to tease and tussle like that, too. Of course, there hadn't been any parents to interfere, so there'd been more than one occasion when a good-natured wrestling match spiraled into a fistfight. But even in those cases, the family bond never wavered. They were brothers—brothers who would stand together no matter what trouble came calling.

He missed that security, the assurance that someone always had his back. But then, that was part of the reason he'd left. He needed to prove to himself, and to his brothers, that he was his own man, able to make his way in the world without them breaking everything in for him first.

Crossing into the churchyard, Neill guided Mo over to where the other horses stood tethered near some cedar shrubs, nibbling at the few tufts of grass that thrust up from the hard-packed earth. He dismounted, pulled his Bible from his saddlebag, and gave Mo a fond pat on the neck before striding toward the church steps.

It was still early, so people were milling around outside, visiting with friends and neighbors while children ran circles around the periphery, releasing their excess energy before they were confined to a pew. Neill inserted himself among a group of men and quickly made an introduction.

"Neill Archer," he said, offering each man his hand in turn. "Fine town you got here. Gives a man hope he might find work with so many folks about."

A portly gentleman in a fine gray suit eyed him speculatively, though not unkindly. "What kind of work you looking for, son?"

Son? Neill bit back his distaste for the term. *Son, kid, boy*—he'd been defined by those terms all his life. He was twenty-eight years old, for crying out loud. Shouldn't he have outgrown such monikers by now?

But getting riled wouldn't help him find work, so Neill shrugged off his pique and addressed the man who'd offered the question. "I've done a bit of everything, really. Ranch hand, cattle drover . . . I've laid track for the railroad, put up windmills, built barns, repaired roofs, dug wells."

The sound of an indrawn breath behind him drew Neill's head around. A willowy blond woman jerked her head away the instant his gaze landed on her, but he'd caught a glimpse of interest lurking in her light blue eyes before she'd shuttered them.

He turned back to the men and grinned. "I'm open to any honest labor with a decent wage attached."

The men returned his grin with genuine warmth and nods of understanding.

"Old man Johnson might need some help around his place," one of the men suggested. "His gout's been acting up, and he ain't been able to finish fencin' off that back pasture like he wanted."

Neill's spirits lifted, only to plummet when a third man

shook his head. "Naw. His boys rode in from Amarillo last week and finished stringing the wire. Good boys, Thomas and Grant. Wish mine helped out half as much around our homestead."

"They got their own farms to tend, Yancy. You know that. You can't expect them to work both your spread and their own."

Apparently Yancy could, and that was all it took to veer the conversation off course. Neill held his tongue while the men debated the level of involvement sons owed their fathers. Maybe he'd have a chance to bring the issue up again later. Besides, the parson had started waving people into the building.

As he passed through the doorway into the sanctuary, he scanned the crowd for the woman he'd seen outside. Perhaps *she* knew of some work in the area. He spotted a woman with pale blond hair and a dress that looked vaguely familiar, though he couldn't have said for sure that it was the same one he'd seen outside. She was already seated in a pew, so all he could see were her shoulders and the back of her head, but he decided it wouldn't hurt to look for a place to sit in her vicinity. He spotted a vacant seat in the row in front of her, so he slipped into it and turned to introduce himself—only to find her immersed in a whispered conversation with the child seated next to her. Not wanting to intrude, Neill twisted to face the front and bit back an impatient sigh. He'd just have to wait until worship concluded to speak to her.

Except when worship concluded, she'd disappeared again.

It was probably his fault he'd missed her. Feeling a tug on his heart, he had kept his head bowed for an extra moment or two after the preacher's *amen* rang through the church.

He'd add a few thoughts of his own to the prayer before rising—requests for patience and greater trust in the Lord's provision. He guessed he shouldn't be surprised then to find himself in particular need of those qualities when his one hope for an employment lead had vanished.

Neill shook his head and smiled at the irony. *Well, Lord, the Good Book says you know what we need before we ask. Guess I just proved that, huh?*

He visited a bit with the people around him, then reached for the Bible he'd left sitting on the pew. Odd. He didn't recall that piece of paper protruding from the pages. He pulled it free and turned it over to find a message written in an elegant hand.

> *Roofer needed to repair widow's home. Salary to be paid half up front to cover supplies, half when job is completed. Only men of upstanding character need apply.*
>
> *Interested parties should meet at the schoolhouse at 7:00 p.m. Monday evening for more details.*

Neill jerked his head up and scoured the chapel for anyone who might have left the note. Had it been the mysterious vanishing woman? The note's script certainly appeared feminine. And refined. But she was nowhere in sight.

He turned back to the scrap of paper in his hand. It was worded like a newspaper ad. Perhaps whoever had placed the ad in the paper had heard that he was looking for work and stuck the original copy in his Bible to make sure he saw it. Or maybe God's provision moved faster than he'd anticipated.

Neill grinned as he stuffed the note into his coat pocket. He needed to see about a hotel room for the night. He had a job interview tomorrow.

———•———•———

A dim light was flickering inside the schoolhouse when Neill arrived promptly at seven o'clock the following night. At the door, he pulled off his hat and took a minute to smooth his hair before entering. The door swung in easily at his push, the hinges well oiled. But when he crossed the threshold, he frowned.

The place was empty.

Where were the other applicants? Neill's gaze swept over the empty student desks to the front of the room, where a lantern sat on a table, its muted glow casting shadows on the floor and into the corners. Had the man doing the hiring been called away unexpectedly?

Neill took a tentative step down the deserted aisle. Should he wait? See if the man returned? Setting his hat atop one of the student desks, Neill glanced back out the door standing open behind him. He saw no one. He half expected some kid to slam the door shut and lock him in, then run off laughing with a wild tale to tell his friends about the prank he played on the stranger.

But that wouldn't fit with the handwriting on the note. It had been anything but juvenile.

He took out his watch and checked the time: 7:05. Might as well wait. Someone had left that lantern, after all. The student desks were too small for his long, lanky frame, so he strode to the front of the room, thinking to borrow the teacher's chair. That's when he saw the envelope.

It lay on the table, a few inches in front of the lantern. His name, slightly misspelled—people often left off the second *l* in *Neill* when they didn't know him—was scrawled across the front. He picked it up and glanced inside. A twenty-dollar banknote and directions to the home of a widow Danvers.

Who would leave twenty dollars just lying around like this? Anyone could simply take it and leave the widow high and dry. Or wet, he supposed, since the woman needed a new roof.

Neill had never known his mother, but his best friend's mother had filled that role for him later in life, not caring a whit that his skin was white where Myra's was brown. What if *she* were in the widow Danvers's position? Aged and frail, no husband or sons to take care of her? Neill would go to the ends of the earth to see she was provided for. Apparently this Danvers woman had no menfolk around to fill that need.

Well, the envelope was addressed to him, which meant the widow and her leaky roof were his responsibility now. And Archers never shirked their responsibilities. Neill slipped the envelope into a pocket in the lining of his coat and turned down the wick of the lantern until it sputtered and went out.

Whoever had put this little scheme in motion had hand-picked him for the job, and he aimed to see it through.

✳ Chapter 2 ✳

Neill took the third turnoff as instructed and guided the rented team over a narrow bridge that spanned one of the waterless gullies that must have inspired the town's name. Spotting the widow Danvers's windmill, Neill flicked the reins over the horses' backs and urged them to a quicker pace. Harness jangled and wheels creaked, adding harmony to the rhythmic clacking of the windmill's spinning blades as the house came into view.

Shack might be a better term. The weathered building listed to one side, like a sapling buffeted by constant wind. The thing didn't need a new roof. It needed to be torn down and completely rebuilt.

Too bad there weren't any trees around. He might have been able to shore the thing up a bit with some chinked logs, but all his wagon carried by way of supplies were shingles, a keg of barbed nails, a few rolls of roofing felt, cement paste, and a handful of tools. Somehow he doubted he'd be able to do much with a hammer, jackknife, and cement brush. Maybe the late Mr. Danvers had some tools or scrap lumber Neill could put to use. He hated to think of some frail gray-haired lady putting her foot through a rotted step or having part of a wall collapse on her. He wouldn't mind spending an extra day or two making sure the place was habitable before he left.

Neill pulled the wagon to a halt and set the brake. "Hello, in the house!" he called as he climbed down from the bench. "I'm here to fix your roof."

The door inched open far enough to allow the twin barrels of a shotgun to emerge through the crack.

"I don't know who you are, stranger," a feminine voice rang out, "but I made no arrangements for any roofing to be done. I'll thank you to get back in your wagon and leave the way you came."

Neill stilled. Mrs. Danvers sure held that gun with a steady grip for a widow lady. And that voice sounded none too frail, either. Neill raised his hands, the leather work gloves itching against his empty palms. He took one step back toward the wagon—and the rifle waiting beneath the driver's seat.

"I was hired by someone in town, ma'am," he explained. "They paid up front for the supplies and gave me instructions on how to get to your place. Unless you're not Widow Danvers."

The implied question hung in the air for several tense heartbeats. Finally, the shotgun lowered and the door opened wide enough to give the widow room to step through.

"I'm Clara Danvers."

Three things registered in Neill's mind simultaneously. The widow Danvers wasn't old. She wasn't frail. And she sure as shootin' hadn't been a widow very long.

◆━━━◆━━━◆

Clara maintained her grip on Matthew's old shotgun while she took the stranger's measure. Tall, lanky, a friendly enough smile. The few lines he sported around his eyes from years of squinting against the sun were the only indication of his age. Well, that and the way his stance radiated readiness. This was a man who'd seen trouble and had learned to be wary. Strong of spirit as well as body. But could he be trusted? What if her father-in-law had hired a new hand? It would be just like Mack Danvers to send the man to prod her into agreeing to his demands.

Her hand instinctively lifted to cradle her rounded belly. She'd die before she gave up her child.

Swinging the shotgun up in front of her, Clara caught the barrels in her free hand. She didn't take aim at the stranger, simply held the weapon across her body, letting him know she wasn't a helpless female. "You tell Mack Danvers that my answer hasn't changed since the last time he visited. I'll not be taking him up on his offer. Now, be on your way."

The stranger cocked his head, furrows etching his brow. "I don't know any Mack Danvers, ma'am. A lady in town wrote out instructions on how to find your place and gave me funds to purchase supplies. Here, I'll show you." He reached inside his coat.

Clara tensed and had both barrels pointed at his gut faster than he could blink. "Keep your hands where I can see 'em, mister."

He eased his hand back out. "I don't mean you any harm, Mrs. Danvers. Tell you what. Why don't I step a few paces over here"—he nodded toward an area an equal distance from the wagon and the house—"and you can come take a look at what's in the wagon. See the roofing supplies for yourself. Then if you want to see the note, I'll give that to you, as well."

Clara hesitated. It could be some kind of trick. Yet the man had no weapon on him that she could discern. If she kept an eye on him, she should be able to check out his story safely enough. She nodded her agreement.

With hands lifted in the air, the man took four long strides away from the wagon. Clara adjusted her position as he moved, keeping the shotgun trained on him until she reached the porch steps. Her overlarge belly made navigating the three stairs awkward since she couldn't grasp the railing for support, but she took her time and made it to the ground without incident.

Once at the wagon, she flashed a quick glance into the bed. Roofing supplies. Just like he'd said.

"Who'd you say hired you?" Her grip on the shotgun relaxed. She lowered the weapon, then reached around with her left hand to rub at the sore spot on her lower back. Tension was taking its toll.

"I don't rightly know, ma'am." The stranger made no attempt to approach her, and she found her suspicions waning despite his lack of clear answers. "I rode into Dry Gulch on Sunday and attended worship. I let it be known that I was looking for work, and after services, I found a note regarding a roofing job stuck in my Bible. I followed the instructions, and the next evening found an envelope with your name and directions inside, along with enough funds to buy supplies and the promise of further payment when the job is complete." His shoulders lifted in a shrug. "I think your benefactor wants to remain anonymous."

Clara leaned against the side of the wagon, hope struggling to find purchase in her battered heart. For the last month she'd been slaving over the worthless pile of sticks her wastrel of a husband had left her, trying to make it safe for her baby. She'd patched cracks with sod to keep the wind and vermin out, repaired the broken step with a scrap from the busted barn door, and scoured the place from top to bottom. Twice.

If she'd learned nothing else over her twenty years of life, she'd learned that a woman carrying Comanche blood in her veins couldn't depend on neighbors to lend a helping hand. Or husbands. Or men who were supposed to be family.

So she tended to things herself. But the one thing she couldn't fix on her own was a leaky roof. She'd only endanger her child if she tried.

Did you send this man, Lord? Dared she believe it was even a possibility? Heaven knew she'd prayed often enough for protection for her babe, yet she was afraid to hope that God might actually be answering. He hadn't protected her parents from the smallpox outbreak that took their lives the summer she turned eighteen, after all. Nor had He guarded her husband from the bullet that ended his career as the worst card player in the Red River Valley.

Yet a man she'd never met now stood on her property with a wagonload of roofing supplies and just enough swagger to convince her he knew how to use them. Who else could have orchestrated such a scenario?

She couldn't send him away. Not when the welfare of her child hung in the balance. She needed that roof.

"Let me see the note." Clara marched toward the stranger with her palm outstretched. Well, *marched* might be too grand a description. *Waddled* was probably closer to the truth with as ungainly as she'd become over the last month. But she refused to let this man intimidate her. She was in charge of this interview, and he would dance to her tune or leave.

The stranger met her halfway and handed over the paper for her inspection. No smugness lurked in his approach. Only concern and caution, as if she were a high-strung mare he feared spooking with sudden movements. And wasn't *that* a flattering comparison.

She snatched the paper from his hand and examined the writing. Definitely not the slashing strokes Mack Danvers preferred. The stranger was right. It looked feminine. And the only woman on the Circle D was the housekeeper. Clara had seen Ethel's handwriting on the supply lists that Matthew used to bring into her father's trading post before they'd started courting and could safely rule her out. Ethel's chicken scratch was barely legible.

Handing the paper back to the stranger, she scrutinized his face. Strong jaw. Direct gaze. None of the shiftiness she'd come to recognize in her husband nor the condescension or scorn she detected when her father-in-law deigned to look at her. No, this man's eyes were warm and honest. Kind. And they had lovely green flecks that added a sparkle to the brown depths.

Clara took a step back. No need to look *that* close. He was a workman, nothing else.

So why did she suddenly have the urge to make sure her hair was in place?

Bah! It wasn't like he would see anything beyond her belly, anyway. A belly that was fixing to burst with another man's child. For all she knew, he had a wife back home somewhere. She was a job to him. And that was the way she wanted it. Three or four days and he'd be gone.

"I guess if you're going to be repairing my roof," she

said with a defiant lift of her chin, "you might as well tell me your name."

"Neill Archer, ma'am." He touched the brim of his hat and bowed slightly in acknowledgment. But it was his boyish half smile that did her in.

Her heart did a foolish little flip in her chest. The reaction scared her so badly, she started backing toward the house.

"Go ahead and unload your supplies." She waved a hand toward the wagon, hoping he wouldn't notice the trembling in her fingers.

Distance. She needed distance. She was no naïve girl anymore, ready to swoon at a handsome man's smile or charming flattery. She'd been down that road and had no plans for a return trip. The faster Mr. Neill Archer finished this job and left, the better.

"There's a ladder in the barn," she added once she'd reached the porch and had a better grip on her senses. "Not sure what kind of shape it's in, but you're welcome to use whatever you find."

He nodded. "I'll need to take the rig back to the livery in town after I unload, but I should be able to get a start on things before dark. That is, if you don't mind me spreadin' a bedroll in your barn. I could stay in town if you'd prefer."

"No. The barn's fine." He'd lose hours of work time if he had to ride in and out of town every day. Better to get this over with as quickly as possible. "I'll have supper ready for you when you get back."

That crooked grin reappeared, but she steeled herself against it. Neill Archer was a temporary necessity. For her baby's sake. That was all. She'd not allow herself to get distracted.

✳ Chapter 3 ✳

The woman was a distraction of the worst order. He couldn't get her out of his head. Neill tightened his knees and urged Mo to a canter after leaving Dry Gulch and the rented wagon behind. The speed felt good but did little to banish Clara Danvers's image from his mind.

The woman reminded him of an Indian princess reigning over her pathetic shambles of a house as if it were a rich tribal hunting ground. She'd been dressed in the same trappings as any other woman, calico from chin to toe, black hair piled atop her head in a tidy bun. No doeskin fringe. No braids. Yet her dusky skin and fierce pride transformed her into an exotic beauty that captured his imagination like no woman ever had.

Even with her hugely pregnant belly.

A grin tugged at Neill's lips as he slowed Mo to a trot and turned him toward the bridge. When she'd lumbered down from the porch earlier, he'd nearly rushed forward to help her, shotgun be hanged. But her stoic determination kept him rooted where he stood. Clara Danvers was no fragile flower. She was a coyote who'd learned to scrape and scavenge and protect what was hers. No mere steps could fell her.

Neill's smile faded as visions of Clara's foot breaking through a rotted step dispelled any romantic notion that the woman's pride alone could keep her safe. Perhaps he'd better check the soundness of the steps and railing before he started work on the roof.

As he rode into her yard, he could feel Clara—he couldn't think of her as the widow Danvers any longer—eyeing him. He waved at her through the kitchen window, then dismounted and led Mo to the barn. In the time it took him to rub down his horse and do a cursory hunt for ladder and tools, Neill had worked himself into a right fine lather.

If the late Mr. Danvers hadn't already been dead, Neill would have slapped some sense into the lazy no-account. Daylight shone through countless holes in the rotted siding, doors hung busted on their hinges, rust coated the water troughs, and he'd counted at least eight mice nests. No telling how many creatures made their homes in the darker regions beneath the loft. Even if the man had died the night he conceived his child, the place couldn't have deteriorated this fast. It had to have been a run-down mess before the fella kicked off, leaving his wife to pick up the pieces.

Which, of course, she had. Neill ran a hand over the half wall that separated the front two stalls from the rest of the barn. The first stall housed the milk cow that stood munching her hay contentedly, as if blissfully unaware of the ruin around her. The second was where he had stashed his belongings and unsaddled Mo before turning him loose in the corral with the only other stock he'd yet to see on the place, a sturdy little gray mare that immediately set to bucking when Mo entered her territory. Much like her mistress had done with him earlier.

Both stalls were pristine. Fresh straw covered the floor, cracks in the outer walls had been filled with some kind of mud mixture as a barrier to the elements, and clean water buckets, free of algae and bugs, stood cheerfully waiting to be of use. Clara had done all she could to care for her animals. But when was the last time someone had taken care of *her*?

⸻ ◆ ⸻

Clara inspected her table with a critical eye. It had been a long time since she'd fed a man. Matthew had been gone for six months—not that he'd ever graced her table as often as the ones in Dry Gulch's saloon. Still, she couldn't help worrying about whether or not she'd made enough. Fresh meat was in short supply. Her advanced pregnancy didn't lend itself to setting snares, and what chickens she had left were needed for eggs. Thankfully, her cellar had a good supply of vegetables and last year's canned goods, so she'd been able to put together a hearty corn chowder, throwing in extra potatoes for good measure.

She nibbled on her bottom lip as she surveyed the towel-covered basket in the center of the table. Would one pan of biscuits keep a hungry man satisfied? It would have to, she decided. There was no time to bake another. Clara wiped her damp hands on her apron before reaching for the ties at her back. She hoped the simple meal would be to his liking.

Clara tugged off her apron and tossed it over the back

of a chair. She'd soak some beans tonight and make her mother's molasses baked bean recipe tomorrow. It had been her father's favorite. Tickled the tongue and stuck to the ribs, he'd always said.

Neill Archer would need something to stick to his ribs if he kept working at the pace he'd set. He'd been hammering and sawing nonstop since the moment he returned from town, all without setting foot on her roof. Her porch sported three new steps, though, and a railing that no longer wobbled when she grabbed hold. She'd tested it herself when he went to the pump to wash. His workmanship proved sturdy and strong, putting her feeble patching attempts to shame. Though why he felt the need to fix her porch steps when he was hired to repair her roof, she couldn't imagine. No one was paying him for that.

A knock sounded on her back door, breaking her free from her musing.

"Come in, Mr. Archer." She lifted a hand to her hair, then caught herself and immediately brought it back down.

Bootheels clicked softly against the floorboards behind her. "Smells mighty good in here, ma'am."

She turned to find Neill Archer hesitating several feet away. He held his hat before him, plucking at the crown as if uncertain of his welcome. And no wonder. She had yet to converse with him without a gun in her hand.

Clara pulled out Matthew's chair for him. "Have a seat. Please."

He accepted her offer and sat down, hanging his hat on the spindled back of the vacant chair next to him. She dished up his chowder before slipping into her own chair, then paused.

"Would you offer grace?" She ducked her head. What

had prompted her to ask such a thing? Now he was stuck in the awkward position of—

"Yes, ma'am." The definitiveness of his answer reassured her, and she released a pent-up breath.

He bowed his head. "Lord, thank you for this fine supper and for the kind woman who prepared it. May the work of our hands honor you each day, and may our souls find rest in your presence. In the name of Jesus, amen."

The instant he finished, she passed him the biscuits, careful to hide her reaction to his prayer behind a mask of politeness.

The words had been simple, but they'd resonated with a depth that made her pulse thrum. He hadn't just repeated familiar phrases out of habit—he'd meant each one. She'd felt it.

"I . . . um . . . wanted to thank you for fixing the porch steps," she murmured as she passed him the butter crock. "You didn't need to do that."

He shrugged. "I wanted to." He tore open a biscuit and slathered it with butter. "I'll start tearing down the old roof first thing in the morning. I don't expect the job to take more than three or four days." He popped half a biscuit into his mouth.

A contented expression flashed across his face while he chewed, and a rush of pride shot through her chest. She dipped her spoon into her chowder, not expecting to hear from him again until he'd finished his meal, but before she'd even swallowed her first mouthful, his voice resonated across the table. She hid a grin behind her napkin as she dabbed her lips. Apparently Neill Archer was a talker.

"I ain't got anywhere special to be anytime soon," he was

saying. "So if you want to put together a list of chores that need doing around the place, I'll see they get taken care of before I head out."

"That's kind of you, Mr. Archer, but I can't—"

"The name's Neill, ma'am, and yes, you can." His stern tone cut through her excuses. "For the young'un's sake, if not your own." He gestured toward her belly with the hand that held his spoon. "Besides," he said, his tone lightening, "meals this tasty are worthy compensation."

Clara wasn't quite sure how she felt about being badgered into accepting his kindness. Her pride balked a bit, but practicality won out. He was right. She *could* accept his help. For the baby.

"Thank you." The words fell from her lips into her soup since she couldn't quite bring herself to meet his gaze, but it seemed sufficient. She caught his nod out of the corner of her eye before he turned his full attention back to his food.

Several moments passed without further conversation, and Clara began to relax.

"So who's this Mack Danvers fella you thought I was workin' for?" Neill's question shattered the silence along with Clara's peace of mind. "A relative of yours?"

"My father-in-law." And that was all she planned to say on the subject.

Neill scraped up the last of his chowder from his bowl, while Clara prayed he'd not pursue the issue.

"I take it the two of you don't get along?"

She jumped up to retrieve the soup pot from the stove. "More chowder?"

A small chuckle escaped him. "All right—you win. I'll shut up and eat my soup."

"I didn't mean . . ." She froze, the ladle poised above his bowl.

His grin only deepened. "I know you didn't, Clara. That was just my ornery streak coming out. Pay me no mind."

Chowder splashed into his bowl as Clara fought to hide her grin. This man didn't know the meaning of ornery if he thought his teasing comments qualified. "Does it come out often—your ornery streak?"

Mercy. Was she actually flirting with the man?

His eyes warmed, and he smiled up at her. "Only with people I like."

A heat rose to her cheeks that had nothing to do with the steam from the soup pot. Clara spun back toward the stove.

"I'm the youngest of four brothers." His laughing voice followed her. "It was my job to be ornery."

How easily she pictured him making mischief for his older brothers, pestering and getting in the way. Yet he'd grown into a responsible, capable man, if his actions this afternoon were any indication.

What would it be like to spend evenings with a man who worked hard all day only to laugh and tease with his family when the work was done? A little piece of heaven, surely.

Neill proved true to his word and stopped pushing her for answers about Mack. Instead, he told stories about his family—stories full of humor and adventure, about four boys running a ranch on their own after the death of their father, about brothers he obviously idolized and adored.

"Then there was the time I found that skunk behind the woodpile," Neill said, leaning back in his chair, a light of deviltry twinkling in his eyes. "I was probably about ten at the time. I snuck back to the house and grabbed the scrap bucket we kept for Sadie, our bird dog, then laid a trail of the stuff from the woodpile to Jim's workshop. He always disappeared there to work on his carving after dinner. I made sure to leave the door ajar for the visitor I'd invited."

"You didn't!" Clara knew she shouldn't laugh, but a giggle bubbled up in her nonetheless.

The man beside her grinned with a mixture of boyish pride and rueful chagrin that brought a warmth to her heart she hadn't felt in years.

"You shoulda heard him howl. Travis and Crock thought we were under attack. They snatched up their guns and ran across the yard while I stumbled to the porch, bent over with laughter. Jim staggered out of his workshop, took one look at me, and lunged for the railing. I never ran so fast in my life. I didn't venture back till well after dark."

Neill chuckled and shook his head. "Jim stank so bad, Travis made him sleep in the barn for a week. 'Course, he made me scrub down the workshop from floor to ceiling and take over Jim's chores for the week, too. But it was worth it."

He winked at her, and Clara couldn't resist a smile over his antics, even as she ducked her head to focus her attention on her bowl. *Empty.* She chanced a glance at Neill's bowl. It was empty, as well. But she wasn't ready for the meal to end. Slipping quietly to her feet, Clara retrieved the coffee-pot from the stove and refilled both of their cups, hoping to manufacture a reason for them to linger.

Neill had fallen quiet, though, and she worried he'd leave if she didn't find a way to prolong the conversation, so as she eased back into her chair, she gave voice to the first thing that popped into her head.

"I wish I'd had older brothers to lean on after my parents

died. Maybe then I wouldn't have felt pressured to marry the first man who asked." Clara bit down on her wayward tongue. She couldn't believe she'd just blurted that out. Yet a defiant part of her was glad she had. It was true. And no amount of fanciful thinking could change it. She should know. She'd tried for two years.

"How old were you?" His deep voice melted over her, free of accusation, and in that moment, she knew she was going to tell him.

He was safe, she rationalized. A stranger passing through. And she'd been carrying the burden too long alone.

"Eighteen. Papa ran a trading post out here when all that existed were a handful of ranches." The words poured out of her as she stared at the dregs of chowder at the bottom of her bowl. "He was half Comanche, so people weren't all that happy to do business with him, but his was the only outfit around, so they did." She stole a glance at Neill. He didn't appear shocked by the revelation of her heritage.

"I imagine he came to earn their respect," he said, lifting his coffee to his mouth, "since he was able to keep his business even after the town started growing."

"He did." Clara sat a little straighter, pride lifting her chin to face Neill Archer fully. "He ran an honest store and understood the ranchers' needs better than anyone else. Extended credit in hard times, too, when other businessmen refused."

"But his generosity left you without a way to support yourself when he died, didn't it."

Clara nodded. "It wasn't his fault. He and Mama got the fever during the winter and died before the spring crops could be harvested and the debts repaid. I had to sell the remaining inventory to Claasen's General Store in order to pay Papa's suppliers. There hadn't been much left after that. So when Matthew Danvers, son of the wealthiest rancher in Dry Gulch, starting courting me, I thought my troubles were over. Turns out, they were just beginning."

✳ Chapter 4 ✳

Neill's hands clenched into fists beneath the table. "He didn't beat you, did he?"

If he had, Neill would dig the fella up, shoot his no-good carcass full of holes, and then spit on his bones and leave them for the wild animals to carry off.

"No." Clara shook her head, a sad little smile curving her lips. "Matthew was more neglectful than cruel. After our wedding, he set me up in this . . . house." The word emerged as if she weren't quite sure the structure qualified for the description. "I think he won it in a card game. One of the few things he managed to hang on to. I tried to make it a home, but he rarely spent more than a night or two under this roof at any one time. He much preferred the hotel in town. It was closer to the saloon. And the card games."

How could a man be married to this exotic princess and not want to spend every moment of the day with her? Neill couldn't fathom such stupidity.

"He just left you out here . . . alone?"

She laughed softly at the disbelief in his voice. "I didn't understand it at first, either. I thought perhaps I had angered or disappointed him. But then his father paid a visit, and everything became clear."

Neill's jaw tightened. "Mack Danvers."

Clara nodded, looking down to her lap. "Apparently Matthew had been bucking his father's orders most of his life. Not surprising, really, what with Mack being such a hard man. Matthew refused to take his place as the heir to the Danvers ranch, shirking his duties in favor of carousing in town. If Mack wanted him to attend church, Matthew opted for an all-night binge in the saloon on Saturday night. If Mack told him to buy thirty Herefords from a rancher in Amarillo, Matthew would return with two dozen longhorns.

"And when Mack threatened to cut Matthew off if he didn't marry and produce a son, Matthew married the one woman in town most likely to stick in Mack's craw. Me." A brittle laugh escaped her, the sound cutting through Neill's heart like broken glass. "It's rather humbling for a bride to realize she was chosen not for her beauty or intelligence or even her cooking skills, but because she was the woman most likely to be disdained by her husband's father."

Neill couldn't stop himself. He reached out and covered her hand where it lay fiddling with the edge of her empty bowl. She startled slightly but did not pull free of his touch.

"There is nothing about you to disdain, Clara," he asserted fiercely. "I've only known you a day, but I can see evidence of your hard work, your care and concern for your animals and the babe that will be born soon. You are beautiful and strong, and I admire you more than any woman I've come across."

A sheen of tears misted her eyes, but she blinked them away and shook her head. "There's plenty in me to disdain as far as Mack Danvers is concerned. The Comanche killed his wife, you see. His wife and his oldest son, the one who was supposed to be his heir. All they left him was his grief and a boy so full of anger and hurt that rebellion was his only outlet."

Clara tried to ease her fingers from his hold, but Neill tightened his grip. "You're not responsible for the actions of a handful of renegade warriors any more than I am responsible for the actions of the whites who slaughtered Comanche women and children in retaliation. Mack Danvers is wrong."

"He might be wrong," Clara said, tugging her hand free at last and pushing to her feet, "but he's a force to be reckoned with in this county. He sits on the city council and is well respected not only for his wealth but for his dedication to town growth. It's because of his money and influence that Dry Gulch has a school, a sheriff. People listen to him."

She wrapped a protective arm around her stomach for the briefest of moments before reaching to collect the dirty dishes. It was a motion so instinctual, Neill doubted she was even aware she had done it. But he was. More than aware. The telling gesture set off alarms in his gut.

Mack Danvers wasn't through making trouble for Clara.

Clara was amazed at how quickly she'd grown accustomed to Neill Archer's presence. After only three days, they'd fallen into such an easy routine, it felt as if he'd been working on her place for years.

He'd surprised her the first morning by milking Hester and leaving the full bucket inside the back door for her to find when she emerged from the bedroom. He'd mucked the stalls, too, and replaced two broken rungs on the loft ladder before carting it over to the edge of the house and climbing onto her roof. All before breakfast.

The man knew how to work.

Yet it was the evenings she would miss the most when he left, not the labor. For at the end of the day, they'd linger over dinner and coffee, talking about the day and about deeper, more personal matters. Matters they'd probably never have had the courage to put voice to if they didn't know their time together was so fleeting.

She'd told him the tale of how her Comanche grandmother had arrived at her grandfather's trading post with a half-dozen moccasins to barter for food and blankets and how her grandfather had slipped a handful of penny candy into her supply sack when she wasn't looking in hopes that the sweet treat would bribe her into returning. It did. In the course of a summer, he'd managed to teach her English, a few Bible stories, and what it meant to fall in love with a white man.

Neill had spoken about leaving home two years ago, and about how that leaving had hurt his oldest brother, Travis. The man was more father than brother to him and didn't understand why Neill felt compelled to buy his own spread when the family ranch was his home. Clara suspected that leaving had hurt Neill, as well, though he didn't say so. Instead he talked of the land he hoped to buy. About trees that stretched to the sky and lush pastures where his cattle would graze. About his best friend, Josiah, a local sharecropper's son, and their dream of running the ranch together. Josiah had stayed behind to accumulate a starter herd while Neill traveled from place to place, earning the funds necessary to purchase the land.

When he talked about his friend, a light came to his eyes that signaled more than a casual camaraderie. It seemed a deep bond existed between the two. Neill claimed he wanted the spread as a way to prove he was his own man, yet Clara couldn't help wondering if his motives had more to do with Josiah. Sharecroppers had a rough lot—working another man's land for only a fraction of the profit. Few men escaped such a life, never able to save enough from their meager earnings to invest in land of their own. She'd seen Neill's compassionate side, his altruistic nature. There might have been a part of him that chose to leave home in order to escape the shadow of his brothers, but she'd bet her new roof that his leaving had more to do with creating opportunities for his friend than for himself.

Clara leaned back in her bedroom rocker and allowed her eyes to slide closed. Her hands went lax, and the tiny gown she'd been sewing pooled in her lap. The rhythmic pounding overhead lulled her as Neill fastened shingles to the roof. Such a comforting sound. The sound of a man nearby. The sound of protection, provision. Her baby pushed against her womb, a tiny knee or foot bulging against the place where her palm rested on the shelf of her belly. A smile curved her lips. She never tired of feeling her baby move. Such a miracle.

Gently, she nudged the rocker into motion with her foot and rubbed slow circles over the area where she imagined the baby's back was. She caressed her child and hummed one of the tunes Neill played after retiring to the barn each night.

With her eyes closed, she could almost imagine it was

night now, the soft refrains of his fiddle offering her a lullaby sweeter than any bird's song.

She'd taken to sitting in this very chair, a wrapper covering her nightdress, the lantern extinguished as she waited for the soft, lilting music—music that touched her soul like a tender caress—to float to her through the propped-open window.

He said the music eased his loneliness. She feared when he left, the memory of it would magnify hers.

Clara fell into a light doze until the sound of an approaching rider brought her head up with a jerk. Her heart thumped against her chest, as it always did when unexpected visitors paid a call. Until Neill, she'd never experienced a favorable outcome from such a visit.

Neill.

Her pulse steadied. She wasn't alone.

Yet as she moved from the bedroom to the main part of the house, she noticed an absence of hammering. Had Neill left while she dozed to see to some other chore, or had he just paused in his work to take stock of her caller?

Praying it was the latter, Clara took Matthew's shotgun down from above the doorframe and cracked the door open.

A dull pain ripped across her abdomen at the same time she recognized the horse and rider coming to a halt in her yard. She winced and immediately sent her prayers reeling in the opposite direction. *Please let Neill be far away*. For his sake, as well as hers.

Mack Danvers had little patience for men who interfered in his business. And right now, *she* was his business.

✳ Chapter 5 ✳

Neill crouched on the back of the rooftop, careful to keep his head low. As a hired man, it wasn't his place to interfere in Clara's affairs. Nevertheless, instinct warned him to stay close. He didn't recognize the barrel-chested man who had just ridden in, but judging by the scornful glances he cast at the house and barn as he dismounted, Neill had a pretty fair guess as to his identity.

"Hello, Mack." Clara's greeting confirmed his suspicion. The porch overhang blocked her from his view, but he imagined her standing tall and proud as she faced down her father-in-law.

"Clara." Mack Danvers took a few strides closer to the house, then braced his feet apart and crossed his arms over that broad chest. "I see you haven't birthed my grandson yet."

"What do you want, Mack? I haven't changed my mind since your last visit, and I won't be changing my mind any time in the future. So leave me be."

Neill grinned at the way she cut to the heart of the matter. She'd not forfeit control to her adversary, even in conversation.

A scowl darkened Mack's features. "I ain't leaving until you and I come to an understanding." He took a menacing step toward the porch. Neill tensed, muscles coiled and ready to spring into action if needed. But Mack stopped his advance after that single step and just glowered at his daughter-in-law.

"Is it more money you're wanting? I shoulda known you'd be a greedy creature. That's why you married my boy in the first place, right? Thought you'd live out at the Circle D surrounded by finery, didn't you? Ha! Matthew might've loved to thumb his nose at me, but even he knew you didn't belong there. That's why he stashed you out here, away from decent folk."

Neill's jaw clenched so tight his teeth ground together. Pain radiated up his forearm from the increased pressure of his grip on the hammer, now digging into the heel of his hand. He glanced at the tool, then slowly unfurled his fingers from around the handle, afraid he would hurl it at Mack Danvers's head if it remained in his grasp.

"Five hundred," the man growled. "Five hundred and you sever all ties to the child. Go wherever you want. Do whatever you want. But I keep the boy and raise him to take his proper place at the Circle D. I've got a wet nurse ready to take over his care the minute he's born. He'll want for nothing."

"Nothing but a mother's love." Clara's soft voice held an edge of steel.

This was what Mack Danvers wanted? To separate her from her child? No wonder Clara refused to talk about it. The very idea was abhorrent. Neill knew firsthand what it was like to grow up without a mother. His brothers had loved him and filled the void as best they could, but there'd been no softness, no kisses on skinned knees, no lullabies. A piece of his heart had always felt neglected, no matter how he denied it to himself or others. He'd never been able to identify what had been missing until Travis wed Meredith and they'd had their first baby. Watching his sister-in-law lavish affection on his nephew finally opened his eyes.

Perhaps that was what had drawn him to music as a boy. He'd been trying to replicate the comfort of a mother's song.

"Come now, Clara." Mack's condescending tone raised Neill's hackles. "How do you expect to provide for the boy? All you have is a run-down shack that will probably collapse during the next snowfall. You have no money. No way to provide a living for yourself, let alone a child. And even if you could find work, who would tend the baby? Quit being sentimental and selfish. Do what's best for the child. Give him to me to raise."

"Yes, because you did such a great job with your own sons," Clara spat back in retaliation. "One never lived to be a man and the other grew up despising you."

Mack charged the porch, his face livid. "It's only because of you and your heathen kind that my boys are gone!"

Neill shoved to his feet and ran across the roof. When he reached the porch overhang, he grabbed hold of the edge and swung himself over the side, tucking his legs up to his chest in order to dodge the railing. He landed on his feet with a thud and immediately put himself between Clara and her father-in-law.

"What . . . ?" Mack jerked back. "Where the devil did you come from?"

Neill ignored the question. "It's time for you to leave."

The man's eyes narrowed. "This is a *family* matter, mister. Between my daughter-in-law and me. Step aside."

Neill didn't budge. "Where I come from, family supports one another. We don't exploit each other's weaknesses for personal gain." He leaned his face close to Mack's. "Nor do we try to take children away from their mothers."

Mack glowered at him. Neill glowered back, his arms tense and ready should the man require some physical convincing. So focused was he on the threat Mack presented that he failed to notice Clara's movement behind him until she stood by his side, lightly touching his arm.

"Let it go, Neill. This is none of your concern."

None of his concern? How could she say that? No man worth his salt would stand by and let another man bully a woman. A pregnant woman, at that. Maybe he had no claim on her, but that didn't mean he couldn't stand up for what was right.

"I'm not leaving." His eyes never left Mack's. "I won't interfere if you want to have more words with this yahoo, but you'll have to do it with me here. I aim to see that Mr. Danvers keeps a lid on that temper of his."

"That won't be necessary," she insisted, her fingers tightening a bit around his forearm. "I believe my business with Mr. Danvers is concluded. He could offer me five *thousand* dollars, and I'd still not give up my child."

"You're a fool, Clara." A hardness came over Mack's features, a hardness that made Neill's insides go cold. "That boy belongs with me, and I won't give up until he's mine." He turned from Clara to Neill, his mouth twisting into a smirk. "Your guard dog won't be here forever."

Neill's hands balled into fists, but Mack took a step backward, easing himself off the porch.

"Oh, by the way," he added nonchalantly when he reached his horse. "I've given orders for the Circle D hands to take turns watching over your place. I felt it my *family* duty." He speared a quick glance at Neill. "I wouldn't want any harm to come to you in your delicate condition, my dear. And, of course, with my men close at hand, I'll be sure to hear the happy news as soon as my grandson's cry hits the air."

Clara's grip became a vise on Neill's arm, and it was all he could do to stand still at her side when what he wanted was to pummel Mack Danvers into the dirt.

The man lifted his foot to the stirrup, mounted, and then saluted the two of them with an arrogant flick of his wrist before finally taking his leave.

Neill watched him go, the man's words ringing in his ears: "*Your guard dog won't be here forever.*" His gut clenched. Mack Danvers held all the cards. He could just wait Neill out. Wait for Clara to be vulnerable. Unprotected.

The roof was nearly finished, and Clara had yet to give him a list of chores. He might find a way to lengthen his stay by a day or two, but what then? What would become of Clara and her baby when he left?

Clara's hand slid from his arm, and Neill turned to face her. She looked as if a gentle breeze would knock her over. Complexion pale. Arms shaking. He immediately took her elbow and steered her back into the house.

"Come inside. You need to sit down."

"I'm fine," she protested, but Neill wasn't about to let her pride push him away. She needed him.

The notion sunk into his heart like a stone sinking in

mud, surrounded on all sides until it became part of the earth itself.

No one had ever needed him before, not to this extent. The youngest of four brothers, he'd always been included yet never felt truly essential. Until today. Clara needed him. And suddenly nothing else seemed to matter. Not the ranch he and Josiah hoped to buy. Not the roof he was expected to finish. Not his dream of proving himself a man equal to any of his brothers. All that mattered was protecting Clara and her baby.

And he only had two days to figure out a way to do that.

Plotting and scheming would have to wait, though. Right now he had to get Clara settled.

The house only boasted two rooms—the bedroom behind the closed door, and the front room that served as kitchen and small parlor. Neill guided Clara to a faded armchair in the parlor section and urged her into the seat.

"Really, Neill. I'm fine." Her color did look slightly improved, but he found he couldn't leave her. Not yet.

He patted her arm. "Humor me." He saw a footstool against the wall and moved to retrieve it. "Here. Put your feet up." He knelt at the edge of her chair and reached for the heels of her shoes, thinking to help her. She hurried to lift them on her own.

Soft leather brushed against his hand, and swinging fringe danced against his fingers.

He grinned up at her. "Are you wearing moccasins?"

Clara blushed and tried to arrange her skirt to more fully conceal her footwear. "They were my grandmother's," she muttered. "My feet have swollen over the last month, and my usual shoes pinch. These are more comfortable."

"I'm jealous." Neill teasingly tried to get another peek. "I always wanted a pair of moccasins. I figured if I had some, I'd be able to sneak up on my brothers without them hearing me."

Clara shyly met his gaze. "You don't find them . . . heathen?"

"Are you kidding?" He rocked back on his heels. "If God clothed Adam and Eve with animal skins when they left the garden, it seems to me He'd be in favor of such footwear. Don't you think?"

She smiled, and the tension he'd been battling finally seeped out of the room. Then Clara leaned back in her chair and released a heavy sigh.

"Every day I pray that this child is a girl." She wrapped her arms around her stomach. "I pray that she looks so much like a Comanche that Mack will take one look at her and want nothing to do with her."

"Do you really think that would stop him?" Neill watched her hands as they made slow, circular motions over her belly. When she stopped, he leaned closer and covered her hand where it rested on the chair arm, half expecting her to jerk away, but she didn't. Satisfaction surged through him.

"No. Mack is so desperate for an heir of his own blood, he'd probably take a girl, too. But I'm not giving up my child, Neill." Tears clogged her throat. "I'm not!"

Neill rubbed the back of her hand with his thumb, then bent forward and dropped a kiss onto the soft skin. Clara sucked in a shocked breath, her gaze flying to his.

"I know you're not." He spoke the words without a single ounce of doubt. "I'm going to help you."

"How?" she sputtered.

"I'm not sure yet, but I'll think of something."

She curled her free arm around her swollen abdomen in a protective gesture that solidified Neill's resolve. "I have a little money set aside. Matthew never touched the funds I had left from my father's estate. He only gambled with Mack's money. It would be enough to see me through a year or two if I scrimped. Plenty of time to find work after the baby is weaned. But I fear Mack will try to force the issue. He's threatened to take me to court if I fail to go along with his terms. Have me declared unfit."

Her hand trembled as she lifted it to push a piece of hair behind her ear. "What chance would I have against him—a woman with no income, tainted by Comanche blood, against a rich white man who's a pillar of the community?"

Neill dropped another kiss onto her hand. "He must worry that you'd have at least a small chance. That's why he'd rather buy you off than risk a hearing." He wanted to believe that honest men wouldn't take a child from his mother's arms just because another relative had more money, but he'd been out in the world long enough to know that wealth and power could sway a man's ideals.

"Even so," Clara said, the despair in her eyes tearing at his heart, "the odds will still be in his favor."

Determination forged a hard knot in Neill's gut. "We'll just have to make sure we take away that option, then, won't we?"

✶ Chapter 6 ✶

Clara barely slept that night. Every time she drifted off, visions of her father-in-law wrenching her newborn out of her arms rose to torment her. She'd whisper fervent prayers, then huddle under the covers and try to find sleep, but little was to be found.

Her back ached, her head pounded, and the only comforting thought she was able to muster was the memory of Neill's kiss upon her hand. It was comforting to imagine that this strong man with the big heart would step in and solve her problems. Her tattered spirit had soared at his tender touch, at the way he shielded her from Mack's anger, at his teasing smile when he discovered her moccasins. If she had married a man like Neill instead of Matthew, how different her life would be. They'd be awaiting the birth of their child with joy and love instead of her standing alone, plagued with fear and desperation.

Yet no matter how strong the temptation, she couldn't allow herself to rely on Neill to solve her problems. Using a man to solve her problems was what got her into this mess in the first place. No, as soon as the roof was finished, she'd thank him and send him on his way. Though the thought of facing Mack on her own held little appeal. Or likelihood of success.

Maybe she should run. Hitch up the buckboard and ride to Amarillo, where she could catch a train to somewhere Mack would never find her. But where would she go? She had no family. No friends outside of Dry Gulch. If she had to spend her inheritance on new lodgings and town food, her funds would be depleted in months. How would she feed her child then? Here, at least she had a garden, a new roof to keep them protected from the weather, a milk cow, and a handful of chickens. But all of that would mean nothing if Mack ended up with her child.

Lord, what am I to do?

Her mind too agitated to even contemplate sleep, Clara threw back the covers and padded across the cold floorboards. The early-morning air sent shivers from her bare feet up her calves. She grabbed the quilted throw from the foot of the bed and wrapped it around her shoulders. Then she plopped into the rocker and stared out the window into the dark, willing the horizon to lighten with the promise of day so she could finally put this horrific night behind her.

Turning away after several minutes of fruitless staring, she caught sight of the box she'd prepared weeks ago for her babe's arrival. She'd found an old crate in the barn, the wood still strong, the sides and bottom solid. She'd sanded every inch of that crate until it was as smooth and soft as one of her grandmother's fur-lined moccasins. Then she'd padded it with the thick flannel quilt she'd pieced specifically to cushion her child's tiny body. The makeshift cradle lay on the floor in the corner, ready to receive the babe, yet hauntingly empty. Would her child ever sleep in the nest she'd created with such love, or would he be laid in a fancy, impersonal cradle somewhere on the Circle D?

Too weary to hold the tears at bay any longer, Clara finally stopped fighting and let them roll in rivulets down her cheeks. She'd be strong again when the sun came up, but right now—sitting in the dark—she wept.

Neill sat cross-legged on top of his bedroll, his head in his hands, elbows braced on his knees. He'd barely slept. Lifting his head, he grimaced at the sight of stars shining valiantly in the still-black sky. Would dawn never arrive?

Groaning in frustration, he tousled his hair with enough force to leave it standing on end, then tugged his boots over his stockinged feet and shoved his arms into the sleeves of his last clean shirt before pulling it over his head. Leaving his shirttails dangling and the buttons around the collar undone, he strolled out to the pump and worked the handle. Cupping his hands under the water, he let the icy liquid pool in his palms before splashing it over his face.

The bracing cold slapped him fully awake. Dampening his hair with his wet fingers, he found his gaze drawn to the house and his mind drawn to Clara and her predicament.

Only one solution had presented itself with any promise during his tossing and turning last night. He had to take Clara away from here—out of Mack's reach. And not just anywhere. He had to take her someplace she would be protected should Mack track her down. Someplace Neill could guarantee her safety and that of her babe.

He knew of only one such place.

The Archer ranch.

He was still over fifty dollars short on his ranch fund. Twenty of that was supposed to come from this roofing job, but there was no way he'd leave Clara alone long enough to claim his pay. The sooner they left, the better. And with Mack's men watching Clara's place, that would be no easy feat. They'd have to take the train out of Amarillo. It was the fastest way to Palestine. Which meant more money out of his pocket. Not that it wasn't worth it.

Shoot, he'd give up his entire nest egg to keep his woman safe.

His woman. When had he started thinking of Clara as his?

Probably the moment he kissed her hand and she didn't run screaming to the next county. The thought set him to grinning. Clara would never run screaming anywhere. She was a fighter, fierce and brave. Not afraid of hard work, either, as evidenced by her care of the animals and buildings left to her by her no-account husband. She'd make the perfect rancher's wife. And he couldn't say he'd mind growing old looking at her fine-boned face and dark eyes over the breakfast table every morning. Not to mention that glossy black hair of hers. Considering the thickness of the braid she wore coiled at her nape, it must hang clear to her waist. What would it be like to wrap its silky strands around his hand? To watch it sway as she brushed the long tresses out at night? To see it feathered across his pillow?

Neill suddenly choked on the air he was breathing. Best turn his thoughts in another direction before traveling any further down *that* path. He didn't even know yet if Clara would accept his offer.

A tiny noise floated through the predawn air, one that

didn't fit with his surroundings. Instantly alert, Neill focused his attention on pinpointing its source. It came again, a soft cry, from the house. Walking on soundless feet, Neill cautiously crossed the short distance to the side of the house where Clara's window stood partly open.

A small muffled sob escaped the room and pierced Neill's heart. She was crying. His strong, stoic, determined Clara was weeping alone in the dark. He could make out her shadowy outline on the rocker at the foot of the bed, and without thinking he strode around to the front of the house and let himself in.

She'd shouldered this burden too long on her own. It was time for another pair of shoulders to take on the task for a while.

He knocked gently on her bedroom door. "Clara? It's Neill. I'm coming in." He knew if he asked for permission, she'd send him away.

"No, I-I'm fine."

But he'd already opened the door.

"No, honey. You're not fine."

She frantically swiped at her cheeks and nose, as if she could hide the evidence of her weakness. "G-go away, Neill. You sh-shouldn't be h-here."

He hesitated. She was probably right. A man had no business in an unmarried woman's bedroom. But blast it all, he couldn't just stand by and do nothing while she cried her eyes out.

Travis would've already had Meredith in his arms by now if she'd been the one upset. Surely Neill could offer Clara the same comfort. It was better than standing helpless in the doorway watching her try to hide her misery.

Each time she swiped at a tear, it felt like a lash flaying his heart.

Decision made, Neill squared his shoulders and trudged into the room. In two steps he was at Clara's side, scooping her up, quilt and all. He carried her to the bed, sat down on the corner, and cradled her in his lap. She stiffened against him and made a halfhearted effort to push his arm away, but he didn't budge. "Let me hold you, Clara," he murmured in a gravelly voice. "Just until the sun comes up. Things will look better then. I promise."

Her dark eyes shimmered with unspent tears when she finally looked at him. She peered into his face, as if his intentions were written there for her to read. Maybe they were, because after a moment she reached an arm around his waist and laid her head on his shoulder, her forehead coming to rest against his jaw. "Just until dawn." The words escaped on a sigh that filled Neill with a satisfaction so deep he thought he'd drown in it.

Moments earlier he'd wanted to lasso the sun and yank it up over the horizon to end the torture of the night. Now he wanted to tether it to some spot farther east to prevent its rising. Forever wouldn't be too long to hold his Clara. She felt so good in his arms, so right.

Neither said a word as time ticked slowly by. Neill lightly ran his fingers up and down the outside of Clara's arm, enjoying the feel of her even breathing as she relaxed against his chest. Then a different movement registered, a rolling motion that pressed against his belly before advancing to his rib cage. He sucked in an awed breath, his hand stilling in midmotion to hover over Clara's pregnant stomach. *The baby.*

How he longed to lay his palm upon her belly and feel the child move. He recalled Travis doing so with Meredith, the two of them sharing delighted smiles. Such a miracle. Such a bond between parents and child.

But this wasn't his child. And Clara wasn't his wife. Not yet. He had no right to touch her in such an intimate manner. Still, he couldn't drag his hand away. For some inexplicable reason, he longed to be connected to this child he'd sworn to protect.

Then all at once her hand was there. Covering his. Positioning his touch to match the movement of her child and pressing his palm against her abdomen.

Something pushed against his hand. A foot, maybe? A knee? His breath caught. Afraid to break the spell, he kept his amazement to himself, not daring to even whisper. After a long moment, Clara removed her hand, and Neill reluctantly did the same.

He returned to the gentle stroking of her arm, his gut clenching in denial when he saw the hazy glow of dawn creeping over the horizon.

He didn't want to let her go.

Ever.

✳ Chapter 7 ✳

Knowing this would probably be Neill's last day and wanting desperately to give him something in return for all the kindness he'd given her, Clara had offered to do his washing. Of course, he'd only agreed on the condition that she let him set up the tub and tote the water, as if she hadn't been doing such chores throughout her pregnancy. Sweet, stubborn man.

His clothing now flapped in the breeze from her drying line. Three shirts, a pair of trousers . . . and a handkerchief that wasn't really his. Clara reached into her apron pocket and fingered the handkerchief she'd found in his pocket. She'd pilfered it, replacing it with one of Matthew's—an identical white cotton square. Neill would never notice. Or care.

But she cared. She pulled it from her apron pocket and lifted it to her nose, breathing deeply. It carried his scent. Not strong, but just enough to help her recall how it had felt to pillow her head against his chest. His shirt open at the neck, exposing the warmth of his skin. His strong arms supporting her as if she weighed nothing. The tender way he'd stroked her, and the tremble in his fingers when he felt the baby move inside her.

She had never felt more cherished in her life. In those few precious minutes with Neill she'd found everything her heart secretly longed for. Everything she knew she couldn't have. Neill deserved a woman who would come to him untouched, not one carrying another man's child. A woman who would bring him honor among his brothers and friends, not one people would scorn because of her Comanche blood. A woman who could bring him laughter and joy, not one who added to his burdens with the magnitude of her troubles. Even if he were crazy enough to offer her his protection and his name, she'd not take advantage of his compassionate nature. She esteemed him too highly to steal his chance at true happiness.

So she'd settled for stealing his handkerchief instead and would live off the memories of one perfect moment in time when a good man had cared for her.

Stuffing the handkerchief back into her apron pocket, she banished her melancholy thoughts and got back to work. Biscuits wouldn't bake themselves. Clara jammed her hands into the flour-lined bowl and gently kneaded the soft dough until it reached the perfect consistency. Neill deserved the finest meal she could wrangle, and she aimed to give—

A warm gush of wetness between her legs cut off all thought.

No. Her dough-covered hands clutched at her stomach. *Not now, little one. Not now. I'm not ready.*

This couldn't be happening. She hadn't even felt any contractions. Clara massaged her abdomen as if she could somehow hold the baby inside. But a second smaller gush mocked her efforts.

Think, Clara. Think.

The midwife she'd consulted had told her that first babies

took a long time to birth. Hours. So she had some time. Clara drew in a pair of deep breaths, willing the panic away. The midwife had also told her that many women found the birthing easier if they stayed active until the pains grew too intense to stay on their feet. That shouldn't be too hard. Her pains hadn't even started yet. She could finish dinner, feed Neill, then send him out to the barn early so she could retire. He knew how tired she'd been that morning. He'd not argue.

She'd have to close her window. It wouldn't do for him to hear any cries that managed to escape her lips. She'd always planned to have this baby alone. Ever since Mack made it clear he wanted her child. He could easily pay off the midwife, the doctor, anyone in the area who might help her. Not only would they tell him about the birth, but for a big enough bribe, they might be induced to take her baby from her while she was lying abed after the birth. She'd be too exhausted and weak to stop them.

No, it was better to do as Jochebed and the other Hebrew women did when Pharaoh commanded the midwives to kill their sons in the days of Moses. Learn all they could, then have the babies on their own before the midwives arrived. She had no sister or mother to aid her, but she'd not risk losing her child because of such a small matter. She'd made do pretty much on her own for the last two years, handling things she'd never thought herself capable of. This was simply one more challenge. God helped Jochebed. He'd help her, as well. He *had* to.

⋄———⋄———⋄

Neill glanced across the supper table at Clara, trying to find a way to share his plan with her. An unusual tension vibrated in the air around them, though. They'd never had trouble talking over supper before. In fact, it was one of the things he'd enjoyed most about his time with her. But something was off. She seemed withdrawn, distracted. She had yet to meet his eye, despite numerous attempts on his part to garner her attention. Was she distancing herself because she expected him to leave now that the roof was complete? Hadn't he vowed to help her? Did she have so little trust in him?

Neill gave an imperceptible shake of his head at the thoughts running through his head. Why *should* she trust him? Her husband married her to defy his father, and her father-in-law wanted to take away her child. The woman had no reason to trust men. Especially a man she'd known less than a week. She had no way of knowing that he intended to follow through on his rash promise to help her. For all she knew, he was just a big talker, full of wild schemes and good intentions with nothing to back them up.

Well, he could at least put her mind to rest on that score.

Tossing down his napkin, Neill cleared his throat. "Clara, I have a plan. I want you to come with me—"

"You need to leave, Neill," she interrupted, her focus still locked on her plate. "Tonight. Before full dark sets in."

"What?" He couldn't believe he'd heard her right.

She finally raised her chin and looked at him, her face a stoic mask. "Leave. No good will come of you staying."

Neill leaned back in his chair, his focus intent on her face. Something was definitely off. Had their closeness this morning scared her? Dissolved the trust that had been growing between them? But even that made little sense. She'd gone out of her way to do his washing, to bring him refreshment during the day, to bake a fresh batch of his favorite biscuits, even when there were some left over from yesterday's meal. It made no sense that she would go out of her way to be so kind if she truly wanted him gone. She could have just ordered him off her property this afternoon, when he told her he'd finished with the roof.

"Why tonight?" he queried, watching her closely. "Why not at first light?"

Her mouth tightened for a brief second while at the same time, a slight crease marred her brow. At first he attributed it to frustration, but then she swiveled her head aside as if she feared he might have noticed the telling twitch. When she turned back, her face was as smooth and stoic as ever.

"Your job is finished," she said with matter-of-fact precision. "I appreciate all you've done, but it is time for you to go."

Neill crossed his arms over his chest. "I'm not leaving. Not unless you come with me." If she thought she could out-stubborn him, she had a lot to learn about Archer men.

"You're not my protector, Neill. You're just a hired hand who's passing through. I'm not your problem."

"No, you're not." Neill's jaw twitched as he sat forward and did his best to glare some sense into her. "You're my friend. And if you'll let me, I'd like to be even more than that." He softened his voice and reached for her hand. "I want to be a husband to you, Clara. A father to your babe."

"No!" She snatched her hand away from him and jumped up from the table. She spun toward the stove, turning her back to him, but not before he caught the glimmer of tears in her eyes. In an instant, though, her steel returned, as if she had mentally poured molten metal down her spine and cooled it with icy reserve. Her shoulders straightened and her voice emerged without a single warble.

"Marriage doesn't solve problems. It creates more. I'll not make the same mistake twice."

"No, you'll just make a different one." Neill pushed up from the table so fast his chair tipped over and crashed to the floor. Clara flinched but made no move to turn around. "Do you honestly think you and your child have a better chance of escaping Mack on your own?" he demanded as came up behind her. "Or do you think so little of my character that you lump me into the same category as Matthew?"

"It doesn't matter. I'll not marry you. So go. You've done your good deed. You've made your offer. Now you can leave with a clean conscience."

"I already told you," he gritted out, "I'm not leaving." He cupped her shoulder and spun her around to face him, intending to get to the bottom of things once and for all, but the tears streaming down her face stopped him cold.

She stretched her neck away from him, trying with all her might to hide her misery, but it was too late. He'd seen the truth.

His hands immediately gentled on her shoulders. "I'm not leaving, Clara." His voice hardened with resolve even as he snuggled her close to his chest and rubbed soothing circles over her back. "No matter what you say or do to push me away, I'm not leaving. So you might as well get used to the idea and quit fighting me."

"But I'll bring you nothing but trouble." She struggled against his hold until she was able to tip her head back and meet his gaze. "It's no good."

Neill smiled at her, then tenderly forced her head back down to his chest and covered it with his chin. "Oh, I don't know," he murmured, his tone husky. "I think it could be very good."

Again she pulled her head free and looked into his face. The stoic mask completely decimated now, her vulnerability became palpable. "I can't agree to marry you, Neill. Not yet. I've only known you four days. It's too soon."

He started to argue, but she shook her head at him. "Please. I know you are a good man. That's not what I fear. I just don't want to be forced into marriage again because of hardship. If I marry, I want it to be because we both truly want it, not out of a sense of fear on my part or duty on yours. Just give me some time. Please?"

Neill peered into her face and swallowed his arguments. "All right. I'll not pressure you about marriage. But I *am* going to take you home with me. Home to my brother's ranch, where the Archers stand together. Where we can protect you and your child. We can leave at first light, and catch the train in Amarillo. My sister-in-law can help you with the birthing. Everything will be perfect. You'll see."

Clara ducked her head against him, but she didn't relax. No, her entire body tensed, and she curled forward over her belly.

"Neill?" Her voice emerged through gritted teeth.

"Yeah?" He started rubbing her back again, his concern growing over her obvious discomfort. She was practically curling in on herself, the muscles across her midsection pulled tighter than the strings on his fiddle.

"I don't think your sister-in-law is going to help with this birthing."

Neill frowned. "Why not?"

Before she could reply, the answer hit him like a log beam against his thick skull.

"Land's sake, Clara. You should have told me you were in labor!"

✳ Chapter 8 ✳

"How long have you been having pains?" Neill scooped Clara into his arms and made for the other room. The crazy woman should be in bed, not feeding him supper.

Clara pushed at his chest. "Leave me be, Neill. I have work to do."

He ignored her protest and kicked open the bedroom door with his foot. "The only work you need to be worrying about is bringing that baby into the world. I'll take care of everything else. It won't be the first time I've cleaned a kitchen."

He moved to lay her on the bed, only then realizing that she'd already stripped most of the bedding away. Evidence of an oilcloth covering the mattress peeked out from beneath the top sheet. A pile of towels and a basin of water sat ready at the side of the bed, and a blanket made of pieced flannel lay rolled up within arm's reach.

Somehow seeing the preparations she'd made caused the reality of the situation to swell within him until he thought he might drown. He laid her gently upon the bed, then with trembling hands, tugged off her moccasins and covered her with a sheet. "I'll . . . uh . . . go fetch the doctor."

Desperate to race for his horse and bring back someone more competent than he for dealing with the situation, Neill spun toward the door only to halt at Clara's cry.

"No! Please, Neill. You can't. No doctor. No midwife. Mack will have already paid them off. I can't risk it." Her urgent voice flayed him. He stopped and turned back to face her.

"I have to get someone, Clara. You can't have this baby alone."

Her chin jutted out and her eyes glittered with familiar determination. "Yes I can. I will. It's the only way to ensure my child's safety."

Another pain hit her then, apparently stronger than before. She winced and hissed out a breath as she rolled to her side and drew her knees up. "You need to leave, Neill," she managed once the pain had passed.

Neill set his mouth in a mutinous line. "If you think I'm leaving now, you're out of your mind."

Then the crazy woman did something he'd never expected. She laughed. The sound cut straight through his defenses and melted against his heart. Everything about him softened in that moment, and he found himself smiling back at her.

"I'm not asking you to leave the house, Neill. Just the room. I need to change into a sleeping gown."

"Oh." He let out a sheepish chuckle and rubbed the back of his neck before straightening to level a serious look at her. "All right. But I'm going to be on the other side of that door, however long it takes. I'll come running whenever you need me, Clara." He took a step closer to the bed, longing to touch her, to comfort her, to do *something* to ease her pain. "You don't have to do this alone. I'm here."

She held his gaze a long moment. "Would you play for me?"

His brows knit in confusion.

"Your fiddle. The music relaxes me. I think it will help when the pains worsen."

Neill seized upon the idea, thankful to have something tangible to do. "Honey, I'll play all night if you want me to."

"Thank you." Her smile lit up the room and spurred him to action. Barely slowing enough to click the bedroom door closed behind him, Neill rushed out to the barn to collect his violin.

◆———◆———◆

The man was a marvel. Clara paused to breathe between the pains that seemed to be intensifying at a rapid rate now. For two hours, Neill had played almost without stop. The soothing tones had floated to her from the next room, easing her tension and lulling her into a light doze as she rested between contractions. With all her brave plans to have this baby on her own, she couldn't thank God enough for sending her a man stubborn enough to stay. The labor would have been unbearable without the music to remind her that she wasn't alone.

A new pain hit, radiating through her back and abdomen with stunning force. She tried to breathe through it like she had with the others, but this one was different. More forceful. More prolonged. And with it came a staggering need to push.

A groan tore from her throat as she fought her body's instincts. She couldn't do this. Heaven help her! She *couldn't*.

Panic swelled in her breast. What if something went

wrong? She'd be helpless to do anything about it. What if she labored too long and didn't have the strength to tend her child after the birth? What if the babe had trouble drawing his first breath? Scenarios swirled unrelenting in her mind, one more horrible than the next, until she could no longer restrain her cry.

"Neill!"

The lilting music cut off with a screech, replaced by pounding footsteps. A heartbeat later, Neill threw open the door and rushed to her side. He threw himself down on his knees so his face was even with hers and immediately started smoothing back her hair from her sweat-dampened forehead.

"I'm here, Clara," he crooned. "I'm here."

She scanned his face wildly and latched onto his wrist, her fingers nearly going numb with the force of her grip. "I can't do it, Neill. I can't."

"Of course you can, honey. You're strong. The most capable woman I know." He smiled at her, his words confident. "And I'm here to help you."

A tear fell down her cheek. "I'm scared."

He pressed a kiss to her brow. "We'll get through it together. Everything will be fine."

Another pain hit, and she writhed away from him. Away from the softness of his lips, the comfort of his words. But he followed her. His sturdy arms lifted her back and arranged what few pillows she had behind her.

"The babe's coming," she gritted out, needing him to understand the urgency. "You have to make sure nothing goes wrong."

She forced her head around and locked her eyes onto

Neill's, ignoring the pain building across her middle. She needed his promise. His assurance.

He nodded at the same moment a vise gripped her abdomen and demanded she push. She wouldn't ignore the demand this time. Neill was there. He'd make sure her child was safe.

With renewed determination, she curled forward and bore down.

After the first ten minutes of standing helplessly by while Clara labored, Neill shoved aside every high-minded ideal he knew about protecting a woman's modesty and did whatever he could to protect and comfort the woman herself. He climbed onto the bed behind her and supported her back. He dampened one of the cloths she'd laid out for the baby's bath and used it to cool her face and neck. He massaged her lower back with the heel of his hand and held her when the pains struck.

How did she endure it? It had been at least an hour since she'd told him the babe was about to arrive. Her groans and deep-throated cries haunted him. How much longer? Surely the child should have been born by now. Neill scrubbed his palms against his pants legs. Was something wrong? He'd vowed to protect mother and child, but how could he fight an enemy he couldn't see?

God, help her, his spirit pled. *I don't know what to do or how to help. Bring Clara and her child safely through this. Please.*

He wet the cloth again and rubbed it across Clara's face, desperate to do something, *anything* to ease things for her.

Her muscles tensed. Another pain was upon her. He tossed the cloth aside and dug his heels into the mattress. She'd taken to clasping his arms for support and leverage as she pushed, so he extended them on either side of her and braced for her pressure. Her hands found his as if drawn by a magnet. His palms engulfed hers. He leaned his mouth to her ear and whispered encouragement.

She pulled against his hold. A cry vibrated in her chest. Then all at once, she released his arms and reached forward, her body still straining.

"He's coming, Neill!" she panted, excitement warring with fatigue in her voice. "I can feel it."

The next several minutes passed in a blur. Before Neill quite knew what had happened, he was helping Clara lift her son to lie across her chest. The baby's tiny mewling cries created the most beautiful music Neill had ever heard. Tears moistened his eyes, and awe set his fingers to trembling as he cut the cord before covering the babe with a dry towel and starting rubbing him clean.

Clara rested against the pillows, the wonder on her face a sight to behold as she smiled down on her son. The babe's dark hair spiked up in black tufts and his face scrunched into a wrinkled mess as he howled his displeasure over his ordeal. Covered in muck, his head slightly misshapen, the kid wasn't exactly what Neill would call pretty. Still . . .

"He's perfect," Clara whispered. "Absolutely perfect." She caressed the child's reddened cheek with the curve of her finger, and Neill found himself agreeing with her assessment.

"What will you call him?" he asked in a low voice, strangely unable to tear his hand away from the babe's back. It was as if sharing the child's journey into the world had forged an indestructible bond between them. Neill swore he could feel his heart swelling in his chest, making room for a new occupant.

"Harrison." She stroked the black hair atop the boy's head. "It was my mother's maiden name. I've always liked it."

Neill smiled, for some reason exceptionally glad she wasn't naming the boy after her late husband. "Harrison's a good name. Strong. Just like our little fella here."

The word *our* fell from his lips without conscious thought. When Neill realized what he'd said, he immediately sought out Clara's gaze to judge her reaction, but she hadn't seemed to notice. She was too busy cooing over her son—a boy who was rooting like a hungry piglet, his pink mouth open as his head strained backward against his mama's chest.

Comprehension brought heat to Neill's face. "I'll . . . uh . . . give the two of you some privacy and go . . . uh . . . warm some water for the little guy's bath." He backed quickly toward the door. "Just call out when you're ready."

He'd nearly made his escape when Clara's soft voice brought him to a halt.

"Neill?"

He turned. "Yeah?"

She focused wholly on him for the first time in several hours, and the depth of emotion shining in her dark eyes nearly stole his breath. "Thank you."

All he could manage was a nod. Then he slipped from the room and headed to the stove, hoping the mundane task of putting a kettle on would restore his composure. Heaven knew he needed some. Yearning for a family of his own had hit him so hard, he feared his knees would buckle.

And not just any family. He wanted *this* family. This

woman. This child. But he'd promised Clara time, and he aimed to keep his word. Although . . . he'd never promised not to woo her over to his way of thinking. A smile curved his lips as he contemplated the prospect.

So distracted was he by the plans running through his mind, he almost overlooked the shadowy outline of a rider mounting up across the yard. A rider who could only be headed one place. The Circle D.

✴ Chapter 9 ✴

Neill bit back a shout and ran out into the night to give chase, not that there was any chance he'd catch the spy. Especially in his stocking feet. He'd removed his boots hours ago. Nevertheless, he charged as far as the barn, debating the wisdom of collecting Mo and setting out after the man.

With the time it would take him to strap on his gun and collect the horse, even if he rode bareback, the other man would be too far ahead to catch. He'd never be able to track him in the dark, and since Neill had no idea in which direction the Circle D lay, it'd be pointless to try.

No. He'd do Clara more good here. Although they wouldn't be staying *here* very long. They'd have to push up their timetable if they were going to have a chance to make their escape before Mack Danvers showed up at the door demanding his grandson.

No woman should have to do what Neill was fixin' to ask Clara to do, not after laboring for hours to bring a child into the world. But there was no help for it. It was the only way to keep Harrison and his mama safe.

Neill slammed the flat of his hand against the barn wall. Blast it all! If there was any other way . . . but there wasn't.

Not unless he wanted to kill the man. Unfortunately, Neill had a feeling God would frown on that solution.

So that left running. And they'd need to make their departure before the sun had fully cleared the horizon.

Blowing out a heavy breath, Neill pushed away from the barn and headed back to the house.

———◆——◆——◆———

A son. I have a son. Clara marveled at the miracle of it as she gazed upon the drowsy babe at her breast. He had suckled for a while, but now his mouth hung lax, his tiny tongue smacking slightly as sleep claimed him.

"Mama loves you, Harrison," she whispered, lifting him slightly so she could press a soft kiss onto his head. "And no one is ever going to take you away from me. I swear it."

Clara's eyes slid closed, a flood of protectiveness surging through her. *God, give me the strength to keep that vow. Guard my son. Keep us together.*

A quiet knock at the door brought her eyes open. Neill.

"Just a minute." She adjusted her sleeping gown, refastened all the buttons, then bid him come in.

He carried a basin before him with a towel slung over his shoulder. "I made sure not to get the water too hot. It's just one degree above tepid." He approached the side of the bed and held the basin out for her inspection. "Do you want to test it?"

She smiled and shook her head slightly. "I trust you." The words tumbled out before she had a chance to think them through. Yet she found she did trust him. Completely. Even with the well-being of her child. How could she not after he had proved himself over and over? Honorable. Reliable.

Capable. Compassionate. Neill Archer was everything she needed in a protector for her child.

And everything you need in a husband? The perverse thought clung tenaciously to the edge of her mind, despite her efforts to shake it free.

Neill slowly lowered the basin to the floor, resting it on the braided rug she'd fashioned as a young bride in a hopeless effort to make her house more of a home. Then he turned to her and held out his hands. "May I take him?"

Clara swallowed hard, her arms instinctively tightening around Harrison's small body. She didn't want anyone else to hold him. Not even Neill. But such thoughts were irrational. All she had to do was look at the awe still stamped on Neill's face to know he'd die before letting harm come to her child.

"Be sure to support his head," she cautioned as she reluctantly loosened her grip on her son.

Neill's large hands, tanned by the sun, nicked and scarred from his work, cupped the babe's head, back, and bottom with easy grace and surprising confidence.

He glanced at her, his lips twitching into one of those boyish smiles that always set her heart to fluttering. "I've got seven nieces and nephews back home, remember? I've held babies before."

Harrison's arms and legs flailed as cool air hit his bare tummy while Neill held him out in front of him. "Easy, little man," Neill murmured. "Gotta get you cleaned up and lookin' your best for your mama. Can't be disappointin' the ladies, now, can we?"

His nonsense made Clara smile. Holding Harrison's head securely with his fingers, Neill positioned the babe along the length of his left forearm, then held him over the basin, talking to him all the while. "Your mama, she's a real special lady, and she sure worked hard to get you here." He picked up a cloth that had been floating in the basin and drizzled water over Harrison's chest.

None too happy about being awakened in such a fashion, the boy's face crumpled and his cries hit the air.

"Don't like the water, huh?" Neill shook his head and made a *tsk*ing sound. "That will change. Just wait till I teach you to fish, and swim, and splash through mud puddles. You'll love the water then. You can catch tadpoles, skip stones, all kinds of fun things. You'll see."

Clara's heart twisted. He spoke to her son just like a father would. A true father. Not just a nice man who wanted to help out. If she gave him the chance, would he come to think of her as a husband would a wife, not just someone in need of protection? Could he look past her Comanche blood and see her as a woman? A woman worthy of his love?

Neill finished bathing Harrison, then wrapped him in a towel and snuggled him close to his chest. He pushed to his feet and paced the floor, bouncing Harrison in gentle motions until the baby settled. Clara couldn't seem to tear her eyes away from the sight. There was something about seeing a man—a well-muscled, hard-working man—cradling an infant tenderly to his chest that turned her insides to mush and made her heart long for the impossible.

"Do you have a gown for him?" Neill's question snapped her out of her musing.

She nodded quickly and motioned for him to bring her son to the bed. "I rolled it inside the blanket." She grabbed the bundle from her bedside table and unfurled it. "Lay him here," she instructed, "and I'll dress him."

Neill sat on the edge of the bed and handed Harrison back into her care. He offered the babe his finger to clasp while she fastened a diaper into place, then pulled free of the baby's hold when she slipped the white gown over Harrison's head and threaded his arms through the sleeves. After tugging the long skirt of the garment over her son's bent legs, she swaddled him in the soft flannel blanket and cuddled him near her heart. When Harrison ceased his fretting and relaxed against her, it dawned on her how quiet Neill had become. Eerily quiet.

"What is it?"

His gaze lifted from the babe to her face, his expression grim. "I spotted a man in the yard—one of Mack's men, I assume. He rode off before I could stop him."

A great weight pressed in on Clara's chest, making it difficult to breathe. Neill lifted his hand and fingered a tendril of her hair before pushing it over her ear. The soft touch comforted, even as the news filled her with dread. Her father-in-law was probably hearing the report of Harrison's birth this very moment.

"We have to leave, Clara. By first light. I have to get you to my brother's ranch before Mack catches up to us, which means we've got to get to Amarillo before he realizes you've gone. It's the only way to ensure he doesn't try to force the matter. He can't threaten you if he can't find you." His voice echoed with gentleness and regret, yet she recognized the steel behind the softness and was grateful for it. His conviction gave her courage. Hope.

"Bring me the baby crate," she instructed, willing her weariness away. "I'll put Harrison down and see to the packing."

Neill laid a staying hand on her shoulder. "Not yet. I've

74

got extra water heating for your bath. All I want you to do is see to yourself. I'll take care of everything else."

And he did. He filled a tub with gloriously warm bath-water, settled Harrison in his crate-bed, and then left her to her privacy while he packed up his belongings, whatever food he could stuff into a burlap sack, and all the shotgun shells he could find to accompany the only additional weapon at their disposal. She saw the evidence of his industriousness when he carried her to the parlor and laid her on the settee. The daft man insisted she not wear herself out with walking and instead carted her around like an invalid.

Although, truth be told, she was as weak as a newborn kitten after pulling herself out of that tub and dressing. Still, it was shameful to be toted around like a helpless lamb. Even if such action left her feeling delightfully cherished.

"Any mementos or geegaws you want me to pack up with your clothes?" he asked on his way to her room, a small trunk tucked under his arm—the trunk that had once carried her trousseau.

She'd banished the leather case to the barn loft, packing away the table linens and embroidered pillowcases she'd lovingly crafted as a young woman, after she realized the true reason Matthew had married her. A tiny act of rebellion, one he'd never even noticed, but an essential one for her. She'd had to preserve her hopes, protect them from the withering forces of reality. Somehow it made it easier to endure a loveless marriage if her dreams were packed into a trunk for safekeeping.

Now they were back and in the hands of another man. Would he care for them? Or simply dump them on the floor to make room for clothing and supplies?

"Clara?" he asked again. "Anything special you want me to pack?"

Feeling rather like Gideon laying out a fleece, she said nothing about the linens. "Just the photograph of my parents and my mother's Bible on the bedside table."

He nodded crisply, then disappeared into her bedroom. Drawers opened and closed, and a blush rose to her cheeks as she imagined him stuffing her undergarments and stockings into the trunk along with her two good skirts and shirtwaists.

Then a great rustling ensued. What on earth was he doing in there?

A moment later the answer became apparent as he carefully navigated the doorway with her mattress, minus the soiled bedding, tucked under his arm.

"What are you doing with *that*?"

He gave her a stern look. "You are going to rest in the wagon on the way to Amarillo. I'm not about to have you come down with childbed fever because you were forced from your home hours after giving birth. Harrison needs his mama, and I aim to see she stays around to watch him grow up."

Clara opened her mouth to protest, then promptly shut it as she recalled that Neill's mother had died from such a fever mere days after he was born. His high-handed orders were symptoms of his concern. She supposed she could let him coddle her a bit if it made him feel better, though there was no way she'd actually sleep with the threat of Mack Danvers hanging over their heads.

But sleep she did. Nearly the entire way to Amarillo. She woke when the buckboard's wheel hit a rut and she found herself under a pile of blankets. Harrison's crate lay beside her, sheltered from the wind by the sides of the wagon and her trunk.

She craned her neck to peer up at Neill. He was facing forward, his wide shoulders and broad back exuding strength as he somehow managed to keep the two mismatched horses to a steady gait. Mo towered over her little gray mare, but the two seemed to have settled into a rhythm.

Clara's gaze darted to her trunk, curiosity compelling her forward. Was her fleece wet or dry? Biting her lip, she cast one last glance at Neill, then quietly levered herself to a sitting position and began working furiously at the trunk straps. Once they were loose, she opened the lid and dug her hand down past the petticoats and nightdresses until her fingers stroked a neatly folded fabric edge. Her heart did a little flip as she latched onto the piece and tugged it upward. Embroidered flowers of blue and yellow danced across white cotton. Her eyes misted as her lips curled upward.

He'd kept her linens.

✶ Chapter 10 ✶

Neill ran a weary hand over his face as the train rattled along the tracks. Whiskers scratched his palm. His lids closed over eyes that burned from a combination of too much soot and too little sleep. They'd been on this train for the better portion of two days. Two days of hard wooden seats, stale air, and noise that never seemed to end.

He hadn't been able to afford passage in a sleeping car, as much as he wished he could give Clara that luxury. Still, she never complained. She leaned against the window using his coat as a pillow and slept as much as she could manage. When darkness fell and the cabin grew chilled, however, Neill gathered her into his arms and urged her to rest against him, where it was warmer. He tended Harrison while she slept, and when she awoke and took over, he grabbed what rest he could, knowing he'd need all his wits in the coming hours.

Mack was on their trail.

He'd said nothing to Clara. She already looked behind her enough as it was. She didn't need more worry heaped on her shoulders. He'd tell her when the need arose, but until then, he'd carry the burden on his own.

He'd spotted Mack Danvers in Amarillo. And worse,

Mack had spotted him. Clara, thank God, had already been onboard the train with Harrison. Neill had been seeing to the trunk when he heard a shout from down the street. Mack Danvers stood in front of the livery, kicking up a fuss and gesturing wildly at the gray mare and worn buckboard the owner had just purchased. From Neill.

Clara had insisted he sell the wagon and gray mare, not knowing when or if they'd return. She'd encouraged him to use the funds to purchase their tickets, but when she wasn't looking, he'd slipped the money into her handbag. Should she decide not to marry him, he wanted to make sure she had a bit of money to make her own way. But with Mack so close, he wished he'd just turned the old mare out to pasture somewhere outside of town. Somewhere void of people so no one could give out his description or point Mack in the direction of the train station. He'd been careful not to mention their travel plans, but when a stranger wandering through sells his horse and wagon in a railroad town, there was only one logical conclusion to make.

He'd hurried onto the train after that and whispered a prayer of thanksgiving when the final whistle blew. The train started its slow chug out of the station as Neill made his way to his seat. But halfway down the aisle, he spotted a man on horseback racing to catch the train. Neill bent low to peer out the window, his gut telling him the man's identity before his eyes confirmed it.

Mack.

The horse came alongside the car, and Mack's gaze bored into his. There was too much noise to hear what he yelled, but Neill had no trouble reading Clara's name on Mack's lips or the threat raging across his features.

Mack Danvers hadn't been able to pull them from the train, but Neill knew the man wouldn't be far behind. There was another departure on the Amarillo schedule, slated for the afternoon. He and Clara had a few hours' cushion at best.

Pulling his thoughts back to the present, Neill peered over Clara's head to the window, his bleary eyes drinking in the sight of pine trees zipping past. Home wasn't far now.

"Have a biscuit, Neill. It's a little stale but still filling." Clara held the golden roll out to him with a tired smile.

He glanced down at the burlap sack in her lap. The thing was pitifully flat. He shook his head. "You take it. You and Harrison need it more than I do."

"I ate while you were resting," she said. "Please, Neill. You've barely slept and hardly eaten. I promise I won't waste away if you have the last biscuit."

Neill exhaled a heavy sigh at the same time his stomach let out a lusty growl. Clara's eyes widened, her mouth twitching suspiciously. Suddenly they both erupted in quiet laughter.

"Give me that thing," Neill groused between chuckles. He took it from her hand and bit into it with comical relish. Clara grinned at him with such affection that it was all Neill could do to swallow the biscuit bite without choking as a new hunger emerged. Only their lack of privacy kept him from leaning forward to taste her lips.

Clara must have sensed the change in him, for she quickly glanced away, a touch of pink coloring her cheeks. She set the empty sack aside and lifted a fussing Harrison from his crate at her feet to her shoulder.

Neill ate the rest of his biscuit in silence.

"Do you think Mack will follow us?" Clara finally ventured.

He nodded, knowing the time had come for candidness. "Yep. I spotted him in Amarillo before we left. A few well-worded questions around the depot would let him know our destination. He's probably just a few hours behind us."

Clara worried her bottom lip with her teeth and lifted her hand to shelter Harrison's head, tucking the babe close to her neck. "Is there a chance he could catch us before we get to your brother's ranch? He'll be able to travel much faster as a single rider than we will in a wagon."

Neill wrapped his arm around Clara's shoulder and drew her into his side. He pressed a chaste kiss to her forehead and held her tight. "I wired Travis before we left Amarillo yesterday. He'll be expecting us. And the trouble on our tail. We'll have reinforcements."

As long as the telegraph had been delivered.

Neill kept that worry to himself. Oftentimes the telegraph office in Palestine held on to messages for those who lived on outlying ranches and farms. They didn't have the manpower to deliver messages out of town. He'd used the word *Urgent* at the beginning of his message, hoping that would spur the telegrapher to hire someone to deliver it immediately, but he couldn't be sure it had.

If Jim happened to be in town, they would no doubt deliver the message to him, but Neill had been gone so long, he had no idea what Jim's schedule was anymore. He used to make regular town visits to oversee his carpentry shop and to let his wife, Cassie, visit with her folks, but he much preferred the solitude of their homestead near the Archer ranch, and spent most of his time there.

"I'll take care of you, Clara," Neill vowed. "Mack will

never get his hands on Harrison as long as I have breath in my body."

She turned her face so far into his chest that he nearly missed her whispered words. "That's what I'm afraid of."

Neill's heart slammed against his rib cage as the rest of his body grew unnaturally still. Had she meant that the way it sounded? Could she actually be coming to care for him more as a man than a protector?

He prayed it was so. Because it'd tear his heart out if he ever had to let her go.

◆   ◆   ◆

When they finally disembarked from the train late that afternoon, Clara worried that her legs would collapse beneath her. Neill's strong grasp at her elbow kept her upright, but she couldn't quite contain her sigh of gratitude when he guided her to an empty bench on the depot platform and directed her to sit while he fetched his horse from the stock car.

She glanced around the busy station as she straightened Harrison's blanket around his neck and head. Passengers mingled with friends and family, businessmen collected shipments, porters carted trunks and luggage. She scanned every face that came within view, ever diligent in case Mack should appear. Yet more than fear drove her to attend to the details around her. This was Neill's home. He could probably greet many of these people by name. His history lay here, and at his brother's ranch. That in itself made the place fascinating. It was part of the man she was coming to love.

Clara spotted Neill crossing the platform, his long strides propelling him quickly through the milling crowd. "Mo's unloaded," he said when he reached her. "One of the stable boys will bring him around for us. I'll need to ride over to the livery to hire a wagon, so I thought it'd be better for you to be inside. I should only be gone a few minutes, but I don't like you out here on your own. Once the crowd disperses you'll be too visible."

She nodded and reached for the hand he offered her, but a low voice boomed across the platform, freezing her in place.

"Neill!" A monster of a man barreled his way toward them. Clara instinctively clutched Harrison tighter to her chest in an effort to shield him from whatever danger this man presented, but then she caught sight of the enormous grin spreading across Neill's face.

"Jim! Am I ever happy to see you." He held out his hand to the man only to be yanked into a bear of a hug.

"You been gone too long, kid," the other man groused, not more than a hint of a smile warming his countenance, yet the affection between the two was undeniable. Jim stepped out of the embrace after a moment and regarded her with stoic eyes, his gaze traveling from her to the bundle she held. One brow lifted in question. "This the trouble you wired us about?"

Heat flamed in Clara's cheeks.

Neill frowned. "Watch it, Jim." His growled warning drew another raised brow from the large man.

"Clara Danvers," Neill said, taking her hand and helping her to her feet before wrapping a decidedly possessive arm about her shoulders, "this mannerless brute is my brother Jim." Neill gave her a squeeze, probably to help shore up her courage. She found her chin ratcheting a few degrees higher in response, and she could have sworn she saw the barest flash of a twinkle in Jim's eyes.

Heavens, she really must be tired. Now she was seeing things.

"The trouble is on our trail," Neill explained in a voice low enough not to carry to any passersby. "I'm not sure how far back. Clara's father-in-law wants to confiscate her babe so he can raise the boy as his own without her interference. Her husband is dead, and his father insists she give up all claim to the child, which, of course, she's not willing to do. I offered her protection and figured the ranch was the best place to make a stand."

"You figured right." Only three words, but they carried a simple acceptance that had Clara's spirit soaring with gratitude and relief. Maybe the man wasn't as hard as he appeared.

Jim grabbed her small trunk and started walking toward the edge of the platform. "Come on. I've got a wagon waiting."

Neill gathered Harrison's empty sleeping crate, then steered her into his brother's wake. "How'd you know which train to meet?"

Jim never broke stride. "Didn't," he called over his shoulder. "This is my third train today."

Clara stared after the man, amazed at the matter-of-fact statement and all it conveyed. The Archers were a dedicated, loyal bunch, it seemed. Neill had told her as much, yet she never imagined such loyalty would be extended to her after such a short association. Yet Jim hadn't argued with his brother for even a moment or complained about him bringing trouble to their door. He'd just picked up her trunk and marched on as if the slapdash explanation Neill had offered was good enough for him.

When they reached the wagon, she noticed a tall black

man tying Mo's lead line to the rear of the bed. He glanced up at their approach and beamed a smile at Neill. Clara felt a new energy surge through Neill's arm in response.

"Josiah! I wasn't expecting to see you here."

"And why not?" The man crossed his arms over his chest. "We're partners, ain't we? If trouble's houndin' you, it's houndin' me, too."

Neill handed her off to his brother and leapt forward to embrace his friend. The man uncrossed his arms, and the two thumped each other good-naturedly on the back.

This was Josiah? Neill's partner and closest friend? A black man? Clara's arms trembled as the ramifications shattered her composure. Thankfully, Jim handed her up into the wagon seat just then, and she was able to support Harrison's weight upon her lap without fear of dropping him.

All this time she'd worried that Neill, despite his good intentions and kind heart, would come to resent her Comanche blood. Even if her heritage didn't matter to him, she'd feared it would matter to others, and that would affect him. Wear on him. Lead to resentment.

Yet here he stood embracing a black man—a man with a heritage as prone to prejudice as her own—without a single inhibition or care about what others might think.

Perhaps marriage wasn't as impossible as she'd thought. She ducked her head to hide the smile she didn't want to explain when Neill returned to her side.

"Are the kids safe?" Neill asked Jim as his brother swung into the saddle of a waiting mount. "I don't want to put Travis and Meri's brood in harm's way."

"Cassie and her folks have them all corralled at our place. Joanna's there, too."

"So Crock's here?" Neill slid a quick glance in Clara's direction. "Good."

She didn't know what to make of the oddly intense look until she remembered his second brother, Crockett, was a preacher. Her heart gave a little leap. Was Neill still hoping to persuade her toward marriage? Because if he were, she doubted she'd need much convincing to change her answer. After all, she was falling more in love with the man by the minute. But what did he feel toward her? Obligation or something deeper?

The wagon dipped as Neill climbed onto the seat beside her, sandwiching her between himself and Josiah, who was taking up the reins. She was about to ask why Josiah was driving when she noticed Neill's ready grip on the rifle draped across his lap.

"Just a precaution," he said when he noticed her concern. His calm smile did little to impede the shiver coursing down her spine. The gun might be a precaution, but it also announced in no uncertain terms that Neill was prepared to fight for her, and the thought of what could happen to him if he did drove shards of terror through her heart.

✶ Chapter 11 ✶

Neill scanned the trees lining the road as they slowly made their way through the hills, straining his ears for any rustle or stirring in the underbrush that might signal an attack. He hadn't been this vigilant since he'd been a boy, training under Travis's watchful eye to guard the family and their land from all intruders. At least then they'd had the safety of the house and barn to retreat to when needed. Out here in the open, he, Clara, and Josiah were much more vulnerable. Neill bit back an impatient sigh. If they'd been on horseback, they could have been at the ranch by now, but Clara could never have mounted a horse, and it wouldn't have been safe for Harrison, either. So instead they plodded along in the wagon, surrendering precious time to the man pursuing them.

Clara fidgeted beside him, lifting her head from where she'd been lightly dozing against his shoulder for the past hour. She stretched her neck, twisting it forward and back as she rubbed at the soreness with her hand. "How much longer?"

He watched her movements, simple, yet unconsciously

alluring as she exposed the side of her slender neck to his view. Neill cleared his throat. "Thirty, maybe forty-five minutes if we keep this pace." He itched to cup her nape in his hands and massage the tension from her neck and scalp, to release the weight of her hair by tugging her pins free, and to press his lips against the provocative freckle hiding behind her right ear.

Swiveling his head away from her, he ordered his attention back to the trees. As delectable as the prospect of kissing Clara was, he couldn't afford the distraction. Not when her life and her son's future depended on him.

"Where is your brother?" Clara asked. "I thought he was riding to the ranch with us."

"Jim's scouting our back trail." Neill tossed a look over his shoulder. "He'll let us know if anyone is following."

"Do you think Mack could have—"

"Shhh!" Neill held up his hand, a sound having caught his ear. Clara immediately fell silent.

Josiah met his gaze over Clara's head. He'd heard it, too. The Archer family signal, a bird call they'd perfected as children to communicate while hidden in the trees. It came again, and this time Neill placed it. Up ahead and to the right.

He caught a movement in the trees in the same location. Just to be sure, he raised the rifle he'd borrowed from Josiah and tucked the stock into his shoulder but lowered it again when Jim emerged, his horse loping toward them.

"Keep the horses moving," Neill instructed when Josiah started to rein them in. Jim's horse was lathered. That didn't bode well.

Jim came abreast of them. "Older man that matches your

description is heading up the path. Got another rider with him. I took the game trails to cut out some distance, but they'll be upon us in a matter of minutes."

Neill had played this scenario out in his head over and over during the last hour. He knew what had to be done. He gave Jim a sharp nod, tucked Josiah's rifle under the seat and slid it down to where his friend could easily reach it, then climbed over the bench into the wagon bed.

"Neill?" Clara tried to grab his arm, but he evaded her grip. "Where are you going?" Harrison started fretting at his mama's sharp tone. Neill hardened himself against it.

Coming up behind Josiah, he clutched the man's shoulder. "As soon as I get Mo clear, race for the ranch. All out. Got it?"

"I'll get 'em there. Don't worry." Josiah adjusted his grip on the reins, ready to whip them over the horses' backs.

He trusted Josiah with his life, but somehow it still tore his gut out to leave Clara and Harrison in another's care. He glanced back at Clara. A mistake. She'd turned in her seat, her eyes full of fear. For him. Shutting down his emotion, he pivoted away, grasped the side of the wagon, and started edging his way to the rear.

But he couldn't leave yet. Not without . . .

Neill spun and lunged toward Clara. He wrapped his hand around her nape and kissed her with all the passion and love he'd been storing up over the last several days. She clutched his arm and kissed him back with a desperate enthusiasm that nearly buckled his knees.

"I love you, Clara Danvers." His husky voice rasped between them. "And when I get back, I aim to make you mine."

Her eyes shimmered. "I'm already yours."

Neill pressed his forehead to hers, his eyes scrunching tightly closed at the sweetness of those words. Then he shoved away. He'd already delayed too long.

Whistling to Mo, he made his way to the side of the wagon, his step unsteady as the wheels continued rolling over uneven road. He untied the horse's lead line and tossed it over Mo's neck. Then, bracing one booted foot on the side of the wagon while he murmured encouragement to his gelding, Neill stood straight and grabbed for the saddle horn as he leapt onto the animal's back.

"Go!" he shouted to Josiah.

The man needed little urging. "Hyah!" He slapped the reins against the team's back, and the wagon lurched forward.

Neill forced himself not to watch. Instead he turned Mo around to face whatever came down the road, pulling his own rifle from the scabbard on his saddle.

"We stand together, brother," Jim said, guiding his mount into position beside Neill.

"Together," Neill confirmed.

A rumbling echoed from the south, growing louder as hoofbeats thundered closer.

Mo snorted and sidestepped. "Steady, boy." Neill leaned forward and patted his horse's neck. "Steady."

All at once, Mack Danvers and his companion surged around the bend. Capitalizing on the element of surprise, Neill jammed his rifle butt against his hip and fired a round into the sky. The loud crack spooked the horses. They whinnied in distress and reared up, their hooves pawing the air. Mack and his comrade had their hands full just trying to stay in the saddle.

"You're not welcome here, Danvers," Neill shouted above

the melee. "You made your offer and Clara declined. Leave her be."

Mack wrestled his mount under control. "You want the little squaw, you can have her," he spat. "But the boy is mine. I won't leave without him."

"You won't leave *with* him." Neill narrowed his focus. The man had made no move to go for his gun since he and Jim already had theirs out and ready, but there was something about his demeanor that made the back of Neill's neck prickle.

"That boy's my flesh and blood, Archer. The heir to the Circle D." Mack's mount started dancing nervously again, as if sensing his rider's rising temper. "You'll have to shoot me to stop me from retrieving my grandson."

A war cry burst from Mack's lungs, and he charged.

Neill clutched Mo with his knees and took aim with his rifle. He couldn't let Mack steal Harrison from Clara. He couldn't. His finger tightened on the trigger.

But he couldn't shoot a man in cold blood, either.

And Mack seemed to know that, the blackguard. He'd taken a calculated risk, and it had paid off.

Neill wavered. The man would be upon him in a blink. He could see the light of victory glowing in his eyes.

No!

He might not be able to shoot a man in cold blood, but that didn't mean he was helpless to stop him.

Neill flipped his rifle around, grabbed the barrel with both hands, and the instant Mack came into range, swung it like a club. Mack's eyes went wide. Left with no choice, he dodged sideways to escape the blow, his frantic momentum toppling him from the saddle as the rifle butt grazed his skull.

Neill followed, launching himself atop Mack, trusting Jim to deal with the second man.

Fists crashed into flesh. Bone slammed against bone. Hardened experience battled youthful vigor, desperation lending both men enhanced strength.

Neill's head pounded from multiple collisions with the ground. Blood oozed from his nose, and his left eye was nearly swollen shut. His ribs ached, his hip throbbed, and he thought his right shoulder might have been knocked out of joint when Mack had flipped him over his head. Mack was in equally poor shape, gasping for air between blows. Yet when he threw his weight atop Neill and pinned him to the ground, he gained the advantage.

Neill kicked out at Mack's gut even as the older man's hands came up to crush his windpipe. Thoughts of Clara and Harrison darted through Neill's mind as dark spots began to cloud his vision.

His family. *God above, don't let me fail them.*

⋆ Chapter 12 ⋆

Clara held on for dear life as Josiah whipped the wagon around a corner and down a private drive. Bracing her feet against the front board and gripping the side of the seat with her right hand, she clutched Harrison to her chest with her left and prayed they'd somehow get to the ranch without the wagon flipping.

They raced through thick stands of trees that nearly blocked the sun. Only when the pines began to thin did Josiah rein in the frenzied horses. He lifted off the bench slightly, using his weight to bring the team under control. At the same time, he let out a piecing whistle that left her ears ringing. The wagon hit a clearing and Clara gasped. Two armed men stood in their path, legs braced apart, rifles raised. She immediately twisted sideways and curled her body around Harrison, shielding her son as best she could.

Her eyes squeezed tightly closed, Clara jerked when Josiah cupped her shoulders with his hands.

"Come on, Miz Danvers. We got to get you into the house. I promised Neill I'd keep you and the little one safe. I can't do that so good out in the wagon."

She grabbed hold of Josiah's arm with her free hand. "But those men . . ."

A smile broke across his features, his teeth shining brightly in his dark face. "Travis and Crock ain't gonna shoot you, ma'am. They's just making sure we don't got any unwanted comp'ny on our tail."

"Travis?" Clara twisted abruptly toward the man approaching her from the opposite side of the wagon. With his gun now pointed harmlessly at the ground, she saw past the threat of the weapon to the face behind it. He was an older version of Neill. Tall, lean, and a bit more weathered, but definitely capable of lending aid.

"You've got to go after Neill," she blurted.

In a blink, his expression changed from one of curiosity to a hard stare that nearly froze her to her seat. It didn't stop her, though. Nothing would stop her. Not when Neill's life hung in the balance.

Dodging Josiah's grip, she leaned toward Travis and seized his shoulder. "Please. Mack is obsessed with taking my son from me. Neill stayed behind to head him off. But Mack will stop at nothing. Not even killing. Not if it means getting control of his grandson. You have to help Neill. Please!"

"Josiah?" Travis looked past her, a brow raised.

Clara glanced between the two men. Why wasn't Travis rushing to fetch his horse? Did he not realize how little time they had?

"Jim is with him," the driver said, his voice frustratingly void of urgency. "I promised Neill to look after his woman, so I'll be here to watch the house."

Travis nodded once, then finally started issuing orders. "Crock, take the lady in to Meri. Josiah, see to the team.

I'll saddle the horses." Then he turned back to her. "You'll be safe here, ma'am. If you belong to Neill, you belong to all of us. No matter what happens, you and your child will be protected."

"Thank you, but please go. Neill needs you more than I do right now." She released his shoulder, barely restraining herself from shooing him on his way.

He grinned at her impatience, then set off at a jog toward the barn. Another man immediately stepped into the void he'd left and smiled up at her. The warm, natural charm he exuded softened the edge of her distress. "I'm Crockett, ma'am. Let me help you down."

She thought to put Harrison back in his makeshift bed before alighting, but strong hands circled her waist and had her feet on the ground before she could blink. "Th-thank you." He held her steady while she braced her wobbly legs beneath her. "I'm Clara, by the way. Clara Danvers."

He winked at her. "Soon to be Clara Archer, I'll bet."

She lifted her chin. "Yes."

"Excellent!" He took her arm and led her to the log house standing a short distance away. "It's about time that boy settled down. Maybe now he'll quit galavantin' all over the state and stay put for a while."

They hadn't even reached the porch yet when a lovely blond woman bustled out the front door. She had a slight hitch in her step, but the enthusiastic welcome glowing in her blue eyes erased all else from Clara's mind. How long had it been since she'd had true female companionship?

"Meri, meet Clara," Crockett announced as he assisted her up the stairs. "Neill's intended."

The instant she reached the top step, Clara found herself

wrapped in a fierce hug. "Welcome to the family, Clara. I've been praying for the Lord to lead Neill to the right woman. And here you are."

The right woman? Tears welled in Clara's eyes. She carried Comanche blood and was the mother of another man's babe—yet this beautiful, kind-hearted lady took one look at her and not only accepted her but called her an answer to prayer. Her knees did buckle then.

"Whoa." Crockett grabbed hold of her elbow and steadied her.

"I'm fine," Clara insisted, waving away his help once she had her feet back under her. "I'm just a little worn out from the trip."

"Of course you are." Meri held out her hands. "Could I take the baby for you? Mine have gotten so big, it would be such a joy to hold an infant again."

Clara hesitated only a moment, then nodded. "His name is Harrison," she said as she handed her son into Meri's arms.

"He's beautiful," the other woman enthused. "Such a dear. And so tiny. Why, he can't be more than a couple weeks old."

"Two days."

"Two days?" Meri gasped. "Good heavens! You came straight from childbed, didn't you? What was that boy thinking?"

Clara stiffened. "That *man* was saving my son. Leaving was necessary." Why did they all speak of Neill as if he were still a child?

Meri looked taken aback, and then a slow smile spread across her face. "Yes. You are *definitely* the right woman."

"Crock!" Travis's shout drew all eyes to the barn, where he emerged leading two horses. "Mount up."

Neill's brother placed a hand on her shoulder. "We'll bring your *man* back to you safe and sound, Clara. Don't worry."

She glared at his teasing grin. "See that you do."

His chuckle warmed her, but the sound quickly dissipated as he bounded down the steps and across the yard to the waiting horses.

The men disappeared in a flurry of dust as they kicked their horses into a run. Meri led the way into the house, so busy cooing to Harrison that she didn't notice Clara's hesitation to follow.

She peered into the trees as if she could actually see Neill if she just tried hard enough. "Bring him back to me," she whispered, the prayer lifting from the depths of her heart. "I need him."

⸺◆⸺◆⸺

Mack's fingers tightened their grip on Neill's throat. Consciousness ebbed.

Then a vision of Clara swam through his mind. Clara alone. Abandoned. Her son lost to her. *No!* Neill forced the darkness back, a new ferocity thrumming in his veins.

Mack shifted position to press more weight against Neill's throat, and Neill seized the opening. With a surge of strength that could only be God-given, he raised both knees and jammed his boots into Mack's gut. He twisted and shoved with all his might, launching Mack sideways. Neill gulped blessedly sweet air.

Not taking any time to savor that sweetness, Neill immediately threw himself on top of Mack and slammed his fist into the man's body and face again and again until his adversary finally stopped swinging back.

"Clara is to be my wife," Neill shouted down at the man moaning beneath him. "Harrison will carry *my* name. Be *my* son. You no longer have any claim to him. Do you understand?"

Mack stilled. Eyes that had been rolling back in his head suddenly sharpened their focus. "She named the boy Harrison?" His grunted words were barely decipherable, but Neill made them out.

"Yes." Odd that the boy's name would have such an effect on him.

Mack lifted his head an inch off the ground, then collapsed back down. "My grandmother's . . . maiden name."

Neill's brows rose. What were the chances? True, Harrison was a rather common surname, but for it to belong to both Clara's mother and Mack's grandmother smacked of something stronger than coincidence. Providence, perhaps? After all, he doubted Clara would have named her son Harrison had she known the family attachment Mack had to the same name. There was too much animosity between them for her to choose a name that reminded her at all of her overbearing father-in-law.

"Can I at least see him?" Mack murmured, his words slurring slightly. "He's all I've got left of my boys."

Neill's gut screamed no. The man wasn't to be trusted. But stealing a man's grandson from him was no better than what Mack had tried to do to Clara. Harrison deserved to know his entire family, warts and all.

"Only on my terms," Neill growled, "and only if Clara agrees."

Mack's eyes slid closed, and the lines of tension etching his face eased. "Thank you."

Neill rolled off the man and tugged him to his feet. "Harrison will be my son in the eyes of the law, an Archer, with all the protection of the Archer family. I will love him like my own and raise him accordingly. He'll know ranching, hunting, horses, weapons, and . . . if you can see your way to cooperating, he'll know his grandfather, too."

Mack sucked in a harsh breath. "You . . . you won't keep him from me?"

"You'll only be allowed to see him on Archer property, and only with me or one of his uncles in attendance. But understand this." Neill grabbed Mack's shirtfront and brought the man's face even with his own. "If you ever attempt to take the boy or if anything suspicious occurs while you are with him, your welcome will be revoked. Permanently. You'll never see him again. Understand?"

"What of the Circle D?" The man's shoulders stiffened slightly, a hint of the old belligerence creeping back into his voice. "Would you keep the boy from what is rightly his just to spite me?"

Neill shook his head. "When Harrison is old enough, we can discuss a visit. But I won't force it on him if he is unwilling. If you want to name him your heir, that's your business. However, don't be thinkin' you'll have long summers together to train him in the ranch's management. Not unless you prove yourself trustworthy first."

"Sounds reasonable to me," a voice behind them said. "Don't you think, Crock?"

Neill turned to find Travis and Crockett astride their

horses, wrists crossed over their saddle horns as if content to watch the show from that vantage point.

"Yep. Plenty reasonable." Crock winked at him. Neill grinned.

"'Bout time you two got here," Jim groused, his own face sporting several new bruises as he shoved Mack's hired man in front of him to join the gathering.

Travis pushed back the brim of his hat. "Seems to me you two young'uns had things well in hand."

Jim scowled. Crockett chuckled. And Neill could only think how good it was to be home.

"We'll take care of Danvers and his man for you, Neill," Travis said in his usual take-charge way. "Go home to your woman and let her know you're all right."

For once, Neill felt no urge to argue. He hobbled toward Mo and hefted himself into the saddle, ignoring the protest of his muscles.

"Send Josiah back with word on whether or not Clara's willing to let Danvers see the babe," Travis called out. "If not, we'll escort him back to town and see him on the train."

Neill raised a hand to let his brother know he'd heard, then nudged Mo into a canter. The faster pace sent pain radiating through him with every stride, but Neill didn't care. All that mattered was getting to Clara and assuring her that Harrison was safe.

✳ Chapter 13 ✳

Clara paced the parlor, unable to sit. Her exhausted body begged her to join Meri on the settee, but her fretful mind wouldn't allow it. Not until she knew how Neill fared.

Josiah stood guard on the porch, one hip resting against the railing as he scanned the drive. Every time Clara paced by the window, she glanced his way, searching for a clue in his demeanor that might tell her how dire the situation truly was. But the man kept lounging there as if he weren't the slightest bit concerned. Such a stance should reassure her, but instead all she could think was that he knew she was watching him and was purposely projecting a relaxed air to ease her worry. Which only served to inflame her anxiety.

"Come sit, Clara," Meri urged. "You're going to wear yourself out with all that pacing. You won't be any good to Neill if you collapse."

That last argument stilled Clara's feet. Neill had been strong for her through all of this. She owed it to him to be strong in return. The stoicism that had been her strength for so many years fell back over her like a familiar gown, rolling from her head to her toes in one long wave. No more pacing. No more fretting. Whatever came, she'd deal with it the best she could. Hadn't God proved He could be trusted, even in the darkest times? He'd brought Neill to her, after all.

And didn't Neill deserve her faith, as well? She'd been angry when Meri and the others had referred to him as a boy, but had she done any better—immediately assuming he'd not be able to hold his own against Mack? Neill had proven himself capable, honorable, a man worthy of her trust. And where trust led, her heart had followed—right into Neill Archer's keeping.

Clara made her way to the chair nearest the window and lowered herself onto the cushion. No matter what happened, she'd not disgrace him with hysterics. She'd be a rock, a steady fortress, a . . .

"Rider comin' in."

Josiah's shout spurred Clara from her chair, heart pounding. She rushed to the window, all thoughts of rocks evaporating like insubstantial mist.

"It's Neill!"

That's all she needed to hear. Clara ran for the door, her heart sending prayers of gratitude heavenward even as her feet flew across the porch and down the steps. God had brought him back. He looked like he'd been run over by a freight wagon, but he was alive and fit enough to sit a horse. God was good.

He'd barely dismounted when she threw herself into his arms. He groaned, but tightened his arms around her waist and drew her even closer into him.

"It's over, Clara. Harrison's safe."

Clara gazed up at his face, bruised and bloodied, yet the most beautiful face she'd ever seen. "I love you, Neill

Archer," she said, echoing the words he'd left her with in the wagon, and infusing them with the truth of her own heart. "And as soon as that preacher brother of yours returns, I plan to make you mine."

Neill grinned that crooked, boyish grin that always turned her insides to melted butter and lowered his head toward hers. "I'm already yours." The husky murmur echoed in her ears as his lips met hers in a caress so tender, a tear of sheer wonder slid past her lashes. Her palms moved up his chest and her fingers clutched at his shirt as if she could hold him to her forever.

"I'll . . . uh . . . just take care of your horse," Josiah said from somewhere behind them.

Clara broke away from the kiss and buried her face against Neill's neck, embarrassed to have forgotten they weren't alone.

"Thanks, partner." The deep sarcasm in Neill's voice made Clara smile against his collar. Then he shifted his stance a bit and called after his friend. "Oh, by the way, it might be a while before we can make an offer on the ranch. I'm still over a hundred short."

"Don't worry about it," Josiah answered. "Travis said we could run our herd on his back acres as long as we need to. We'll make do."

"No. Wait." Clara raised her head and looked from Neill to Josiah and back again. "Remember when I told you about the inheritance I had set aside? I always planned to use that money to provide for Harrison. What better way to provide for my son than to invest in a home for him and a livelihood for his future? All I have to do is write a letter to Mr. Whitfield at the bank back in Dry Gulch, and he'll transfer the funds to your account here. *Our* account. He can even see about selling my old cabin for me."

Neill's fingertips stroked her cheek. "Are you sure, honey? That's your money."

"No, Neill. It's *our* money. *Our* dream. Let me share it with you."

"You're an amazing woman, Clara Danvers." His fingers trailed from her cheek down along her neck and toyed with a stray piece of hair that had come loose from her pins. Her skin tingled in response. "What did I ever do to deserve you?"

"What did you ever do?" A laugh bubbled out of Clara before she could stop it. "Well, let's see." She ticked her answers off on her fingers. "You fixed my roof, you delivered my son, and, oh yes, you saved me from an obsessed man set on stealing my child. I'd say you've done plenty."

Instead of the smile she'd been expecting, his face grew solemn at her words. "About Mack . . . I need to ask a favor of you."

"What?"

"I think you should let him see Harrison."

"No!" How could he suggest such a thing? After all Mack had done, there was no way she'd let him anywhere near her baby.

"Hear me out, Clara." Neill's soft voice penetrated the haze of her indignation. "Hear me out, and if you still don't feel comfortable with the idea, I'll send him away. I told him you would have to agree. That I wouldn't go against your wishes."

Clara exhaled a long breath, giving her mind a chance to catch up with her emotions. This was Neill. The man she loved. The man she trusted with her life. With her son's life. He wouldn't ask her to do anything that would put Harrison in jeopardy.

"All right," she conceded. "I'll listen."

He led her to the porch, to a pair of rocking chairs, and held her hand as he explained the bargain he'd proposed to Mack. A bargain made in Harrison's best interest. To reserve the boy's chance to inherit the Circle D. The chance to know his only living grandfather. The chance to restore relationships that Clara had believed beyond mending. All while under the watchful eye of the man who would be his father not by blood, but by choice. A choice inspired by love.

"I trust you, Neill," she finally said, squeezing his hand. "I trust you to protect our son and to guide our family. Mack can come."

He lifted her hand to his face and kissed the back of it, holding his lips there for several long, delicious seconds. "Thank you," he murmured against her skin. "I think it's the right thing to do."

"But he can't stay for the wedding," she blurted. "Archers only."

A deep chuckle rumbled in his chest, shaking his body as laughter overflowed into the air between them. "Archers only, huh?" Slowly, the amusement faded from his gaze, replaced by a love so intense, her lonely heart ached from the pure belonging it inspired. Bending his head, he laid another kiss upon her hand. "Sounds perfect."

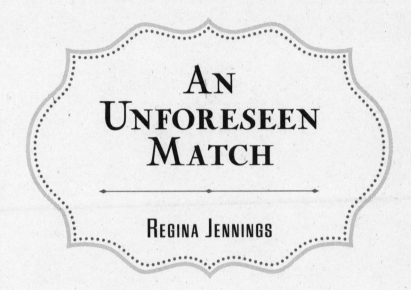

An
Unforeseen
Match

Regina Jennings

✶ Chapter 1 ✶

Dry Gulch, Texas
Late Summer 1893

Grace O'Malley heaved her last box of belongings onto the table and peered inside, forgetting it did her little good. With her failing vision she could see the curves of the book spines, but the gold lettering was lost to her.

A shadow passed through her light. Her friend Emilie stepped near. "Your books? Where do you want us to put them?"

Grace trailed her fingers over the leather covers. "I no longer have any use for them, do I? Give them to your children. In a few years they may enjoy reading them."

"Oh, I hate for you to—" Emilie snuffled, then spoke with determined brightness. "Thank you. They'll cherish them."

Grace turned to where she thought the three other women stood. "What is left to do before this place is suitable? Should I scrub the basin?"

"I've already done that," Hannah answered, hesitation corking her voice.

"Then I'll make the bed." Grace inched forward, hands

outstretched. Her shoe bounced against the chair leg. She grasped the back, reoriented herself, and set forth again to the lone bedroom.

"Honestly, Grace. Why don't you scoot on out?" The broom whisks paused for Mrs. Stevenson's scolding. "You'll only be in the way."

Grace's neck tensed. A year ago she could've been considered the most capable woman in Dry Gulch. Now she was less help than a child. Well, she had to rectify that situation.

She clasped the metal footboard of the bed and swept her hand over the cool feather tick until she found the stack of folded linens. She fingered the pile. A sheet on top. No, two cotton sheets, then a well-worn quilt. Leaving a sheet on the bed, she moved the pile of blankets to set them on the dressing table, but when she released them, they dropped to the floor.

"My dust pile!" Mrs. Stevenson erupted in coughing. "And those blankets were just laundered."

Grace rubbed her own itchy nose. "You moved the dressing table. How was I supposed to know?"

"Well, I had to sweep beneath it."

Quick steps neared. A muffled pounding and more dust. "Don't worry. We'll air them out and they'll be as good as new." Hannah spoke in the same patient tones she used for the students at the school where she and Grace taught together—*had* taught together before the darkness stole Grace's profession. "Let me help you make the bed."

"Or even better," Emilie said, "I'll help and Grace can rest."

"Rest?" Grace crossed her arms. "I'm not tired. I'm not sick. I canna sit in a rocker for the next fifty years, waiting for me life to end."

Silence. She cast about, trying to catch a glimpse of a face but couldn't land on anything recognizable. Were they watching her? More likely they were exchanging significant glances, shaking their heads, and communicating pity right in front of her because she couldn't see it.

"If that's how it's to be." She felt her way past the bed and grasped the rocking chair. Benny, her new puppy, yipped as she stomped past. "I'm going outside." She shoved the rocker before her, enjoying the bustle as the ladies jumped out of her way. Wrestling it past them, she picked up speed until it crashed into the doorframe. The gasps behind her only encouraged her recklessness. She might not be able to see, but she could still make decisions for herself. Even blind, she was a force to be reckoned with.

Finally the chair cleared the threshold, and the punishing heat of late August assaulted her. From the angle of the sun, she assumed the house faced south. Were there any trees on the plot? Doubtful, knowing the ruggedness of the canyon lands. She spun the rocker to face away from the house and sat, prepared to bake in the dry shade of the porch. Prepared to pretend she liked it.

And the pretending had only begun.

Grace hadn't needed the school board to tell her she couldn't teach anymore. She'd known before they had. And since Dry Gulch hadn't grown as predicted, they could do without two teachers. Grace wouldn't be replaced. Merely removed.

What stung was their practical solution to her upkeep. Unlike Hannah Taylor, Grace didn't have any family in town, and boarding her in the homes of her students inconvenienced the parents, especially with the additional burden of her blindness. They needed a place to stash her—like a dilapidated homestead somewhere out of the way, but close enough they could administer charity. Naturally they expected her to sell it, take the money, and move somewhere more convenient, if only she knew where. The young school-teacher with her whole life ahead had been set aside, but she wouldn't go quietly.

"I think you'll want to keep this book." Emilie laid a heavy block on her lap.

Her Bible. Grace wiped the dust from it. She hadn't picked it up since the encroaching darkness had obscured its words, and although she would never again be able to read it, she had to admit the weight of it in her hands comforted her.

She had her faith, her intelligence, and her health. Surely her life still counted for something.

Grace rocked furiously, her mind searching for any small pocket of hope that had been left to her. "Did you say there's a barn?"

Emilie's skirt swished as she turned. "Yes, and a ramshackle mess it is. I don't know how Clara Danvers kept any cattle in it."

"If I set out straight from here will I find it?"

"Don't you dare! You could wander away and never be found."

Grace stopped rocking. "Sooner or later I have to take care of myself."

"Then what excuse would I have to visit my friend?"

From inside the cabin Mrs. Stevenson called out, "While I'm thinking of it, don't fire up your stove. This cabin could go up like a tin of paraffin and you might not be able to find your way out."

Grace jutted her jaw forward. "I'm not to cook. I'm not to leave the cabin. Next thing I know you'll be telling me to stay in me chair unless I have someone aholding me hand."

Another silence. Grace fidgeted, full of energy and no place to expend it. "Don't fash yourself over me. I won't be on your charity long. I'm mulling over a plan."

"A plan?" Emilie's voice held a smile as big as the canyon. "Do share."

Grace expelled the breath she'd held. "Well, it's a mite personal, but since you asked, I'd like a husband, and I'd like to find one while I still have enough sight left to see his face."

A shadow moved between her and the light, too tall to be Mrs. Stevenson. "Your sight could return at any time, Grace. God could work a miracle. Don't despair."

"I'm not despairing, Hannah. I'm planning ahead. While I'm grateful that the school board bequeathed me this homestead, I don't relish the idea of living alone here for the rest of my life. A husband would be useful."

"Possibly, but no guarantee." Emilie's wry smile flashed but a moment before Grace lost sight of it again. With a house filled to the brim with children and a doting husband, Emilie couldn't complain over much.

"Don't you have a brother?" Hannah came nearer. "He'd want to know about your ailment."

Grace searched until a portion of Hannah's concerned face appeared in the fuzzy circle. "Before I'd apply to my brother for help, I'd take a husband on the luck o' the draw."

"I don't know that anyone is raffling off men." Emilie straightened Grace's collar.

Grace slapped her hand away. "Not a contest. I was thinking about an advertisement. I've heard that men do such

113

things. They have land, but want a bride. Why couldn't I do the same? I already have the homestead."

"This homestead brought luck to Clara Danvers. No reason it couldn't happen again," Hannah murmured.

"And with the Cherokee Strip land run next month, there'll be a plethora of land-hungry men passing through," Emilie added. "Dry Gulch will be crammed with potential husbands who lost out in the race."

"What will they think of her condition?" Mrs. Stevenson asked. "And how could she marry a perfect stranger?"

The three figures had converged before her, their forms creating a dark block. "If the stranger is perfect, he won't be too disappointed that my eyesight is failing. I still have much to offer."

But no one spoke up to affirm her statement. Grace's grip on her Bible tightened.

Emilie recovered first. "If you place an advertisement, be sure to mention your charming Irish lilt."

"And your stunning beauty," Hannah said.

"And the homestead. After all, that's what those men are really after," Mrs. Stevenson said.

Grace turned her face to the east. The golden light blurred what lay beyond, but she'd chosen to believe her land overlooked a beautiful canyon, with multicolored layers as far as healthy eyes could see. "If the farm is what they're after, then it'd better be in tip-top shape." But if her guardians were correct, it wasn't, and she could never repair it on her own. She needed help.

❖

In all the world there was no sorrier sight than a cowboy carrying his saddle. Clayton Weber surged forward, sheer determination propelling him through the early September evening toward the dusty town. He had to find a shovel, had to bury Sal before the coyotes got to her. You didn't leave your best friend to be picked apart by scavengers, no matter how many miles you'd carried your gear.

Except for the schoolhouse, the town appeared deserted. Tightening his grip on the pommel, Clayton trudged the last quarter of a mile toward the lit building, thankful for the darkness. He'd stay in the shadows as much as possible if there were ladies present, so his face wouldn't elicit the usual questions.

He rubbed his marred brow. Of all the luck. He'd planned his journey for a year—ever since he'd heard about the Cherokee Strip land run. Already, most all of Oklahoma Territory had been parceled up and given away to those swift enough to outrace their peers. If he wanted a ranch of his own, this could be his last shot. But then Sal had stepped in that jackrabbit hole. The second he heard the horse's leg snap, Clayton knew. He'd have to find work fast if he wanted to replace Sal in time for the race.

He dropped his saddle at the hitching post. Startled by the noise, a skittish horse tugged against the reins that secured her. Poor Sal. No one should have to put their own horse out of her misery. He started to rub the mare's muzzle to calm her, but an old memory stopped him. With a last rueful glance at the horse, he stepped into the open doorway of the schoolhouse.

"Plenipotentiary." The young lady at the front of the classroom chewed her lip with a nervous glance to the boy at her side. "P-l-e . . ."

Behind the two youngsters sat what amounted to local

dignitaries and a schoolmarm. Clayton slung his saddlebag off his shoulder and leaned against the frame. Spelling bees had the potential to drag on longer than a leap year.

"... n-i-p-o-t-e-n-t-i-a-r-y. Plenipotentiary."

There was silence as the moderator bent her thin frame over a hefty book. At her nod applause erupted. The girl broke into a smile and turned to her opponent, who awaited the next word.

"Tergiversation." The teacher's voice sounded uncertain—almost as uncertain as the young man looked.

"Tergiversation." He clasped his hands behind his back. "T-e-r ..."

Clayton scanned the room. Who would most likely have a shovel at hand? Who would be most likely to rustle him up a supper before he returned to his tragic duty? Who wouldn't ask questions about Clayton's rough appearance?

In one giant breath, the room gasped. The boy's head drooped. The girl bounced on her toes before she remembered to act like a lady. Applause erupted as the slender teacher handed the winner a blue ribbon.

Clayton retreated out of the lamplight. The gathering was sure to break up soon, and people would swarm out of the building. No one wanted to find him blocking their path.

But before he could get out of earshot, a man's voice rang out, calling the assembly to order.

"Before we have a benediction, the school board would like to inform you of the latest on Miss O'Malley's situation. In our attempt to provide for our former teacher, we purchased Mrs. Danvers's homestead, and we'd like to remind you that it's our Christian duty to aid her while she's still in the community. To that end we'll have coffee cans at the back of the building for donations to her upkeep. I'm certain that you, as parents of her former students, will see the need for our continued support of Miss O'Malley, even when she is unable to be of use to us. Thank you."

As they prayed, Clayton moved around to the side of the schoolhouse, well out of the way. So they gave a homestead to a poor old schoolmarm who'd been put out to pasture? If only he could get one so easily.

A boy's snuffling reached his ears. Clayton stepped around the rain barrel and found the evening's second-place speller huddled against the wall.

Clayton looked both ways, but no one else was in the alley. He couldn't leave the kid crying all alone. He inched closer, almost stepping on the boy's shiny new shoes.

"Congratulations on a fine performance."

The boy raised miserable red-rimmed eyes. "I got beat by a . . . by a girl." He dropped his face into his hands.

If Clayton's worst problem was being outspelled by a girl, he'd wear a wig and dance the cancan. "No matter what your friends tell you, girls can be quite clever. I bet your schoolteacher and ma are smart enough."

The boy groaned. "I hate spelling. I hate school. I'm going to quit and become a cowboy like you. Nobody ever asks a cowboy to stand in front of people and spell."

Clayton scratched his scruffy cheek. "True. A cowboy might go hungry, get banged up by a stampede, and grow so lonesome that he sings to his cows, but he won't have to spell nothing."

"Anything," the kid corrected.

Clayton nodded. If the boy felt good enough to fix his grammar, he'd be fine. "Run cows if you'd like, but get your lessons done first, because you might get tired of eating dust and swatting mosquitoes. And don't worry about that smart girl. She'll probably become a schoolteacher and won't know what fun is even if it whops her upside the head."

"Oh?"

Clayton spun at the feminine gasp. How long had the blond woman—the teacher, he assumed—been listening? He ducked his chin, praying the darkness obscured his face.

"Beg your pardon, ma'am. I didn't mean any disrespect." From the corner of his eye he could tell she was studying him.

She crossed her arms. "Andrew, your parents are looking for you. They're at the front."

Andrew scrambled to his feet and trotted away. The teacher continued to regard him.

"Good evening to you." Clayton tipped his hat and followed Andrew, only too aware of her steps close behind.

Two men, ranchers from the looks of them, were taking his measure as he rounded the building. As expected, an outsider didn't go unnoticed for long. Fortunately for him, his situation was easily explained and verifiable, and he lost no time marching up to them and sharing his tale of woe.

"A broken leg, eh? That's too bad." The man hooked his thumbs beneath his belt. "Without a horse you don't have much shot at a stake in the land run, do you?"

Clayton tugged his collar and bandanna higher on the left side of his face. "I have some savings, but if I buy a horse I'll be hard-pressed to outfit my claim. If there's any work to be done around town, it'd surely help me make ends meet this winter."

"Do you realize that only one out of every fourteen men is liable to get land in the race?" the rancher asked.

Clayton kept his face turned from the gathering, as if they could read the accusation that had accompanied his injury. "Yes, sir, but if I don't get to Goodwin quick, I won't have any chance at all. I hear that the registration lines are days long."

Grunts affirmed his statement. "Well, I'll be willing to help you bury your horse tonight," the rancher said. "Then in the morning we can ask around."

"I'll give you a hand."

"Me, too."

Nice of them to help out. Dry Gulch seemed a right friendly place.

"Are these your saddlebags?" The circle parted for young Andrew, who stood with the smiling teacher at his shoulder.

"Yes, but . . ." Clayton frowned. The saddlebags were his, but the newspaper stuffed beneath the leather flap he'd never seen before.

* Chapter 2 *

Gripping the tablecloth, Grace flung it high and then settled it over the table. She smoothed the worn fabric and wondered which family had donated it. Evidently they didn't think she'd be able to tell how threadbare it was. Well, she shouldn't be ungrateful. At least the tablecloth hid the gouged face of the table. Because she'd always boarded with her students' families, Grace had never accumulated the necessities for housekeeping. Who would've thought she'd live in a home that she'd never seen . . . and would never see?

From the corner, Benny yipped in his puppy dream. It'd been Emilie's idea to get the puppy. As long as he drowsed on his mat, his grumblings anchored the room. Without a reference, Grace's world floated in endless possibilities.

Benny stirred. His breath stopped, then his nails clicked across the floor.

"What do you see?" Grace followed him to the door and pulled it open, the sun painfully bright on her eyes. Benny's tail thudded happily against the frame, but he didn't run outside.

Footsteps on the hard-packed earth alerted her that she wasn't alone.

"Hello there. Miss O'Malley?"

Grace clutched the door. A chill went up her neck at the man's unfamiliar voice. She hadn't heard a horse, and her allotment of food had already arrived for the day. Who else would come looking for her?

"Hello? Who is it?"

"I don't mean to startle you, ma'am. My name is Clayton Weber. I'm new to town, but I saw your advertisement in the paper. I understand you're looking for a man."

Grace's jaw dropped. "I didn't . . . How did you . . . ?" Who had sent him? She hid her hands behind her back. Grace hadn't declared her request for a husband to more than her three friends, and she certainly hadn't placed a notice in the paper. She stepped back. Benny yelped at the contact, further discombobulating her. "I'm sorry, but there's a mistake."

"Aren't you Miss O'Malley? I have the paper right here."

Footsteps echoed on the porch. A draft of air fanned her neck as he waved the paper, sending the smell of newsprint aloft. Her throat tightened at his nearness. Was this Emilie's mischief? Grace would wring her neck.

Cautiously, Grace eased outside, shut the cabin door behind her, and shaded her eyes. She couldn't catch the entire swath of his butternut shirt in one pass, but he looked able-bodied. She followed the line of his buttons up to a scruffy jaw and crooked smile over straight teeth. At first she thought the white line blazed across his cheek was another void in her vision, but when he turned away it disappeared, as well.

"You know I can't see much and you came anyway?"

"I don't mind. I'm more bothered by the fact that you're Irish, but I decided to give you a chance." His words held a chuckle.

She choked back a retort, putting all her efforts into getting a look at him. Just when she found the wavy blond hair at his temple, he shifted, and she lost her place again. Grace lowered her eyelids, allowing the burning sensation to ease. Obviously she'd made him uncomfortable.

But so was she. A real live potential husband at her door, and she had no notion of what to do with him.

❖

Her stare reminded him of a house cat watching a mouse hole. Clayton scratched the back of his neck and told himself those piercing brown eyes saw nothing. The color of strong tea, they'd already lost their usefulness, which was a shame. Still, protecting the ladies from the sight of his unbecoming mug was a habit. It'd take a bit to remember he didn't need to bother hiding from Miss O'Malley.

Not that he intended to spend much time with her. He had to get registered and on the starting line before the gun sounded at noon on September sixteenth. The handyman advertisement didn't specify the exact tasks to be completed, but this place needed more work than he had time for. Well, he'd do the best he could, working sunup to sundown, and see how much he could earn—hopefully enough to supplement his savings after he replaced Sal.

"I'm sorry for my hesitation." Miss O'Malley's hands folded before her, her impeccable posture sending a message of calm and control. "You caught me unaware. I need a bit of time to think this through."

"What's there to think about? You don't have another man bidding for the job, do you?"

Bright spots appeared on her cheeks. "Well, no, but it's not a decision I take lightly."

Oh bother. Not one of those persnickety headmistress types. He didn't have time for a lengthy consideration. "I've done this before," he said. "I'm very experienced, so if you're not satisfied, just send me packing. I won't take it personal."

Her eyes widened and her jaw dropped. "You've been married before, Mr. Weber?"

He drew back. "I don't know that that's any of your business."

Her chin firmed and her brow wrinkled. Talking to women never got him anywhere. Although she didn't do the normal woman stuff most did when they saw his face—look away or pretend not to notice—he still couldn't make any sense of her conversation.

Clayton shook his head. "If you must know, I'm not married, but let's not meddle in private affairs."

"One's marital status should not be kept private."

"Why does it matter? You obviously want my services, whether you're hitched or not. Now, let's get down to business." Ignoring her sputters, Clayton spun on his heel. His fists rested on his hips as he surveyed the barnyard. "That sow's going to have piglets soon, and they'll run right through the slats. The pigpen would be the first improvement I'd make."

She fumed in silence. Well, she couldn't see what he was talking about anyway.

"You've got a nice roof on the house, but the barn could use patching, and your windmill is spinning catawampus.

That's all I see from here. Did you expect me to look about the house?"

For being blind, she sure knew how to glare. "The house is my domain. I'll allow you to sleep in the barn loft for now if you promise to behave as a gentleman."

His head snapped. Was she addled? Why would he act ungentlemanly? "Of course. I'll go about my business and stay out of your way. Then as soon as this place gets put together—"

"Mr. Weber." If her cheeks were pink before, they were blooming now. "I've never been in a discussion such as this, but I feel something is amiss. You take no pains to hide your interest in the land, but could you at least pretend I have something to do with this transaction?"

Schoolteacher, they'd said. He could see it in her posture, the commanding tone of her voice. She demanded his respect, even though she was making as much sense as a two-story outhouse.

"Ma'am, I don't mean any disrespect, but I'm not sure what you expect. I've been a hand at a variety of spreads, and I've never had such a . . . personal . . . interview."

She sucked on her lip. Her eyes floated across the horizon. "'A hand,' you say?" Her voice had lost most of its thunder. In fact, she sounded downright uncertain. "That advertisement . . . would you mind reading it to me, in its entirety?"

His eyebrow cocked. The ad contained nothing unusual beside the fact it had been circled with thick strokes so he couldn't miss it. He snatched it out of his back pocket and spread it dramatically.

"Wanted: a handyman to assist at Grace O'Malley's homestead. Money has been set aside at the Whitfield Bank to compensate anyone willing to be of service to a woman in need. Basic carpentry skills required."

The lady stumbled backward, bouncing into the wall of the house. Before he could reach for her, she'd righted herself.

"A handyman? That's what the ad says?" The pup's head cocked at her incredulous tone. To be honest, Clayton was scratching his noggin, as well. "A handyman?" Her eyes sparkled at some private joke. "Wait until Emilie hears about this."

Clayton didn't want to interrupt, but his curiosity got the better of him. "What did you think it said?"

She touched her lips before folding her hands before her, much like the spelling bee winner the night before. "That's unimportant." She cleared her throat. "I approve of your suggested improvements. If more is required, please discuss it with me first. And since the money has obviously been collected by the school board, I'll ask them to inspect your work before you are given your pay. Am I clear?"

Her dark hair shone in measured perfection. Her skin, so startling white in contrast, had regained its original fair shade. And she was treating him like an errant schoolboy. Clayton read again the words on the newspaper before him. Whether she admitted it or not, she was a woman in need, and he was beginning to see why it was easier to set up an account and pay a stranger to look after her than it was for the local men to lend a hand.

No matter. He needed money and he needed it fast.

"I'll get started immediately."

She nodded and stood still, face to the sun, for a long moment before entering the house.

✳ Chapter 3 ✳

Grace paced the room, trailing her hand over the kitchen table, chairs, stove, and rocker. She repeated this short loop incessantly, memorizing the number of steps from one piece of furniture to the other, noticing where her footsteps echoed on the floor and where they thudded, assuring herself that nothing would vanish when her back was turned, closing her eyes and imagining that even the porthole of light that remained was lost. Was her world reduced to this? Not only had the canyon vistas been stolen from her, but also every printed word that had transported her to lands unknown. Her hand lingered on her Bible. How she wished she had committed more Scripture to memory. If God would give her another chance, she'd never take for granted the privilege of reading His Word again.

A rap sounded at the door. Grace fixed her location in mind and counted the steps. She swung the door open, although she might as well have spoken through it for all the help it was.

"Miss O'Malley, it's well past suppertime." The boards creaked beneath his feet. "Were you wanting my help in the kitchen, too?"

The handyman. She'd wondered if he'd return or just fade away like so much of her world.

"Don't be ridiculous. I've eaten already."

He didn't leave. She waited. Should she shut the door in his face?

"That's dandy, but I haven't had a bite. It's nearly two miles into town. Were you planning . . . ?" His unfinished question ended with a self-conscience cough.

Grace's fingers tightened on the knob. What kind of woman couldn't put dinner on the table? What must he think of her? "I had cheese and bread for supper with some pickled okra. My fare depends on who brings it out and what they have available."

"You mean leftovers?"

Grace didn't like the word or its connotation. "It's more than they have to do."

He rapped his knuckles against the doorframe. "And more than they want to do. How're you set up for cooking? Can you use the stove?"

When she didn't answer, he grasped her wrist. Grace recoiled at the sudden touch, but then it was gone. The air stirred as he marched past her. Pots clanged together. The stove door creaked open, then snapped shut. Cabinet hinges protested and heavy jars thudded on the table.

"You don't have much here, but it's a start. This winter will be lean, but once your pigs get big enough, you could trade for a goat and have milk and butter. Chickens would be easy for you to handle—"

"I beg your pardon?" Pulled as if by a magnet, Grace pushed between him and the pantry, forgetting to count her steps. "What are you doing in my house?"

"Starving."

"I'm not prepared to split every meal with you." After a day of solitude, she was itching for an argument. "I've barely enough to eat as it is."

"A man's got to have food. If you couldn't afford me you shouldn't have—"

"I didn't place that ad. I have no way of feeding myself, much less you."

The plate next to her clattered. She felt the vibration through the countertop.

"Cheese? Cheese and bread? Those are slim rations, ma'am." He clomped to the table and dropped into a chair, scraping it against the floor. "If I had time I might scare up some game. A man can't work without meat in his gizzard."

Grace was on the verge of telling him that humans didn't possess that anatomical item when he started in again . . . with what sounded like a mouthful of cheese.

"So you didn't want a handyman?"

She rubbed her elbow, unsure what she wanted him to know, but definite on what she had to hide.

"I can't afford one, especially one with a voracious appetite. That notice in the paper, it's none of my doing."

"But when I stepped on your porch, you warmed up to the idea quick enough, or were you expecting something else?"

She could feel his eyes on her. She turned to close the squat door of the pantry. "From what I can tell by my limited senses, this place is a dilapidated disgrace. No matter what my plans are, being burdened with this property in its present condition is a liability."

He grunted. "Do you have any coffee?"

She'd hired him and he expected her to be the maid.

"Does it matter? I can't tend a stove."

His chair creaked. "What can you do? It's going to get cold this winter. Unless you expect someone to sit by your fire—"

Her hands clutched her skirt and her voice rose. "You know, you're a great one for pointing out the obvious. Going blind was not my idea, and now I'm torn between riding out my days in solitude, inconveniencing friends, or finding a stranger and—" Her mouth popped shut. While the husband option seemed the most logical to her, she'd not air it for him to ridicule.

A chair screeched across the floor. "Have a seat," he said.

"You'll not be telling me what to do in me own house."

"Ah, there's more of that Irish. Should've known I'd hear it plain when you got riled." He munched as she paced, never more than a few steps away in the small cabin. What could she do? Throw him out? But he had to eat. Send him away? The work needed to be done. At the least she could insist on his taking the rest of his meals outside.

Benny's tail thumped in the corner, reminding her that although she might not be able to see the invader, her actions could be very entertaining to him.

She stopped and found her place by the pantry, clearing his path to the door, should he decide to use it.

And he did.

"I'll be right back," he said.

"I don't think so." But she was talking to his back as his footsteps faded.

Supper was over. Why should she let him back inside? She'd throw the bolt and teach him a lesson. Grace rushed toward the door. Two steps and her knee collided with a low open cabinet door. Her skirt had protected her from direct contact, but when she reached to steady herself, she sent a canning jar careening off the countertop and crashing onto the floor.

Vinegar. Okra. No matter how disorganized her house had been, at least it had smelled good—until now. She dropped to her knees, only to gasp and roll away. The skirts didn't protect her from the broken glass that sliced her leg.

Grace sat on the floor, collapsed against the cabinet door, and turned her face to the ceiling.

Why?

She'd gone from a productive, respected leader in Dry Gulch to a needy, helpless bother who couldn't even throw a tantrum without help. What did God expect her to do? She'd go mad circling her room, waiting for Emilie to bring her food like some animal in a menagerie.

Boots clumped through the door. Grace sniffed and turned her face away from the man.

"I turn my back and look at the mess you've made." He walked past her and dumped a load of firewood next to the stove. Legs turned toward her. "Be careful. You'll cut yourself."

She kicked his direction, gratified to see him hop. "If you hadn't left the cabinet door open and the jar—" A dishrag dropped into her lap. A bowl clinked on the floor next to her.

"You'll have to touch lightly to find the pieces. Go slow or you'll tear your hands up, and you can't afford to damage your fingers."

Grace's lips pinched together. He expected her to clean it by herself? Her chest swelled with indignation. Insufferable.

The door to the woodstove swung open. Wood rattled into the mouth.

"I might be able to see a person's outline move in the sunlight, but I cannot find shards of glass in the dark."

A match flared. A light glowed momentarily before she lost it again. The scent of sulfur mixed with the vinegar. "Where do you keep your coffee?"

"You, sir, have some nerve."

"The name is Clayton—Mr. Weber if you prefer—and I get ornery when I'm hungry."

"I'm not calling my hired hand by his given name."

"That's fine, Grace. I suppose the coffee is in your pantry. I'll have you a strong cup in a jiffy."

If only he'd leave so she could throw a decent fit. Something shimmered. Using the rag she plucked a jagged piece of jar off the floor and dropped it into the bowl. This would take all night. The glass had mixed evenly with the sopping okra. Once the rag got wet . . .

"Would you hand me a spoon?" she asked. "The wooden one . . . please." It didn't kill her to be polite, although she felt plenty sick about it.

She nearly sputtered the question again when he didn't answer, but then he took her hand and pressed the slender handle into it. "There you go."

Grace leaned as far as she could and scraped the spoon toward her. Methodically she began her next sweep just to the right of where she'd started before. The spoon grew heavier as it hit the pile of glass and okra she was amassing. By the time she tilted the bowl and swept the mess into it, the coffee was boiling on the stove.

"Not bad work," he said. Coffee gurgled out of the spout and splashed into a mug. "It's a good start."

"I'll sweep tomorrow when it's dry." She stood, but before

she slid the bowl onto the counter, she performed a tentative brush to make sure it was clear.

"You cut yourself," he said. "There's blood on your skirt."

She brushed her knee. "I'll tend to it later."

"But how are you going to see—"

"I'll tend it later." Her voice rang with a volume unreached since leaving the classroom.

"Just trying to help." He slurped on his coffee.

She turned and found the pump handle. Having a man in the house was unnerving. She couldn't tell where he was looking, what he was doing. How did she ever think she could run an ad for a husband? On the other hand, wasn't Clayton proving how helpful one could be?

———◆———◆———◆———

Now that the insides of his stomach weren't rubbing against each other, Clayton repented of his foul mood. He'd been tough on her, but he wanted to know whether she was worth it or not. Why repair the place if she'd never appreciate what she had? Sure, she hadn't been there long, but it would chap him if he was willing to risk his neck in a land run for a homestead and she wouldn't lift a finger to keep hers.

Grace dried her hands and the motion drew his eyes. She was much younger than he'd expected, and the problem of being with a blind woman—there wasn't any reason to stop staring. Her long white fingers looked out of place on the rustic spread, but they sure were nice to gaze at. Those hands connected to slender arms, and her figure curved where it ought, straight shoulders, and a narrow waist. She probably hadn't had much experience running a household even before her affliction.

Well, he couldn't waste time woolgathering. Besides, the way she searched for him when he spoke gave the eerie impression that she saw more than was possible. He rubbed his brow, feeling the familiar dent where the scar began before skipping through his cheek and ending at his jaw. He'd always avoided the ladies on account of his appearance. Eventually, they would ask what had happened, and if he answered vaguely they were insulted. If he told them . . . well, he'd never do that. He couldn't stand their pity, their polite conversation while they looked over his shoulder for someone to rescue them from the marred man. But Grace had no problem speaking directly to him. He had the feeling she'd go toe-to-toe with him and like it.

She folded the towel. "Is it dark already?"

"Sure is. Your mug is here on the table."

She took her chair, graceful once she knew where she was headed. Her hands skimmed the tabletop until she found the mug. Her eyes lowered. "Thank you. I haven't had anything warm to drink for days."

Grace didn't know to hide the struggle that warred across her face. Clayton watched, fascinated. She was proud but practical. Could she set aside her pride and accept his help?

"The people here are kind to look after you." He took a sip.

Her mouth turned down. "They are. I only wish they didn't have to. I don't see what good this disease can accomplish."

"Disease?"

"If that's what it is. But it's not contagious. The doctor had to convince a score of concerned parents."

Her rueful smile covered a pain he could relate to—being

cast out of society, viewed with suspicion. And then he'd marched in, treating her like she should be doing better. Shame on him.

Yet she'd taken his challenge. Hadn't she cleaned the glass herself? And she didn't seem to hold a grudge for it.

"When did it happen?" he asked.

Grace wrapped her hands around the steaming mug. "For years I couldn't see at night. Stumbling around after dusk was normal for me, but last winter I realized that even in the light my sight was narrowing. By February, I couldn't see all five rows of my students from my desk. I had to turn my head to catch those on the edge. By the time summer break commenced I could barely make out two rows side by side. I finally had to admit I couldn't continue to teach. When I saw a physician, he said it was only a matter of time."

"And now?"

"It's like looking through the bottom of a pill bottle—as narrow as a spool of thread and cloudy most of the time. If I search I can find something, but it's hardly worth the effort. The second I set my fork down, it's gone. I look and look . . . and it's only going to get worse." Her chin rose as if daring him to offer a soggy platitude. Probably too many had already overdone the pity.

"Sounds like a challenge, figuring out how to make it on your own. If we put some thought to it, there are probably ways to make this place friendlier for you." He drained his mug. "For instance, how are you supposed to know what's in the pantry the way those jars are all jumbled in there?"

"Usually Emilie sets dinner out for me."

"But Emilie has better things to do than to be your nursery maid." Her eyes flashed, but she kept her mouth shut. "You'd

134

rather succeed on your own than cause more work for her, wouldn't you? Surprise everyone with what you can do?"

"They're more likely to be mad than surprised, but I'd prefer their disapproval to being helpless."

Already he sensed her resolve forming. How could the town of Dry Gulch have expelled this vibrant woman? Instead of sending her out to some isolated homestead, they should've elected her mayor. He didn't have long, but he'd do his best to see her conquer this malady before he left.

∗ Chapter 4 ∗

The jangling traces of Emilie's wagon woke Grace. Morning already? She and the hired hand had stayed up late, talking through plans and ideas for the place. Without a clock for reference, the time had passed too quickly. Grace rolled onto her back, relieved to see a golden glow. Another night defeated by morning. How many more would she witness?

She reached for the dress thrown across the rocker and then stopped. Last night she'd undressed in total darkness. This morning—well there was a man outside who could see, even if she couldn't. She'd wait on Emilie's assurance that no one was peeking.

Just another thing she couldn't do without Emilie's being there. Last night's conversation had hurt. She didn't like being told that she wasn't achieving all she could, and yet she had more hope now than at any moment since that dreadful visit to the doctor. At least someone believed she could do better and treated her like the intelligent woman she was. After months of being cosseted, she was ready to adjust—even if it meant picking up glass and getting cut in the process.

What was taking Emilie so long? Grace grabbed her brush and stroked through her black hair, twisting and pinning the thick cord until it felt secure. She'd never had much use for a mirror, a quirk that proved convenient now.

At the knock, Grace went to the door and threw the bolt. "You're late. Are the children well?"

"They're fine, just took extra effort to get them headed to school this morning." Emilie traipsed into the house and pecked her cheek. "And I'm not going a step further until you tell me about that man out there."

Grace closed the door behind her. "Don't pretend you're surprised to see him. You can't imagine how close I came to humiliating myself over that newspaper notice you placed."

"Newspaper? I don't know what you're talking about."

Emilie sounded sincere, but then again, without seeing her expression, Grace was a poor judge. "Let me get dressed first. Will you keep an eye on the windows and make sure Mr. Weber is nowhere near?"

Emilie's dark form blocked the front window. "He's hiding in the barn. Seems afraid of his own shadow. I had to hail him three times before he'd acknowledge me."

Grace went to her room and pulled her skirt on beneath her nightgown. Clayton, shy? He hadn't hesitated to speak to her. "What did you say to him?" she called through the doorway.

"I asked him if he was your brother, and he said he was your handyman. Well, as you can imagine, I nearly gave up the ghost right then and there, but before I could get another question in, he turned and skedaddled to the barn. Left me sputtering in the wagon." The lid of her crockery jar rattled.

"If you didn't place the ad, who did?"

"What ad?" She set the crock on the counter with a satisfying thud.

Grace buttoned the last of her shirtwaist and returned to the front room. "Oh, you'll love to hear of me being so daft. Mr. Weber came with a newspaper and said he was answering an ad. . . ."

When it came to appreciating a story at Grace's expense, Emilie did not disappoint. She hooted and guffawed until even Grace was wiping tears from her face.

"You asked him if he'd been married before?"

Grace clutched her side with laughter and nodded.

Emilie blew out a strong breath. "If you could see him, Grace, he's a strapping specimen."

"Even I made out that much. What's his face like . . . if an old married woman like you notices such things?" Grace filled her lungs with the savory smells wafting from Emilie's delivery.

"Handsome, at least what I could tell. Like I said, he was bashful. Didn't look me directly in the eye. Come to think of it, maybe it's not a good idea to have him here. What if he's a murderer? What if he's a drifter who robs blind women because they can't identify him?"

"Then he would've robbed me last night before anyone knew he was here. Besides, someone in town gave him the newspaper and directed him to the place. Someone must trust him."

Emilie jangled the silverware drawer open. "If I were you I'd break windows, tear shingles, pull fences down, and do anything I could to give him more work. Keep him around and you might not need to advertise for a husband after all."

◆——————◆——————◆

Grace waved good-bye, spirits boosted from their chat. So little of interest had happened to her since moving to the farm that she'd much rather joke about the new handyman than give another report on her worsening malady.

She hummed as she removed all the canned goods from the shelves. If she would've told Emilie her plan, Emilie would've insisted on doing it, but Grace was looking forward to the task.

A knock sounded on the door. Benny yipped.

"Clayton?"

"Yes, ma'am."

"Come on in. You're probably looking for your dinner."

"Saw your friend come to the door, but I didn't want to interrupt your visit."

Grace dimpled. Their fun would've been dampened with him present. Couldn't speak with the object of the conversation across the table from them.

Slowly but steadily she found a bowl and spoon for him. Carefully she ladled out the stew while he took his seat. Emilie had moved the tin cups after washing, and it took Grace a moment to find them. She stretched on her tiptoes to reach the back of the shelf. Clayton's chair groaned just as her fingers brushed the cold tin.

"You got it?" He was closer than she remembered.

She filled the cup with water, turned, and waited for him to take it from her.

"Thank you." His fingers brushed over hers. He sat.

She could wait in her room until he was finished, but Grace couldn't bring herself to leave. Wouldn't she get enough solitude in the future? He might be shocked at her forward-ness. He might think it inappropriate that she converse with the help, but what did it matter? He wouldn't be in Randall County much longer.

"I've had time to think over your suggestions, and I'm taking your advice about rearranging the shelves. I should know what I have in my pantry."

He grunted. "All right, then. What's your plan?"

Grace settled her backside into her chair and leaned her arms against the table. "Obviously, writing descriptions would be a waste, so I'm going to use string. I'll use vary-ing thicknesses of string and ribbon. One will denote okra, one tomatoes, one green beans, and so on. Then I'll group them together on the shelves."

"That could work." His spoon clinked against the bowl. "What else do we need to brand?"

We? Grace couldn't help the warmth that spread through her at the single word. He wasn't doing it for her, and he wasn't leaving her to do it on her own. They were working together.

"I can't think of anything offhand."

He stood and placed his dishes in the sink. "Do you know your spices?"

"I can smell them." Walking all the way around the table to avoid bumping into him, she reached the pantry.

"How about the flour and sugar?"

"The canisters are different. For now, it's only the Mason jars that trouble me." Grace reached above her head for the top shelf, but the furthest jars were just beyond her grasp.

She felt rather than heard him. Warmth, a presence—how could she know exactly where he stood when he hadn't touched her? She remained motionless, afraid that any movement would bring contact with the stranger. And he was a stranger.

The jars slid across the top shelf, then plunked onto the countertop.

"That's all of them."

She could breathe again. Carefully she turned, still sensing his nearness. "If you wouldn't mind . . . I need help sorting them."

Maybe he nodded. He stepped away and soon he was humming a happy tune while Grace rifled through her scrap bag. With her scissors she sheared the strings, then began tying them on as Clayton told her which group was which.

"Umm, this string doesn't match the other tomato jars," he said.

Grace searched for the mismarked jars. Clayton took her hand and guided her to them. She ran her fingers over the yarn. "They feel the same."

"Then I reckon it'll do," he laughed.

Grace smiled but couldn't relax until the warmth of his touch had faded.

"I'm starting on your barn this afternoon." Clayton's voice echoed inside the small pantry. "Some of the gaps have been mud patched, but they won't hold the winter out. There's new lumber left over from the roof, but I need more nails and hardware to shore the pens up. Tomorrow I'll go to town—"

"I could go with you." The words had shot out before she could stop them.

The floor groaned beneath his feet. "It's a long walk."

"There's nothing wrong with my constitution, and I've

141

been stranded here for a week. Besides, I used to live in town, and it'll be good to be around people again."

His shoulder brushed hers as he picked up the jars. "I didn't peg you for a homesteader, but I'm not sure you strike me as a socialite, either."

"So I can't make it on my own, but no one wants to be around me? Is that your impression?"

Clayton chuckled. "Your friend mentioned your brother. Is he coming to help you?"

"Not if I have anything to say about it. We're not close." Grace tied the last string and rued the day she'd ever let her brother's name fall on the ears of anyone in Dry Gulch. "He came to America before I was born. When my parents died on the journey from Ireland, I was left with him." She fiddled with the frayed ends of the thread. "He wasn't pleased to have a child to raise, so as soon as I was old enough, I struck out on my own."

"From where?"

"Fort Worth."

She pushed the last of the jars toward Clayton. So vivid were her memories of being presented to her grieving, scowling brother that she almost missed Clayton's next words.

"I'm from Fort Worth."

At the trepidation in his voice, she turned. What did he fear? Why did his statement ring of confession?

"It's unlikely our paths crossed." She ran her fingernail along a split in the countertop. "My brother was a tinker, so most of the time we traveled through the countryside repairing pots and pans. When he came to town, he was up to no good and left me behind. Occasionally I attended school in communities as we passed through, but never for long. We weren't your typical family."

His voice dropped. "My dad died when I was young, too. I lived with my grandparents." He walked away to stand near the pantry. The physical distance seemed to echo a distance between them that hadn't been there before.

"Is that all? The way you say it sounds dire."

The hinges of the pantry door creaked as if they were bearing weight. "So you didn't go to school," Clayton said, "but you're a schoolteacher?"

Because she heard respect instead of mockery, she'd allow him the misdirection this once. "I loved school. Couldn't understand why other students complained about attending. Along the way I met generous teachers who gave me books and checked on my progress the next year when I came through. Reading was my escape." One that was no longer available.

"So what now? I think with some planning, you could learn to manage the house on your own, but wouldn't you be happier in town?"

"Perhaps, but this situation became available."

"Are you resigned to living here alone? Forever? I've got to wonder what you hope to accomplish by fixing the place up."

She didn't have to defend herself, but it irritated her that he thought her impractical, as if her actions had no ultimate aim.

"Everyone wants land. Look at all the men gathering to race for a free homestead in the Cherokee Strip land run in a little over a week. Those who lose will be milling about by the thousands, and if the harebrained fools are willing to gamble their lives in a race, maybe one would just as soon settle here." She filled the basin with water and sprinkled soap flakes into it.

"You do understand the reason the *harebrained fools* are willing to risk their lives is because they can't afford a homestead? You don't think one of them could pay you enough to buy you out, do you?"

"No," she snapped. "I'm not daft. I'd live here, too."

"With a man? A stranger?" He sucked in his breath with a low whistle. "Exactly what kind of deal do you hope to strike?"

Grace's face burned. She tucked her chin. "Never you mind."

"You can't leave me to imagine the worst, can you? Come on, Grace. Maybe I can sharpen your strategy, clarify your terms."

She spun toward him. "Leave me be, Clayton Weber. You have no right—" But then she caught sight of a pair of twinkling hazel eyes. "Oh, I see you!"

A white line creased his brow, but didn't lessen the intensity of his gaze. "You see me? But it's foggy?"

No fog could dull his warm, intelligent eyes. She drank them in as long as she dared. Not only was he beautiful, but he could possibly be the last man she ever saw. "Yes. Of course. I meant that I found you." Quickly she tried to take in his high forehead, curly hair, crooked nose—all the qualities she could catch before this window of sight closed again.

"You have advice for me?" Grace couldn't care less about his input. She only wanted to see his mouth work, to tie it to the voice that had already become familiar.

His generous lips widened into a smile. "I'll do you the honor of assuming you'd marry, no sharing a homestead otherwise. So the question is how do you lure these reckless ne'er-do-wells to your lair? Perhaps an advertisement?"

"Mm-hmm." How could she attend his words when so focused on drinking in his features? Emilie hadn't exaggerated in her praise.

"Now, the danger of placing a notice would be guaranteeing the quality of your applicants. You don't want them showing up on your porch with a newspaper in hand—" His mouth formed a circle, then spread into a satisfied grin. "You placed a notice, didn't you? That's why when I got here . . ."

Before Grace could stop herself, her eyes had traveled again to his. They practically snapped with laughter. She spun around, turning her back to him.

"I did not place that ad. Don't be ridiculous."

His voice dripped with amusement. "Not for a handyman, but maybe another ad. Had I not read the paper to you, we'd be an old married couple by now."

A slippery mug sprang from her grasp and bounced across the countertop. Clayton caught it before it crashed to the floor.

"I did not place any notices," she sputtered, "so cease with your vain speculation. Now, why don't you get back to work? I'm too busy to continue this conversation."

"There's only my bowl to wash. If you want me to—"

"Not just that. I have to—" Grace's thoughts flitted around the room trying to think of anything left undone. "I have to give Benny a bath."

"You bathe the dog?"

"Just . . . just go."

He tapped the countertop one last time and headed toward the barn, whistling Wagner's "Bridal Chorus."

Grace listened to him stride away and wondered how long the clarity—as narrow as it was—would last. Her eyes burned from the effort of splitting the veil, alerting her that the reprieve could only be temporary.

Of all the times for her eyesight to clear, this conversation would've never been her choice. True, his rakish eyes were a sight to behold, but she'd rather the amusement not be at her expense. Grace bent and called the dog. And now she had to wash the little thing. What a mess.

Being embarrassed over Clayton's discovery felt childish. She wanted to get married. Who didn't? Perhaps what had mortified her was that she'd thought he was presenting himself as an option, when he had no intention of doing such a thing.

But what about now? Grace scratched beneath the squirming Benny's chin. Was she the only one captivated by the thought of them being an old married couple?

⋆ Chapter 5 ⋆

The wet nose of the sow pushed through the gap in the slats and sniffed Clayton's pant legs as her new piglets tottered after her on quick hooves. Would he ever have a place of his own? The odds of his winning a 160-acre homestead in a race and holding on to it through the winter weren't promising. He couldn't leave to register in Goodwin until he'd completed his job here, and now he'd lose a half a day going to town for supplies.

Just the thought of appearing in Dry Gulch made his head hurt. When a stranger walked into town, people bristled. They steered their children away, held their bags closer. If something went missing, he'd be the first accused. If something broke, he'd be the first questioned.

But this wasn't Fort Worth.

Here, no one knew that he was the son of a horse thief. No one in Dry Gulch remembered the hanging. They had no reason to suspect him of wrongdoing. In Fort Worth, he never knew if it was his appearance that caused people to recoil or his family's reputation, and truthfully, even he couldn't separate the two. Not when the attackers had screamed accusations against him as they struck.

But didn't he believe that his standing in God's sight held more significance than human opinion? Then why couldn't he look people square in the eye?

He slid his jaw from side to side, feeling the familiar catch. Grace hadn't seen the scar, and she'd never hear the charges. Her openness to him gave him hope that a fresh start in Oklahoma Territory awaited him. And while he couldn't imagine another woman that'd measure up to Grace, he'd do well to find someone less pretentious to love.

And maybe the next lady wouldn't be Irish. He couldn't keep the smile from breaking out on his face. Grace wanted a husband. How surprised she must have been to find him on the opposite side of her door. He must've seemed like a gift dropped from heaven. Especially when she couldn't see. He shooed away a fly. Would Emilie tell her about the scar? Did they talk about him at all?

The door opened. Grace stood at the threshold in a smart rust-colored getup. The ribbons of her bonnet caught in the wind and streamed like happy fish tails flapping in a cold stream.

"Good morning," he called.

She turned her head in his direction. "Good morning. I hope you're ready to start out."

He pushed off the fence. "Yes, ma'am, but I didn't know if you wanted my company this morning."

"I'm stuck with your company regardless. I might as well dilute it with some variety." Her head tilted saucily. The red of her shirt heightened the color in her lips.

"Do you know the way?" he asked.

She shook her head. "I haven't been to town since they brought me here. I'm relying on your navigation."

"Never fear." Too bad he didn't have Sal. But his reminiscing was cut short as he noticed that she hadn't budged off the porch. "Have you ever left the cabin?"

"Not yet. I've meant to acquaint myself with the grounds, but I didn't want to be in your way."

Truly, or was she afraid? He strode to her. "Once we finish up our errands today I'd be glad to take you around." He gently touched her shoulder to warn her of his intention, and then slid his arm through hers. "There are three shallow steps down. There you go. You can catch the handrail here, but we need some way for you to find the barn and house. Wouldn't want you missing them and wandering into a gully."

Her arm tightened. "I've been thinking about that. Could you hang some wind chimes on the house and barn? Then I could find them."

"I'll do that. Of course you won't hear them when the wind dies. We could string up a guide rope."

"But what if Emilie didn't see it and her horse got tangled? Besides, once I gain my confidence, I won't want to hang on to something to find my way."

He couldn't help but look at her slender hand clutching his sleeve.

"Perhaps we could put down some paver stones," she said. "I'd know the second I stepped off the path."

"What about snow?"

"If it snows, we'll hang up a guide rope."

"We? Did you plan to employ me throughout the winter?" But the thought of seeing snow with her warmed him.

Her lips curled in a modest smile. "I misspoke. Naturally, you won't be here that long, because you have to— What exactly are you doing, Mr. Weber?"

He turned his mind from foolish imagining and scanned the grassy road ahead as it wound between mesas and around gulches. When would he learn that such dreams weren't for him?

"I'm buying a horse. Mine broke her leg just outside of town."

"Oh, the poor thing." Grace grasped his cuff. "I'm sorry."

"I loved that old horse, and I won't do much good in the land rush without her."

"Land rush? You're not—"

His steps slowed. "Running in Oklahoma Territory with the rest of the harebrained fools?"

She stopped. Her neck tightened with her grimace. "Oh dear. I hope I didn't—"

"I'm not offended."

"I hope I didn't entrust the upkeep of my farm to a howling lunatic." Her dark eyebrows animated her statement.

"Ah. Why would I expect an apology out of you?"

She grinned and he winked before remembering it was wasted.

⸻

Even with Clayton at her side, Grace's first steps in town terrified her. She could picture her surroundings, but she also remembered the chaotic nature of Dry Gulch. Horses might race down the road. People hurried from building to building. Like them, she'd enjoyed the hustle, but now it left her confused and disoriented.

"Good day, Miss O'Malley."

She turned to catch the voice. Whose was it? "Good day. I'm afraid I can't—"

150

A touch at her elbow and Clayton whispered, "He's gone. He just spoke in passing."

"Can you believe all the covered wagons passing through for the Land Rush?" another man intoned.

"Covered wagons?" Grace stopped. "You don't say? I thought since the railroads came through no one—"

"Poor suckers," a gruff voice interrupted. "Packing up their families and traveling all this way for nothing. I heard there were over fifty thousand camping around Ark City alone."

Grace's hand fell limply to her side. "He isn't talking to me, is he?" she whispered to Clayton.

"No, ma'am." He moved her on down the sidewalk until the conversation faded.

She'd passed hours in her cabin wishing for someone to talk to, but now that she was surrounded by people, she'd never felt more alone. She couldn't see who was speaking to her, couldn't tell when they approached or when they left. Not only had her navigation been compromised by her blindness, but also her communication. Was anything left untouched?

Clayton's hand remained steady beneath her elbow as they moved forward.

"Step up. You're in front of the diner now." Through the din his voice penetrated, firm and sure. "Smells good, doesn't it? I suppose the hardware store is near."

"Claasen's store will have what you need. It's just across the street." People muttered greetings to her but forgot to introduce themselves. Why wouldn't anyone slow down?

"Here comes your friend," Clayton said. "The one who visits you."

Grace strained against his arm. "Emilie? Where?"

"I'm here." Emilie grasped her by the shoulders and kissed her cheek. "You look beautiful, by the way. How do you manage without the benefit of a mirror?"

Grace smoothed her skirt. "Walking two miles in this heat was a trial. I'd forgotten the convenience of living in town."

Clayton cleared his throat. "If you don't mind, I'll drop by Claasen's while y'all catch up."

"That'd be dandy." Emilie took Clayton's place at Grace's side. "So is your hired help all you'd hoped for?"

Grace frowned.

"Don't worry. He's gone. I wish you could see the looks he's getting walking down the sidewalk. If I'm not mistaken, Danielle Fowler will find an excuse to go into Claasen's . . . yep. Like a bloodhound on the scent." Emilie giggled. "Has he told you what happened to his face? Was it a duel? An Indian attack?"

Grace turned in at the milliner's without asking, guessing where Emilie was headed. "He never mentions it, and I don't think he'd want me to." But Danielle would have the nerve to ask. Would Clayton talk to her?

"I've tried to get a good look at it, but he keeps his face turned. Lucy and I decided that if given a chance we'd ambush him from opposite sides. Then he couldn't hide from both of us."

"Who all knows he's at my place?"

Emilie opened the door for her and released her arm, leaving Grace floundering just inside the establishment. "Everyone, I suppose. After the spelling bee he asked around until Mr. Stevenson gave him directions to the homestead. And I might have mentioned a stalwart gentleman working for you at the sewing circle yesterday." Emilie paused to exclaim over the ruby lushness of a bonnet.

The sewing circle. No use for Grace there—or anywhere. Grace stepped timidly toward the display table, relieved it hadn't been moved since her last visit. While she couldn't appreciate the hues, she luxuriated in the richness of the velvets against her fingertips. Greedily, she traced a wide brim, spiked with starched lace and topped with a billowy feather. In many ways, her blindness had erected a barrier between her and the sighted. On the other hand, it pushed her into close physical proximity with anyone who wanted to help. Contact reserved for family and close friends became necessary to communicate, or even to find her way around.

When Clayton first appeared, Grace hadn't expected they'd spend much time together. Now, with him taking his meals inside and their growing interactions, she felt as if she should have a chaperone. If she were still working at the school, the school board would definitely have objections.

She stepped to Emilie's side. "What do people think about his being here? Isn't it scandalous for us to be alone on the homestead together?"

"No one will think a thing of it," Emilie assured her. "You aren't in any kind of disreputable arrangement."

"Why not? No one knows his character."

"But they know yours. Despite my encouragement, I doubt the proper Miss O'Malley would consider carrying on with her hired hand . . . would she?"

Grace tucked her chin at Emilie's laugh. "It's just that I don't want to take my reputation for granted. We should be vigilant against temptation."

Emilie patted her hand. "No one suspects you of being a temptation, my dear. We're just glad that someone is getting that place fixed up for you."

Grace bit the inside of her lip. If her friends couldn't imagine her with a beau, why would Clayton consider it? And when had a good reputation felt so insulting?

✳ Chapter 6 ✳

The pavers had been laid, the boards on the pigpen replaced, and the walls of the barn repaired. Clayton wiped his forehead with his kerchief as he surveyed his work. The place looked a sight better than it had when he'd first come a week ago, but not good enough. Not yet. And no doubt thousands of people were already crowding the lines at the registration office in Goodwin. Time was slipping away, but part of him didn't want to leave. What would Grace say if he told her he wanted to stay? She'd say something—that's for certain—but would she consider his request?

He stuffed his kerchief into his shirt pocket. There was only one way he could live at the homestead with her, but he wouldn't name it, even to himself. What was the use? A fine woman like Grace wouldn't want to be tied to a man like him.

Clayton stopped beneath the windmill and pumped up some water to splash on his face and hands. While in town he'd spoken to a rancher, a Mr. Mack Danvers, about acquiring a new horse. From the sound of it, the Circle D ranch was close by. He hoped the man would give him a reasonable deal so he could skedaddle once he collected his payment. The squawking windmill brought to mind one project he still had ahead of him before he could go.

Grace stepped outside, cradling a large ceramic bowl. Her black hair shone glossy in the sunlight, her cheeks pinked from the warmth. She waited, as pretty as a china doll, listening for him.

"Clayton?"

"I'm here."

She adjusted to speak to him, her brown eyes forgetting that their searching wouldn't be rewarded. "I'm attempting dinner rolls tonight. I think I have the dough right, but would you mind looking after the baking? I can't judge when they're done."

Clayton paused. As much as he'd like to, the sand was spilling from the hourglass. No one would save him a spot at the starting line in Oklahoma. Besides, her confidence would never grow if she didn't accomplish it on her own. "Sounds delicious, but I'm fixing to climb this here windmill. You'll do fine without me. Take them out and poke at them every now and then."

She frowned. "I don't want them filled with holes. And I can't see how brown they are. Why don't you come inside and rest a mite?"

His stomach rumbled at the thought of the rolls, but he didn't have time to waste. "I can rest once I've staked my homestead. I'd rather get this windmill looked after before a breeze kicks up."

He ducked his head beneath the lowest brace and pulled on his leather gloves. His foot hadn't hit the first rung when she spoke again.

"But the windmill does not concern me at the moment. I worked hard mixing the dough and I don't want it ruined."

Hurt had replaced her winsome smile, and the tender feelings she stirred up reminded Clayton that he'd already tarried with her too long.

"My employment consisted of carpentry and handyman work, not sitting watch at the oven on baking day. The school board won't pay me for that, so I'll fix the windmill instead. If you'll excuse me."

She settled the bowl against her stomach and clasped her hands around it. "You offered your advice on finding a husband, so I ask you, which would go further toward attracting a man—a good windmill or good rolls?"

Enough. Clayton tugged the gloves off his hands. Why was she goading him with all this husband talk? Didn't she realize how the subject made his hackles rise? "Are you sure you want a husband? A husband might not take orders as well as a hired hand. He might not appreciate your interfering if he's not getting paid."

Her head jerked. "He wouldn't work for free. I'll cook and clean in exchange. There's nothing wrong with an amicable partnership."

"As long as he knows what he's getting. You'd better tell him up front that he's signing his life away for clean laundry and burnt rolls." The thought of another man taking his place made his knuckles itch. He clomped away, all thought of working on the windmill abandoned.

"Are you leavin'?" Grace asked.

"Yep," he said, even though he hadn't realized it until he answered. "I've worked for a full week. I reckon I'm entitled to a few hours off."

"But . . . but where are you going?"

"Wherever I like." He bumped through the barn door, dug through his saddlebag until he'd found his canteen, and then headed to the water pump. He'd make up for the lost time, but he wasn't worth squat as long as she was yammering on about finding a husband.

Curse those pavers. She'd left her bread dough in the house and followed him to the windmill. "That's fine. You just go and do . . . whatever."

"I aim to." He thrust the canteen into the cascade of cold water.

"I won't miss your company." But still she stood there. She seemed to gulp the fresh air as she turned her face toward the sun. Her chin tilted up and her eyes closed.

She glowed. Her agitation seemed to burn away, leaving her porcelain complexion dewy and fresh. Her lips parted in a worshipful trance while the wind chimes rang their mellow notes. Clayton didn't want to interrupt, but he couldn't just stand there gazing at her like a love-dumb ox.

"Can you see the sun?" he asked.

She nodded. "And I can feel it. Even if I'd always been blind, I'd have to know it was golden, wouldn't I? What other color could feel this rich?"

Clayton cranked the lid of the canteen down. How could she make him feel so rotten one minute and wring his heart the next? God sure hadn't done His menfolk any favors when He'd made women such a puzzlement.

"I reckon you can find your way to the house. I'm taking out."

She opened her eyes. "When are you coming back?"

"When I'm done being gone."

Grace's brow wrinkled. "You've worked so hard lately, we've barely spoken. Well, please don't be gone too late. I'll worry if I don't hear you banging around in the barn before nightfall."

Clayton looked at the canyon ridge past the pasture. He had worked long hours lately, and he needed to burn off some steam, but hadn't Grace worked hard, as well? Wasn't she even more a prisoner?

Resignation, pure resignation, had him kicking dust with his pointy-toed boot. "Would you like to come along?"

She smiled. "Me? I'm apt to slow you down . . . and yet I've oft wondered how the land lies beyond the corral."

He waited, afraid she'd join him . . . halfway wishing she would.

"Of course, dinner would be late," she said.

"I won't starve."

Grace turned again to the sun. "And this jaunt won't put you behind in your work?"

Clayton slung his canteen over his shoulder. "Let me be clear. I'm throwing off the yoke. If you come, I don't want no gabbing about my work. You'll be my guest, and I expect you to behave."

Grace's eyebrow arched. "You're telling me how to behave?" A grin danced on her lips. "Very well. Will you wait while I fetch my bonnet?"

Clayton nodded before remembering to answer aloud. She strode off, confident on the smooth stones they'd placed to direct her to the house, so far from the uncertainty that'd plagued her when he'd arrived.

His chest stretched. He'd done that. He'd helped her regain her assurance. Every day she more resembled the woman she was born to be.

159

What would he think of her if they'd met under different circumstances? Certainly she wouldn't have been so demanding on a man she only knew socially. On the other hand, neither would she have been so transparent. As her help, Clayton saw both sides of her—the determined worker who expected excellence from herself and those around her, and the scared girl who worried she was inadequate to the challenges ahead. Knowledge of her fear gave him more sympathy for her demands. Although he didn't feel guilty taking her down a peg when necessary.

She stopped before him, still tying her bonnet strings.

"It's remarkable how you know where I am." Clayton took her arm and directed her away from the barnyard. "Do I need a bath?"

She laughed. "No, but you're not far from the truth. You do have a scent . . . a warmth . . . and when I get close enough, it's like I've stepped into your presence. I feel it."

Clayton almost stumbled. His temperature rose a few degrees.

"And it helps that I can usually spot something as big as you in broad daylight," she said.

Had she been pulling his leg with all that "presence" talk? He braved a glance, something he was doing more frequently, and saw her eyes crinkling at their corners.

He blew out the breath he'd been holding. "Has your sight improved?"

"It's worse, as if I'm inside a drawstring bag and the strings are being pulled tighter and tighter. Soon that little bag will seal up, and I'll be left with only memories."

The vibrantly striped walls of the canyon jutted above the rolling fields, their orange, white, and red bands contrasting against the short evergreens dotting the view. She would lose this—had already lost it. Her world consisted of less than he could see through a buttonhole. He couldn't imagine how she could continue. What would her future bring? Who would care for her after he'd gone?

Why was he leaving anyway?

Clayton would've never presumed to court Grace. A woman as beautiful as she with a homestead of her own wouldn't have any use for him. But after hearing her plans, or lack of, he couldn't help but wonder. If she would settle for a man she didn't know, why not him?

"Are you dead set on marrying a stranger?"

Her lashes fluttered. "I'm giving it some thought."

"But to never see him? He could be an old goat."

"How old are you?" she asked.

Clayton blinked. "Twenty-three." He took four steps before getting the courage to ask why.

Grace dipped her head. "That's barely older than me. I wondered if you were hiding something."

Of course he was. His arm stiffened. He'd say something fast before she noticed.

"Were you looking for a husband before?"

Grace leaned more heavily against him as the ground rose beneath their feet. "I took my first teaching position when I was fifteen years old. It gave me freedom from my brother—what I most desired. I always assumed I'd marry someday, but I had no urgency about it. Catching a man's eye didn't seem too difficult, so I thought I'd wait until teaching no longer interested me." She ran a finger beneath her bonnet string and swallowed. "You think I only want a husband so I'll have someone to work for me, but that's not true. I might be demanding, but I want to be loved, too. I want someone to think I'm special."

Clayton's boots felt like he was wading through quicksand, but he'd plod along no matter how deep he got. "And how will you know if someone loves you?"

She drew in a long breath. "If he can put up with my sharp tongue, that'll be a good start."

"So you've no plans to soften your tone?"

She stopped. "My natural personality is imperative."

"I don't understand those twenty-cent words. Does that mean the same thing as bossy?"

Her lips pursed. "So a woman isn't allowed to make suggestions?"

"Certainly, if she's paying for help. But if she keeps up that overbearing attitude, well, most men would rather risk their necks in a juvenile land run."

Grace's head dropped. She resumed her walk. "Point taken. I must remember that the fragile male ego—"

"Careful now . . ."

She patted his arm. "You see, Mr. Weber, I am a teacher, but I'm also a student. I love to learn, even when the truth is painful. Thank you for caring enough to speak plainly."

"Why did you call me Mr. Weber? What happened to Clayton?"

"You said I wasn't your employer during our excursion. The proper forms should be observed."

"As you wish, Grace."

She pressed her hand to her mouth but was too late to hide her smile. "Very well, Clayton. Would you mind telling me where we are?"

Safe ground.

"We're coming up to a canyon wall. I thought we'd find some shade now that the sun's being rude. That and I'd like to get a closer look at the layers of colors. I've never seen such fancy dirt and rock." He did his best to describe it to her, but she seemed preoccupied.

"Meeting a woman while working cattle must be difficult," she said at last. "It's no wonder you haven't married."

He gritted his teeth. "I've done the trails and worked odd jobs here and there, but I need a place to put a family before I can go about getting one. As soon as your windmill is finished—"

"You promised no talk of chores." She smiled. "Now, surely, you've had a sweetheart. Maybe a childhood friend?"

He used to tease the girls. That was before.

"A gentleman doesn't kiss and tell."

Her cheeks pinked. Her fingers extended their full length before settling against his arm again. "Do you have the tools you need to fix the windmill?"

Grace prided herself on controlling her realm. Now that she had the inside of her homestead organized she walked taller, and soon she'd be familiar with the barn and garden. But out here on the tableland . . . out here she was at Clayton's mercy, and being under his protection wasn't nearly as distasteful as she'd feared.

They lingered in the shadows of the canyon wall while the afternoon sun baked the earth. Clayton dozed in the grass while she walked her fingers over the cool rock wall, memorizing the texture. Grace had heard of Monsieur Braille's innovative coding for the blind even before she'd been stricken, but she'd be lucky to ever hold one of Braille's books. Not many would pass through Dry Gulch. Still, she imagined reading through touch, pretending that the uneven wall held messages invisible to the sighted yet detectable by her. Had God carved a message for her here? What would it say?

He would tell her something about being healed in heaven, promising her that she would see her Savior's face through unclouded eyes. And until that day, God no doubt wanted her to know that He saw her, loved her, and wouldn't abandon her. Even though she couldn't see, His words would light her path so that she would have nothing to fear.

The rock crumbled beneath her fingers, dashing chips around her feet. She believed, even if she needed continual reminders. Her fear wasn't a foe easily vanquished, and as long as she still had light, she hadn't faced the worst. As long as Clayton was with her, she hadn't had to fight alone. But he wouldn't be here long.

On the way home, neither of them spoke much. When possible, Grace followed a few steps behind. She needed the space, for Clayton's presence disrupted her thoughts.

She smelled the sow first, and then the smoke from her cookstove.

"I want to cook tonight," Clayton said above the wind chimes.

"Are you tired of my cooking?" Grace reached for the door, but Clayton swung it open for her and ushered her inside with a hand at her back. Benny rushed out, scampering around Grace's ankles.

"Maybe I need the practice more than you do."

It was on the tip of her tongue to remind him that they

were home and once again she was in charge, but she wasn't ready to resume command. Not when he carried it so well.

No longer needing to count her steps, she hung her bonnet on its peg. The pump groaned, and water gushed into the basin.

"Your turn." Clayton handed her a towel.

While she washed her hands and face, he poked at the fire until it crackled, and soon the ham was sizzling in the skillet. Grace's stomach grumbled, so she pinched a piece of corn bread from Emilie's tin.

"I saw that." Clayton slid the bread away from her.

Grace popped the stolen bit in her mouth and sat at the table. "I wish my rolls would've taken. They'd go perfectly with that delicious ham."

"Stop your bellyaching," he said, but there was a smile in his voice. The table groaned under the weight of the iron skillet. The heat rolled over her face like the ripples of a sun-warmed stream. A plate slid to her.

Grace skimmed her hand over the table until she found a knife and fork. After a few empty jabs, she laid her knife aside and located the food with her fingers.

"Here. Let me cut it." Clayton tugged at the plate.

"No." She caught his hand. "I need to do it myself. You won't always be here."

Or would he? The room grew quiet. Clayton didn't release her plate, but neither had she released his hand. Grace had spent the day on his arm, but touching his skin, the cords spanning from his wrist to his sturdy knuckles, sent heat through her. At times Clayton seemed little more than a voice to her, but he was real—sitting in her kitchen, seeing her, seeing how she kept house, how she walked, what she did with her face. While she knew very little of him physically, her appearance was no doubt familiar to him. For all she knew, he was watching her now. She glided her thumb along the side of his finger and noticed his callouses. His breathing grew slow and deliberate. Yes, he most certainly was watching her and waiting for her to explain herself.

"I'm sorry." She left her hand resting atop his. "I've gotten into the habit of touching when I'm . . . curious about something."

She lifted her hand and found her knife, but instead of using a fork, she held the ham steady with her left hand while she cut. Her trembling increased the difficulty of the task. Why was he so quiet? Shouldn't he be eating? She wished he'd wear a blindfold so they'd be on even footing.

"What were you curious about?" he rasped.

"Nothing." She took a bite of ham and prayed he'd not ask again.

His utensils clicked against his plate. "Do you want to know what I'm thinking?"

Grace's throat tightened. She reached for her drink, but it wasn't where she'd expected.

Clayton touched her wrist and slid the cool mug into her hand before speaking. "I'm wondering how you could trust a person you've never seen. I can't imagine talking to someone without knowing how they were listening. Not being able to see if they were leaning forward, watching each word leave your lips. Not knowing if they were watching you as you crossed a room. You wouldn't realize how much their happiness depended on you. You might completely miss their interest."

Grace straightened. What had she missed? Was he *flirting*

166

with her? He sounded too serious to be teasing. The corn bread crumbled in her hand. "Since losing my sight, I haven't been exposed to much socializing, but if such looks were going unnoticed, I'd hope you'd inform me."

They ate in silence, although Grace was now crackling with curiosity. What had he meant? If only she could watch him as closely as she felt him watching her.

"Would you truly place an advertisement for a husband?" he asked finally.

Grace ducked her head. "What choice do I have? Without someone to help me, my life will be so limited. I can't go anywhere. I can't read anything. I wouldn't be helping anyone, just be a burden to tend, and so much of life would go unexperienced."

His fork clunked against the table.

"Are you finished?" Grace asked.

Clayton grunted.

Although she knew he was studying her, she slipped her apron on and carried the dishes to the basin. A quick sweep of his plate let her know that he'd left a rind for Benny. She tossed it in the pup's direction and filled the basin with water.

His footsteps sounded behind her. "What exactly are you afraid of missing?"

<hr />

Clayton had plenty of fears of his own. Fears of being accused. Fears of being judged. Mostly he tried to avoid new experiences, not search them out. But Grace was adventurous. As poor a hand as she'd been dealt, she still wanted to play again.

She remained bent over the basin, her heavy black hair caught in a twist at the nape of her neck, her apron strings tied in a pretty bow at her slender waist.

"I want a family," she said. "I spent years taking care of everyone else's children and have never had my own to dote on. While a teacher, I lived in house after house. I'd like to choose my own meals and arrange furniture that I selected. I'd like to make a home for myself . . . and to share."

"Oh." He had dreams of his own homestead, so he could understand. "If that's all—"

"All?" She turned to face him, her skirt squashed by the cabinet behind her. "Clayton, not only do I want those things, I'll probably never have them. How am I going to meet a man living out here? Who is going to court me? Who would marry me now? I fancy myself educated, yet my education is sorely lacking. I've never even been kissed."

Times like this made him grateful she couldn't see him. "It's nothing," he stammered. "A bunch of foolishness over nothing."

She chewed her bottom lip and, having reached a decision, nodded. "Then you wouldn't mind showing me? It could be a sort of scholarly exercise, just to see what all the fuss is about."

His stomach dropped. Oh, he'd asked for this, him with all his sweet talk. He should've known she'd demand action, but how could he refuse? "I'm telling you, don't expect too much."

She squared her shoulders to his voice and backed even more firmly against the countertop behind her. There were hundreds of reasons this was a bad idea, but not one of them could stop him. Clayton clasped his hands behind his back and leaned forward. He aimed carefully, but hearing his approach, she moved, causing him to brush the side of her mouth.

Her eyebrows drew together.

"That was your own fault," he said. "You moved."

Again he leaned in.

"I'm sorry," she said just as his mouth glanced off of hers. Another failed attempt.

"Listen, woman. You can't be jumping all around like that." He placed his hand on her cheek. "Be quiet . . . be still . . . and . . ."

There'd be no missing this time. Her lips rose and waited just beneath his. He brushed against them, and then once more just to make sure the job was done correctly. She gasped and because he didn't want to hear her criticism, he kissed her again—this time more deeply. Her lips softened beneath his in a most curious fashion. His hands found their way to her shoulders, slid around her back, and pulled her close, amazed at the way her body shaped to his own. He hadn't realized it, but there was more kissing to be done. There were different kisses, tastes, depths—and he wanted to try them all. Immediately. With Grace. His heart thudded against his ribs. His core burned. He realized he was devouring her, but he couldn't stop. Not as long as she was so compliant, so willing.

He had to breathe, but he didn't go far. His mouth found her cheek, her neck. What had come over him? She wasn't a piece of cobbler to be nibbled on.

With a grunt he sprang from her. She clutched at the countertop with iron fingers, obviously outraged.

"My stars!" she exclaimed. "It can't always be that way."

He was gasping air as he croaked, "What way?"

"So . . . so wonderful! Is it like that every time?"

His chest filled at the sight of her—eyes half closed, mouth ripe and inviting. No, he couldn't do it again or there'd be no telling what would happen.

"How would I know? I've never kissed a woman before."

Grace's jaw dropped. "But . . . but you acted like you had. You said it was a bunch of foolishness."

He shoved his chair beneath the table, scooting it a full foot. "Evidently I was wrong." And he stomped outside.

✳ Chapter 7 ✳

All evening Grace had dreaded her next meeting with Clayton—the awkwardness, the disbelief of what had transpired between them—but by morning she couldn't wait for him to come to her. She'd relived the kiss half the night, her heart fluttering every time. Had Clayton stopped the first or the second time, she'd still be addled, but then he'd jumped the moon, and now Grace feared her knees would buckle at the sound of his steps on the threshold.

But he hadn't stepped on the threshold. The bright glow in the window told her that it was past breakfast. Emilie would be by soon. Grace turned the lid on the canned pears and returned them to the pantry.

What was Clayton thinking this morning? Had he stopped to consider that her homestead could be nicer than any he might find in the Cherokee Strip? Did he remember that she'd originally thought he was answering an ad for a husband? At this point Grace was nearly ready to ask him point-blank.

When she finally heard hooves approaching, the hour was well past Emilie's usual arrival. The wagon wheels turned more slowly than Emilie's quick buggy. Grace waited at the door for the person to disembark. Heavy footsteps meant it must be a man.

"Miss O'Malley, how are you?"

The voice was familiar. The barn door swung closed, alerting her that Clayton was on his way.

"Fine," she said, "but as you know, I can't see you. To whom do I owe the pleasure?"

"It's Albert Newman, ma'am. Miss Emilie mentioned that she was coming out today, so I asked if I could have the honor and bring the food in her stead— Eh . . . hello, there."

"Good day."

Grace's toes curled at the sound of Clayton's voice.

"Mr. Weber," she said, "this is Mr. Newman. I had his two youngest boys in class. Mr. Weber was commissioned by the school board to spruce up the homestead."

"The school board?" Mr. Newman expelled what sounded like a juicy glob of spittle. "I don't remember any such discussion arising at the meetings."

Grace frowned. "They didn't place an advertisement?"

"Not that I've heard tell of."

Clayton cleared his throat. "Miss Grace, I'm going to climb the windmill now. Just wave if you need me. I'll be watching."

Wasn't he always? Grace's stomach twisted. So intent was she on his departing footsteps that she missed Mr. Newman's first words, and he was obliged to repeat them.

"I'd like to go inside. I could use a drink after being in the sun."

Grace could only imagine how sweaty Mr. Newman was. His fancy white shirt made an appearance at every school function, complete with yellowed crescents staining the underarms. "Right this way." She would refrain from breathing through her nose.

"I'll put the food on your counter here," he said.

"That's just fine," she said, and then pointed him to the table and two chairs. Benny padded over to inspect their visitor while she got a cup of water from the jug on the counter next to her.

"Nice little fellow you've got." The small chain around Benny's neck jangled. "There should be some scraps for him, I'd imagine." He took the cup she offered. "You're finding your way around here pretty easily, aren't you?"

Grace clasped her hands in front of her. "I'm learning. It's an adjustment, but even being able to see light is a help."

His foot tapped the floor. "Well, I don't want to waste my time. The reason I came was to see if you'd allow me to call on you. The children are nearly grown. They take care of themselves, so there'd be no worrying about them, but I get lonely and I can imagine that maybe you would be—"

"Excuse me." Grace held up a hand. As a school-board member Mr. Newman had never supported her, always questioning her methods and dedication. Had something changed? "I'm sorry, but I'm at a loss. You've never expressed any interest in me before. Why now?"

"Look, Miss O'Malley. You're a beautiful lady. I'm humble enough to admit I couldn't turn your head, but now, well, maybe looks don't matter so much. The balance could've tipped for me after all."

There'd sooner be a snake in Ireland.

He snuffed, and she imaged the sleeve of his white shirt getting even dingier sopping up his nose.

"I thank you for your offer, Mr. Newman, but I'm still adjusting to my affliction and don't want to make any hasty decisions. I'm afraid I must deny your request."

The cup clinked against the tabletop. "You'll be lonely soon enough, so don't let your pride get in the way. You just let me know when you're ready. I'm not one to hold a grudge."

"That's a comfort." He'd held a grudge when his son had failed his sixth grade examination. Or maybe this was his way of reconciling. "Thank you for bringing dinner, and I hope you'll send my greetings to your children."

"Yes, ma'am. They are sorely worried about you, and that's a fact."

She only prayed they didn't know the nature of his visit. She'd hate to have the story spread throughout town, but she couldn't consider Mr. Newman's offer. Especially not with the way her heart soared at every thought of Clayton Weber.

Grace followed Mr. Newman outside and waved as the wagon rolled away. What had she expected? A lot worse than the perspiring Mr. Newman could answer any notice she decided to run. Somehow, she'd grown more particular recently. If only Clayton weren't afraid to speak to her again.

Grace noticed the squeaking wheel of the windmill wasn't raising its usual fuss, so she lifted her head and shaded her eyes. If he was watching as he claimed to be, he'd know she was looking for him.

Boots thudded to the ground, raising a cloud of dust. Grace covered her face.

"You need me?"

Yes. Oh yes.

"Mr. Newman brought dinner, and you already missed breakfast. Aren't you hungry?"

Silence. Grace lowered her hands to search before her but couldn't make out anything besides Clayton's dark form.

"I'll bring you a plate outside if you're too busy." Was he even there? Her eyes stung from squinting.

"Do you want me to come inside?" His voice was tight. Uncertain. "I didn't know how you'd feel after last night."

Grace's heart did a somersault. Elated. Giddy. Even more curious than before. "I want you to come inside." She bowed her head, too embarrassed to show her face. She should've been outraged by the liberties he took, but she was fair. Although she'd asked him for a candle and he'd given her a lightning bolt, she was willing to admit she shared the blame.

"I'll wash up out here," he said.

Grace followed the wind chimes to the house. She pulled the cheesecloth cover off the tin and took a deep whiff. Onion soup. By the time Clayton had taken his seat, Grace had ladled a bowl for him, eager to get past this initial awkwardness.

He paused.

"You're awfully quiet," Grace said.

"I'm praying."

"Sorry."

She wasn't hungry. She'd kept the pears and toast out all morning, waiting for Clayton, and had consumed more than she'd intended, but maybe she could eat a few crackers for an excuse to sit across the table from him.

"What did the man want?" Clayton slurped a spoonful.

"He brought the food from Emilie."

"He wore a fancy going-courtin' shirt for that?"

175

With yellow underarms? Grace grimaced. "Now that you mention it, he did ask if he could call on me."

Clayton's spoon splashed in his soup. "And you said . . ."

Judging from his voice he wasn't smiling, but she hadn't done anything wrong. Why should she feel defensive? Grace rocked in her chair.

"I told him absolutely not. He never would've got the courage to speak to me before. Why does he think I'd accept him now?" Maybe she was overdoing it, but obviously Mr. Newman's visit had upset Clayton. She'd set things aright. "Just because I can't see doesn't mean I want a husband who'd be rejected by everyone else."

"What do you mean by that?" His voice had cooled to January ice.

"His appearance is disgraceful. I'd be ashamed to be associated with a man whose—"

"Is that your criteria? You'd reject a man on his looks even though you can't see him?"

Grace's mouth dropped open. "You want me to court Mr. Newman? Is that what you're saying?" Did Clayton regret kissing her? Why else would he be so eager to get her off his hands?

He stood. His bowl dropped into the sink.

"I don't know Mr. Newman, but if you're going to find him lacking, it should be for his character, his personality, or his situation. Don't mock him for his appearance."

"I'm not mocking him. He might make a fine husband for someone else, but that doesn't mean I'm obligated to accept him. There's a difference between tolerating someone and wanting to marry them. Shouldn't I wait for a man who's a better match?"

Like you, she wanted to add, but didn't have the courage. If only she could see Clayton. Was he glaring at her in disgust? Was he looking at the door, longing to leave?

"I understand," Clayton said. "Now if you'll excuse me. I can't afford to waste any more time."

Just as she'd feared. He'd recognized his mistake. Clayton had plans in Oklahoma Territory, and one kiss wasn't going to change them.

By the time Clayton reached the top of the windmill, he was out of breath. He stood, hands in fists, and looked down at the square cabin, all the hopefulness and sentiments from earlier that day vanished.

She still didn't know. She didn't realize that the man who'd kissed her with abandon was himself disfigured. That if she wasn't blind, he, like Mr. Newman, would have only admired her from a distance.

A husband who'd be rejected by everyone else. Sooner or later she'd find out. Emilie would tell her. Someone would tell her. Or maybe she'd wonder why he avoided crowds and why he rarely spoke up in public. She'd wonder why her husband hid when people were around.

If he had any hope of making the land run on Saturday, he'd better finish up and hit the trail.

Clayton sat on the platform, his heels swinging in midair. He hadn't thought about the land run all day. Hadn't worried about getting the horse or running for a stake. No, his thoughts hadn't left the little homestead outside of Dry Gulch. He loved Grace, possibly had loved her from the first moment she stepped outside and surprised him with her prying questions. And while he'd been prepared to love her from afar—admire her, help her, and then move on—at some time he'd come to the conclusion that this love was worth fighting for. Here was a place he could belong. And after last night's kiss, he'd thought that she believed so, too.

He was a fool. How could he fault Grace when he was so taken by her beauty? *Hypocrite.*

And once again he cursed the men who'd scarred his heart even more than his face. When the son of a horse thief is accused of stealing a horse, no one believes his innocence. When he's disfigured, no one gives him sympathy. Even worse than the actual damage was the shame it represented—his dead father's crime forever imprinted on him. If Grace couldn't respect a man because of the grubbiness of his shirt, she wouldn't endure a man whose charges and punishment were visible for all to see.

But what would become of her after he left? Maybe she'd finally post the notice and would have some candidates to choose from. Maybe Emilie would help. Either way, it wasn't his concern.

Clayton sat until his frustration demanded action. He'd get the windmill done, then he'd go to the bank and inform them that his task was complete. By tomorrow he'd collect his money and quit town. He'd already failed at this contest. The race was his last chance.

⋆ Chapter 8 ⋆

Grace hefted the rocker, hooking her arm through its back, and made her way outside. While she didn't have the nerve to approach Clayton, she wanted to be outside—to hear his labor, to know there was another human soul within miles. Her hopes of winning his regard had shriveled, so she wouldn't get in his way, but she wasn't ready for her isolation to begin.

She'd just stepped onto the porch when he hailed her from the barn.

"Where are you headed?" he asked.

Her courage all but fled at his dark tone. "Needed some air."

He stepped onto the porch. "By my account, the work here would pass inspection from your mysterious donor. It's time for me to buy a horse, get settled up at the bank, and move on. I've been underfoot long enough."

Was he watching her for a sign of encouragement or was he resolute? Oh, the frustrations of not being able to read him! But her memory of his dismissal reminded her that this man—as helpful as he was—wanted her off his hands.

He had plans for a new start in the Cherokee Strip, and she was obviously in his way.

"Are you coming back?" How she wished they were inside. Standing outside, the sounds of his movements were swept away by the wind, leaving her no clue to his stance.

"Do you want me to?"

How could he even ask that? She was practically throwing herself at him. Her arm gave way, and the rocker crashed to the ground. "Yes, I do. I mean, you might have to wait until someone inspects the work. There's no reason for you to waste your funds on a hotel when you could stay here."

The rocker clattered against the porch as he positioned it for her. "If I get a horse you wouldn't mind me keeping him in the barn while we wait, would you?"

"Of course not."

He touched her arm and guided her to the rocker, still a gentleman even when irritated. "Let me see you settled then before I leave."

And leave he did. No lingering to explain what had upset him. Just an eagerness to put distance between the two of them, a distance her wounded heart felt keenly.

With Clayton gone, Grace sat alone on the homestead, which was only a dot in the middle of the tableland. The dry, hot wind carried the smell of drought over the empty fields—fields that would be one man emptier by tomorrow.

With a sigh, she went inside to tidy the house and let the day pass as quickly as it would. Without Clayton, her world would've been as small as the space inside her cabin. She owed him for expanding it to include the barn and grounds, but he'd also shown her that her borders weren't only physical. Whole unexplored territories existed in her soul. Could she find the way on her own, or was she destined to be disappointed with the barren plot he was leaving her?

From outside Benny yipped. His growl purred when it should've rumbled, but he'd gotten the message to her. A horse was approaching.

Clayton couldn't have gone to town and back yet. Grace locked the door as a precaution. She'd rather have it between her and her unknown caller until she knew who it was.

"Hello? Be this the home of Grace O'Malley?"

The sound of his voice carried Grace back to the wagon swaying across central Texas and to an emaciated waif fresh off the boat—hair tangled, clothes reeking, newly orphaned—thrust on the mercy of a big brother she'd never met. He'd been none too happy to see her then. Why had he traveled all this way to see her now?

"Brian? Is that you?"

A saddle creaked and the ground thumped as he dismounted. "Aye, lass. Come on out so I can take a look at you."

Grace straightened her collar. She wouldn't cower to him. No longer did she need his begrudging help to survive.

She opened the door, positioning herself squarely in the doorway. "I can't fathom what's brought you here." She crossed her arms. "I don't need your help, you know."

He cleared his throat, and when he spoke again, his words were measured, careful. "That's good to hear, but I came on the off chance you might, after I received a letter from the school board."

"They sought you?" Grace shook her head. "It wasn't my doing. I would've told them not to bother."

"Grace, don't worry yourself. It's glad I am to make this

journey and ashamed that I didn't make it sooner." The voice was the same, but the tone had changed.

What was he doing there? Throughout her childhood her brother reminded her daily that her care taxed his resources. That his life would be better without her. She'd never regretted her decision to leave. He'd never wanted her. Why was he here now?

"You can pen your horse if you'd like. There's water on the back side of the barn."

"Thank ye."

Grace waited for him to finish before she entered the house, mentally adjusting the image in her mind to the reality of the day. Seven years had passed since she'd seen him. His fair face would be fuller, his black hair thinner, perhaps . . . although Da hadn't lost any before his death. Were Brian's eyes as hard? Were his hands as impatient to strike? She'd know soon enough, although she didn't fear him anymore.

"You're blind, they say." Brian stepped inside and followed her gesture to the chair opposite hers. "That's a blow to shake a mountain."

"Aye." Grace smiled to hear the tones of her motherland, even if the speaker brought her no joy. "It's a fearsome prospect, wondering which day will be the last that I see the sun. Still, I'm learning to get on without sight. Clayton—the man who helps me—insists I can make a go of it right here."

"And I don't blame you for wanting to, especially considering how ye fared at my hands, but things have been different since you left."

"Oh?" She crossed her arms. "So tell me, what's changed in Fort Worth?"

Fabric whisked as he rested his elbows on the table, causing it to groan and slope toward him. "It's not the town that's changed, but me. To start, I realized how much I had to amend for. You remember those years of traveling. I couldn't get past that Da and Mam never made it here, after all me hard work." The familiar edge to his voice emerged and then just as quickly retreated. "I lashed out at everyone, kept the company of rough lads. I didn't care who I hurt, but feeling entitled to me wrath, like the rest of the world owed me something. It was nearly my undoin'."

Whatever Grace had expected from a reunion with her brother, this wasn't it.

"Go on," she said.

"Before you left, I'd go out carousing with the boys of the evenings. One night we were burning over something—angry over a slight, angry over a hand of cards—I don't remember, but we stoked it up until we had a rage going, picking a fight with anyone who stumbled into our path. At first we had a jolly time of it, but then I saw my hate on the faces of me mates, and it frightened me. I'd used my anger to control people, but it had grown until it controlled me, and it would destroy me if I didn't check it."

Was this her brother? Grace had given up on him, never looked back, never considered the possibility that for all the maturing she'd done over the years perhaps God had refined him, as well.

"Naturally I didn't burden you with me troubles," he continued, "but once you left, I couldn't help but realize I was truly alone, and who would want something to do with a nasty piece of work like me? Then one day a lady stopped me, an angel from heaven. Said she'd watched me, knew I was troubled, and that God wouldn't leave her in peace until she'd talked to me."

Grace could see the scene as clearly as if she were standing on the streets of Fort Worth with her brother. "And you fell in love with her."

"Not hardly. She was an auld hag, more fit to be me nana than me wife, but her heart brimmed with a kindness that weren't from this earth. It was she who showed me to take the cross and the Savior who bore it."

"Truly?" Grace balanced on the edge of her seat. "But that's wonderful, Brian. I hope you're not embarrassed for me to say it's welcome news."

"Not a mite. And while I'm glad to hear you've no need of aid, I had to come offer it just the same . . . and to offer an apology, as well. You were only a wee lass when you came over. It weren't your fault that Da and Mam died, and I showed you no kindness. I was tight in my dealings, and I come to ask your forgiveness. If you ever have a need, I'll see to it."

She extended her hand across the table and smiled as he took it. Here was a miracle she hadn't even known to pray for. In heaven someday she'd find out who'd been interceding for her brother and thank them for the gift they'd given her.

"I cried many nights over your cruel words," she said, "but once I fled, they didn't haunt me. As much as I hated our situation, I think I realized that you were hurting, too."

"'Tis no excuse, but good of you to say." He released her hand and slapped the table. "Enough o' me weepy tale. Does my story affect your decision? My wife is all after me to bring you home to the wee ones."

Grace's fingers danced over the tablecloth. Nieces and

nephews? Better than anything the lonely homestead offered her. She could sell the ranch and perhaps afford to erect her own place on their land. She'd have some independence, but not be alone. It was the most sensible solution, if a suitable husband didn't present himself. And it sure seemed like Clayton didn't want the job.

"Can I think it over? I don't want to burden your family."

"Grace, would I have made this trip if I weren't altogether certain? Ever since I received the letter from the school board, I've known that God wanted me to find you. He has a plan here. You just wait and see."

Did He? Grace leaned into the back of her seat. Going home with her brother had never been her first choice. Had God made it her only choice?

———◆———

The mid-September sun baked the hard ground beneath his feet and radiated its strength up beneath the shade of his hat. Clayton swiped his forehead. In a couple of months the heat would disappear and freezing gales would whip across the canyon lands. He wouldn't have long to make a shelter in Oklahoma Territory. The money he'd made working for Grace, combined with his other savings, would have to stretch to get him the supplies he needed to ride out the winter, especially now that the price for his new mount had been set.

Speaking of horses, he saw the strange one before he was within shouting distance of the house. Clayton quickened his steps. Emilie didn't have a bay horse, and he'd not met anyone on the road. Who could it be? Another suitor? Perhaps it was for the best.

But still, a stranger on the premises required looking into. Clayton came to the house, slowing as he approached the door. He could hear Grace speaking cheerfully, evenly, with no distress. Then a man answered. Clayton's brow lowered and his stomach knotted. Another Irishman. They'd brought him nothing but trouble.

"Grace?" Clayton clutched the door handle. At her answer he stepped inside. The man at the table was sitting calmly, both hands atop the table. No threat that Clayton could detect.

"This is Clayton Weber." Grace swept her arm toward him until she caught him by the sleeve. "If you see anything good about this homestead, he can take the credit for it. He's repaired the barn, fixed the windmill, and organized the house. Without him . . ."

Her words blurred beneath the roaring in his ears. His skin pricked, telling him that something was wrong. From long practice Clayton kept his scar hidden. He tilted his head and peered down at Grace as he tried to puzzle out the man's identity. What was he doing there? Had they met before?

"Aren't you going to say something?" Grace blinked, obviously curious to what she was missing.

To what? He hadn't heard half of her words.

"He can't take his eyes off you." The man smiled. "And I'm happy for ye if he has good intentions. Otherwise, it's another reason for you to come live with your brother."

Her brother? Clayton's throat lurched. The brother she'd fled years ago? What kind of trouble had he brought? Clayton jerked his arm free of Grace's grasp and looked the man straight on.

The man's eyes widened. His face drained of color. Recognition shone in his eyes, too. But from where? Clayton's hands clenched into fists.

"What's happening, Clayton? Why are you so quiet?"

The man rose out of his chair. "You—the lad from Fort Worth? I can't believe you're here in the flesh."

Clayton tasted bile. This man? He'd been one of them? The scene flooded back over him. The angry taunts, the gang surrounding him, accusing, attacking. This man's actions had changed Clayton's life forever. All the pent-up rage of an adolescent boy falsely accused threatened to spew over, but no longer was he a scrawny child caught unaware. He was prepared this time.

"You remember me?" His throat clenched. "You remember, and you have the gall to stand before me?"

"I'm glad to see you, lad. I'd always wondered what happened to ye. It's a mercy that you healed so clean."

"That's all you have to say? You think I'm pleased with your handiwork? I've dreamed every day that I would get a chance to pay you back."

"Clayton? Brian? What's this about?" Grace turned in her chair and gripped its back. "Do you know each other?"

O'Malley stood, his hands raised, palms out. "If I could take back that night, I would. It's no untruth to say how I regretted my part. I should've stopped them—I wish I had. My horror over what happened to ye is what brought me to me knees. It showed me what a filthy scoundrel I'd become."

"Congratulations." Clayton balled up the word and threw it at him. "You stayed safe instead of speaking up for me. You satisfied your anger, and then you satisfied your guilt. Unfortunately, I had to live with the consequences. It'd be fair, don't you reckon, if I lost my temper now? Maybe I can repent at a more convenient time."

Grace stood and angled herself in front of him. "Clayton, what's the matter? Brian's not here to cause trouble. He's offered me a home." Her brow creased with confusion, and the fact that she couldn't understand his anger only made it grow.

"You would go with him? You would trust him after what he did to me?"

"What did he do?"

She'd lifted her face to his, gazing where no one wanted to look. Was he willing to destroy her acceptance? Did he want her to know that she'd been tricked into admiring a man that no one else would want? Apparently he had one scrap of pride left, for he couldn't bring himself to ruin her image of him. Clayton was at a loss.

"Aye, this is a conundrum," O'Malley said. "To think I had a chance to help the man who'd someday fall in love with Grace."

"Love? What are you talking about?" Grace's hands shook as she held them out, begging for answers. But Clayton wouldn't acknowledge either charge.

"Lad"— O'Malley's brown eyes implored with a directness that Grace's could no longer muster—"there's nothing I can do to cure the harm I've done. Nothing I can say besides I'm sorry and tell you I'm not the same man. Grace knows full well how selfish and small-hearted I was, and that's why I'm here—to make amends. I never imagined God would give me a pass at both of ye at the same time."

Tears quivered on Grace's lashes. Clayton stabbed O'Malley with his glare. "For what you allowed them to do to me and for what you put Grace through, you don't deserve another chance."

"Don't judge him for my sake," Grace said. "If I can forgive—"

But Clayton wouldn't hear any more. He spun around. The room blurred away—the cabin, the barn . . . they all fell behind as he stalked across the rough land, fleeing the pain that had chased him even to this isolated homestead.

◆ ◆ ◆

Grace reached, but Clayton had fled before she could touch him. The scorching wind blew through the open door, carrying the sound of the wind chimes angrily crashing into each other.

"I don't understand," Grace said. Had Clayton changed for the worse as much as Brian had turned toward good? How else could she explain the furious man who'd threatened Brian and stalked out?

"I told you that I'd played a hand in brutality." Brian's chair creaked as he lowered himself into it. "Well, the man we cornered, he was a lad, more like."

Grace's heart dropped. She fell into her chair, nearly missing the seat. "Clayton?"

Brian cleared his throat. "When we got our horses at the livery that night, the stable owner had words for us. Called us drunken Paddies and hooligans. We were seeing red, we were.

"We stumbled to the stables, and there was a lad with the horses. I didn't recognize him, but someone claimed he was a known horse thief. That's all it took. We couldn't strike at the livery man, but this boy was defenseless. They got ahold of him and took their turns beating him. I spurred them on, feeling good that finally I'd found someone who was even lower than I was. But then they held him down while Kennedy got a riding whip. He said he'd mark him so everyone who saw him would know what kind of criminal he was. That's when I lost the stomach for it. I slunk away, but not before I heard the blows."

A sob wrenched from her chest. She could picture the young man, her young Clayton, and his surprise, his frustration at the unwarranted attack. "What a shock for him to find you here."

Brian grunted in affirmation. "I wish I would've found him after, but I fled. Never thought I'd meet him like this."

Grace had no answers. She'd seen evidence of Clayton's scar. Emilie had mentioned it, too, but she hadn't guessed how it represented a wound much deeper.

"I thought I'd finished causing you pain, and here I've hurt you again."

Grace stood. She couldn't reassure Brian, not yet. First she had to look after Clayton. Her loyalty was with him.

She motioned Brian to the door.

"I'll be back in the morning." He huffed as he pulled himself into the saddle. "My offer of a place still stands."

And she must consider it. It was perhaps her only option.

How was it that one of his monsters, the villain of his nightmares, had the same fair coloring and proud features of the woman he loved? Clayton watched by the barn as O'Malley rode away. Grace stood with her arms wrapped around herself, her brow creased with worry. Or was it pity?

O'Malley had told her, no doubt. Now she could imagine Clayton as she had Mr. Newman—pathetic, unattractive, and unwanted. O'Malley hadn't protected him back in Fort Worth, and once again he was marking him so even a blind woman would see his shame. Well, Clayton's time with Grace was at an end. The arrangements for the inspection of his work had been made, and after tomorrow he'd have no business messing with this family any further.

Clayton's heart clutched as Grace took the first tentative step away from the house. Her feet touched the stone pathway and she sped toward him. He barely had time to dodge into the barn before she reached him.

He couldn't face her. Couldn't speak. Not yet. His thoughts clashed as they tried to reconcile the events of his past with the meek man he'd confronted. Through his confusion, though, one thing was clear. Clayton didn't want to hear Grace's plans. He couldn't promise her that he'd be all right. That he'd forgive. Not when O'Malley's deeds were the only things keeping him from declaring his love for her.

Easing to the wall, Clayton leaned heavily against it. She still wasn't comfortable in the barn. If he didn't move, maybe she'd leave him alone with his regrets and self-pity.

The sun squeezed through the gaps in the rough construction, striping Grace with gold. "Clayton? Are you here?"

He filled his lungs with the stale air and waited. Her dark brows pinched together. One hand extended as she slid her foot forward. "Can you hear me? I want to talk."

His tan shirt blended into the wall. He wasn't talking. Not yet. Her coiffure had slipped astray, allowing her dark hair to frame her face. Her slim figure advanced another step.

"I want to tell you that I understand your shock. Brian

191

told me about your encounter. He confessed the worst, and I'm not surprised. I knew him then, too."

His fists clenched. Grace tilted her head. Her jaw rose as she leaned in his direction. Two more steps.

"No one expects you to forget what he did. We just want . . . I want . . . what's best for you. Forgiving Brian will do more for you than for him."

Perhaps, but was it possible to forgive him? Not yet. Not until he forgot about Grace and the love his scar had cost him.

A low trough rested before her. Another five feet and she'd trip over it. Should Clayton move it? He straightened. Her body tensed. "I know you're here," she said. "I can sense you. Remember? I can feel you looking at me." She turned left, directly toward him and stepped forward. Her arm extended until it touched the wall not a foot from him.

Clayton couldn't turn away. Her eyes held enough sadness for both of them. The clean scent of her kitchen soap caught him unprepared. He filled his lungs with it and then didn't dare release the breath he'd been holding.

"I wish you'd speak." Her usual confident demeanor had broken. "You know I don't want to live on charity. Brian's coming solves several needs of mine, but it also creates one. I hate to leave Dry Gulch without knowing that you're going to be fine. I don't want to leave until you find peace."

She waited. So close, so beautiful. So beyond his reach.

Grace ducked her head. The hem of her skirt brushed against his boots. Years of hiding from the ladies, keeping quiet when he wished to speak, and bowing out just when life got interesting kept Clayton welded to the wall. He'd become a master at fading into the woodwork, and now his skills were being put to good use.

192

"I'm sorry that knowing me reminded you of past harms," she said.

Did she have any idea of how beautiful she was?

"I won't bother you again." Using the wall as a reference, she turned and made her way out of the barn.

Clayton covered the wall where her hand had been, imprinting his palm in the very spot she'd just left. He'd had almost a week and a half of promise. A week and a half of possibilities that he'd relinquished along with his innocent optimism. That time had passed. He could now go to Oklahoma Territory and pray God would let him start anew. At least Grace would be cared for.

But he was left wondering why God would afflict him so. The woman he loved, the man he hated—they were of the same blood. Could he make peace with the man who'd stolen his appearance and reminded him every time he saw his reflection that he was the son of a thief? Could he give up the grudge he'd nursed for years over a woman he'd known such a short time?

He could, but there was no call to. Grace wouldn't have him either way.

His work was completed. Although the banker seemed confused by the situation, there was an account set up for Miss O'Malley, and he agreed to help Clayton claim the amount due him. After an inspection, Clayton could buy Mr. Danvers's horse and head to Goodwin to register for the race.

He took an ax off its pegs in the barn. He wouldn't get any sleep tonight. He might as well get a store of firewood set by for Grace, or whoever would spend the winter here.

✳ Chapter 9 ✳

Clayton hadn't come in for supper. With movements dulled, Grace returned the clean dishes to the shelf. Lack of sight couldn't hide Clayton from her. He'd been in the barn, but he hadn't answered her. While their spats had always been spirited, perhaps he now saw them in a different light. Did he wonder if the family resemblance ran deeper than dark hair and a fair complexion?

And then there was the issue of Mr. Newman. Grace still didn't understand Clayton's reaction. She'd hoped he would be pleased that she rejected the man. Either she'd misread the growing intimacy between her and Clayton, possible since she couldn't see him, or Clayton desperately wanted her married and off his hands. How could she not believe the second?

She wouldn't go outside again. Better to leave well enough alone.

Judging from the lack of golden squares on the wall, the sun had already set. Grace rubbed her temples. Her eyes stung. Her head throbbed. She hoped it wouldn't be a sleepless night, but how could she rest knowing Clayton was troubled? Knowing that their time together was so short? She would always wonder what life would've been like if Clayton had answered a husband notice instead of one for a hired hand. She should've asked him from the first day.

Grace changed into her nightgown and removed the pins from her hair, placing them carefully on the dressing table next to the bed. Could she go with Brian without Clayton's approval? She climbed into bed and kicked the quilt to the foot, knowing she'd be drenched in sweat in the stuffy room, if she could sleep at all. Instead, she found herself going over every conversation, every discussion she'd had with Clayton. She'd seen the narrow white valley that cut through his brow and cheek, but she'd thought nothing of it. Perhaps seen in its entirety, it was gruesome. But no. Hadn't Emilie raved about Clayton's good looks? Hadn't she described how the ladies noticed him?

But she'd said something else, too. She'd called him bashful. Said that he wouldn't look her in the face, but as far as Grace could tell, he'd never failed to face her.

Until now.

As long as he thought her blindness covered him, he interacted openly. Now that she knew, he wanted to hide.

She punched her feather pillow up and rolled to her side, afraid of what the morning would bring. Afraid to say good-bye, or even worse, to leave without a good-bye.

◆━━━◆━━━◆

And morning came too soon. Clayton was already at work, ax ringing. Grace rolled to her back and fought against the syrupy drag of exhaustion. She had to wake up. Get dressed. Get breakfast. Why was she so tired?

She opened her eyes. Nothing. No light. No glow. Were her eyes truly open? Grace touched her face, felt her lashes. Her fingers met the wet orb of her eye, but all was black.

With a jolt she sat up, searching for the illuminated squares that marked the windows. Nothing. Nothing to anchor to. She wrapped her fists in her sheets, holding on. Afraid that the whole room had disappeared. Afraid to stretch her foot downward, wondering what else had evaporated with her sight.

The darkness had finally come, but this time it was permanent. Nothing more than she could see at this moment. No more searching. No more hoping to catch a glimpse. Just her alone in darkness.

But there was one person who'd grown close enough he could stand in the circle with her.

"Clayton?" She had to find him. She had to hear a voice, to know if the world remained unchanged for someone. The ax slammed again into a log. "Clayton!" she cried. What if the racket was her imagination? What if her hearing had become unreliable, too? What else would be taken from her?

"Grace!" he called. "What is it?"

Forgetting her hesitation she ran toward his voice and threw the bolt. With arms outstretched she rushed outside.

* * *

The desperation in her cry burst through Clayton's reserve. He ran to the house, ax swinging, ready to confront Grace's attacker. Reaching her, he tucked her beneath his left arm and stepped inside, prepared for whatever had chased her, but there was only sleepy Benny blinking from his pillow.

"What is it? What's wrong?" The sun was gone, but even

in the moonlight he could make out her white gown and tear-stained face. His heart thundered, partly from his readiness to fight and partly from having her close again.

"I can't see. It's all dark. Everything is gone." Her arm wrapped around his back, her head pressed against his chest.

A quick inventory of the dark room told him they were alone. He leaned the ax against the wall and cradled her head, her black hair cascading over his hand.

Dark? Sometimes he forgot she was blind. She wasn't a disadvantaged woman. She was the woman he loved. But now her loss splashed over him afresh as he imagined all that she'd lost. "I'm so sorry. So, so sorry."

Her back jerked with short, sudden breaths. "How long before I forget what my world looked like? Will I forget my friends' faces? Will I forget light? Colors?" She shuddered. "Now I won't even know if it's day or night."

Maybe being isolated was the natural order of things. For a brief period he'd escaped his loneliness, but it'd only been temporary. He rocked her, a low-pitched hum rolling from his chest to replace the promises he wanted to make. But his promises wouldn't help her. Not if she didn't want him.

"Maybe your light isn't all gone. Come morning you might be surprised."

"Morning?" Grace's spine straightened. "It's not morning? But I heard you at the woodpile—"

Taking a last deep breath of her fragrance, he released her and found the kerosene lamp. "It's not morning. It's still the middle of the night." The match flared. He adjusted the wick and flooded the room with light.

"Oh!" Grace covered her mouth. The flame reflected in her tear-washed eyes. "I see it. I can still see it."

And he saw her. Her soft cotton gown skimmed the tops of her bare toes. Her hair curled around her shoulder. As pleased as he was to vanquish her fears, he regretted that she wasn't still in his arms.

"That's a simple enough fix." He moved the lamp to the table. He might wish he could, but he had no right to stay. "I apologize for waking you."

Her gaze didn't wander from the dancing flame. "I didn't realize how frightened I'd be. I've known this was coming, but still I'm terrified. And now I understand why you want me to marry Mr. Newman. I understand now how hard it will be to face this alone."

Clayton's head tilted. "I don't want you to marry Mr. Newman, but does it matter that he's not handsome? Does that mean he can't provide and care for you? Does that mean he can't love and cherish you?"

She wrenched her face from the flame toward his. "But I don't love him. I couldn't love him, and it has nothing to do with his appearance. He's slovenly. He's careless with his children. He's spiteful. Truthfully, I don't know that I've ever noticed Mr. Newman's features. It's his lack of character that makes him unattractive. Besides, I'm surprised at you for taking his side. You haven't let your scar affect you."

"My . . . my scar?" Clayton's stomach turned inside out. He swallowed. "I knew your brother would tell you."

Her eyes narrowed. "He told me about its origin, but I already knew of its existence. I saw it myself, or bits here and there. That, along with your sea-green eyes and curly hair."

His mouth opened. Then closed. "I thought . . . if I'd known, I would've done a better job of hiding."

"Don't hide. My sight may fade soon, but I want to see your face as much as I can before then."

She took the lamp by the base. Clayton stepped back.

"Please," she said.

Clayton lowered his eyes. Would she regret her decision? Would seeing his face change her opinion of him? His throat hopped. What did it matter? He planned to leave by sundown. Too late to hide now.

"I'm here," he rasped.

Grace held the lamp aloft. The flame warmed his cheek. He could taste the burning kerosene in the air.

Her brows lowered and her eyes narrowed. She swung her head, trying to locate the injury. When she caught sight, he flinched.

"No, don't move." She handed him the lamp and laid her palm against his cheek. Her eyes closed and she seemed to soak away all the bitterness that clung to the thin white line.

He didn't think he could speak while she touched him, but once started the words spilled out. "I was just a lanky, overgrown kid who loved horses. I hung around the livery stable all the time helping out. I never did any harm." So many years of pain from an innocent pastime. "But that night some men took offense. Friends of your brother's who thought I'd insulted them for being Irish. They accused me of being a horse thief." He placed the lamp on the table. "My pa was hanged for horse thieving."

He waited for her to step away, for her face to harden in disapproval, but her expression softened. Now she held both sides of his face. "So brutal. So unnecessary."

"No one came to my defense. No one spoke up for me. They marked me for a thief, and from then on everyone who saw the mark would suspect it was the lash of justice I deserved."

"So that's why you didn't like my brogue?" Her fingers walked their way from his brow to his chin and met at his mouth.

"I don't mind it so much anymore."

"And when you see me, are you going to always think of my brother's cruelty?"

Her giant brown eyes, mostly unseeing, waited on his answer. O'Malley's friends had taken much without his consent, but would Clayton give away even more? How could he deny Grace this peace at their parting?

Or maybe this wouldn't be a parting. Did he dare hope?

"He's your brother, and after today I doubt I'll think of the incident much at all."

———◆—◆—◆———

Grace traced his lips. She wanted him to speak. Anything that would cause them to move against her fingertips again. "And you're sure you don't want me to marry Mr. Newman?"

She waited, expecting to feel a smile, but instead his throat worked as he tried to swallow.

"I want you to marry *me*," he whispered.

She felt the words leave his mouth. She heard them, too, and while her mind couldn't believe, her heart soared. His lips parted once again. His head lowered, and Grace barely had time to slide her hands around his neck before his mouth met hers.

Whether it was from their one rehearsal or because they were already so close, Clayton didn't go awry on this kiss.

He wasn't experimenting but declaring all he wanted and all he offered. A happy sob rose in her throat. His arms tightened around her.

"Marry me, Grace. There's nothing I want more."

"You'd stay here with me? You'd be content with this homestead?"

"I don't care about the homestead. You can come with me to Oklahoma Territory, if you'd like. It doesn't matter, as long as we're together."

Her fingers reached the wavy hair at his temples. "Marrying you would make this all worth it."

Now she felt a smile so strong his ears moved. "Even losing your sight?"

"If I could see, I would've never met you."

Before he could stop her, Grace stretched on her tiptoes and kissed his cheek. He halted, stood stock-still as she followed his scar, covering it in gentle kisses all the way up to his brow. She pressed her cheek to his and held him until his breathing had evened.

"I'm glad your brother found you." Clayton burrowed his face into her unbound hair. "It's not often we see the demons of our past defeated, but sometimes God lets us see them redeemed, and that's even better."

"You can forgive him?"

His chest rose and fell in a giant sigh. "I already have."

◆━━━◆━━━◆

The sun pushed above the canyon, spilling its warm light over the backs of the two men riding toward the homestead. Clayton drove the ax blade deep into the stump and called Grace. At the doorway she untied her flower-printed apron and lifted it over her head before joining him. Her smile provoked his, even if she couldn't see it. He positioned her to face the horses and wrapped his arm around her waist as they waited for them to reach the house.

"There are two horses." She wrung her hands.

"You can see them?"

"No. I'm getting better at listening."

Grace's brother reined in before the banker's son, Marcus Whitfield, reached them. One look at Clayton's protective stance at Grace's side, and Brian's eyebrow rose.

"Looks like you and I be needing a serious talk."

"Yes, sir." Clayton said. "But first, it's only fair to tell Mr. Whitfield that his inspection is unnecessary. Miss O'Malley and I are getting married, and it wouldn't be right to take money for fixing up my own place."

Grace leaned into him, her shoulder digging warmly into his ribs.

O'Malley tilted forward over the horn of his saddle. "Does he speak the truth, Grace?"

She beamed. "Yes, he does. While I'd like to stay with your family, my future is with Clayton. From here, I'm his responsibility."

The face Clayton had detested eased into an amicable expression. "If it means anything, you have me blessing. And you'll need a horse. I'll see that you get one. It'll be a wedding present to you, Grace. A gift to start afresh on, although I do wish me kids had a chance to meet their Auntie Grace."

How could Clayton deny anyone happiness when he'd been given so much? "I'll bring Grace to visit. I promise."

The man ducked to hide the tears welling in his eyes. "You

are compassionate, sir. A good man, and I'll be honored to call you me brother."

"And about your payment," Marcus Whitfield said, beaming, "this new development may affect your claim on the funds, but I assume you can still collect. I imagine the trustees will be very pleased with the outcome."

"The trustees?" Grace's head lifted. "I've been wondering who set up that account. Did they place the advertisement, too?"

But it was Mr. Whitfield's turn to look puzzled. "I don't know what advertisement you're talking about."

As usual, Grace had her face lifted to the sun, but she turned to smile at Clayton, her happiness brimming over. "The advertisement that brought me a troublesome hired hand"—she nestled under his arm—"and a man I'm proud to marry."

Her arm slid behind Clayton and rubbed generous circles on his back. Clayton didn't have words to express his thanks—not to the woman he loved, not to the man he'd hated, or to the God who'd mended the scar in his soul and made something beautiful from it.

No Match
for Love

Carol Cox

✳ Chapter 1 ✳

Lucy Benson cleared her throat. "Walter proposed to me this morning."

Not one of the members of the Dry Gulch Ladies' Sewing and Prayer Circle gathered in Prudence Whitfield's parlor missed a stitch.

One corner of Dottie Jackson's lips quirked up. "Again?"

Lucy jabbed her needle into the dresser scarf she was embroidering. "Again. And to tell you the truth, it scared me a little."

Emilie's good-natured laugh echoed throughout the room. "This makes the sixth time Walter has asked for your hand. Or is it the seventh? I've lost track by now. It's about as surprising as the sun coming up every morning. Predictable, but hardly frightening."

"It wasn't the proposal that scared me," Lucy shot back. "It was the fact that I was tempted to say yes."

Dottie and Emilie gasped.

Mrs. Whitfield's finely arched eyebrows soared toward the white hair coiled atop her head.

Hannah Taylor, who had stopped by for a moment just to say hello, plopped into a chair and stared.

Dottie found her voice first. "You can't be serious! Marry *Walter*? How could you even consider such a thing?"

Lucy pressed her lips together. "It isn't like I have much choice, Dottie. It was wonderful of your family to take me in and give me a home after Papa died and left me penniless. But your wedding is only a month away. Once you're married, I can hardly expect your parents to let me continue staying with them."

"That's where you're wrong. You're my oldest and dearest friend, and Mother and Father love you like a daughter. I know they would be happy to have you stay on. It would keep the house from seeming empty after I'm gone."

Lucy knew from long experience there was no point crossing Dottie once she'd made up her mind—even when she was wrong. She forced a smile to her lips and tried to lighten the mood. "You'll be in charge of your own household soon. Maybe you should consider taking me on as your maid once you're Mrs. Richard Brighton."

A ripple of laughter ran around the room, and Lucy flinched. She hadn't intended her remark to be quite so humorous.

Gertie Claasen laid her needlework down and wiped tears of mirth from her eyes. "What an idea! I can just see you trying to iron linens or clean a floor. Face it, Lucy, apart from embroidery, you're utterly unsuited for doing anything along domestic lines."

Lucy ducked her head and focused on the dresser scarf,

hoping her irritation didn't show. Still, she had to admit the truth of Mrs. Claasen's statement. "You're right. I have no domestic skills . . . or any other prospects. Which is why I may have to take Walter up on his offer."

"Oh, my dear." Mrs. Whitfield laid her knitting on her lap and reached over to press her hand on Lucy's arm. "It takes more than money and land to give you happiness and a true home."

"I know, and believe me, that isn't my first choice." *Or my second. Or my tenth.* Walter Harris's tightly controlled approach to life meant everything had to be done the right way—*his* way. If she gave in to his demands and agreed to marry him, her every action would have to fit that narrow mold, as well. Just the thought made her feel as though her chest were being squeezed in a vise.

"But I don't have any other place to turn. I simply can't impose on Dottie's family indefinitely. I've prayed about this ever since I learned about the bad investments Papa made, but God hasn't opened up any other doors." Lucy drew a deep breath. "Maybe marrying Walter is His will for me."

Dottie clicked her tongue. "Pastor Eldridge keeps reminding us that God is a loving Father. I can't imagine marrying Walter Harris being His will for anybody."

Hannah leaned forward, concern shimmering in her light blue eyes. "You truly have no other prospects?"

Lucy shook her head. Hearing her predicament put into words made the situation seem even more disheartening. "I'm afraid not."

Mrs. Whitfield drew herself up and folded her hands. "Ladies, we need to take Lucy's problem to the Lord."

After a round of heartfelt prayers, Hannah excused herself

to go tend to her three little brothers, and the rest resumed their needlework.

While the group chattered about a new shipment of fabric that had just arrived at the general store run by Mrs. Claasen and her husband, Lucy's attention remained focused on her dilemma. And on trying to choke back the lump in her throat.

It wasn't her fault she'd never learned to be useful about the house. Being raised by a doting father who catered to her every need, she never had to acquire such knowledge. It wasn't that she was unwilling to work hard. She just didn't know how to run a home. But surely she could learn, if only someone would give her the chance.

Dottie's wedding was only a few short weeks away. The Jacksons could hardly be expected to extend their hospitality after their only daughter left the nest. Which meant Lucy needed to find another place to stay . . . and soon.

She wrapped the navy embroidery floss around the tip of her needle to form another French knot. Was marriage to Walter the answer God had for her? A vision of her insistent suitor swam into her mind. Walter, with his watery blue eyes and the jutting Adam's apple that made him look like a tom turkey. Walter, with the controlling nature that made her feel unable to breathe freely in his presence. True, his family had plenty of money. He could offer her a fine home and servants, every comfort her heart desired.

But would that be enough?

◆———◆

Over the next week, it seemed as if Lucy stumbled across Walter every time she turned around.

Carol Cox

On Sunday, he sat across the aisle from her at church and sent meaningful glances her way during the sermon.

On Monday, she spotted him coming out of Claasen's General Store just in time for her to beat a hasty retreat down a nearby alleyway.

On Tuesday, she spied him loitering across the street when she and Dottie emerged from the dressmaker's shop.

Was God trying to tell her something?

When Dottie's mother tapped on Lucy's bedroom door on Wednesday afternoon and said she had a visitor, Lucy felt almost resigned to her fate. She checked her appearance in the oval mirror and descended the staircase, feeling a bit like a French aristocrat walking to the tumbrel.

To her surprise, Pastor Eldridge awaited her in the parlor.

"I'm here on a mission of mercy." He smiled. "Shall we sit down?"

Mystified by his cryptic statement, Lucy gestured to a wingback chair and settled herself on the settee opposite.

Pastor Eldridge folded his hands and peered at her over his pince-nez. "It has come to my attention that you are in a rather desperate situation. I want you to know you're in my prayers. . . . Although, I must say I'm a bit saddened that you didn't confide in me about your plight."

Lucy's eyes widened. Pastor Eldridge knew all about her dire financial straits. What else could he mean, unless . . .

"Walter came to see me yesterday and asked me to talk to you. He wanted me to help plead his case."

"He didn't!" Lucy gasped and half rose from the settee.

The pastor waved her back to her seat. "Don't worry. As your pastor—and friend—I don't believe it would be in your

211

best interests to be joined to Walter in matrimony. Unless, of course, that is where your inclination lies?"

"Heavens, no!" The words blurted from Lucy's lips before she could stop them, and she felt her face flame. "That is . . ."

Pastor Eldridge shook his head. "Say no more. I've known Walter since he was barely out of knee breeches. I understand your feelings completely."

"Oh." So maybe God wasn't trying to coerce her into an unwanted match?

"That being the case . . ." Pastor Eldridge reached into his coat pocket and drew out an envelope. "Walter wasn't my only visitor this week. I was asked to deliver this to you." He tapped the envelope on his knee, then handed it to Lucy. "This just might be the answer to your prayers."

Thoroughly baffled, she took the sealed envelope. Without pausing to find a letter opener, she wedged her finger under the flap and tore it open. A single sheet of paper lay inside. When she drew it out and unfolded it, a slip of cardboard fluttered into her lap. Lucy picked up the small rectangle and gave it a quick glance. "A train ticket?"

Her pastor nodded. "Read the note."

Lucy smoothed the paper and began to read:

Andrew Simms of North Fork, Texas, is looking for a companion for his widowed aunt, Martha, whose dearest wish is to remain on the ranch she owned with her late husband. Andrew is concerned for her welfare, but he can't be at the ranch all the time. Finding someone trustworthy to stay at the Diamond S with his aunt would relieve Mr. Simms's concerns for her welfare.

If you choose to accept this position, you would be helping not only yourself, but this dear saint who would love to finish out her years in the place that holds so many happy memories for her.

Lucy took her time folding the paper, pressing the creases into sharp lines while thoughts tumbled through her mind. She looked back at Pastor Eldridge. "Where did this come from?"

"I'm afraid I can't tell you." He answered Lucy's incredulous look with a rueful smile. "I realize that sounds odd. I do know where the note came from, but I promised not to reveal the identity of the person who wrote it."

Lucy pressed her hand to her throat and tried to slow her racing heart. A ticket. The promise of a job—one far away from Walter's unrelenting pursuit. "It sounds like an answer to prayer."

Then common sense asserted itself. "It also sounds too good to be true. How could I accept this offer without knowing anything about it? It would be like buying a pig in a poke."

Pastor Eldridge tented his fingers. "I understand this puts you in an unusual position. While I'm bound to keep the writer's name a secret, I *can* tell you I have the utmost confidence in this person's integrity. In addition, I made inquiries of my own, and I can assure you that Andrew Simms is a respected member of his community, and his need for a companion for his aunt is genuine."

He leaned forward. "You've been a member of my flock since you were a little girl, and I've watched you grow into a young woman any parent would be proud of. I would never advise you to do anything I thought might endanger you. I can't say this will solve all your problems, but I think it may be a wise course of action—for the time being, at least."

Lucy studied him gravely. Could it be? Was it possible to receive an answer to prayer right out of the blue? Skepticism colored her voice when she spoke. "Why did you bring this offer to me? You mentioned a 'mission of mercy.' Do people see me as some sort of charity case?"

The pastor settled back in the chair and shook his head. "I don't believe it stems from pity. Think of it as a means of gaining time to find out what God really does have in mind for you."

She picked up the ticket again. "North Fork," she whispered, then felt a flutter of panic. "I don't even know where that is! And what does Mr. Simms think of this arrangement? He doesn't know a thing about me."

Pastor Eldridge sat forward again. "North Fork is east of Amarillo, only a couple hours from there by train. According to the writer of this note, Mr. Simms has already heard about you and agreed to take you on. Once you agree to accept the job, he will be alerted to meet you upon your arrival." His eyes glinted behind his spectacles. "Does this mean you'll do it?"

Lucy looked back at the ticket and traced the lettering with her fingertip. "I've been asking God to show me what to do, but I never expected anything like this."

"You mean having your prayers answered in an unexpected way?" Pastor Eldridge chuckled. "God is in the business of taking care of His own, you know. And think of it this way—you'll have an opportunity to be the answer to someone else's prayer, as well."

Lucy caught her breath and let it out on a soft sigh as a long-forgotten peace settled over her. God still cared, was still watching over her. Not only that, but she could be a blessing to somebody else. Joy bubbled up inside her while she calculated how long it would take to pack her trunk and say good-bye to Dottie and the ladies of the sewing circle.

Lifting her head, she returned Pastor Eldridge's smile. "Please give the author of this note my deepest thanks and let Mr. Simms know to expect me on Friday."

* * *

"I can't tell you how much I appreciate you bringing me all the way to Amarillo." Lucy smiled at Pastor Eldridge and his wife as the three of them alighted from the Eldridges' buckboard in front of the Amarillo train depot. She glanced off to the southwest, where a haze of rain laced the sky in the direction of Dry Gulch. "I hope that storm moves past quickly so you don't get soaked on your way back home."

The pastor's wife clasped Lucy's hands. "Don't you worry about that, dear. It was our pleasure to bring you, and it's a blessing to know you have a chance for a new start in life."

Lucy smiled and nodded, wondering for the hundredth time about her anonymous benefactor. Try as she might, she couldn't think of anyone who could have set all this in motion. Pastor Eldridge remained true to his word about keeping the note writer's identity a secret. She might never know who orchestrated the events that led to her leaving Dry Gulch, but she did know that God was in control. Perhaps she would simply have to thank Him for His provision.

Her one regret would be missing Dottie's wedding, but her friend had taken Lucy's sudden change in plans with grace . . . and a show of excitement. "What an adventure!" she exclaimed when Lucy outlined the opportunity Pastor Eldridge presented. "Maybe you'll meet some handsome rancher and fall in love yourself. And if not, at least you'll be away from Walter."

Pastor Eldridge lifted Lucy's carpetbag from the rear of the wagon and motioned to a porter to see to her trunk. "Now all that's left is to get you settled on—" He broke off, staring at a point over Lucy's right shoulder. "Oh no."

Lucy whirled around to see a gangly figure loping along the platform. Her mouth dropped open. "Walter? You followed me all the way to Amarillo?"

Her would-be suitor raced up to them, his skinny chest heaving. "I couldn't believe it when my father told me he saw you leaving town with your bags packed. What do you think you're doing?"

Mrs. Eldridge moved closer to Lucy. Her husband stepped forward, putting himself in Walter's path. "Calm down, son."

Walter evaded the pastor with a neat sidestep. His face took on a stony hardness. "How can you think of leaving Dry Gulch . . . leaving *me*? We are meant to be together."

A cry of "All aboard!" cut through the end of his plea.

Pastor Eldridge gripped Walter by the shoulder in a fatherly manner and turned him in the opposite direction. "Why don't we step over here and talk for a moment. It seems God may be leading Lucy in a different direction than the one you have in mind." He glanced at the two women and jerked his head toward the waiting train.

Mrs. Eldridge tugged on Lucy's arm and led her to the passenger car.

Lucy felt a flutter of panic. "What if he follows me again?"

"Don't worry about that. This train goes all the way to Fort Worth. He'll have no way of knowing where you get off." The pastor's wife gave Lucy a quick hug and a peck on the cheek. "Let my husband deal with Walter. All you need to do is get on board."

She nudged Lucy toward the step. "Remember what Paul said in his letter to the Philippians: 'Forgetting those things which are behind, and reaching forth unto those things which are before.' Let that be your watchword as you begin your grand adventure."

Lucy said good-bye through a mist of tears and found her way to a seat. She had barely settled herself before the train jerked and started to move. She watched the door of the car until the depot was out of sight, half expecting Walter to leap inside at the last possible moment, but Pastor Eldridge apparently had taken control of the situation.

She leaned back against the seat and breathed a quick prayer of thanks. Her journey—her grand adventure, as Mrs. Eldridge put it—had begun.

"Forgetting those things which are behind . . ." Mrs. Eldridge's parting words echoed in her mind. That would include not only her narrow escape from Walter, but her entire life up to this point.

And what was it that lay ahead? A new life as companion to a lonely widow. Lucy envisioned the two of them chatting about patterns and needlework as they sipped tea together, or holding a skein of yarn while the dear woman rolled it into a ball before beginning her next knitting project.

She swallowed hard. Tea and needlework were well and good, but what else would there be to occupy her time in an isolated ranch house with no near neighbors? Looking back through the window, she watched Amarillo fade into the distance and felt a pang of apprehension. Had she just made the mistake of a lifetime?

The image of Walter's angry face sprang into her mind, and she pushed her fears away. Even if the days ahead bordered on mind-numbing tedium, that would still be better than a life as Walter Harris's wife.

* Chapter 2 *

Andrew Simms scanned the horizon as he paced the board-walk in front of the North Fork depot. The sight of trailing smoke as the train came up out of the Red River Valley brought him to an abrupt stop.

What had he been thinking? When he'd written to an old friend in Dry Gulch asking for prayer about Aunt Martha's situation, he'd never expected an immediate response suggesting Miss Lucy Benson as the perfect solution. Had he been out of his mind, agreeing to have a stranger take up residence on the ranch?

The train rumbled into the station, and Andrew stepped back to avoid the plume of steam that hissed from beneath the wheels.

What kind of person would volunteer to take on the task of watching over his unpredictable aunt, sight unseen? He hoped she would be intelligent and congenial. It had been hard enough to sell Aunt Martha on the idea of having a companion foisted upon her. Showing up at her door with someone she found unacceptable would only make matters worse.

The conductor leaped from the car to the platform and set a small wooden box at the bottom of the steps. Andrew's stomach knotted, and he ran his finger around his collar as if the action would help him breathe easier. It didn't.

The first passenger to alight was a young woman Andrew guessed to be a few years his junior. She smiled her thanks as she took hold of the conductor's proffered hand and stepped down to the platform, where she smoothed the skirt of her blue dress and adjusted her flowered hat. She looked around, as if she expected someone to be waiting for her.

Andrew glanced behind him and frowned when he saw he was alone. The new arrival wasn't anyone he recognized from the North Fork area. Why hadn't someone come to welcome her?

She looked his way with a questioning expression. Embarrassed at being caught staring, Andrew shifted his gaze back to the passenger car, waiting for Lucy Benson to alight. To his surprise, the conductor picked up the wooden box and jumped back on board. A moment later the train gave a lurch and chugged away.

"Wait!" Andrew stepped forward with one hand raised and realized the newly arrived young lady was standing at his elbow.

"Mr. Simms?"

"What?" Andrew stared into her wide blue eyes, an impossible idea forming in his mind. No, it couldn't be. In his wildest imaginings, he couldn't picture this refined creature in a setting like the Diamond S.

"Miss Benson?" His voice came out in a dry croak.

A smile wreathed her delicate face, and she extended her right hand. "That's right. I can't tell you what a godsend this opportunity is."

Andrew shook the hand she offered, and continued to stare. So this was Lucy Benson, the woman who was going to ride herd on his cantankerous aunt. *Dear heaven.*

❖

Lucy gripped the seat of the buckboard as it jounced along the dusty road—up one gentle swell of land and down another. A weary sigh escaped her lips despite her best efforts to hold it in. First the train ride from Amarillo, now this jarring trail, barely more than a track through the sagebrush. She felt more than ready for her interminable journey to end.

She cast a sideways glance at Andrew Simms. His dumbfounded expression when she introduced herself announced more clearly than words that she wasn't what he'd been expecting. But how could that be, given that he'd agreed to the arrangement orchestrated by the anonymous letter writer?

She glanced down at her gloved hands, clasped on the skirt of her royal blue traveling dress, and wondered what he'd expected. A sturdy farm girl, perhaps? One who could rope and brand cattle or cook for a crew during roundup? Surely not. The job offering hadn't mentioned anything of the kind, only serving as a companion to his much-loved aunt.

Looking up again, she saw that his attention seemed focused on guiding the horses and took the opportunity to examine him more thoroughly. His appearance was pleasing enough, but outward features didn't always give a clue to the character that lay within. What kind of man would her new employer turn out to be? Lucy shifted on the seat, uncomfortably aware that they were miles from the nearest town or dwelling. Right now, Andrew Simms was the only person on earth who knew where she was. The thought left her feeling vulnerable, and a bit nervous.

The moment she read the letter describing her new position, a mental image of Martha Simms had formed in Lucy's mind—a gentle white-haired soul who passed her days in a rocking chair, lost in happy memories of the past. A picture of her nephew had come less readily. His concern for his aunt's welfare put him in a positive light. Underneath his taciturn exterior, he must have a good heart, though his gruff manner upon their meeting hid it well. He'd barely said a word since asking if she wanted to stop for lunch in town. At that point, her taut nerves had driven thoughts of hunger from her mind, but now she felt her stomach rumble.

"How much farther is it to the ranch?"

Andrew started as though he'd forgotten her presence. "Another thirty minutes or so." He shook the reins, urging the horses to pick up their pace as though he felt every bit as eager as she to see this uncomfortable ride come to an end.

Thirty minutes. Lucy sighed and dug in her carpetbag. Rummaging through its contents, she pulled out two apples and held them up. "Would you like one?"

Andrew glanced at the fruit in her hand, and the lines in his forehead deepened. "Thank you. I should have insisted on getting you a meal in town before we started. You had no way of knowing how long the drive would be." He accepted one of the apples and took a bite.

"I'm not famished. I just thought it would be nice to have a little snack." Lucy bit into the crisp apple and savored the juicy tartness. With the ice thus broken, she plunged ahead. "Tell me about your aunt. I'd like to know more about what's expected of me."

Andrew chewed thoughtfully for a moment, then turned to look at her full on for the first time since helping her into his buckboard. She felt a flush rise up her neck under the impact of his gaze, and she studied his face more closely. When he wasn't gaping like a poleaxed steer or driving along in moody silence, he was rather nice looking. With wavy chestnut hair framing chiseled features and a tanned complexion that spoke of long days spent outdoors, he could easily fit the role of the handsome rancher Dottie had teased her about. His lips were firm, but not clamped tight like Walter's when he was displeased with her. A crease marked his cheek just beyond the right corner of his mouth. Lucy wondered if it deepened into a dimple when he smiled. Her eyes moved a few inches lower and focused on the cleft in his chin. The indentation would just fit the tip of her finger, if she pressed it there.

"My aunt is a wonderful woman." Andrew's voice jolted her back to the moment. He seemed to choose his words with care. "She and Uncle Ebenezer pretty much raised me. Since he passed away three years ago, she and I are the only near family either one of us has left."

Lucy's breath caught in her throat, and she knotted her hands in her lap.

"Are you all right?"

Lucy bobbed her head in a brief nod. "It's just that I know how that feels—being alone in the world, I mean. My mother died when I was young, and I lost my father just a few months ago."

She took a deep breath and tried to steady her voice.

"Shortly after the funeral, I learned he made some bad investments and lost everything. Not only was my father gone, but the house and all our possessions, as well. I don't have a penny to my name." The confession brought a bitter taste to her mouth.

Andrew remained silent a moment. "That's why you spoke of this job as being a godsend?"

Lucy looked away and sighed. "I was living on the charity of a friend's parents. I had to find some way to get out of there and make my own way." Pulling herself together, she squared her shoulders and faced him again. "Enough about me. You were talking about your relationship with your aunt."

Andrew studied her before he continued. "We've always been close. Aunt Martha has been good to me, and I want to make her remaining years as happy as possible. I've offered to buy a small house for her in North Fork, but she's stubbornly independent. She absolutely refuses to leave the ranch."

Lucy looked out over the gently rolling landscape. "I can understand not wanting to leave the place where she's lived for so many years." She felt a pang at the memory of her childhood home, now in someone else's hands.

"So can I. The Diamond S has been her home since she and my uncle built it up nearly twenty years ago."

Lucy polished off another bite of her apple. "I'm sure she treasures your visits. Are you able to see her often?"

"Not as often as either of us would like. Especially not since I started a business in North Fork a year ago. I sell and install windmills to ranchers and farmers all over this part of the state." His face took on a glow, and he seemed to grow taller on the buckboard seat. "There's something about the look on a rancher's face when the wind turns the vanes and the pump jack starts sucking up water and pumping it into the tank for the first time."

Lucy's lips parted. "Streams in the desert. That must seem almost like a miracle."

A smile lit Andrew's face. "That's it exactly. This is a wonderful land, filled with promise. All it needs to be a paradise is water—and I can help supply that. It means a fair amount of traveling, though. I like to direct things myself when a windmill is being installed. I can leave the business in the care of my foreman while I'm gone on those trips, but I still have to stay on top of day-to-day operations."

He finished his apple and tossed the core to the side with an easy overhand motion. "That's why I'm hoping this works out for Aunt Martha. I would hate to force her to leave the ranch, but it's gotten to the point where I can't leave her out there on her own much longer."

Lucy nodded, making mental notes. Martha Simms might be a frail, gray-haired widow, but she sounded spirited enough to dig in her heels and take a stand when she needed to. And that was a good thing. Lucy didn't relish the thought of spending her days with a meek shell of a woman.

"Is your aunt's health sound?"

Andrew let out a sharp bark of laughter. "Oh yes. She's healthy enough. You won't be dealing with an invalid, if that's what you're asking."

Lucy furrowed her brow. "I don't understand. If she's in good health and doesn't mind being on her own, why does she need someone to stay with her?"

Andrew's smile faded, and he shifted on the seat. "It

isn't her physical condition I'm worried about. It's more . . . mental."

Lucy sat bolt upright. "You mean she's unbalanced?"

"No, nothing like that." Andrew patted the air as if warding the thought away. "She isn't deranged—exactly. It's just that she's been . . . imagining things."

Lucy eyed him narrowly. "What sort of things?"

Andrew cleared his throat and fixed his eyes on the road ahead. "Over the past couple of months, she's claimed to see some pretty peculiar things going on around the ranch house. She says . . ." His voice trailed off, and Lucy almost missed the next words.

"Excuse me? Did you say something about a cow jumping over the moon?"

Andrew paused a moment, then went on as if he hadn't heard. "There's nothing to it, of course, but I can't persuade her it's all in her head. As much as this has been preying on her mind, I'm concerned she might get herself in a situation where she could get hurt. That's why I thought it would be a good idea to have someone around to keep an eye on her."

A heavy weight settled in Lucy's stomach. "So my staying with her is all your idea? How does she feel about it?"

"She seemed fine when we discussed it." Andrew jiggled the reins and clucked at the horses again.

Lucy waited for him to elaborate, but that seemed to be the extent of his conversation for the moment.

✶ Chapter 3 ✶

"We're almost there." Andrew pulled the buckboard to a stop at the top of a low rise. "That's the Diamond S." He swept his arm in a broad arc, indicating the panorama below them, a broad valley ringed by cedar-studded hills. In the center of the valley, Lucy could see a cluster of buildings.

Andrew clicked his tongue, setting the horses in motion again. Lucy leaned forward on her seat and scrutinized the buildings, trying to take in every detail.

As they drew nearer, she focused her attention on the ranch house, a white two-story structure with shiplap siding surrounded on three sides by a wraparound porch. A brass weather vane glinted from the rooftop, and a windmill turned gently in the breeze. A flock of chickens scratched the ground near what Lucy assumed was the hen house, and a horse in the corral nickered when they drove up into the ranch yard.

Beyond the buildings, scattered groups of cattle grazed the hillsides. All in all, a peaceful, charming scene. She could understand Martha's reluctance to exchange this tranquility for the bustle of town life.

Lucy eyed the livestock. "How does your aunt manage to run the ranch on her own?"

Andrew tightened his lips, and the crease in his cheek stood out in sharp relief. "The ranch is still in operation, but Aunt Martha isn't running it anymore. It became too much for her to handle after Uncle Ebenezer died, so she sold the stock off to Carson Murphy, whose ranch adjoins the Diamond S. Their agreement lets him run his cattle on her property. I think it gives her a sense of comfort to be able to look out across the hills and still see them out there. It's almost like nothing has changed."

Lucy nodded. That would also explain why Andrew felt the need to have someone else stay out here. With no workers living on the place, it left his elderly aunt alone—isolated and vulnerable.

Andrew stopped the horses near the broad front porch. He sprang to the ground with a lithe movement and circled the buckboard to help Lucy alight. Once she was standing on the ground, he stepped back, allowing her a moment to collect herself.

Lucy did her best to brush the wrinkles from her skirt, then she ran her fingers through her hair, trying to push the windblown curls back into place.

"Ready?" Andrew asked.

She settled her hat in place and nodded. Her breath came more quickly as Andrew stepped up to the front door. A new chapter of her life was about to begin. Up to now, her thoughts had been focused on getting away from Dry Gulch and Walter's unwanted attentions, and she hadn't given too much thought to her first meeting with Martha Simms. Now that the moment had arrived, her nerves felt as if they were stretched as tightly as piano wire. She clasped her hands in front of her waist to keep her fingers from trembling and wondered what kind of greeting she should offer.

Martha wasn't just a lonely old woman who was hungry for company, as she'd assumed at first. From what Andrew said, it sounded as though she suffered from some sort of delusions. Lucy felt a pang of sympathy. She could only imagine how upsetting that must be . . . for both Martha and Andrew.

Another thought struck her. With these unsettling events going on—however imaginary they might be—how would Martha feel about taking a complete stranger into her home?

She would probably be nervous, even a bit fearful. That meant Lucy would need to present herself as someone to be trusted so Mrs. Simms could understand right from the start that she was there to help. To that end, she must appear to be calm and gentle, yet in control.

Turning to the door, Andrew raised his hand and gave it a loud knock. "Aunt Martha, we're here!"

Lucy squared her shoulders and curved her lips into a bright smile. Perhaps a reassuring hug would be a good way to establish herself as a comforting presence.

The doorknob rattled and Lucy stepped forward, ready to spread her arms wide. The next moment, the door flew open and a tall, rawboned woman dressed in faded calico strode onto the porch.

"What brings you out here?" she said in a raspy voice. "I didn't expect to see you again so soon." Her gaze flitted from Andrew to the buckboard. Her eyes narrowed down to slits when they lit on the trunk in the wagon bed. She glanced back toward him and seemed to notice Lucy for the first time.

"What in thunder is all this?"

Andrew stepped forward and laid his hand on her shoulder. "Aunt Martha, allow me to introduce Lucy Benson. She's traveled here from Dry Gulch, and I brought her straight from the station."

The woman turned the full force of her glare on Lucy, who felt as though she had just been blasted by an icy blue norther. *This is Andrew's aunt?* The picture Lucy had built up of a fragile, bewildered old dear shredded into a thousand pieces. She could envision the fragments of her mental image blowing across the wide Texas plains like miniature tumbleweeds.

Martha Simms snorted. "All right, that tells me who she is and where she came from. It doesn't tell me what she's doing here."

Andrew cleared his throat and fingered the cleft in his chin. "Now, Aunt Martha, you know we talked about having someone come out to stay with you."

"*You* talked about it, you mean. I never agreed to anything. I thought it was a lot of nonsense at the time, and I haven't changed my mind."

Lucy sucked in her breath and stared at the stony-faced woman before her, taking note of the jutting chin and the lips set in an uncompromising line. *What's happening here?* Andrew's aunt was the one who was supposed to be confused and fearful, but Lucy felt utterly at sea.

Wasn't her coming to the Diamond S supposed to be the answer to two prayers? But it was all too apparent that Martha Simms didn't want her there. What would happen next? Was she going to be loaded onto the next train bound for Amarillo and sent packing?

Andrew shot a sidelong glance at Lucy, then leaned toward his aunt and lowered his voice. "You know how worried I've been about you being out here all alone . . . especially with what's happened lately."

The glare faded and an indulgent smile creased Martha's weathered cheeks. "Boy, in the years I've lived out here, I've faced up to rustlers, bandits, and Comanches. I know you care about me, and don't think for a moment I don't appreciate that. But I don't need anybody to nursemaid me."

Lucy's thoughts whirled. She didn't have a nickel to her name to pay for food or lodging. And her mysterious benefactor had provided only a one-way ticket. Even if Martha Simms ordered her back to Dry Gulch, she had no way of getting there.

She turned to Andrew and tried to keep her chin from quivering. "Mr. Simms, I was given to understand we had an agreement, but it's obvious your aunt had no idea I was coming. It seems I've been brought out here under false pretenses."

Andrew's face paled beneath his tan. "No, no. It'll be fine, really. Just give me a minute."

He turned to his aunt. "Could I speak to you in private?"

The two of them walked to the far end of the porch, leaving Lucy standing alone. When they stopped, Mrs. Simms glanced back over her shoulder. Seeing Lucy's attention fastened upon them, the woman nudged Andrew around the corner of the house.

Lucy's anxiety overcame her sense of propriety. Treading softly, she edged along the front of the house in silent pursuit. Eavesdropping might be frowned on in polite circles, but she simply had to know what Andrew and his aunt were saying. Her future depended on it! She reached the corner of the house and pressed herself against the wall, straining to hear.

Even though Martha spoke in hushed tones, her rasping whisper carried to Lucy's new position. "What were you thinking of, bringin' that prissy little gal all the way out here? I know you're a grown man, but I have a good mind to cut myself a switch off the big cottonwood and march you out to the woodshed."

Despite her concern, Lucy had to suppress a smile at the thought of muscular Andrew Simms being disciplined like a six-year-old.

"I know you're upset," Andrew said, "but please hear me out. My business is growing, but I can't concentrate on keeping up with it when I'm worried about you. It would help put my mind at ease if you had someone else out here."

"And I already told you there's no need for you to fret."

"When we talked, I knew you weren't happy about the idea, but I thought you'd be willing to give it a try."

"Well, I'm not." Martha's tone held a note of finality. "Last I heard, the train runs in both directions. You can ship her right back home again."

"That's the problem. I can't."

"And why not?" Martha demanded.

"She has nothing to go back to. She explained it to me on the drive out here. Her parents are dead, and her father lost everything in a bad investment. She has no home, no money, no family. She's completely on her own with no one to turn to."

Lucy felt her face flame at hearing her predicament laid out in such blunt terms. Had it sounded so pathetic when she told her story to Andrew? She'd only meant to give him the facts, not make a bid for his sympathy.

A long pause followed, during which she wished the ground would open and swallow her up. Finally Martha spoke.

"Seems like I don't have any choice. The only Christian thing to do is let her stay—at least until we can figure something out."

"That's wonderful." Relief was evident in Andrew's voice. "Just give this a chance. That's all I ask."

Lucy scurried back to her original position before Andrew and his aunt appeared and tried to look at though she hadn't heard every word they'd said.

"It's all settled." A smile wreathed Andrew's face, and the crease in his cheek folded into a dimple—just the way she'd thought it would. "You're going to stay."

Lucy put a hand on the porch rail to steady herself as a wave of relief swept over her. Then she caught sight of Martha Simms's grim expression and reminded herself the respite was only a temporary one.

———◆———◆———◆———

Andrew stepped over to the buckboard and hefted her trunk. "I'll carry this inside. I need to head back to town before it gets too late."

Panic clutched at Lucy's throat. He was leaving already?

"Guess I'll need to find a place for you to stay," Martha grumbled. "I wasn't expecting company."

Andrew grinned as he maneuvered the trunk through the

front door. "Come on, Aunt Martha. You know you always keep a guest room ready."

A flicker of amusement crossed Martha's lined face. "Take her on up to it, then. You know the way."

Lucy followed Andrew upstairs, where a turn to the left put them at the doorway to a cozy bedroom. She took in the colorful Irish Chain quilt on the bright brass bedstead, the braided rag rug, and the comfortable-looking armchair. The room exuded warmth and welcome—totally at odds with the frosty reception she had received from Martha.

Andrew set the trunk down beside the bed and dusted his hands. "I'll be on my way now. I hope you'll be comfortable here."

He made his way downstairs with an easy stride, and Lucy clattered along in his wake, feeling unexpectedly bereaved. Though they had met only a couple hours before, the thought of him leaving her alone with crotchety Martha Simms made her feel as though she were losing her best friend.

"When will you be coming back?"

Andrew didn't seem to notice her distress. "I try to make it out here several times a week." He paused with his hand on the knob of the front door. "Why? Do you want something from town?"

What she wanted was for him to stay until she felt comfortable in Martha's company . . . but that might never happen. She folded her arms across her waist and tried to look more confident than she felt. "No, thank you. I have everything I need."

They stepped out onto the porch, where Martha leaned

against the railing. Andrew bent to kiss his aunt's cheek, then climbed aboard the buckboard and set the horses on their way. As she waved good-bye, Lucy couldn't help but notice that Martha didn't seem one bit happier than she was to see him leave.

✳ Chapter 4 ✳

Martha planted her hands on her hips and eyed Lucy as though she'd found a weevil in her flour bin. "Appears you're going to be here for a while. I still can't see why Andrew came up with this harebrained scheme. I don't need anybody nursemaiding me, but as long as you're here, you might as well make yourself useful."

Lucy nodded eagerly, ready to do anything that might soften that gimlet-eyed gaze.

Martha pursed her lips. "I like to sit out here on the porch of an evening and enjoy a cup of tea. Why don't you brew up a pot and we can visit a bit. Might as well get to know each other if we're going to be spending time together. I'll show you to the kitchen . . ." She lifted one eyebrow. "Unless you'd rather change out of your traveling clothes first?"

Lucy looked down at her dress. "Is there something wrong with what I have on?"

Martha shrugged. "I just thought if you're going to be working in the kitchen, you might want to hang up your fancy clothes and put on one of your plain dresses."

Lucy pressed her hand against her stomach to quell the

sinking sensation in her midsection. "Actually, this is one of the sturdiest dresses I have."

Martha's *harrumph* left no doubt of her opinion as to the suitability of Lucy's attire. Leading the way to the kitchen at the north end of the house, she pointed out the pump and the kettle waiting on the stove, then reached up into a cupboard and pulled down several tins. "What kind of tea do you like?"

Lucy brightened. "Do you have any Darjeeling?"

Martha grimaced. "I don't have any of that fancy stuff, just what I gather from what grows around here and whatever the mercantile has in stock when I make a trip into town." She plunked the tins down on a square wooden table. "There's dandelion, sassafras, rose hip, chamomile, and pennyroyal. Take your pick."

Lucy stared at the assortment.

Martha *harrumphed* again. "I'm partial to sassafras. Let's try that this evening." She strode over to the stove and held one hand above the surface. "Good, there's still some heat from when I was baking bread earlier." Reaching into a wooden box beside the stove, she pulled out a chunk of wood, then lifted the stove lid and tossed the firewood inside. "The best way to get to know a kitchen is to pitch right in and locate things yourself. You'll find cups and the sugar bowl in the cupboards. Spoons are in that drawer over there. The stove will be plenty hot for boiling water by the time you get the fixings ready."

With that, she turned on her heel and headed back toward the porch.

Left alone in the kitchen, Lucy stared around her, feeling as helpless as a newborn kitten. *Fix the tea.* It sounded so simple when one uttered the words, but how exactly did one *do* it? Gertie Claasen's teasing words about her lack of domestic ability came back to taunt her. Shaking off her dejection, she squared her shoulders and hiked up her chin. She'd drunk hundreds of cups of tea over the years, and she'd never heard anyone describe brewing it as a complex task. Surely she could figure it out.

After filling the kettle at the pump, she set it on the burner and held her hand above the stove's surface in imitation of Martha, wondering just how hot it had to be to boil water. While she waited, she picked up the tin of sassafras tea and pried off the lid. Inside the tin she saw what looked more like a heap of wood chips than anything resembling tea leaves.

She picked up a pinch and eyed the woody texture doubtfully. How much should she put in? The amount she held between her fingers didn't look like it would be enough to do more than add a tinge of color to the water, let alone create a bracing brew.

Lucy reached into the tin, scooped up a handful of sassafras, and dropped it into the kettle of water. Gauging from Martha's reaction to her arrival, both of them would need all the bracing they could get.

While the water heated, she rummaged through the cupboards until she located two teacups and matching saucers. Her throat tightened when she pulled them down and saw the Blue Willow pattern. She traced the blue-and-white design with the tip of her forefinger. Not quite the same as the Spode china she'd grown up with, but close enough to make her heart ache. Lucy blinked back the tears that sprang to her eyes and continued her preparations, opening and closing more cupboard doors until she located a tray and the sugar bowl, plus spoons and napkins.

She was in the middle of arranging the pieces on the tray when she heard a harsh sizzling behind her. Lucy whirled around to see water spurting out of the kettle onto the hot stove like a miniature geyser. She grabbed a dish towel she spotted lying on the counter, wrapped it around her hand, and snatched the kettle off the stove.

Steam rose up and tickled her nose when she poured the deep red liquid into the delicate cups. She set the cups and saucers on the tray and arranged the other items beside them.

Feeling a flush of pride at having already mastered one household task—*wouldn't Gertie be amazed!*—she picked up the tray and carried it out to the porch.

Martha had seated herself on one of the two rocking chairs. Lucy set the tray down on the small table between the chairs with a sense of accomplishment. Maybe serving as Martha Simms's companion was going to work out, after all. Despite what her unwilling hostess seemed to think, Lucy had no desire to be a useless ornament.

She spread one of the napkins over her lap while Martha reached for the cup nearest her and raised it to her lips. Lucy lifted the remaining cup and watched over the rim for Martha's reaction to her first culinary endeavor.

She didn't have to wait long. After the first sip, Martha's eyes widened, then she gulped hastily, as if she'd swallowed a bug. The corners of her mouth drew down, making her look more like she'd been sucking on a lemon than sipping her favorite tea.

Lucy lowered her teacup and stared. "Is anything wrong?"

Martha didn't answer. Without a word, she flicked the hand holding the cup to one side and sent a shower of tea spattering across the dust beyond the porch.

Baffled by the odd behavior, Lucy raised her own cup to her lips again and took a tentative sip. She felt her mouth twist into an expression that surely resembled the pucker on Martha's face.

Martha clinked her empty cup on the tray and held it out to Lucy, who added her own cup to it. Then Martha rose and carried the tea tray toward the front door, mumbling. As she nudged the door open and disappeared inside the house, Lucy caught the muttered words, "Land sakes. I never knew a body could burn tea."

What went wrong? Lucy had time to think back over each step in her tea-making process a dozen times before Martha returned bearing the tray, this time with a matching teapot sitting between two empty cups.

She plunked it down on the table. "Just so you know, the tea makings go in the teapot. About a teaspoon per cup. *Nothing* goes into the kettle but water." She drew her eyebrows together. "Understand?"

Lucy gulped and nodded.

Martha settled back into her rocking chair. "When the water in the kettle boils, you pour it over the leaves in the pot and give it a few minutes to steep." She lifted the teapot and poured a stream of pale yellow tea into each cup.

"The color is much lighter this time." Lucy sniffed the steaming brew. "It doesn't even smell the same."

"I wasn't in the mood for sassafras any longer. This here's chamomile. It's good for the nerves."

Lucy decided it was time to turn the conversation in a

new direction. Looking out across the hills, she said, "This is a beautiful setting. How long have you lived here?"

Martha took a long sip of tea, then let out a contented sigh and set her rocker into motion. "Ebenezer and I moved here in '76. He always wanted to try his hand at ranching, and he turned out to be right good at it."

A gentle smile lit her face, and she stared off into the distance. "When we first married, he had all sorts of grand plans—promised me he'd show me the world. After he saw how well the ranch did those first few years, he thought he'd be able to make good on his word. The way he figured it, we'd keep on saving up and eventually have enough to see the sights and travel in style. Bless his heart, he didn't count on the lean years, with rustlers, drought, and tick fever cuttin' into our profits."

Martha closed her eyes, and the creases in her forehead deepened. "A few years back, he upgraded our stock and thought we were getting back on track. He was all excited, told me to start thinking about the places I'd like to visit first. Then he up and died." She pressed her lips into a tight line.

The silence stretched out for several moments before Lucy spoke again. "Andrew said you aren't operating the ranch yourself anymore?"

Martha opened her eyes and folded her hands in her lap. "Carson Murphy—he owns the Two Bar M just north of here—and Ebenezer knew each other for years. Carson bought my cattle and brought in a bunch of new breeding stock, so he needed more graze land. He and I worked out an agreement where he runs his cattle on Diamond S land. The rent, along with his payment for my cattle, allows me to keep living on my own place, and I still get to look out and see cattle on the landscape. It's been a good arrangement for both of us."

She took a last sip of chamomile tea, then set her cup back on the tray and pushed herself up out of the rocking chair. "I don't usually eat much of an evening, but I can round up something for you, if you're hungry."

Lucy shook her head and got to her feet. "I don't want to be a bother. I still have a couple of sandwiches left in my carpetbag. I can eat them while I unpack."

Martha grunted. "Suit yourself. I'll bring some water up so you can wash off the trail dust."

Back inside, they separated in the parlor, with Lucy heading for the stairs and Martha turning toward the kitchen. A framed drawing near the stairs caught Lucy's attention, and she stopped for a closer look. "Is this a scene from Paris?"

Martha walked over to join her. The lines on her face softened when she gazed at the picture. "That's the Eiffel Tower. Ebenezer saw it in a magazine about that big fair they had in Paris in 1889. It's one of the places he planned to take me when we'd saved up enough. After he died, I put it in a frame and hung it there. It makes me feel like I still have a bit of Ebenezer with me every time I look at it."

Lucy's heart squeezed, feeling an unexpected kinship with Martha. "Something like that happened with my father. He and I talked about going to the World's Fair in Chicago this summer." Her eyes misted. "But then he died, and everything changed."

Martha nodded, and a tight smile stretched her lips. "Life is full of changes—that's for sure." She turned back toward the kitchen, and Lucy continued up the stairs to her room.

By the time Martha came up with a pitcher of steaming water, Lucy had unloaded all her dresses from the trunk and spread them across the bed. Martha set the pitcher on the dresser next to the basin and watched Lucy attempt to shake the wrinkles out of a blue paisley frock. Stepping over to the bed, she eyed the other dresses and gave a *tsk*.

"One thing for sure, these fine clothes were never meant for ranch life."

Lucy tilted her chin. "These are the only clothes I own, so they'll have to do. I'll make them work. You'll see."

Martha clicked her tongue again and started for the door. "I'll loan you one of my aprons. That'll help protect them. Even so, they'll never look the same again." She looked back over her shoulder as she left the room. "Better use that water before it gets cold. If you need anything else, I'll be up a while longer. It's a full moon tonight."

Lucy nibbled on her sandwiches while she hung her dresses in the wardrobe and stowed her other belongings in the dresser drawers. By the time she finished, the sky had darkened, but Lucy felt too keyed up after the day's events to think about sleep.

Taking off her traveling outfit, she washed up before slipping into her nightgown and brushing her hair. Then she walked over to the window, raised it a few inches to catch the evening breeze, and stared out across the moonlit landscape. *Such a peaceful, idyllic scene!* If only she could draw on that peace to soothe her mind.

A passage of Scripture would be perfect for calming her spirit. Lucy pulled her Bible from her carpetbag and climbed into the inviting bed. Settling back against the pillows, she propped her Bible against her knees. A yawn stretched her mouth wide as she thumbed through the well-worn pages. Her fingers stopped on Psalm 121.

"I will lift up mine eyes unto the hills, from whence cometh my help. My help cometh from the Lord. . . ." Before she reached the end of the sentence, the words began to swim before her eyes. Maybe sleep would come more easily than she'd thought. Lucy closed the Bible, laid it on the bedside table, and blew out the lamp. She hadn't gotten very far in her reading, but she could meditate on the Lord's ability to help in her current situation while she drifted into slumber.

She pulled the sheet up around her shoulders and stared into the darkness, her thoughts on the way the Lord had brought her to Martha Simms and her nephew. Andrew seemed utterly convinced that his aunt suffered from some form of delusions, yet after studying Martha all evening, Lucy hadn't seen anything to suggest that. Martha might be grumpy at times, even grouchy. But crazy? No.

Lucy's eyelids refused to stay open, though her mind continued to mull over the situation. She would keep a close watch on Martha until Andrew's next visit and see if she could spot any unusual behavior. Wouldn't he be glad if she was able to tell him his fears were all for naught?

The next instant, her eyes flew open. *But what about me?* While it would surely be a relief to Andrew to learn his concerns were groundless, the good news for him might spell calamity for her.

If Martha proved to be every bit as sane as the next person, there would be no reason for Lucy to stay on. And in that case . . .

Her apprehension mounted. Would Andrew see that as a reason to ship her back to Dry Gulch?

"'My help cometh from the Lord,'" she whispered, wishing she felt the full conviction of her words. She half expected her turbulent thoughts to keep her tossing and turning for hours, but despite her fears, the strain of the past few days took its toll, and sleep claimed her.

———◆———

A loud cry startled her awake. Lucy lay perfectly still, trying to get her bearings. *I'm at the Diamond S*, she recalled with sudden clarity. As she propped herself up on one elbow and strained to listen, she heard the cry again.

Martha. The sound was muffled, as though coming from a distance. Maybe she was still downstairs. Was she hurt—perhaps ill—and calling for assistance?

Shaking her head to clear her thoughts, Lucy pushed herself upright and started to swing her legs over the side of the bed when a loud blast shattered the night.

She let out a shriek and tried to scramble out of bed, but her legs became entwined in the sheets, and she landed on the floor in a heap. Pulling her knees to her chest, she curled into a ball and wrapped her arms around her head. *What is going on?*

Martha's voice rang out again. Lucy couldn't make out the words, but the sharp, angry tone came through clearly enough—definitely not that of someone pleading for aid.

She remembered Martha's account of standing off rustlers and other marauders. Could it be happening again? Was the ranch under attack?

If that was the case, Martha would need help. Lucy tore free of the sheets and sprang to her feet. Without taking time to put on her wrapper, she charged out the bedroom door in her nightgown and felt her way down the stairs with one hand on the wall and the other gripping the stair rail.

Another blast echoed from below, and Martha hollered again. Lucy flinched but pressed on.

The front door stood open. Through the doorway, she could see the moonlight bathing the landscape in a silvery glow. Martha stood in front of the house, breaking open a shotgun. A tendril of smoke curled up from the breech as she shoved in a new round of shells.

A floorboard creaked under Lucy's bare feet as she approached the doorway. Martha snapped the shotgun barrel closed, raised the gun to her shoulder, and swung back around toward the house.

Lucy ducked behind the door. "Don't shoot, Mrs. Simms! It's me, Lucy!"

"Did you see it, too?"

"See what? What's happening?"

Martha gestured skyward. "The cow jumping over the moon."

Lucy sucked in her breath at the reminder of Andrew's muttered comment, and her throat tightened. "You were shooting at a cow?" She pointed overhead. "Up there?"

Martha grunted. "Nah, over there." She jabbed the shotgun sideways. "Cows don't fly. Somebody has been making this happen. I saw a shadow near the corner of the barn and let off a round."

Lucy scanned the area Martha indicated. She saw no movement, only streams of water gushing out from holes in the side of the rain barrel.

Martha followed her gaze and sniffed. "The varmint must

have ducked behind it when I swung around. Then I heard someone else up on the roof."

Lucy padded her way across the packed earth to Martha's side and peered up at the top of the house. Moonlight glinted on the mangled remains of the brass weather vane she'd noticed on her arrival.

She laid her hand on Martha's arm and spoke in a soothing tone. "Mrs. Simms, it's only the weather vane."

"I'm pretty sure I winged him. He must've ducked behind the chimney when he saw me take aim." Martha shook her head. "They pulled that stunt the last two full moons, with a cow floatin' up there in the sky. The first couple of times, it took me by surprise, but this time, I was ready for them. They probably didn't expect that." She gave a dry chuckle.

"But there's no one there now. Where could they have gone?"

Martha peered into the shadows. "Guess I scared them off. They probably kept the house between us and them and hightailed it out of here while we were talking." She lowered the shotgun, looking mildly disappointed. "Might as well go back inside."

Despite the warmth of the summer night, Lucy shivered as she stood in the parlor and watched Martha drop the heavy bar across the door. The older woman walked to a nearby cabinet, where she pulled more shotgun shells from a box and dropped them into the pocket of her robe.

She glanced over at Lucy. "Just in case. Always best to be prepared." A yawn stretched her lips wide. "We might as well go back to bed. Now that they're gone, we should be able to get a good night's sleep."

Lucy merely nodded, unable to think of any appropriate response.

Back in her room, she closed the door firmly and leaned against it. Then, remembering the perforated rain barrel and the mangled weather vane, she tugged the chair over to the door and propped it underneath the doorknob. Moving over to the window, she folded her arms and leaned on the sill.

Flying cows? She raised the window all the way to the top of the frame. Talk of levitating livestock was enough to make people question Martha's sanity, but the ranch woman seemed convinced an intruder had been skulking about.

Had someone really been lurking outside? Resting her arms on the sill, Lucy held her breath, listening for any hint of stealthy movement. All she heard was the creak of the windmill and the soft lowing of cattle.

Climbing back into her rumpled bed, she curled up under the sheet. Martha might be looking forward to untroubled slumber, but Lucy fully expected a long, wakeful night. She rolled onto her side and punched her pillow into a more comfortable shape.

At least the night's episode had removed one worry. There was no longer any question of telling Andrew his aunt's mind was clear. Martha undeniably needed someone to keep an eye on her, so Lucy's place at the Diamond S was assured.

But with cows jumping over the moon and Martha unleashing shotgun blasts at invisible marauders in the middle of the night, the question now was whether Lucy could survive her stay there.

✳ Chapter 5 ✳

Andrew waved good-bye to Harvey Duncan and slapped
the reins against the horses' rumps, setting the buckboard
back toward North Fork at a good clip. Half an hour later,
he pulled back on the reins when he came to a fork in the
dusty road. The Diamond S lay only a few miles out of his
way. He might as well make a slight detour and see how
Aunt Martha and her new companion were getting along.
He guided the horses to the right and headed for the ranch.

He'd seen the look of panic on Lucy Benson's face when
he announced his departure three days before. That, coupled
with Aunt Martha's irritation at having unwanted company foisted upon her, made him feel guilty about leaving
so abruptly.

Maybe he hadn't made things as clear as he should have . . .
to either of them. He'd honestly thought he and Aunt Martha
had come to an agreement about the need for someone to
stay there with her—but she obviously hadn't seen it that
way. Hopefully, three days spent in each other's company
had given the women a chance to work things out.

He checked the position of the sun and shook the reins.

If he hurried a bit, he could make it to the ranch house in time for dinner. With any luck, Aunt Martha might have made one of her mouthwatering peach pies.

Andrew noted Carson Murphy's dun gelding tied to the hitching rail when he pulled up in front of the house. Wrapping the reins around the brake handle, he hopped down and trotted up the front steps.

Lucy answered his knock, wearing a faded calico apron over her pale blue dress. Her hair, pulled into a loose coil at the back of her neck, bore little resemblance to the fussy style she'd worn the day she arrived. With her sleeves rolled up halfway to her elbows and her forearms streaked with traces of flour, she looked the very picture of domestic life. The notion sent an unexpected surge of warmth through him.

A flush tinted her cheeks when she saw him. "Won't you come in?" She stepped aside so he could hang his hat on the peg near the door. "It seems today is our day for visitors. Mr. Murphy stopped by a little while ago."

Andrew followed along as she led the way into the parlor, where Aunt Martha and the neighboring rancher were getting to their feet.

Aunt Martha looked toward the doorway when he approached. "You always did have a good sense of timing. We just invited Carson to stay for dinner. From the way you're grinning, I expect we ought to set another place." She nodded at Lucy, who scurried off toward the kitchen while the rest of them made their way to the oak dining table.

Andrew watched Lucy carry another place setting to the table. He held her chair for her and smiled at her as he took his seat. "Did you do the cooking today?"

A muffled snort came from Aunt Martha's direction. He

shot her a puzzled glance, then looked back at Lucy, whose cheeks had turned pink again.

"I'm afraid I'm not much of a cook . . . yet. But your aunt says she's going to teach me."

Aunt Martha threw back her head and laughed aloud. "'Not much' is right. Would you believe she managed to burn the tea the first night she was here?"

Murphy snickered and smothered a grin.

"Burned the . . ." Andrew glanced back at Lucy, whose face had gone from pink to brick red, and decided not to pursue the matter.

"But she's a quick learner," Aunt Martha added. "I'm sure she'll get the hang of things before long."

"I will," Lucy said with a determined tilt to her chin that Andrew found utterly endearing.

They loaded their plates with roast beef, mashed potatoes, and creamed peas. Andrew forked in a mouthful of the beef and closed his eyes. "Mmm. Delicious as always, Aunt Martha. Nobody makes a pot roast like you."

Aunt Martha beamed. "What brings you out this way, Andrew?"

"Harvey Duncan's windmill needed a new part, so I took it out and put it on for him. Since I was out this way already, I thought I'd swing over here on my way back to town and see how the two of you are getting along."

Aunt Martha laid down her fork. "I hate to admit it, but it's been right pleasant having company around. Lucy fits in just fine, and everything's going smoothly . . . except for that little set-to we had the other night."

Andrew choked on his potatoes. "What happened?"

"Another one of those floatin' cows on the night of the

full moon. This time I heard somebody skulking around over by the barn. There must've been two of 'em, because I heard someone else scrambling around on the roof."

The succulent pot roast felt like a lead weight in Andrew's stomach. "What did you do?"

His aunt shrugged as if she were discussing nothing more exciting than her recipe for peach pie. "I let off a couple of blasts from my shotgun. Haven't had a lick of trouble since."

Andrew's fork slipped from his fingers and clanked against his plate. He stared back and forth between the two women.

Lucy focused on her plate, apparently absorbed in slicing her pot roast into small bites.

Andrew cleared his throat to catch her attention. "Did you see any sign of these intruders, Lucy?"

She took her time swallowing, dabbing her mouth with her napkin before meeting his eyes. "I was upstairs. I only came down after I heard the shouting . . . and the shooting." Her gaze slid away. "There wasn't anyone around by the time I joined your aunt."

Andrew glanced back at Murphy, who shook his head and offered a sympathetic smile.

Aunt Martha looked up as if nothing out of the ordinary had occurred. "Carson stopped by to talk about fencing off several areas of the ranch into big pastures. That way he can rotate the grazing. He's already done it on his place with good results, so I told him I'm willing to give it a try."

Murphy began describing the project to Andrew, and talk continued along those lines until Lucy went to the kitchen and brought out a peach pie for dessert. Andrew's mouth watered. As he raised the first bite to his lips, a knock sounded on the front door.

Lucy set her napkin down and went to answer it. She returned almost at once with two cowboys in tow. "These gentlemen say they've come to see Mr. Murphy."

"Jasper!" Andrew got to his feet and shook hands with the wiry cowpuncher who had ridden for the Diamond S during Andrew's growing-up years, then went to work at Murphy's Two Bar M after Aunt Martha sold the cattle. He gave a nod to Jasper's companion, Curly, another of Murphy's riders.

Jasper wrung his hand. "Good to see you, Andrew. I've been hearin' good things about those windmills of yours."

"Glad to hear it," Andrew said, feeling a glow of pride. He gestured toward Lucy. "This is Lucy Benson. She's come to stay with Aunt Martha. Lucy, these are Jasper and Curly, two of Murphy's cowboys."

Jasper beamed. "Glad to hear you'll be stayin' around, miss. You sure do brighten up the scenery." Turning to Murphy, he said, "We checked out that draw over to the west. Looks like we're gonna need more fencing than we thought. Maybe as much as a wagonload."

"That sounds like my cue to head for town and pick up more supplies." Murphy thanked Aunt Martha and Lucy for dinner, nodded to Andrew, and went on his way.

The cowboys lingered. Jasper hooked his thumbs in his belt and assumed a feigned innocence that wouldn't have fooled a child. "Is that peach pie I smell?"

Martha smirked. "You know good and well it is. You also know I always make extra, in case someone drops by. Go help yourselves."

A few minutes later, Lucy looked out the window and laughed. "Look at those two! They're out there with huge slabs of pie, and there's a cow nosing at Jasper's slice."

"A red cow with a big white splotch across her shoulders?" Aunt Martha chuckled. "That's Maybelle. You'll see her around here a lot. Her mama died when Maybelle was born, so we brought her indoors and fed her from a bottle. She's more like a pet dog than a cow."

She yawned and pushed her chair away from the table. "If you'll excuse me, I believe I'll go upstairs and lie down for a spell."

Lucy rose and began collecting their dishes. Andrew stood and cleared his place, earning himself a grateful look. Taking his cue, he picked up Murphy's plate, as well, and followed her to the kitchen.

Lucy stacked the plates on the counter, then lifted the kettle from the back burner and poured steaming water into the wash pan. She shaved a few pieces of soap into the water and began scrubbing the plates.

Andrew spotted an apron hanging over the back of a nearby chair and tied it around his waist, bringing a giggle from Lucy. He poured hot water into the rinse pan and accepted the clean plate she handed him.

"It sounds like your business is doing well," she said.

"It is." He dipped the plate in the rinse water and polished it with a dish towel. "Even better than I dared to hope. If word keeps getting around about the improvements a steady source of water can bring, I'll have more business than I can handle."

Lucy's blue eyes sparkled as she passed him another plate. "So progress comes to west Texas?"

"It does indeed. And more than just windmills are in our future. Have you heard about Edison's electrical wonders at the exposition in Chicago this summer? Before long, there will be electric lights in every home across the country. A new century is right around the corner, and the possibilities are nearly endless! I can't wait to be a part of it all."

Catching himself, he gave a sheepish laugh. "Forgive me. I get a little wound up when I think about what the future holds."

"No, I think it's wonderful! Listening to you, I could easily get caught up in it myself."

With an effort, Andrew tore his gaze away from her shining face and cleared his throat. "Changes are coming fast. That's for sure." He glanced up toward the second floor. "Speaking of changes, I can't remember Aunt Martha ever sleeping in the middle of the day before."

"She's been tired lately. I expect that's the result of sitting up half the night to watch for intruders." Her voice trailed off and she fell silent.

"You really didn't hear anything?"

Lucy handed him a saucer without meeting his eyes. "What I heard was that shotgun. It scared me to death! At first I thought somebody was attacking the house."

"But now?"

"I can't say they *weren't* here, but I didn't see anyone." Lucy ducked her head and scoured away at a serving bowl. "I want to believe her—I know *she* believes someone was there. I really like her, you know. Underneath that gruff exterior, she's a very caring person."

Andrew's stomach knotted. Despite his decision to bring in a companion for his aunt, he had hoped he'd been wrong in his assessment of her mental state. "When she first told me about these 'cows,' she said it was just like the nursery rhyme, where the cow jumped over the moon. I assumed it was some sort of hallucination—I never thought she'd let off that shotgun with you around. If this is going to escalate, I don't want to put you at risk. Do you feel like you're in any danger?"

"Maybe a little that first night." Lucy offered a weak laugh. "But since then, we've gotten along fine."

"I'll make it a point to stop by more often." He only hoped that would be enough to assuage his conscience. "I do feel a lot better knowing she has someone out here keeping an eye on her."

"There's only been that one incident since I've been here," Lucy said. "Maybe all she needed was someone to talk to and get her mind off these imaginary intruders. And I enjoy her company, too. I'm glad I came." She handed the serving bowl to Andrew. When he reached out to take it from her, their fingers touched. The tingle he felt could have powered one of Edison's electrical gadgets.

Lucy's eyes widened, and Andrew felt like he could stare into those pools of cornflower blue forever. His voice was husky when he spoke. "I am, too."

Yes indeed. He would definitely be stopping by more often.

✳ Chapter 6 ✳

Lucy set a recently laid egg in the basket she held over her arm and reached back into the nest, probing for more. While she checked the other nests, her thoughts went back to her conversation with Andrew the week before. There had been no further instances of mysterious goings-on in the night. Maybe they'd been right in their conclusion that Martha was lonely and needed a bit of company to set her mind at ease.

She put one last egg in her basket and looked down at the chickens, pecking away at the cracked corn she'd spread out for them. A swell of pride swept through her. Two weeks ago, who would have guessed that she, Lucy Benson, could feed chickens or gather eggs? On top of that, Martha had shown her how to bake a pie, pluck a chicken, and clean the ranch house. She was feeling more domestic by the day.

Andrew rode into the ranch yard just before noon. Lucy went out to meet him, marveling that the already sunny morning seemed to have brightened even more.

She grinned at him as he swung down from the saddle. "You're early. Dinner won't be ready for another hour or so."

"Good. I was hoping for a chance to talk to you." The

corners of his eyes crinkled when he smiled, and Lucy caught her breath. "Have you gotten to see anything of the ranch yet, besides the house and outbuildings?"

"Not really. I've been so focused on learning things in the kitchen, I haven't had a chance to go exploring. Why?"

Andrew pointed toward the top of the nearest hill. "You can see one of my favorite views from right over there. Care to take a look?"

Lucy calculated for a moment. Dinner was in the oven, and she didn't really need to do a thing for the next half hour. She looked up at him and smiled. "Why not?"

A light breeze fanned her face as they walked up the hillside, matching strides. At the top of the rise, Andrew turned toward the northeast and swept out his arm. "Look at that. Those plains just seem to go on forever . . . rolling along like a vast ocean."

Lucy's lips parted as she stared at the majestic sight.

"Over there," he continued, pointing off to their left. "Do you see that rock wall sparkling in the sunlight? Just below that is a ravine with a creek running through it. The dark line of trees beyond it shows where the creek meanders out across the prairie."

Lucy heard the warmth in his voice and caught the emotion behind it.

"There are miles of country like this in west Texas," he went on. "Imagine what it could be like with water enough to support more grazing. With enough windmills out here, we could triple—maybe quadruple—the number of cattle the ranches could sustain."

His excitement was contagious, and Lucy's heart quickened. "I can see why you love it. And why your aunt has enjoyed living here so long. Speaking of your aunt . . . there have been no further incidents, and we've been getting along splendidly. I've already learned a lot from her. In fact, the meal you'll be eating today is one I cooked myself." She slanted a teasing look at him. "Assuming you'll still want to stay and eat after hearing that."

A grin tugged at Andrew's lips. "I wouldn't miss it."

This time it wasn't talk of windmills that made Lucy's heart beat faster. When he turned to look out over the vast expanse again, she took advantage of the opportunity to study his strong profile.

"You couldn't learn cooking from a better—" The words died on his lips when he swung back around and caught her staring. He held her gaze, his eyes darkening.

Lucy couldn't move. Her heart tripled its pace, and she felt her throat go dry.

Andrew raised his hand and tucked a strand of hair behind her ear. The touch of his fingers sent a shiver of excitement through her, and her knees threatened to buckle.

With an effort, she looked away and cleared her throat. "We'd better get back down to the house. I need to check on dinner."

◆――――◆――――◆

A week later, Lucy settled into her rocking chair with a grateful sigh and poured cups of chamomile tea for herself and Martha. It felt good to get off her feet after such a busy day. But it had been a rewarding one, as well. She smiled to herself at the memory of the way Andrew had praised her pot roast after he'd "just happened" to stop by for dinner . . . again. After he left she'd put the kitchen to rights while Martha went upstairs for a brief nap, then the rest of the afternoon had been spent with Martha giving Lucy a lesson in bread making.

By the time the loaves came out of the oven, it was time for evening chores, followed by a cup of tea on the porch as the stars came out.

"You're a quick learner," Martha said. "I have to admit when I first saw you standing on the porch in that prissy dress, I didn't think there was any way you'd be such a help around here."

"Neither did I." Lucy took a sip of fragrant chamomile and leaned back in her rocking chair, wrapped in a sense of utter contentment. She chuckled. "And my father would be shocked. He objected to my learning anything he considered manual labor. His goal was for me to marry into a station he felt would be suitable for me."

"One that wouldn't involve cleaning the hen house or baking your own bread?"

The chuckle became a full-throated laugh. "Definitely not cleaning the hen house."

Nothing disturbed the silence for a long moment but the creak of the rockers. Then Martha spoke again.

"From what you've told me, I'd guess this isn't anything you would have imagined doing at this point in your life."

"No, I'm sure my father expected me to be planning a wedding by now. But things didn't work out quite the way he thought they would."

Martha grunted. "You mean once your daddy's money was gone, nobody was interested in marrying you?"

"That isn't entirely true. I did have a suitor after my father passed away . . . a rather persistent one."

Martha arched one eyebrow. "Oh?"

"Walter Harris. His father owns a lot of property around Dry Gulch. I'm sure my father would have considered Walter an excellent prospect . . . from a financial standpoint, at least."

"Something tells me you didn't."

"To be perfectly honest, the man makes my skin crawl. When the opportunity arose to come here instead, it was a welcome reprieve."

Martha drained her teacup and set it back on the tray. "I can't see you spending the rest of your days dancing attendance on the likes of me. You have your whole life ahead of you. What do you want from it?"

Lucy looked out at the low hills silhouetted against the darkening sky. Inky spots along the hillsides showed cattle getting ready to bed down for the night. Off in the distance, an owl gave a plaintive hoot. Nearer at hand, she spotted Maybelle ambling along near the barn.

She shook her head slowly. "Maybe that's my biggest problem—I don't really know what I want." Her voice trailed off, then she added, "But I do know it isn't marrying Walter Harris."

They fell silent. Then Martha said, "Even when you do know what you want, that doesn't always mean you'll get it."

The wistfulness in her voice tugged at Lucy's heart. "Are you thinking of the trip you and your husband planned to make?"

"Mm-hmm. It was his dream to begin with, but the more he talked about it, the more the idea took hold of me." Martha pushed herself out of the rocker and looked out at the night sky. "Even though he's gone, I have a hankering to do it anyway, just to see those places that meant so much to him."

After gathering up the tea things and bidding Martha good-night, Lucy went up to her bedroom and changed into her nightclothes. An enormous yawn stretched her mouth wide.

She walked over to the window and leaned against the casement with Martha's question still running through her mind. "What *do* I want?" she whispered.

She stared out at the night sky, seeking an answer that didn't come. Martha's words had stirred up an unexpected line of thought. In leaving Dry Gulch, she'd thought only of escaping Walter's unwanted attentions and having a roof over her head. Thoughts of anything further in the future hadn't entered her mind.

At the memory of her abrupt departure, she wondered for the hundredth time about the identity of the anonymous letter writer who made her getaway possible. Who could it have been?

Only a handful of people knew of her plight—Dottie Jackson and the ladies of Mrs. Whitfield's sewing circle. Since the letter had arrived on the heels of the women's fervent prayer for her, it seemed likely one of them had a hand in it. But which one?

She pressed her forehead against the window glass, thinking of the dear faces she'd left behind. Could it be Dottie? Doubtful, since her friend's thoughts had been consumed with her upcoming wedding.

What about Gertie Claasen or Prudence Whitfield? Lucy gazed into the darkness, considering. She could picture either of the older women as capable of making the kind of connections that sent her to the Diamond S. But why would either hide her identity? It seemed either of them would have just told her about the job and handed the train ticket over in person instead of having Pastor Eldridge deliver the news.

Emilie? Hannah Taylor? Lucy discarded Emilie as a possibility almost at once. But Hannah . . . Though the quiet schoolteacher never called attention to herself, she was always looking out for the welfare of others. Lucy nodded slowly. Yes, Hannah seemed a likely candidate. How she wished she could know for sure!

If . . . or when . . . she ever learned the identity of her benefactor, she would find a way to let that person know of her heartfelt gratitude. The Diamond S had provided a much-needed haven.

But how long could she expect that to last? And how long did she want it to?

Martha certainly seemed hale enough. The sturdy ranch woman was likely to live a good many years longer. As much as Lucy had grown to love being on the ranch and treasured the developing camaraderie between them, the question had to be asked: Was serving as Martha's companion all she wanted out of life? Would a home and family ever be hers?

"What I want, Lord, is whatever you have planned for me. But I don't know what that is. Am I going to miss out on finding your will, stuck out here in the middle of nowhere?"

Pushing the window up, she leaned out to look up at the stars. Just as her head cleared the frame, she heard Martha's voice raised in a harsh shout.

"Consarn it! What are you no-goods up to now?"

Lucy sagged against the window frame. *Not again!*

This time she paused long enough to put on her slippers

and snatch up her wrapper. She thrust her arms into the sleeves as she made her way down the stairs, bracing herself for the sound of a shotgun blast. None came by the time she reached the ground floor, but once again, the front door was standing wide open.

Lucy crept up to the door and peered out into the darkness. "Martha?" she called in a hushed tone. "What's going on?"

"Over here. At the south end of the porch."

Lucy followed the sound of Martha's voice, stifling a yelp when she barked her shin on the rocking chair Martha had vacated only a short time before. She hobbled the rest of the way to the corner of the house and stood next to Martha. "What's wrong?"

"They're at it again."

Lucy rubbed her throbbing shin. "Who?"

"Those varmints who've been skulking around here."

A wave of disappointment swept through Lucy. Things had been going so well since the night of her arrival, and now this. Andrew was due to visit again in the next day or two. She couldn't bear the thought of having to break the news to him.

Martha clutched Lucy's arm in a grip that made her wince. "Up there! Do you see it?"

Lucy glanced in the direction Martha indicated and stared openmouthed. A glowing shape moved slowly across the night sky, tracing an eerie path toward the barn.

A prickling sensation ran up the back of her scalp. She didn't believe in ghosts, not for a minute. And yet . . .

Martha's grip tightened even more. "You see it, don't you?"

Lucy pulled her arm free and rubbed it gently. "Yes." She

stood beside Martha in silence and watched the apparition continue on its way. "You don't think it's a . . ." Her voice trailed off, unable to form the word.

"A spook?" Martha snorted. "Never believed in 'em, and I'm not about to start now." She raised the shotgun to her shoulder as she spoke.

Lucy clamped her hands over her ears, which only partially muffled the roar of the gun. The unearthly specter picked up speed and hurried along in a jerky manner, disappearing behind the corner of the barn.

She gasped. "Do you think you hit it—whatever it was?"

"Let's find out." Martha hiked her skirts up and scuttled around the end of the barn.

After a moment's hesitation, Lucy ran after her. "Where is it?"

Martha stared into the darkness, holding the shotgun at the ready. "That just doesn't add up. It's gone." Lowering the shotgun, she replaced the spent shell with a fresh one and looked around. "I guess that's all the excitement we're going to see tonight. Let's go inside and try to get some sleep."

✶ Chapter 7 ✶

"Good morning, ladies." Carson Murphy stepped inside as Lucy held the front door open. "I rode over to see how Curly and Jasper were getting along on the fence. As long as I was in the area, I thought I'd stop by and say hello."

Martha snorted. "You didn't come by just to see an old woman. I'd be willing to bet you caught a whiff of my dried-apple pie and thought you could snag a piece."

Murphy laughed. "Guilty as charged. If you have an extra slice, I wouldn't turn it down."

Martha grinned at Lucy. "Havin' cowboys around all those years, I learned early on to make extra whenever I baked."

Lucy went to the kitchen to fetch three slices of pie, still warm from the oven, and carried the tray out to the porch, where Martha and Mr. Murphy sat rocking. The rancher jumped up to give Lucy his seat.

She smiled her thanks and handed him a plate before asking, "Is the fencing project going well?"

"Smooth as can be." He forked a bite into his mouth and closed his eyes in a show of pure enjoyment.

Martha's plate rattled when she set it down. "Wish I

could say the same for things around here. We had another visit from those no-goods who've been skulking around."

"Oh?" The rancher half turned to give Lucy a conspiratorial wink, then smiled at Martha in a patronizing manner that set Lucy's teeth on edge.

Martha didn't seem to notice. "I spotted something movin' along like some kind of specter—right up there." She pointed to the space between the windmill and the barn. "But it quit as soon as I let off a round in that direction, and I couldn't find a trace of anyone after that."

She leaned back in her chair. "I don't know what they're up to, but if they think it's easy to hoodwink an old widow woman, they've got another think comin'."

Murphy shook his head and shot a quick glance at Lucy. "Martha, we've talked about this before."

Martha drew herself up ramrod straight. "Carson Murphy, don't go acting like this is all in my head. I know what I saw."

Lucy sprang to her defense. "She's right. It wasn't just—"

"Don't get your dander up, Martha." Murphy set the plate back on the tray and walked to untie his horse from the hitching rail. Putting one foot in the stirrup, he swung himself into the saddle. "But you might as well admit this is all in your head, and all you're doing is wasting ammunition." He swung the horse around and dug in his heels.

Stung by his dismissive tone, Lucy jumped to her feet. "I saw it, too!"

But Murphy was already out of earshot.

"I don't like him," Lucy told Andrew when he stopped by later that afternoon.

He paused in the act of tightening a bolt on one of the barn door hinges. "Who?"

"Mr. Murphy."

Andrew gave the wrench another turn and swung the door back and forth. "There, it shouldn't drag anymore." He turned back to Lucy. "What do you have against Murphy?"

"I don't like the way he talks down to Martha."

Andrew shook his head and walked over to a shelf on the wall to return the wrench to the toolbox. "That doesn't sound like Carson. What did he say?"

"It isn't so much what he says. It's like he's laughing at her when he knows she isn't watching. He was out here earlier today. When she told him what happened last night, he came right out and said he thought she was making the whole thing up."

Andrew flinched. "What happened last night?"

Lucy recounted the story of Martha shooting at a ghostly apparition.

"She's at it again? I hoped we were getting past that. Especially since there's only been one episode since you arrived." He looked at Lucy. "As for Carson, I think you're wrong. He's been a friend to Uncle Ebenezer and Aunt Martha for many years, and I've never known him to treat her with anything but the utmost respect."

Lucy bristled. "I know what I saw."

Andrew eyed her with concern. "I brought you out here to keep an eye on Aunt Martha, not so she could pull you into her delusions. Next thing you know, you'll be seeing ghosts in the night, too."

"But I did see it."

Her statement stopped him in his tracks. He turned and gaped at her. "You mean she convinced you—"

"She didn't have to convince me of anything." Lucy glared at the clueless man. "I stood right next to her and saw the whole thing. It isn't just your aunt's word anymore—I'm a witness. Something strange is going on."

Andrew continued to the door. Lucy followed him and watched him drop the bar in place. He looked over, his brows knitted in a worried frown. "Let's get over to the house. I think you've had a little too much sun."

"Too much sun?" If Lucy had been holding anything heavy in her hands, she would have been sorely tempted to use it to knock some sense into him. Barring that, she put her hands on his shoulders and shoved.

Andrew stumbled backward, astonishment written on his face. He spread his arms wide. "What was that for?"

"For looking at me like I'm as loony as you think your aunt is. Well, she isn't crazy, and neither am I." She spun on her heel and marched off across the packed earth of the ranch yard.

Halfway to the porch, Andrew caught up to her and snagged her by the elbow. "I never said anyone was crazy. I just think she's imagining things."

Lucy whirled on him. "There is no reason for you to raise your voice like that, especially when you're standing barely a foot away."

"What makes you think you know Aunt Martha better than I do? I've known her my entire life, and you've only been here a few weeks."

Lucy raised her own volume to match his. "Maybe you don't know her as well as you think you do. Do you know her greatest dream is to travel the world, but she doesn't want to part with the ranch because it means so much to you?"

"That proves it, you really are deluded. What she wants is to live out her life right here on the Diamond S. Why would you possibly think she wants to be anywhere else?"

"Because I *listen* to her! Something you apparently don't take the time or trouble to do."

The front door swung open and Martha stepped out onto the porch, planting her flour-covered hands on her hips. "What in thunder is going on? I could hear the shoutin' clear back in the kitchen. Sounded like someone was getting skinned alive."

Lucy searched for some answer that would satisfy. She could hardly tell Martha they'd been debating her sanity. "Nothing much. I was just talking to Andrew."

Martha's focus shifted to her nephew, who shuffled his feet and shrugged. She stared at them a moment longer, then broke into a low chuckle. "You two remind me of Burt and Bessie."

The abrupt change of subject broke the tension. Lucy turned her back on Andrew and flounced over toward Martha. "Burt and Bessie who?"

Martha grinned. "A young bull and heifer Ebenezer and I brought with us when we first came here. Those two were like oil and water, buttin' heads with each other every time their paths crossed. Just like you two were doing out there." Martha turned her head and coughed, then pressed her hand against her forehead.

Lucy stepped forward. "Are you all right?"

Martha waved away her concern. "Felt a bit dizzy for a moment. I'm fine now." She swiped at her apron, sending up a cloud of fine white powder. "Since it appears nobody's getting skinned after all, I might as well go back to my pies. Carson and those cowboys of his have been eatin' them up as fast as I can bake them."

When the door closed behind her, Lucy turned back to Andrew, suddenly at a loss for words.

He pulled off his hat and raked his fingers through his hair. "I need to apologize. I never should have let my temper get the best of me like that."

Lucy ducked her head. "Me too." She stepped up onto the porch and wrapped her arm around one of the upright posts. "All the same, there really is something strange going on around here. If that glowing object was real—and it was—can't we assume those other things your aunt saw really happened, too? And if that's the case, we need to ask ourselves who's behind it . . . and why. That's the part that puzzles me. I can't imagine why anybody would go to all the trouble of doing this."

She caught her breath. "What about Mr. Murphy? Maybe he wants to scare Martha off so he can buy the ranch and increase his holdings."

The corner of Andrew's mouth curved up. "I know you don't like him, but there's no reason for him to do that. The arrangement he has with Aunt Martha gives him all the access he needs, and for far less than he'd spend to own the property outright. I'm afraid you'll have to find another suspect."

Lucy swallowed her disappointment. "All right. But if it isn't him, there's still someone who's making these things happen. It's up to us to find out who it is and the reason they are doing it."

Andrew regarded her thoughtfully, then nodded. "Okay. What do you want me to do?"

It wasn't much as far as concessions went, but Lucy decided it would suffice. "Why don't we join forces. I can keep watch here. Maybe you can do some investigating and try to find a reason anyone would want to torment your aunt like this. Can we agree on that much?" She held out her hand.

When he didn't respond, she added, "I'm not saying you have to believe I'm right. Let's just work together to prove or disprove these assertions of Martha's once and for all."

Andrew drew a deep breath and gave a decisive nod. "That much I can do." He took her hand, sealing the bargain.

The moment his hand enveloped hers, Lucy felt a tingle run from her fingers down to her toes. She stared into his melting brown eyes and watched the crease in his cheek deepen into a dimple. Had she really wanted to bash him over the head only moments before? The sudden transformation in her feelings took her breath away.

✳ Chapter 8 ✳

"Are you sure you're feeling better? Jasper and Curly are working on that new section of fence. If you want me to, I could go fetch one of them and send him for the doctor." Lucy waited until Martha scooted herself up in bed, then set the tray of tea and toast on the older woman's lap. "I should have realized something was wrong when you said you felt dizzy the other day."

"Don't you fret—I'm much better this morning. I should be back on my feet tomorrow." A smile wreathed Martha's creased cheeks. "This is the first time in years I've been cosseted like this. It's a comfort to have you here." She sniffed at her tea, then took a sip. "That's a sight better than the first pot of tea you made for me."

Lucy laughed, remembering the disaster with the sassafras tea on the evening of her arrival. "If you don't need anything else, I'll see to the chores."

She went about feeding the horse and then got cracked corn for the hens from the barn. Maybelle rounded the corner, eyeing Lucy's bucket with curiosity. Lucy grinned at the cow but kept her distance. As docile as Maybelle seemed, Lucy had no intention of getting near those long, pointed horns. She reached in her bucket, tossed a handful of corn onto the ground, and went on toward the hen house, leaving Maybelle nosing the unexpected treat.

While she gathered eggs, she made a mental list of tasks to be done. She needed to bring in firewood for the stove and tidy up the kitchen before she tackled the rest of the housecleaning.

Lucy sighed and wiped the back of her hand across her forehead, thinking how glad she would be when Martha was back on her feet again. Trying to manage all the chores and household duties on top of taking care of the older woman was almost more than she could handle. At least there hadn't been any sign of intruders since the night they saw the glowing "phantom" near the barn.

She hooked the egg basket over her arm and went back into the house. Maybe she would fix some eggs for Martha's midday meal. She pulled four from the basket and was reaching for a bowl on the cupboard shelf when a loud clatter made her jump.

Lucy hurried to Martha's room and peeked inside. Martha lay curled on her side, fast asleep.

Lucy's stomach knotted. That noise had been close. If it hadn't come from inside the house, what had caused it? She glanced out the front window, hoping to see Maybelle lumbering past the porch. Nothing stirred. But she *had* heard something—a noise that seemed utterly out of place.

And that meant something—or somebody—was outside.

She started for the front door, then turned back to pull the shotgun from the rack. She held it gingerly, knowing Martha made a point of keeping it loaded, and hefted it in her hands, surprised by its weight.

With her heart pounding, Lucy stepped onto the porch and scanned the ranch yard from one end to the other.

No one was there. Nothing moved.

Lucy edged along the front of the house toward the north end, where the kitchen was located, and peered around the corner.

Nothing.

Where had the sound come from? She swept her gaze across the outbuildings. The barn door stood slightly ajar.

Lucy swallowed and breathed a quick prayer. Forcing her stiff legs into motion, she crossed the distance to the barn with the shotgun at the ready. Using the tip of the barrel to nudge the door open, she stepped inside.

◆ ◆ ◆

Andrew smiled when the Diamond S came into view. Since Lucy's arrival, Aunt Martha had seemed happier than he'd seen her in ages. Maybe she had been far lonelier than he'd realized. In which case, his decision to provide a companion had been a good idea, regardless of the reason for doing it. Yes, bringing Lucy Benson to the ranch had been a wonderful thing for his aunt.

For him, too, if he wanted to be honest with himself. He hadn't felt so lighthearted in ages. And that was just at the prospect of seeing Lucy.

Lucy, with her golden hair and the smile that seemed meant just for him. Lucy, whose cornflower-blue eyes sparkled when she laughed and flashed when she was angry. And how they had flashed on his previous visit, when she'd shoved him with all her might!

It had been all he could do to keep from reaching out and

taking her in his arms right then and there. Andrew grinned. Maybe he could find some other way to antagonize her so she would push him again.

He pulled his horse to a halt in front of the hitching rail and noticed the barn door standing partway open. *Lucy must be out there tending to some chore.* Maybe he could have her to himself for a few moments before he went inside to visit Aunt Martha.

Treading softly, he eased his way across the packed dirt and peered into the dimness of the barn, wondering if he could catch her unaware. But Lucy was nowhere in sight.

Andrew frowned. It wasn't like her to leave the door standing ajar. She had to be inside somewhere. He heard a stir of movement from the direction of some unused stalls. Grinning, he eased his way toward his objective, anticipating her look of surprise.

Halfway there, his foot scuffed against some loose pebbles, and they rattled across the dirt walkway. The next instant, Lucy appeared in the opening of the last stall.

"Hold it right there!" she said.

Andrew's glee turned to panic when he realized she was holding Aunt Martha's shotgun to her shoulder, pointed straight at him.

"Whoa!" Andrew stopped dead. From the expression on Lucy's face and the way her hands shook, he could see she was terrified. She might not even realize who he was, but that wouldn't matter if her finger tightened on the trigger.

"Lucy, it's me." He froze, not daring to breathe, while she registered his presence.

"Thank goodness!" The words came out in a choked voice. "I didn't hear you ride up."

"I'd be much obliged if you'd take your finger off the trigger and point that somewhere else."

"Oh!" Lucy looked down at the gun in her hands. When she swiveled the shotgun away from him, Andrew stepped forward and took it from her grasp. Easing the hammers down, he laid it on the ground.

When he straightened, Lucy hadn't moved. She could have been a statue, except for the trembling that shook her whole body. She stared at him with a dazed expression. "I could have shot you."

"But you didn't." Andrew tried to keep his voice low and soothing. He took her by the shoulders. "Want to tell me what's going on?"

Instead of answering, Lucy flung herself into his arms and buried her face in his chest. Andrew wrapped his arms around her, cradling her as he would a child while she melted against him and sobbed.

He caught his breath. Hadn't he been dreaming of holding her in his arms only moments before? He tightened his arms around her and savored the experience. Having her cling to him like this was nicer than having her push him away. *Much* nicer.

Lucy's sobs eased a bit. She looked up and gave a quick gasp, as if realizing their proximity for the first time. She took a step back and swiped at her tear-stained cheeks.

"Are you all right?" he asked. "Where's Aunt Martha?"

"She came down with a bad cold just after you were here last time. She's resting right now. That's why I came out here on my own."

"With the shotgun." Andrew picked up the gun with his

left hand, wrapped his right arm around Lucy's shoulders, and led her toward the barn door. "Tell me what happened."

———————◆———◆———◆———————

Lucy knew propriety called for her to push Andrew's arm away. But she didn't. Having him so close felt comforting . . . it felt right. Another tear trickled down, and she swiped at her cheeks again. "I was working in the kitchen, and I heard a noise outside. I thought those intruders were back."

His arm tightened on her shoulder. "I didn't see a soul when I rode up."

"Somebody had to be around to make a noise like that," she insisted. They reached the barn door, and Andrew closed it tight. "I don't know what they were up to, but someone was here. I'm sure of it."

Seeing a smile flicker across his face, she twisted away and widened her stance, planting her hands on her hips. "Don't you look at me that way. I know what I heard."

Andrew held up his hands. "I believe you heard something, and I can see it frightened you. I'm only saying there's no sign of anyone here."

"I thought we had an agreement. I thought you were going to take this seri—" She broke off, realizing Andrew was no longer looking at her, but at a point beyond her shoulder.

She spun around but saw only the windmill. "What is it?"

Andrew pointed toward the top of the windmill. "Do you see that string trailing out behind the tail fin?" He walked past her to the base of the windmill, where a bucket lay on its side. A dozen or more fist-sized rocks lay scattered nearby.

Andrew loaded the rocks into the bucket, then held it aloft and poured them out on top of the pipes and the pump jack.

The rocks struck the metal with a loud, clanging sound. "Is that what you heard?"

"Yes!" Lucy brightened, then her spirits fell. "You mean I got all worked up over a bucket tipping over?"

Andrew shook his head. "I don't think this happened on its own." Mounting the ladder on the side of the windmill, he climbed to the platform under the vanes to take a closer look at the string. He bent to pick up another large rock from the platform and nodded.

When he climbed back down, he held out the rock. "It appears someone loaded the bucket with these rocks, tied one end of that string to the tail fin, and looped the other end around the bucket. When the wind shifted and the fin swung around, it tipped the bucket over and let the rocks fall down onto the pipes."

Lucy scrunched her forehead. "So that means . . ."

"It had to have been set up deliberately."

"Then I was right! Somebody *was* here."

"Yes, and no." Andrew flinched when he caught her exasperated look. "Yes, someone had to be here to do it, but it doesn't mean they were here when the bucket dumped the rocks. This could have been set up hours—even days—ago. It was just a matter of time until the wind changed and sent those rocks tumbling. It wasn't meant to do any harm, but it would surely jangle the nerves of whoever was around." He added in an almost inaudible whisper, "Just like those other times."

Lucy perked up. "So you do believe me?"

"It looks like I have to." Andrew bent over with his hands on his knees and peered at the dirt.

"What are you doing?"

"Looking for tracks. Whoever did this had to leave some

sign." He moved around the windmill in ever-widening circles. Eventually, he straightened with a disgusted expression.

"What's wrong?" Lucy asked.

"I can see scuffs here and there, but not enough to make
out individual prints."

"Show me what you're looking for. Maybe I can help."

"I'm looking for boot tracks—but not yours or mine or
Aunt Martha's. Whoever climbed onto the platform had
to have walked over to the windmill, or ridden their horse
right up to it."

He put his hands on his hips and turned in a slow circle.
"But there aren't any other tracks around here, except for
Maybelle's."

Lucy nodded. It would make sense to find Maybelle's
tracks around the house and ranch yard. The cow was like
a friendly puppy, wandering up close to the house whenever
she was in the mood for company.

Andrew swept off his hat and fingered the cleft in his chin.
"Unless whoever did this sprouted wings and flew in, I don't
see how it was done."

"There's one good thing in this." Lucy gave him an imp-
ish grin. "We may not know how he did it, but at least you
don't think Martha and I are crazy anymore."

Andrew reached out to stroke the backs of his fingers
along her cheek. His touch sent a shiver through her, and
his slow smile warmed her down to her toes. His voice was
husky when he spoke. "I think about you a lot, Lucy Benson,
but I don't think you're crazy."

✳ Chapter 9 ✳

"Are you sure?" Andrew leaned over the plat map spread out before him.

The county recorder nodded and pointed to a series of crosshatch marks running northwest to southeast on the map. "This line marks the route of the Forth Worth and Denver City Railway Company. And this"—he traced an intersecting line with his finger—"is where the Atchison, Topeka, and Santa Fe proposes to put in a new line connecting with their main route up in Kansas."

Andrew followed the line leading to the edge of the county—straight through the Diamond S. "And you say all these ranches along the new route have been sold?"

"That's right. And all within the last few months." The other man gave Andrew a curious look. "Only a handful of people knew about the new plan."

"And all those properties were purchased by the same buyer?"

The recorder nodded. He leaned toward Andrew and lowered his voice. "Between you and me, he got them all at rock-bottom prices, and he stands to make a killing if the proposed line does go through." Straightening, he added in a normal tone, "Does that answer your questions?"

Andrew set his mouth in a grim line. "Yes, I believe it does."

Back outside, he mounted his horse and started off in the direction of the Diamond S. Getting the information had been the easy part. Now he had to figure out how to break the news to Aunt Martha.

The horse shied when the wind sent a string of tumbleweeds spinning crazily across the trail. Andrew tugged his Stetson down on his forehead. After all Aunt Martha had done for him while he was growing up, how could he have assumed her mind was off balance? Remorse ate at him. And the idea that she needed a keeper . . . A harsh laugh tore from his throat, to be carried away on a gust of wind.

On the other hand, if he hadn't been concerned enough to write that letter to his friend in Dry Gulch, Lucy never would have entered his life. The way it all came about remained a puzzle. A query to his friend brought a mystified response, with the friend claiming he had nothing to do with recommending Lucy for the job. He hadn't gone any farther than mentioning Andrew's dilemma to a couple of friends and the local schoolteacher. It seemed the story of how God put it all together might remain a mystery. One thing Andrew did know for certain—he was mighty glad it happened.

He wondered what Lucy's reaction would be when he told the women what he'd learned. With proof that his aunt hadn't been imagining things, would Lucy feel duty bound to find employment elsewhere? He knew she didn't want to accept charity. He also knew he couldn't stand the thought of her leaving.

But he knew one way to keep that from happening—if only Lucy would agree.

◆————◆————◆

A steady breeze teased at Lucy's hair as she picked another handful of horehound leaves and dropped them into the basket she was carrying over her arm. She'd used up most of their supply making tea for Martha during her illness, but foraging for the herb had only been an excuse to get away from the house. Her real purpose in coming out was to see if she could find any signs pointing toward the devious person who'd set up that prank at the windmill. If she could find horse tracks leading away from the windmill, she might be able to follow them to the perpetrator's lair.

That task proved easier planned than done. She'd been searching for over an hour and had covered a good bit of territory, wandering back and forth and scanning the dimpled earth for a sign. She'd seen cattle tracks aplenty, and some belonging to smaller creatures, but no sign of a mysterious horseman.

It was time to head home so Martha wouldn't worry. She'd already stretched her time away from the house longer than any excursion for plants would account for. She turned back to retrace her steps and caught her breath when she spotted a pillar of smoke obscuring one corner of the barn.

Lifting her skirt clear of the ground, Lucy set off toward the barn at a run. The dry framework of the barn would go up like a tinderbox, and with the direction of the wind, the house would be next. Tendrils of panic twined up her spine. She let the basket fall from her arm and redoubled her speed.

283

The wind swirled, sending the smoke into a spiral. As she neared the barn, she saw forks of flame shooting up from the dry prairie grass, still some distance away. *Thank heaven!* The fire hadn't reached the structure yet. If she could circle around in front, get to the leading edge, maybe she could do something to keep the flames from spreading to the buildings.

She raced pell-mell, her lungs straining for air. Just short of her goal, the wind shifted again, enveloping her in an acrid cloud of smoke. She whipped her apron off and used it to wave away the billowing mass. Through the haze, she spotted a figure on the other side of the fire. Had Martha come out to help? No, this person wore a large hat—a Stetson. Squinting, Lucy recognized Curly and went limp with relief. Help was at hand.

As she opened her mouth to call out, the smoke cleared for a moment and Lucy squinted, unable to believe her eyes. Instead of coming to her aid, Curly was heading off at a good pace in the opposite direction—away from the fire— astride . . . a cow? She blinked her eyes, but nothing changed. The animal Curly rode was indeed a cow . . . with a white splotch across her shoulders.

"Maybelle?" Lucy whispered. She shook the confusing image from her mind. There was no time to wonder about that. She couldn't count on help from Curly—she had to get Martha. Spinning around, she sprinted in the direction of the house, but the toe of her boot caught on a clump of grass, and she stumbled and fell headlong.

✦ ✦ ✦

Andrew tried to settle his nerves as he trotted his horse up the last hill before reaching the ranch house. Could he follow his heart and lay his hopes for the future at Lucy's feet, or was there someone whose permission he needed to ask first? Lucy had no family, so he didn't know who that could be. Maybe his best option would be to consult Aunt Martha.

He reached the top of the rise, and his throat constricted when he saw a plume of black smoke coiling up from the valley floor. Breathing a prayer, he bent low along the horse's neck and spurred his mount for all it was worth.

Aunt Martha stumbled from the barn when he slid to a halt in the ranch yard, a stack of empty grain sacks in her arms. "Help me soak these in the horse trough," she panted. "We've got to get that fire out before it reaches the barn."

Andrew glanced toward the barn. "Where's Lucy?"

Aunt Martha pressed her hand to her chest and gasped for breath. "She went out a while ago to gather some herbs for me. She headed off that way." Worry creased her forehead as she pointed in the direction of the smoke.

Her statement hit him like a fist in the gut. Leaping from his horse, he grabbed an armload of the burlap sacks and dunked them in the trough. Gathering up the water-soaked bags, he raced off toward the fire, calling back over his shoulder, "Bring more sacks if you've got them, and a shovel, too."

As he ran, he searched the terrain, straining for a glimpse of Lucy. He doubted she would have gone out of sight of the buildings. In that case, she had to have noticed the smoke and would be on her way to help. But he couldn't see any sign of her. Where *was* she?

Sprinting up to the edge of the fire, he dumped the sodden

pile of sacks on the ground, snatched up the top one, and started to beat out the flames.

——— ◆ ———

Lucy shook her head and fingered the lump on her forehead. She sat up but then realized it was easier to breathe closer to the ground. She lay still for a moment to catch her breath, then remembered the urgency of her situation. She had to get out of the shroud of smoke, had to make it to the house and get help.

Wadding up her apron, she pressed the crumpled fabric over her mouth and pushed herself to her knees, ready to press on. But which way? In the moments she'd lain stunned upon the ground, the smoke had thickened. If she chose the wrong direction, she chanced running straight into the fire.

Scrambling to her feet, she blinked back stinging tears and fought down the panic that rose up in her. She had to think! The wrong choice could prove fatal.

Heat pressed against her, and the sound of crackling flames smote her ears. She had to get out while there was still time—before there was no longer a chance of escape. A few feet away, a clump of sagebrush burst into flame. Lucy leaped back and a ragged scream tore from her throat.

——— ◆ ———

Andrew tossed the smoldering sack aside and grabbed a wet one from the pile. Aunt Martha raced up beside him with more sacks in one arm and a shovel in the other. Without a word, she took the sack from his hands and handed him the shovel.

Gripping the handle, he threw a scoopful of dirt on the

flames, then froze. Had that been a cry? He glanced at his aunt. "That sounded like Lucy."

Aunt Martha nodded, her face pale. Trading her wet sack for the shovel, she said, "Go find her. I'll keep working here."

Andrew circled around the edge of the smoke-filled area, shouting Lucy's name again and again. Fear clamped his heart at the thought of her being trapped in the flames. Hearing a racking cough, he turned toward the direction it had come from, took a deep breath, and plunged into the black cloud. He'd taken only a few steps when he nearly stumbled over her, down on all fours with her head hanging low. Covering her head with the wet burlap, he scooped her up and ran back the way he came.

Emerging into the clearer air, he carried Lucy out of harm's way before he set her on the ground and mopped at her face with his bandanna. "Are you hurt?" he asked.

Lucy gasped for air, then took a deeper breath. "Thank God you're here! I didn't know which way to go. I thought I was trapped . . . until you came along."

They clung together. Andrew cradled her against his chest, his cheek resting on her head.

"I was so scared," she whispered. "I thought I was going to die." She shifted so she could look into his face. "I've never felt so alone in my life. I kept hoping someone would come, but all I saw was Curly riding Maybelle."

Andrew brushed his fingers across the lump on her forehead. "How hard did you hit your head?"

Lucy pulled his hand away. "Not that hard. It seemed strange to me, too, but I know what I saw—even if it sounds a little crazy."

His lips twisted into a grim smile. "No crazier than the

other things that have been going on around here lately." He looked back toward the smoke, where Aunt Martha flailed away, struggling to make headway against the fire. "I have to go help her," he said. "Will you be all right here?"

She nodded and waved him on. "Go ahead. I'll come as soon as I catch my breath."

✳ Chapter 10 ✳

Andrew brushed his lips against the top of Lucy's head before he ran off. His heart ached to stay and hold her, to tell her how he felt, but that would have to wait. Right now, there was no time to waste.

He sprinted to Aunt Martha's side and took over the digging again, throwing one shovelful of dirt after another to smother the flames. Over the crackle of the fire, Andrew heard the pounding of hooves. He spun around to see Murphy and his cowboys riding up, with shovels strapped to their saddles. The three men leaped from their mounts and set to work with vigor.

With the additional help, the tide was finally turned, and the flames surrendered. Andrew stared at the blackened expanse before them, scarcely able to believe they'd managed to stop the blaze. He glanced over at Aunt Martha, with Lucy beside her. Like the men, both women were streaked with soot and looked utterly exhausted.

Aunt Martha let out a shaky sigh. "Thank the Lord. When all was said and done, there was more smoke than fire, but it still could have wiped us out."

Andrew nodded and watched Curly and Jasper tote buckets of water from the horse trough and upend them over the smoldering scrub brush. He picked up his shovel and stirred the wet ashes to make sure the fire was out. Then he leaned back on his heels and turned to Murphy. "We appreciate your help."

The rancher smiled, looking as relieved as Andrew felt. "Glad we were close by. The minute we saw the smoke, we grabbed up the shovels and headed over here. It looked for all the world like the house and barn were aflame."

Jasper raked his fingers through his hair, leaving it standing up in blackened spikes. "Curious how that happened. The wind's blowing up a storm, but there's been no lightning. I can't figure out how a fire got started in the first place."

"That is a puzzle." Andrew eyed Murphy as he spoke.

"I'm just grateful no one was hurt." Aunt Martha's voice choked. "When you went looking for Lucy, I wasn't sure I'd ever see the two of you again." She dabbed at her eyes with the corner of her apron.

Murphy tugged on his Stetson. "Since everybody is in one piece, the boys and I better head back to work." The three men turned and started toward their horses.

"Hold on a minute," Andrew said. "There's something we need to talk about."

◆———◆———◆

Something in Andrew's tone put Lucy on alert. She watched as he stepped toward the departing men, his mouth set in a grim line.

Murphy and the cowboys turned to face him.

Andrew hooked his thumbs in his belt. "I rode up to the county seat this morning. Had a nice chat with the county recorder."

Murphy's brow crinkled. "Oh?"

Keeping his focus locked on the rancher, Andrew said, "Aunt Martha, did you know the Santa Fe is thinking of running a new line of track out this way?"

Lucy swiveled her head to look at Martha, who seemed every bit as puzzled as Lucy felt.

The older woman shrugged. "I hadn't heard anything about it. I guess it's a sign of progress, but it doesn't really affect me any."

"It might not," Andrew agreed, still keeping his eyes on Murphy, "except that the new line they're proposing would come straight through your property."

Martha's jaw sagged. "Through the Diamond S?"

Andrew nodded. "Through the Two Bar M, too, according to the plat map I saw."

Murphy spread his hands. "That's all very interesting, but I assume it's just talk at the moment." He started to turn back toward his horse.

"Unless you happen to have inside information." Andrew's words stopped the rancher in his tracks. "In that case, it's a situation made to order for someone who wants to do a little land speculating."

"I suppose it would be." Murphy shifted from one foot to the other. His eyes darted from Andrew to Martha and back to Andrew again.

"In fact," Andrew went on, "it seems someone has been doing just that—buying up property along the proposed line at a rock-bottom price. It's a clever scheme. All he has to do is hold on and then make a killing when the railroad comes through."

Murphy's face grew deathly pale. Martha took a step toward the rancher. "What's he talking about, Carson?"

Andrew jabbed his finger toward Murphy. "I'm saying your good neighbor is the one who bought up that land on the quiet, working his way right along the path the new line will take. The Diamond S is the last piece he needs in order to own it all."

Murphy snorted. "It shouldn't come as any surprise that I've been buying up land. You both know I've wanted to expand my holdings."

Martha shook her head at Andrew. "Those are mighty strong words without anything to back them up. Carson and I have known each other for years, and he's never breathed a word to me about wanting to buy the Diamond S."

"Because he knew you wouldn't consider selling." Andrew flicked a glance at his aunt. "It seems awfully coincidental that he started buying up those other properties about the same time you started seeing all those strange things around the ranch. The timing seems just a little too convenient. . . ."

Turning back to Murphy, he raised his voice a notch. "Especially since you're the one who gave me the idea that Aunt Martha wasn't quite right in her mind, and I might need to move her off the place for her own good."

Martha's eyes glittered. "Is that so?"

"There's nothing wrong with buying land," Murphy protested.

"But there's plenty wrong in trying to intimidate someone to get it . . . especially an old friend."

Lucy held her breath when Andrew clenched his hands

and stepped forward. His face was tight with the effort to control himself.

"Was that your plan all along, Murphy? You knew she'd never leave willingly, so you tried to come up with a way to make me force her to move into town. Once she was off the ranch, you could take the place off our hands . . . at a price favorable to yourself, of course. Flying cows, glowing specters—it must have taken a bit of doing to pull it all off."

Jasper backed away from Murphy, looking as though he'd bitten into something sour. "You did all that to Miss Martha?" He turned to Andrew. "You know I'd never have a part in anything like this, don't you?"

Andrew studied the cowboy for a long moment, then nodded. "I've known you most of my life, Jasper, and you're a good man. I can't see you stooping to that kind of double-dealing." He turned an assessing gaze on Curly. "Jasper worked for Uncle Ebenezer all those years. He truly cares about Aunt Martha. But you're Murphy's man, through and through."

"This is preposterous!" Murphy blustered. "Think about it, Andrew. You told me yourself you haven't found any sign of intruders. Martha has been letting her imagination get the best of her. It could happen to anyone . . . especially someone who's getting up in years."

Martha sputtered, but Lucy saw a flicker of doubt in Andrew's eyes.

Murphy pressed his point. "As I recall, the only horse tracks you've seen are your own or where the boys and I have ridden straight up to the house. There's hardly anything suspect about that."

Riding up to the house. An image flashed into Lucy's

mind. She stepped forward and seized Andrew's arm. "It's Maybelle."

Andrew scrunched his brows together. "What?"

Lucy pointed at Curly, whose face took on a pasty hue. "I saw you out there, on the other side of the fire. You were riding Maybelle. That's how you came around without leaving telltale tracks, isn't it?"

The cowboy's eyes grew round. He took a quick step back and held up his hands. "It was the boss's idea, not mine. He paid me extra—said it wasn't doing any harm. That cow is as tame as anything, and she's up around the house all the time. He figured if I rode her in here, you'd never know anyone had been around."

"No harm?" Lucy echoed. "You made Martha's nephew doubt her sanity and stole her peace of mind. You're no better than a thief!"

Curly hung his head.

"So you're the one Martha shot at the night I arrived?"

The cowboy nodded. "I didn't know anyone else was around. Not until you ran outside." He sent a sidelong glance toward Martha. "You almost got me, over by the rain barrel. It like to scared me to death."

Martha's expression looked as though it had been etched in stone. "I knew none of that business with the flying cows was real. It was quite a stunt, though. How did you manage it?"

Curly looked down at his boots. "I tacked a tissue paper cutout to a Chinese lantern. It floated up in the air as pretty as you please, as long as the candle stayed lit."

"But there was somebody else with you that night. Who was up on the roof?"

"Nobody." Curly gulped. "Once you let off that shotgun, I hid behind the barn and started lobbing pebbles up there with a slingshot. They made quite a noise rattling around on that tin roof, and it kept you from looking over where I was. I just sat real quiet until you went back inside and things settled down. Then Maybelle and I made our getaway."

"What about the 'ghost'?" Lucy asked.

Curly met her eyes, then looked down at his feet. "I painted a sheet with some stuff Mr. Murphy gave me. It doesn't look any different in the daylight, but in the dark it glows a spooky green. I rigged it on a line I stretched between the windmill and the barn, then I climbed up into the hayloft and tugged it along. Figured it would scare you enough that no one would do any shooting . . . but I was wrong." He ran his finger around his collar. "I barely managed to tug the sheet in through a crack in the barn before you both came around the corner. I thought sure you were going to catch me that time."

"And the fire today?" Andrew took a menacing step toward the cowboy. "Were you behind that, too?"

Curly's eyes widened, and he took a step back. "It wasn't supposed to blaze up like that, but the wind gusted and it got out of hand. I only meant to put up some smoke, enough to draw the two of them out of the house so I could get inside and look for the deed to the place. When I saw it catch like that, I got on Maybelle and lit out to fetch the boss and Jasper to help put it out."

Martha's eyes blazed. Balling her hands into fists, she advanced on Carson Murphy. "Of all the rotten scoundrels! To think you could do something so underhanded after all the years Ebenezer and I considered you a friend!"

She waved her fist under the rancher's nose. "You oughta be grateful I don't have my shotgun in my hands right now. I'd show you a thing or two. In fact . . . you'd better get on your horse and hightail it out of here before I go inside and grab it. I am sorely tempted to fill your britches with buckshot." She watched while her former friend scrambled onto his horse and loped away.

"As for you two . . ." She wheeled on the cowboys, who stumbled over each other in their haste to back away. Curly sprinted for his horse and followed in Murphy's tracks.

"I had nothin' to do with it, Miss Martha!" Jasper took a step toward his former employer, then appeared to think better of it. "All the same, I expect I ought to be heading off, too." He swung up into his saddle and gave her a plaintive look. "Does this mean I won't be gettin' any more of your pies?"

"We'll talk about that after I've had time to cool off. Come back in a day or two." The shadow of a smile touched Martha's lips. "Better make that three or four."

She stared after the departing riders and shook her head. "Carson Murphy—who'd have thought it? Ebenezer always thought he was the salt of the earth. Such a shame, what greed can do to a man."

She let out a long sigh, then turned to Lucy and Andrew. "If you two don't mind, I think I'll go upstairs for a spell. All this excitement has tuckered me out."

"Are you sure you're all right?" Lucy asked. "Do you want me to come up with you?"

Martha patted Lucy's arm. "Thanks, but I need some time to pull myself together and do some praying so the Lord and I can get this sorted out. I'm havin' some real un-Christian thoughts right now."

∗ Chapter 11 ∗

Lucy watched her disappear inside the house, a welter of emotions wheeling through her. What a relief to know the truth had come out at last and Martha's mental state was no longer in question. At the same time, she grieved for the pain Martha must feel after being betrayed by someone she'd long considered a friend.

And what's going to happen to me? Now that Andrew no longer needed someone to keep an eye on his aunt, was there any reason for her to stay?

When the door closed behind Martha, Lucy turned around to face that question head on, to ask Andrew straight out. She squared her shoulders . . . and caught him watching her with a serious expression. When he continued to stare without speaking, she suddenly realized how she must look, with her ash-covered dress and her hair straggling around her face. She clapped her hands to her cheeks. "I must look a fright. Let me go inside and freshen up. Then I need to discuss something with you."

"There's nothing wrong with the way you look." He stepped closer, and his expression took on an intensity that left her breathless. "For a moment there, I was afraid I'd lost you," he whispered.

Lucy brushed a strand of hair away from her face and gave a shaky laugh. "But you found me. And thanks to you, I'm safe." She took a deep breath and plunged ahead. "Now that we know Martha wasn't imagining things after all, I don't suppose you'll be needing me here any longer."

Andrew closed the distance between them and cupped her cheeks in his hands. "I can't think of anything further from the truth." His breath stirred a tendril of hair above her left ear. "It nearly tore me apart when I thought I might have lost you. I couldn't stand it if that really happened."

The simple statement took her breath away. Lucy's heart stopped, then started up again, hammering like the hooves of a runaway horse.

He slipped one arm around her waist. "I only know one way to keep you with me always, and that's to ask you to be my wife." He dragged his thumb across her cheek, sending a shiver of delight through her. "Lucy, will you marry me?"

Her lips trembled so, she couldn't speak. Resting her hands on his shirt, she looked up into his soot-streaked face and knew this was what she wanted for the rest of her life . . . to spend it at Andrew's side.

Raising herself on her tiptoes, she wound her arms around his neck and answered him with her kiss.

Fingers of gold and crimson wove across the western sky. Lucy sat beside Andrew on the top porch step and nestled her head on his shoulder as they watched the sunset. She closed her eyes and let a sense of pure contentment wash over her. They had spent the hour since Andrew's proposal marveling at the way God brought them together and dreaming of the future.

The doorknob rattled behind them, followed by a startled exclamation. "What in thunder?"

Lucy sprang to her feet, with Andrew right beside her. He was the first to find his voice.

"How was your prayer time, Aunt Martha?"

Martha regarded them with an unreadable expression. "The Lord and I got everything worked out. Looks like you two got a few things straightened out, too."

Lucy felt Andrew reach for her hand, and she wrapped her fingers around his.

"We have some news for you," he said.

Martha chuckled. "And I'll bet I can guess what it is."

Lucy's cheeks grew warm. She looked up at the man beside her and smiled. "Andrew asked me to marry him."

A wide grin spread across Martha's face. "I had an idea this was going to happen. Just like Burt and Bessie."

Lucy crinkled her forehead. "That bull and heifer you and your husband brought out here with you?" She glanced at Andrew, who appeared to be stifling a grin, then looked back at Martha. "I thought you said all they did was butt heads."

"That's right. At first, anyway."

"What happened later?"

Martha's hearty laugh rang out, and she waved one arm toward the cattle that dotted the nearby hillside. "Where do you think that line of stock came from?"

"Oh." Lucy nodded. Then Martha's meaning registered. "*Oh!*"

Still chuckling, Martha plopped down in her rocking

chair. "This seems to be an evening for announcements. I have a little news of my own."

"News? Tell us!" Lucy took a seat in the other rocker, while Andrew leaned back against the porch rail.

Martha rocked back and forth with a gentle motion. "I did some deep thinking while I was upstairs. With the railroad coming through, it's going to change everything. As hard as I've worked to hang on to this land, it's difficult to think it won't be the Diamond S much longer. Nothing is going to be the same."

A lump formed in Lucy's throat. She reached over and laid her hand on Martha's arm. "Andrew and I have been talking about that. We want you to come live with us in North Fork. I know it won't be the same, but at least we'll be together as a family."

Martha patted Lucy's hand. "Thank you, dear. That's a comfort." She looked at Andrew with a speculative gleam in her eyes. "So it's pretty much a certainty the railroad is coming through here?"

"I'm afraid so. I know it's going to be hard for you to say good-bye to this place."

"And you think they'll offer me a fair price for the land?"

"I'm sure of it, Aunt Martha. They won't be out to cheat you. You'll be financially secure for the rest of your days."

Martha slapped both hands on the arms of her rocker. "In that case, let 'em come! I'm ready to sell."

Andrew couldn't have looked more dazed if she'd hit him on the head with a two-by-four. "You are?"

"Yep. It's time for me to do what your uncle and I always dreamed of. I'm going to take that money and see the world." She turned to Lucy. "Since the two of us have hit it off so well, I was going to ask you to come along . . . but it appears you've gotten a better offer."

"But . . . but . . ." Andrew sputtered like a teakettle on the boil. "You can't go off on your own like that! There's no telling what you might run up against."

Martha quelled him with a look. "Need I remind you, I've run up against plenty of dangers right here—including that fire this afternoon. I expect I can handle anything—or anyone—I come across."

Laughter bubbled from Lucy's throat. "After seeing you in action, I'm sure you can."

Martha bobbed her head as if that settled the matter. Rising, she walked to the front door. "I'm going to brew myself a pot of tea and let you get back to that conversation I interrupted."

Andrew stared after her. "A lone woman traveling the world? That's the craziest idea I've ever heard of."

Lucy hopped out of her chair and swatted him on the shoulder. "How many times do I have to tell you, your aunt is not crazy?" She slipped into the circle of his arms, which was quickly becoming her favorite place to be, and pressed the tip of her forefinger into the cleft in his chin. A perfect fit, just as she'd suspected. "After all, she knew we were meant for each other, even before we did."

"That she did." Andrew brushed a kiss against her temple, and laughter rumbled from his chest. Framing her cheeks with his hands, he bent his head toward hers. Just before their lips met, she heard him murmur, "I guess Burt and Bessie set a pretty good example, after all."

MEETING HER MATCH

MARY CONNEALY

✶ Chapter 1 ✶

It was downright silly to be the mother to three boys and running a busy household when you were twenty-one and single.

It was a good thing Hannah Taylor was up to it.

"Abraham Taylor, you leave Kevin alone!" Hannah, big sister and schoolmarm, stood at the bottom of the schoolhouse steps. Hannah was a quiet woman and too busy to have much in the way of friends. But when it came to her little brothers, she could melt stubborn with a single glare, and she felt no great need to be quiet with the little varmints. Abe settled down fast. Then she added, "Abe, remember you have to get the clinkers out of the stove."

"It's Jeremy's turn!" Abe wailed.

"You traded with Jeremy for a chance to get out of pitching hay to the horses just yesterday. Now it's time to pay." Hannah went up the steps to the schoolhouse. She paused to wave at Dottie Brighton, who was on her way to Claasen's General Store for supplies. After Dottie smiled and waved

305

back, Hannah hurried inside, leaving her little brothers on the playground. The oldest of them, Jeremy, took charge while Hannah got ready to start the school day. She didn't scold Abe anymore. He was a good boy, just active and noisy. He'd be in to clean out the heating stove soon enough.

Hannah heaved a sigh of relief when she shut the schoolhouse door on the chilly December morning. "Thank heavens I'm back at work so I can get some rest!" She smiled at herself when she thought it. But it was true. The town of Dry Gulch, Texas, halted school for harvest, which was as much work for the women as it was for the men. And Hannah had convinced the school board to give her an extra week of freedom to help prepare for Nelda's wedding. It was Hannah's second little sister to marry. Two Taylor weddings in three years, leaving Hannah the only girl in the family. She had three little brothers, another baby on the way, and a ma who was mighty tired.

As always, Pa was hoping for a boy.

Now here they were, a week before Christmas. There was barely going to be time to organize a school Christmas program, and Hannah loved making Christmas special for her students.

She smiled as shouts of laughter echoed from the playground, all of the noise coming from her little brothers—including two-year-old Kevin, who was too young for school. But Hannah had informed the school board that bringing her baby brother was part of the deal. Hannah couldn't teach if she couldn't bring him along, because Ma wasn't up to it.

She savored the peace of the brisk winter morning in her familiar classroom, enjoying the dusty smell of chalk and the biting odor of ashes from the stone-cold potbellied stove.

She kept her cloak and bonnet on until the stove could be cleaned out and lit, yet she didn't mind that Abe was slow in coming. She needed a few more quiet moments to enjoy her surprising success with helping some lonely friends find happiness.

She hadn't really set out to spark a romance with her meddling. But it was a pleasure to think of her former co-teacher, Grace O'Malley, married to Clayton Weber and already expecting a baby. And word had come back to town that Neill and Clara Archer had married, as well as Lucy and Andrew Simms. Hannah had a hand in all of that and it pleased her to no end. It gave her such a warm feeling that she thought maybe she had a true gift for helping others.

She'd never had much luck helping herself.

Hannah heard the schoolhouse door open and looked up, expecting Abe.

Marcus Whitfield came in with an armful of wood. He'd never delivered the wood before. A member of the school board saw to their wood supply, usually dropping off a week's supply at one time, stacked behind the schoolhouse, but it had never been Marcus. And Hannah routinely assigned the chore of hauling it inside to one of her students.

"Good morning." Hannah had been his classmate in this very school. Now she was the teacher and he was a partner in his father's bank.

Marcus glanced up at her awkwardly and nodded without speaking, then concentrated on where he was walking as if the floor were riddled with holes.

"I hadn't heard that you'd be bringing wood," Hannah said politely, trying not to roll her eyes at Marcus's strange ways.

"Pa's turn." Marcus kept his chin down as he made his way to the stove at the front of the room.

Hannah couldn't imagine Mr. Whitfield, the rather regal president of the town's only bank, ever dropping off wood. And she knew he wasn't on the school board. But maybe he'd volunteered just recently.

From the way he moved along the side of the room, it seemed Marcus was doing his best to stay as far away from her as possible. Marcus was the only unattached church-going man in town. Hannah should probably set her cap for him, but she couldn't quite bring herself to feel any romantic notions about the poor, shy man. Marcus had no interest in her, either. In fact, judging by his effort to keep space between them, he actively disliked her.

Hannah felt a twinge of resentment. She had a sudden desire to march over to him and say, *You can't reject me. I'm rejecting you first, so there!*

She didn't do any such thing, of course. She even had the grace to realize she was having too strong a reaction to a man whose only provable crime was shyness. Why, maybe she'd make Marcus her next project. The man quite obviously needed a wife.

She mulled that over, watching him. So she was gazing right at him when he glanced up at her, saw her looking at him, and fell on his face.

"Marcus!" Jumping up, she rushed over to him. "Are you all right?"

He was sprawled awkwardly on his armload of wood. When he shoved himself up, a piece of kindling under his hand rolled and he fell again. Hannah got to her knees and pulled the small logs scattered under poor Marcus away and tossed them toward the place they'd be stacked. She had most of them removed when Marcus finally managed to get to his knees.

"Your glasses are bent." Hannah's whole life was spent helping people, so it came naturally for her to pluck his spectacles away.

"Here, let me—" she said.

"Hannah, I can fix . . ." Marcus grabbed at her hands.

She looked up to see a streak of blood trickle from the corner of his mouth. "Oh, Marcus, your lip is bleeding." She abandoned his glasses to pull her handkerchief out of the sleeve of her blue gingham dress and dabbed at the small cut.

Marcus rushed to put his glasses on, and his hand tangled with hers as they knelt facing each other. Their eyes locked and held.

Hannah noticed that Marcus, up close, wasn't quite so gangly as she remembered. His eyes were a clear light blue. His hair was blond, almost the same color as hers. His poor lip was mildly swollen and tender looking. The bleeding stopped after only a second or two of pressure from her handkerchief. Not a serious injury and yet she kept glancing at it.

Between looking at his eyes and lips, quite a bit of time passed.

Marcus's hand on hers tightened. He seemed to draw her closer, and she was already very close. "Hannah, I wonder if you'd like to . . . to . . ."

"I have an idea, Hannie!" Abe shouted, charging into the schoolhouse. He stumbled and caught himself against a desk at the back of the room, knocking it out of line.

Hannah surged to her feet and almost ran to her desk,

not sure what had just happened between her and Marcus Whitfield.

"If we don't start the stove, we don't have to clean it," Abe said. "It's warm enough."

Hannah almost laughed out loud. Abe had the earflaps pulled down on his beloved red hat, and his mittens firmly on. Hannah had knitted them for Christmas but made the mistake of telling Pa, who'd insisted on giving the boys their hats and mittens early for the sake of being practical. Abe's cheeks and nose were as red as the cap on his head. But he would rather freeze, and all his classmates along with him, than struggle with the minimal chore of collecting and disposing of the built-up ash in the stove.

Hannah didn't blame him for trying, but it was his turn and he knew it.

Marcus quickly finished stacking the firewood and then nearly ran out of the place. He'd said, *"Hannah, I wonder if you'd like to . . ."* If she'd like to what?

"Nice try, Abe," she said. "Now get to work." She spoke firmly, but her thoughts were drawn back to Marcus and his question. Could he possibly not be quite so indifferent to her as she'd imagined?

Hannah, I wonder if you'd like to go for a carriage ride with me?

Or did he wonder something quite different.

Hannah, I wonder if you'd like to get your own stupid kindling from now on?

Shaking away thoughts of Marcus, she listened with a smile as Abe moaned and groaned his way through the simple job of pulling the cast-iron tray out of the stove and carrying the sooty ashes—along with the hard black "clinkers" of unburned wood—out the door and tossing it all in the ash pile.

Hannah began pulling her books out of the cloth bag she carried. She had fashioned the bag to hang over her shoulder because she usually had Kevin in her arms for most of the three-mile walk to the school.

Hannah prepared for the lessons, making a few last-minute notes. As she worked at her desk, her mind wandered to the reason for this disorganized morning.

Nelda.

The wedding had taken place on Saturday. Hannah had stood up with Nelda, and Marcus Whitfield had been a witness for Rudy. The wedding had gone well, and Hannah was happy for both of them.

She'd been stung by Pa's joke about disguising Hannah, the older sister, and slipping her in as the bride. He'd teased her that he should be like Leah's father in the Bible when he'd tricked Jacob into marrying his older daughter.

As far as a sense of humor went, Pa's left quite a bit to be desired.

Hannah had worked until the wee hours of the morning, setting the house to rights after all the guests had left. Hannah's sister Martha had helped of course, but she had a baby on the way and tired easily. Hannah had shooed her away early. Ma had gone straight back to bed after the wedding, not even joining the guests who came to wish Nelda well.

Ma was frighteningly weak from this baby. Only with the most heroic effort had Ma even attended Nelda's wedding. This would be the seventh Taylor baby. Much as she loved her little brothers and sisters, Hannah fervently hoped this would be the last.

✴ Chapter 2 ✴

Idiot! Mark wanted to slam his head against the school-house wall.

Clumsy, stupid oaf. *Why didn't you just make it perfect and knock poor Hannah over while you were putting your glasses back on?*

The only reason he didn't bang his head against something really hard was because he'd probably knock himself out, then she'd find him, collapsed in a heap, when she came to ring the bell and call the children in to class.

He strode along the street and bitterly noticed that he didn't trip over his own feet, not one single time! Oh no, save that for when he was standing near the prettiest, sweetest woman he'd ever seen. Why did his tongue twist into knots, his feet grow ten sizes, and his face turn flaming red every time he saw her? *Why?*

He was almost to the bank, where he could go in and sit, with paper and numbers. Numbers made sense. He got two and two to equal four every time he tried. With numbers he wasn't an idiot.

He reached for the doorknob on the bank just as the doctor burst out of his office, only a door down, with Hannah's pa a step behind.

Jerome Taylor was moving faster than Mark had ever seen him go.

The doctor rushed for his horse. "I'm not waiting for you, Jerome. I'll see you at the house."

Jerome swung himself up onto his buckboard. The doctor galloped out of town and was gone before Jerome got his horses backed up from the hitching post.

"What's happened, Mr. Taylor? Should I tell Hannah there's trouble?" Mark set aside all shyness as he thought of all Hannah had endured over the years—her fiancé dying, working as a teacher, mothering that huge, ever-growing brood as her ma became a quiet, frail woman rarely seen in town.

Now it looked like more trouble was coming Hannah's way.

Jerome was set to whip his team into motion. Halting, he looked over and said, "The baby came too early. We lost her. Just a girl. But my wife . . ." Jerome wiped his hand across his face for a long moment. Finally he looked straight at Mark. "Whitfield, my wife is dead. I came for the doctor because I need him to see to the body, and he's rushing out there, hoping I'm wrong. But it's too late for him to help. I came inside from morning chores and found the baby born and my wife still and cold. Tell Hannah her ma is dead and to come on home. I'll be needin' help."

Jerome slapped the reins on his horses' broad backs and set off—leaving Mark stunned, mouth gaping. How was he to do such a terrible chore? How could Jerome leave that to someone else? And Mark was supposed to tell Hannah to walk the miles home and bring her little brothers, too?

It wasn't the first time it occurred to Mark that Jerome Taylor was a poor excuse for a father.

He stuck his head in the door of the bank, and his own father looked up from his accounts. "Pa, Mr. Taylor just told me his wife died and her baby, also."

Loyal Whitfield was a stern man with an imperious nature, but Mark was used to him and knew it was mostly bluster. Now Pa set his pen down carefully, his face turning solemn, and why not? A mother dying. A mother with six children, four still at home. It was a solemn business.

"I need to give Hannah the news, then see to calling off school. Can you hitch up the team and bring it around so I can give the Taylor family a ride home? I'd fetch the team, but I'm afraid word will get around and I don't want Hannah to be the last to know."

"I'll get the team right away, son." Pa, usually dictatorial and brusque, looked more upset than Jerome Taylor. "And I'll go over to the general store and ask Mrs. Claasen to come and tend the school. You want to wait for me and I'll come along and help you break the news?"

Mark and his father exchanged a long, sad look before Mark shook his head. "Her pa gave me the job. I'll see to it."

◆———◆———◆

Movement drew her attention to the front door. She'd yet to call the students in, so she prepared to shoo whoever it was back outside.

Marcus Whitfield again. Maybe he'd come to finish that sentence.

This time he looked straight at her. She knew from that

alone that something was wrong. "Come in, Marcus," she said.

Marcus came to the front of the schoolroom. With regret in his eyes he said, "It's your ma, Hannah. The . . . the baby came this morning."

Hannah shook her head. "No, that can't be. It's not due for a long time yet." Even as she denied it, she knew Marcus wouldn't be mistaken about something this important. The very fact that Marcus was speaking in complete sentences told Hannah how serious it was.

"I ran into your pa and the doctor running from his office. Your pa said for me to tell you to come home. The baby was too early, Hannah. She didn't make it."

"A little girl," Hannah whispered sadly. She knew she'd have to call off school and help Ma full time for a few days. Hannah prayed silently for this to be the last baby. Ma just wasn't up to it anymore.

"It's not just the baby, Hannah." Marcus swallowed hard. The gravity of his voice pulled Hannah away from her thoughts about caring for Ma and her sadness over a lost baby sister.

"It's not?" she asked faintly. Her stomach twisted because of the look in Marcus's eyes.

"No, it's your ma. It was . . . she was . . . your pa said she . . . she . . ." Hannah watched Marcus force the words past his lips. "Your pa said it was too late for the doctor to help y-your ma, too. Hannah, I'm sorry. Your ma d-died birthing the baby."

"No!" Hannah rose from her chair and sent it crashing against the wall behind her. She faced Marcus as if he were a wild, dangerous animal. She shook her head. "No, Ma was tired, but she's always tired. No . . ." Hannah's voice got higher and louder. "Don't come in here with that kind of talk."

"Your pa and the doc have already ridden out. Let me get you home, Hannah. Pa's hitching up the team. Mrs. Claasen is on her way to take care of the school. My pa will stay until Mrs. Claasen gets here. It might be best to keep your little brothers away from home for a few hours." Marcus came toward her, his hand outstretched. Hannah backed away until she collided with the blackboard.

Marcus kept coming, and Hannah wanted to run away from him, hit him, hurt him for bringing this hateful news. But Marcus reached her, and instead of striking out, she grabbed at him.

He pulled her close, and she clung to him as the first sob escaped her throat.

✶ Chapter 3 ✶

Hannah knew she was forgetting important things because her little brothers and Pa kept pestering her to make them meals and find them clean clothes.

Kevin cried for his mama all the time. Abe was white-lipped and too quiet. Jeremy was so upset, Hannah was scared for him, afraid he'd turn bad, as he was always lashing out in anger. She needed to help them, but she couldn't gather her thoughts together enough to help anyone.

She found herself turning to Ma for advice, only to be caught by a wicked stab of grief. Ma would never be around again. If there was a conflict between the boys, she settled it the best she knew how. If the gravy didn't thicken, she served it thin with profuse apologies and bowed her head and bore the complaints. Hannah knew how to run a household quite well, but only now did she realize how much she'd depended on her mother.

The winter term of school was lost, and Hannah told them she wasn't up to teaching the spring term. She was just too addled. Rather than replace her, which wasn't easy in a town with few single women, Dry Gulch ended up skipping the spring term, too.

The good folks of Dry Gulch agreed to be patient. It was decided that school wouldn't resume until the next fall.

◆————◆————◆

Hannah had the house running well by then. Pa hadn't wanted her to go back to work because there'd be no one to prepare his midday meals, but perfect Martha and even the grumbler Nelda were each having him over once a week for the noonday meal. To fill in, though he groused about it, Pa stopped in Rosella Bindle's diner in town.

Hannah saw her life laid out before her now, raising her little brothers and caring for Pa. She'd always believed she would marry someday, too, like her little sisters, but now she gave that up. Her family needed her, and she needed them.

She hadn't had the energy to meddle in anyone's life for a while and she regretted that. She'd really helped some people. She knew Neill Archer and Clara Danvers had left the area together, and Mack Danvers, the old tyrant, regaled the town with stories of his former daughter-in-law, Clara, and his grandson. Grace and Clayton Weber were still near Dry Gulch. Hannah saw them every week at church. Grace and Clayton dealt with each new struggle courageously. Word had gotten back to town that Lucy Benson had married Andrew Simms, the nephew who'd searched for help for his aunt. Hannah had sent poor put-upon Lucy.

Hannah had helped those folks. If she ever found any energy, she'd like to help others. But right now she could barely take care of her own family.

Marcus had taken to bringing the firewood every week. So

she saw him regularly, and although he was still awkward, he managed a stilted conversation with her—as long as *she* did most of the talking. Nothing happened again like that moment they'd shared when he'd fallen. But she remembered his kindness when he'd brought the terrible news of Ma's death, and his strong arms when she'd cried. She'd leaned on his shoulder during the long ride home to the ranch. He was a nice man, decent and hardworking. Almost a friend, except he was so quiet.

Her life was the exact opposite of what one pictured as the quiet, lonely life of an old maid. She had three children, for heaven's sake, a crotchety man to care for, and a demanding job that kept her jumping.

If this was spinsterhood, then thank heavens for it, because there was no time for a husband.

✦   ✦   ✦

Winter was tightening its grip on the Texas countryside as Hannah finished the long walk home from school, carrying three-year-old Kevin in her arms. Her brothers tagged along after her. She found Pa sitting at the kitchen table with Essie, the only waitress at Rosella Bindle's diner.

"Essie'n me got married today, Hannie. You're to call her Ma from now on." Pa grinned as he gave her the news.

Hannah stood frozen in the kitchen doorway, unable to think of a thing to say, certainly unable to force the word *Ma* past her lips. Jeremy ran into her back because she'd stopped so suddenly. Kevin wiggled in her arms, and Essie came and plucked him out of her arms. Kevin went easily because he was an outgoing friendly little boy, used to being cared for by all the children at school as well as Hannah. She was too amazed to cling to him, even though the impulse was there.

Jeremy squirmed past her and headed straight for the cookie jar. Abe was right behind and bumped Hannah's shoulders to get by her. She was incapable of movement.

Pa repeated his announcement. "This here's my new wife, boys. We got hitched today and she's yer ma now."

Jeremy and Abe turned to stare at Essie.

Essie had been a widow. Hannah guessed she was around thirty-five. She'd been waiting tables at the diner and living overhead since her husband died years back. Now Essie stood with Kevin on her hip and said to Hannah with a falsely sweet voice, the kind people sometimes used when they were talking down to children, "Two cooks can't share a kitchen—you know that, Hannah. Your pa and I have decided you'll live in my room in town."

Pa grinned and nodded. "You can keep your thirty dollars a month now."

He said it as if letting her keep the money she earned was an act of generosity.

"That, with what you have at the bank, will more'n see to your needs." Pa had banked half of her salary ever since she'd started teaching at age seventeen. He'd kept the other half for the family. Hannah had urged him to take it all. She didn't need any money.

She barely registered the fact that her things were already packed. The team was hitched up and ready to go. She was so stunned she barely noticed herself being escorted out. Only Pa drawing her along, his hand on her arm, made her move.

"Abe, you stay home." He pointed at ten-year-old Abe. "No room for you on the buckboard."

"I'll take Kevin so you won't need to worry over him," Essie said with her perky voice.

"Jeremy, you grab Hannah's trunk and come along. We need help toting. Essie'll ride up front with me. Hannah, you ride with Jeremy in the wagon box."

She glanced behind her and saw Abe in the doorway, white-faced, his jaw rigid, silent. Jeremy had the furious look on his face Hannah recognized from after Ma died. She had hoped that anger was gone forever.

Pa shooed her along as if she were a critter who needed to be herded. When she got to the wagon, because Jeremy hadn't moved, Pa hoisted her trunk in. Essie had Kevin in one arm and a crate full of Hannah's clothes in the other.

What a helpmate she was turning out to be.

Pa took the box from Essie and shoved it in by the trunk. Then he caught Hannah around the waist and boosted her into the back of the wagon. Pa escorted Essie to the front of the wagon and boosted her up.

Essie giggled.

Jeremy jumped into the wagon beside Hannah as if she needed a protector at her side. But it was too late to be protected from Pa's latest folly.

✶ Chapter 4 ✶

Hannah's head still hadn't cleared when she was plunked down in the seedy little attic.

Pa couldn't stop looking at overweight, stringy-haired Essie long enough to notice Hannah's shock or Jeremy's rage. Rosella Bindle, the short, stout, gray-haired woman who owned the diner and had employed Essie for years, was Hannah's new landlady. Mrs. Bindle was no genius of a cook, her voice was loud, and she was given to shouting insults at the bachelor cowpokes she fed daily. But the cowpokes seemed to enjoy Mrs. Bindle's chiding—or at least they pretended to, not wanting to give up their only source of food. And there was no real venom on Mrs. Bindle's part.

She had a pleasant smile for Hannah.

"Welcome." Mrs. Bindle spoke at a near shout, even though the room was tiny and all its occupants were utterly silent. The rumor was Mrs. Bindle was nearly deaf, but most people were too afraid of her to tell her it wasn't necessary to cast her voice quite so wide.

"I'm glad to see you're moving in." Mrs. Bindle slung an arm around Hannah that knocked her forward. "I already miss Essie something fierce in the diner, and I liked knowing she was up here. I hate the idea of the diner being empty at night."

Hannah had no idea what she meant by that. Was Hannah now supposed to guard the place and ward off invaders? That was probably fine. No one much wanted to invade Mrs. Bindle's diner.

Trying one last time to get her pa to think about what he was doing, Hannah said, "Pa, the little ones need time to adjust to this. They already lost Ma. Shouldn't we let them get used to the idea of—"

"They'll see you every day at school," Essie interrupted, smiling and patting her on the shoulder. "And a spinster lady needs to be on her own."

Spinster. Well, that about described her.

"What we need," Mrs. Bindle said, sharing a conspiratorial smile with Essie, "is to find you a husband. It ain't right that a woman lives her life alone. Why, since my Benny died, I've been lonely as all get-out."

"Time to get on home, Essie." Pa held the door for his new bride, his glowering son, and the chipper landlady.

Mrs. Bindle said, "Yep, a man is just what you need. I'll put my mind to it."

Hannah was distracted from her shock at being tossed out of her home by the horror of imagining what kind of man Rosella Bindle might think was a good match.

Hannah had vowed long ago to only marry another believer. Yes, there were plenty of single men around, but she wouldn't consider one who didn't practice the faith, and that didn't describe any of the raucous men who ate at Rosella's diner.

As Essie left, she looked back and said, "A husband is just the thing for you. If you won't see to it, maybe you'd better let Rosella and me scare up a man. Time's a-wastin', Hannah. It's time to grow up."

With that, pushing a recalcitrant Jeremy along in front of them, Pa, Essie, and Mrs. Bindle left Hannah in her attic room, closing the door firmly behind them.

Hannah sank into the threadbare chair Essie had so generously left behind, along with a small bed, a tiny potbellied stove, and a single plate, bowl, and cup—all tin—and one pan.

"Grow up?" Hannah said. "I've been mothering my little brothers and sisters since I was six. I've been running Pa's house since long before Ma died. I've been a schoolmarm since I was seventeen. Grow up?" Her voice echoed in the nearly empty room.

She'd never been alone before. The urge to cry hit her, but she couldn't manage a single tear. The shock ran too deep. She sat in the chair as darkness fell and, still dressed, stared into space, too stunned to move.

◆——◆——◆

Hannah showed up at school out of pure habit. She'd undergone such a radical shift in her life, she was still trying to figure a way to straighten things out.

Jeremy came in with Abe. Essie kept Kevin at home. Of course. Three-year-olds didn't go to school.

Anger etched on his face, Jeremy came up to Hannah and gave her a fierce hug. He pulled away and put strong hands firmly on her shoulders. Hannah realized she was looking straight into his eyes. Jeremy was as tall as she was. "We're going to fix this. You'll be home again before you know it."

Hannah nodded and agreed with him because she wanted to lessen his anger. Then she held the still-silent Abe and told him not to be upset. It wouldn't be long before she was back home. It sounded so good she believed it.

She got through the day by doing what had to be done for her students. But she felt none of her usual joy in teaching, nor even the usual daily aggravations. She was too numb.

After leaving school, she caught herself after just a few steps, walking home to Pa's house. Her brothers always ran straight for home, so by the time Hannah got the school tidied and closed up, she always walked alone. It was not carrying Kevin that jarred her back to reality. She had to stop, close her eyes, and remember where in the world she lived.

Turning toward the diner, she forced her feet to carry her to that drab little room. When she passed the bank, the door slammed open and Marcus Whitfield stumbled out. Poor man. He was so awkward.

Pausing, he met her eyes for a split second. "Hello, Hannah." He came out of the bank, closed the door, and walked up beside her. "I'm going for coffee."

"I'm living above the diner now, did you hear?" Hannah found herself wanting to pour her heart out to Marcus . . . of all people. Better she should talk with her sisters, but they weren't there.

"Yep." Marcus said nothing else. He didn't ask how she liked it there or what happened. He didn't comment on Pa remarrying.

Hannah wondered exactly what form her pa and Essie's

courtship had taken. Had everyone in town known? Had it been going on long? Or had Pa decided yesterday to remarry, picked Essie out from the short list of unmarried women in town, and proposed over lunch, to be married after dessert?

Did Marcus know about this?

He took one step, and Hannah realized she was holding him up on his quest for coffee. He probably only got a short break.

She walked along beside him, aching with loneliness, but nothing about Marcus's demeanor seemed to offer her an opening to talk.

When they arrived at the diner, he reached up, and Hannah thought he was going to tug on the brim of his hat to say good-bye without the chore of actually talking. Except his hat wasn't there.

"Good-bye, Hannah." Marcus went to turn the doorknob, but his hand slipped right off, like maybe his palm was sweaty. He quickly grabbed it again, nearly fighting his way into the diner.

Such an odd man. Good-hearted, but so strange. Hannah remembered her vow about marrying a believer, and Marcus was the only single man left in town who preferred church to the saloon. She should set her cap for him. She'd had such a thought when at Nelda's wedding, noticing Marcus as he stood up for Rudy.

But did being a fine man mean he'd be a fine husband? Hannah suspected he'd never speak to her if they were married, and he certainly would never speak to her enough to ask her to marry him. Why, he'd never speak to her enough to ask her to join him for coffee!

Add to that, as his wife, she'd spend great stretches of time picking him up when he fell over his own two feet.

She went on to her room in the diner's attic. When she got there, it was so dismal it wiped all thoughts of Marcus from her mind.

✳ Chapter 5 ✳

Hannah was practically his neighbor.

Marcus wanted her closer still. He wanted her in his house, as his wife. But he hadn't worked up the nerve to tell her that.

Yet.

But her moving to town seemed like progress, if a man measured progress at the speed of an elderly gout-riddled tortoise.

Or if a man was an idiot.

She walked the length of Main Street at ten minutes after four every afternoon on her way home from school, right past the bank window.

Mark knew because he was newly in the habit of going for coffee at the diner at exactly ten minutes after four.

Even now he was standing near the bank window, watching down the street. If he was attentive—and he was—he could see her coming out of the schoolhouse at the far end of town. The school was set apart just a bit, and there was a livery stable that blocked that end of town, but Hannah was visible for about three seconds as she walked down the steps. Then she vanished behind the livery and was too close to be visible as she walked along the bank's side of the street.

But he knew she was coming.

He had just enough time to get his coat on and step outside casually just as she came up to the bank.

"Marcus, going for coffee?"

"I am. How was school?" Why didn't he ask her to join him for coffee? Why didn't he tell her he'd like her to stay and have dinner with him? Why didn't he tell her everyone in the whole town called him Mark and had for years? Why didn't he stop being such a half-wit?

It had taken him two weeks to come up with "How was school?"

"We had two boys out today with the measles. I think the rest of the students have had it before, so . . ." Hannah always had a story, told in her quiet way. Which was good because it required no talking from Mark's tied tongue. They walked nearly one full block together. The best two minutes of Mark's day.

Then he'd get to the diner door and tell her good-bye and turn in.

One of these days he'd ask her to stay with him, join him for coffee. Except the coffee was so awful it would be an offense to lure Hannah into drinking a cup.

They reached the diner. "Good-bye, Hannah."

"Good-bye, Marcus." Hannah didn't even pause. She took a few more steps, turned, and went down the alley to reach the back door to the diner, which led to a stairway up to her room.

And Mark had to go into the diner and drink that foul-tasting burnt mess they called coffee. It was none too good any time, and by this time of day it was nothing but black sludge and bitter dregs. Not unlike Mark's life. He shuddered through every sip, gulping it fast, like bitter medicine, then carefully did it all over again the next day.

He went back to the bank, and his father was standing just inside with his pocket watch open. When Mark came in, Father snapped the lid shut on the watch. "Two minutes for the walk. Two minutes for the coffee. One minute to walk back. Five minutes of your life, every day." Shaking his head, Father added, "Why don't you just ask the girl out to dinner, for heaven's sake?"

Mark shrugged out of his coat. He'd pretended that he didn't know what Father meant the first time they'd had this talk, and now he was beyond pretense. "She barely knows I'm alive. She only glances at me; she never even slows down. It's like she can't wait to get our little walk over with. No, that's not right—she doesn't walk faster, either. She doesn't even care enough about me to dislike me. She'd pay more attention if a stray dog trotted beside her."

"Well, you could ask her to put a collar around your neck. Buckling it would slow her up a bit." Father laughed.

"Mark, what is wrong with you?"

Wincing, Mark looked past his father. "Ma, I didn't see you there."

"You're clearly not up to the task of asking that woman to spend time with you," she said.

Ma was small and round. She always wore beautiful dresses and had her white hair coiled neatly atop her head. She had a pleasant smile and the temperament of a steaming locomotive that would run you right over if you didn't get out of her way.

"I declare it's time someone stepped in," she said.

Mark felt his face heating up. He knew it would be flaming red in moments. His normal reaction was to run and find a private place until his head turned back to a normal color, but not today—not with his mother saying such a thing.

"You wouldn't say anything, would you?" Mark stood right in his mother's way as if he'd block her from leaving. He loved his ma dearly, but right now he was tempted to drag her home and lock her in the attic, as he would any mad relative. If he had an attic.

His mother of course had no fear of him, which was a terrible shame.

"I would never embarrass you, Mark." She tapped him on one of his red cheeks.

"It's just that she's been through so much, with Charlie dying and all." Charlie was the boy Hannah had intended to marry, one of Mark's best friends. Charlie's death had been such a shock to all of them. Mark wouldn't have dreamed of approaching Hannah as she was grieving his loss. But that had been nearly six years ago now. "Then her ma was ill, and then her ma died. And her brothers needed her after her ma's death."

"Well, they certainly don't need her anymore, now that Essie is caring for them."

"But I can see how being dumped in that attic room affected her. She needs time to get over the shock. I'm waiting until she's adjusted."

Ma snorted. "The earlier reasons may be good ones, but having to live over the diner isn't shocking enough to stop a reasonable man."

"Implying I'm not reasonable?" Mark, who'd excelled in

math and balanced account books for a living, was the very definition of reasonable.

"I'm not *implying* anything. I'm saying it out loud, straight to your face that you, a man I'm proud to call my son, one of the finest, smartest, most handsome young men imaginable, are ridiculous when it comes to Hannah, and you know it."

He'd been enjoying her kind words until she said "most handsome." That was his mother's love affecting her eyesight.

Ma wasn't done. "Leaving her in that room to get over her shock is the very opposite of reasonable. She's a lovely woman living alone in a tiny room. It's probably cold up there. It's probably tainted from years of fumes from Rosella's miserable cooking. It might be infested with vermin. It might even be a firetrap."

Ma was making things up now, but she was good at it. Now there was frozen in Mark's mind a vision of Hannah, cold, dodging rats, dying in flames. Not fair.

"I just want to give her a bit more time." In truth, he needed to give himself a bit more time. But he'd speak to Hannah of personal things soon. He just had to work up the nerve. "Promise me you won't meddle."

"Now, Mark, you know I'd never do anything to cause you unhappiness."

He gave a sigh of relief. She patted his fiery cheek and swept around him, moving very fast for an older woman.

Marcus considered himself a bright man, but for some reason it didn't occur to him until he was lying in bed that night that, honestly, his mother's promise was incredibly vague.

* Chapter 6 *

It was getting harder to believe she'd ever go home as Christmas drew near. Hannah's whole family had gone on without her. Even Jeremy appeared to be getting accustomed to Hannah's absence and had started calling Essie *Ma*. Essie was untidy but she fed the boys well and didn't ever punish them that Hannah could tell. Better than if she was too harsh, but Hannah's little brothers were getting to be a handful at school.

Hannah almost wished Essie would be more of a taskmaster when Hannah had to scold Abe for tromping into the school without wiping his feet.

"Ma don't fuss at me for a few clumps of mud, Miss Taylor." His sass died on his lips. "Uh . . . I mean, Hannie."

It cut straight to Hannah's heart.

She was still fretting over how to manage her unruly little brothers when, walking home from school on a Friday night, Hannah met Dottie Brighton on the street.

Hannah saw Marcus come out of the bank, look her way, hesitate, then turn and head for the diner alone. He would normally have walked with her, but he wouldn't consider waiting, of course. It wasn't like he considered their daily chat important. She thought his shoulders slumped more than usual.

"I just heard at Claasen's that Essie's expecting a baby." Dottie smiled as if chatting about the simplest of happy news.

"A b-baby?" It wasn't simple to Hannah. It was stunning. And Dottie told her as if it were all over town.

"Yes, of course. Hadn't you heard? Well, I'm sure it comes as no surprise. After all, Essie's a fairly young woman, and you know your pa. Always wanting more sons." Dottie rolled her eyes and headed on home, not knowing she'd just blown Hannah's life apart.

Hannah couldn't remember how she'd gotten to her room. She swung her door open and stopped.

For the first time she really saw where she lived. She'd never planned on staying, so she'd paid it no mind. Until now.

It was dingy and untidy. Her flyspecked windows mocked her. The bed in the corner of the single room was unmade. A wooden crate sitting on the floor held her clothes. A single shelf in the kitchen held her plate, bowl, and cup. One of each was all she owned. She'd never needed more, because she'd never invited anyone over for dinner.

The few cooking utensils Essie had left behind were stacked with the plate and the meager supply of foodstuffs Hannah kept on hand. The potbellied stove burned badly because the soot had never been cleaned out.

Hannah realized she'd deliberately chosen to live so poorly because to make the place pretty would be to admit she was staying.

The news about Essie and a baby had torn the blinders off Hannah's eyes. She was never going home. No, better to say, she *was* home.

Well, it was high time to face the facts. Her father's remarriage hadn't been a betrayal to anyone. In fact, to the rest of Dry Gulch, it had been a foregone conclusion. A new baby on the way was the same.

And now here she stood, a woman who'd always taken pride in her home, when all along it had been her pa's. Now that she had her own, it was slovenly and shameful.

With a shudder Hannah admitted she wasn't going anywhere. And that meant she needed to make this tiny attic into a home.

Essie had said it, but it had taken Hannah a long time to hear her.

It was time to grow up.

———◆———◆———◆———

Hannah spent Saturday on her knees, scrubbing. She did plenty of praying while she was down there, too. And if once in a while she caught herself scrubbing with more force than necessary, and realized she was imagining her father's face under her scouring brush, well, she stopped and went back to her prayers.

Her knees ached when she finally finished the last grungy little corner of the room. She lifted the full washbasin, headed down the narrow stairway, and heaved the last of many buckets of gritty brown water into the alley.

She climbed back up the stairs and took stock of the place. Her room was so small the bed took up one whole wall, but it was neatly made with clean linen. The beautiful wedding-ring quilt she'd had stored in her hope chest now covered it.

The gleaming window in the wall between the bed and the newly cleaned stove now had a pretty curtain of tatted lace. Hannah's open hope chest sat below the window, and the embroidered linens Hannah had painstakingly created with her own hands were spilling out of it.

She had several dresses and her cloak hanging from nails on the wall opposite the bed. A wooden crate on the floor under her dresses held her other bits of clothing.

Her only other possession was Essie's chair.

Hannah only controlled the urge to toss the ugly chair down the steps and out into the alley because she had nowhere else to sit. But soon. She had to do something soon. And she knew just what.

She was going to buy herself a Christmas present. She went to the window and looked outside, afraid she'd let the whole Saturday slip past while she worked. It was late afternoon, but the businesses weren't closed yet. She gave herself a quick sponge bath to wash away all the grime, then quickly changed from her housedress to a fresh blue woolen one. With nimble fingers she undid her braid, combed her disheveled hair, rebraided it, and twisted it into a tidy bun at the base of her neck.

She pulled on her cloak against the December weather, tossed one last disgruntled look at the chair, and marched down the stairway and out into the sharp cold of the north-Texas winter. She went straight to the bank.

Marcus Whitfield was seated behind the counter. Hannah considered the man as he sat there. He was her friend even though he never spoke a word that wasn't required of him.

They had their daily walk together, which she realized for the first time he could have avoided with little trouble simply by waiting until she'd passed the bank on her walk home.

He didn't speak much to her, but she knew he could talk just fine. She'd heard him visiting with others after church. But when she wandered near, Marcus always turned quiet.

"Merry Christmas, Marcus."

He looked up from his ledgers reluctantly, as if he were reading a riveting novel instead of columns of numbers.

"Hannah." He nodded with one small tilt of his chin. He silently waited for her to speak.

"I'd like to withdraw ten dollars from my bank account, please. I'm buying myself a new chair for Christmas."

"Claasen's." Marcus went to the cashier's window and opened the drawer in front of him on that single cryptic word, but Hannah knew what he'd meant.

"The general store has chairs, then?" she asked curiously. "I thought I'd need to have one built. I don't remember seeing any chairs in the store."

Marcus stared into the drawer, as usual not making eye contact with her. "Settlers lightened their load. Just today."

"Oh, I hope there's something there I can use. The single chair in my place is so dreary. I want to brighten up the place a bit." Some twist of loneliness made her add, "I'm making some changes, Marcus. I've just now realized that I've spent the last years feeling sorry for myself. Grieving for Ma, raising my little brothers, missing Charles." Charles was the boy she thought she'd marry until he was killed in a fall from a bucking horse. "All in all, I've wasted years of my life. That's a sad thing for a woman only twenty-two to admit, isn't it?"

"They've been tough years." That was a whole sentence, which for Marcus was pretty good.

"Yes, yes, it has been tough. I suppose I earned the right to every tear I've shed in that time. Thank you for reminding me."

Marcus surprised her then by looking into her eyes. She could see the struggle he had lifting his chin, which seemed fastened to his chest when she was around, and she appreciated that he made the effort. She was also a little surprised to notice how pure blue his eyes were. Intelligence gleamed out of his eyes along with his shyness. He'd been smart in school. The two of them always competing for top of the class—Marcus usually bested her.

"I can help get the chair up to your room . . . that is, if you find one," he said politely.

Two sentences. A personal record for Marcus. "Why, thank you, Marcus. I hadn't really thought about how I would carry it, because I didn't expect to find one so quickly. I'll let you know."

Hannah took the ten-dollar coin from him and said again, "Thank you." And then she left the bank, a woman on a mission.

She crossed the street and walked into Claasen's. Essie was there shopping. Pa was nowhere in sight, and neither were Hannah's little brothers. Essie was talking with Marcus Whitfield's mother and Gertie Claasen. Dottie Brighton was there, too, visiting with Grace Weber and guiding her through the store, pointing out what merchandise there was, so sightless Grace could choose the items she wanted.

Every person in the store turned when Hannah came in. Essie and Mrs. Whitfield exchanged a glance that was a bit too sharp. She wondered if they'd been talking about her, but that was unlikely. Dottie and Grace exchanged a few quiet words, too, but Hannah assumed Dottie was telling Grace who had come in.

She greeted them with a special word for Grace, who at one time had taught at the school with Hannah. Then Hannah's gaze fell on a stack of furniture jumbled in the store so that it blocked the shelves on one wall. The first thing she noticed was a wooden rocking chair just like the one she'd rocked her little brothers in.

Hannah asked, "How much do you want for that chair, Mrs. Claasen?" Hannah hoped Essie didn't take offense that her old chair wasn't good enough. But Essie didn't seem like an overly sensitive sort, which was a good trait when dealing with Hannah's pa.

"Two dollars. Like as not these folks thought they could bring their whole house west with 'em." Mrs. Claasen sniffed.

Hannah noticed a small, delicately carved table and two matching wooden chairs. And there was a beautifully polished wooden bed frame leaning in pieces against one wall.

Essie and Prudence Whitfield seemed to be talking about something terribly important. Hannah didn't know the women were overly friendly. Dottie and Grace went and joined in the quiet conversation.

"I have ten dollars, Mrs. Claasen. Would that pay for the table and chairs, too? And how much would you want for that bed frame?"

Essie came and put an arm on Hannah's shoulder. "I'm glad to see you fixing up your place, Hannie. It needed doing."

Hannah had a surprising surge of affection for Essie, and she gave the woman a one-armed hug, glad that Essie wasn't taking offense that she was changing things in the attic room.

"These are pretty pieces," Mrs. Whitfield said, studying the furniture. "You have excellent taste."

She seemed a bit too enthused, and Hannah had no idea why. Especially since this was the only furniture in Claasen's store. It said little about a person's taste when the choices were so limited.

Mrs. Claasen smiled. "You've been real good to our boy at school, Hannah. I know what a handful he is. Ten dollars is just about what I gave those folks for the furniture, and I don't really have a place for it in the store. If you'll haul it away today, I won't have to do a bunch of rearranging. I'll give you the lot for ten dollars."

Hannah couldn't control her pleasure as she pictured the lovely furniture brightening up her room. "Done," she said, and nodded firmly.

Essie smiled so kindly that the last of Hannah's resentment slid away. Hannah doubted she'd ever be able to call Essie *Ma*, but she was part of Hannah's family and it was good they felt kindly toward each other.

"Well, it was nice to see you, but I need to run an errand." The abrupt way Essie spoke seemed to have a deeper meaning, but Essie hurried out before Hannah could find out if something was wrong.

Essie's errand had her running across the street and into the diner, where Hannah could see the owner, Rosella Bindle, through a dirty window. The two women began talking rapidly, and Hannah thought Rosella looked out the window and straight into her eyes.

Mrs. Whitfield whispered something to Mrs. Claasen that pulled Hannah's attention back to the furniture. Mrs. Whitfield stopped whispering.

Mrs. Claasen smiled. "I'll be closing up for the night in about a half hour. I'll wait while you get things hauled away, but if you could make it quick, I'd appreciate it. I've got to get home and put a meal on."

With a strangely sharp look, Mrs. Claasen added, "You could use some help carrying these things."

"I think Marcus is still working," Mrs. Whitfield said as if she despaired of her son ever doing anything but work. "I'll see if he's available." She hurried away before Hannah could stop her from pestering Marcus.

Even though it would take several trips, Hannah knew she could carry these things herself. But it was too late. Mrs. Whitfield was steaming across the street like a locomotive.

Hannah handed the ten dollars over. "I'll get things moved as soon as I can."

Mrs. Claasen smiled a bit too enthusiastically. "Thank you, dear."

Reaching for the rocking chair, Hannah was stopped by a gentle but firm hand on her arm. "I'd like to help you carry that, Hannah," Dottie said, "but Clayton is waiting for Grace at my home."

"That's fine. I can do it myself." Hannah reached again for the chair.

Again Dottie caught her arm as if she wished to delay Hannah for some reason. "We haven't seen much of you lately. Now that you're living in town, you should join our sewing circle."

Hannah said, "I think that's a good idea. I've been too

focused on myself, Dottie. I'm going to try and be more sociable." Hannah had let herself sink into self-pity when she should have been friendlier. Why, she hadn't even taken the time to meddle in anyone's life for a while. Her eyes went to Grace, who was standing by Dottie. Grace looked wonderful. She was round with Clayton's child and glowing with serene contentment, even though she was blind. Hannah had no business feeling sorry for herself when Grace was managing with so many challenges.

"I haven't seen you for a long time." Hannah pulled her old co-teacher into a hug. "I'm happy I ran into you today."

In the moment they hugged, Grace whispered, "I know you were part of bringing Clayton into my life, Hannah. Thank you. I know you'll have your own happy event soon."

Grace released her after that odd comment. Dottie seemed to be looking out the front window, and suddenly she stopped looking and tugged on Grace's arm, and the two them said good-bye and bustled out of the store.

Was every woman who'd spoken to her acting strange or was it all Hannah's imagination? Well, she'd worry about that later. For now she had to get this furniture home.

Her room was just across the street, down an alley to the back of the diner, and up a single flight of stairs. No one piece of furniture was overly heavy, and she could manage alone by taking several trips.

She stepped out of the general store to see that Marcus had just come out of the bank, straight across the street from her. His mother shoved his coat into his hands and he pulled it on. His mother smiled at Hannah and waved, then hurried toward the diner. Hannah could see that once inside, Mrs. Whitfield began talking with Essie and Rosella.

Marcus strode over the packed dirt of the street and climbed the steps in front of Claasen's, his feet thudding on the wooden sidewalk. "Ma said you could use a helping hand."

Hannah smiled at him. "I ended up with more than just this rocking chair. I also bought a table and two other chairs and a bedstead." She pointed into the store to see Mrs. Claasen talking with her husband.

Mrs. Claasen was watching her and Marcus through her window. She saw Hannah point, and Mrs. Claasen and her husband both waved cheerfully. A bit weakly, Hannah waved back, at a loss as to why the couple was so happy. Maybe they really needed the ten dollars.

Marcus reached for the chair. He was six inches taller than she and he had a lanky body that made him seem taller still, but to Hannah he had always been a scarecrow of a man. He hefted the chair away from her as if it weighed nothing, and she noticed his upper arm muscles bulge beneath his coat.

Why, Marcus wasn't a scarecrow of a man at all. He strode straight out onto the frozen ruts of the street toward the diner. Hannah watched him for a few seconds, drawn to the way he moved. She probably should go back for the next piece of furniture, but instead she followed Marcus. He got across the street and went down the alley between the diner and the building next door, to Hannah's door in the back. She hurried to keep up with his long-legged stride.

When he got near the door, she rushed past him and opened it.

"Thank you, Hannah." He waited for an instant before she realized he was waiting for her to go first. She thought of the second door at the top of the stairs and knew she

343

would need to open it. Feeling rude for making him wait with the chair, she stepped in, awkwardly holding the door open ahead of him. He stepped close to block the door open with his body. Very close.

She left the door to him and headed up to her room, with Marcus following her. As they stepped inside, Hannah thought she heard a squeak, like someone else was coming up the stairs. Was Mr. Claasen helping carry the furniture, too? Hannah turned to thank the man just as Marcus said, "You want me to put this where the old chair is?"

Hannah noticed her door had swung shut, which it rarely did. Maybe she hadn't closed the door downstairs firmly and there was a draft.

Marcus set the rocker down beside Essie's old chair.

"No, let me move it." Hannah reached for Essie's chair.

"I can get the chair." Marcus rushed toward it.

Hannah bumped into him. Marcus stumbled.

Marcus grabbed her by the waist to steady himself. Then his warm hands flexed against her sides, which felt unbelievably nice. She glanced up at him and their gazes locked. Time stood still in Hannah's little room. Sounds from outside faded to nothing.

Those strong hands tightened and pulled her closer. Marcus's eyes changed to a darker, warmer shade of blue. A color so intriguing, Hannah felt she needed to study it a bit longer. Then he leaned down an inch at a time and settled his mouth on hers.

✳ Chapter 7 ✳

A thousand wishes and as many prayers, hundreds of dreams that stretched through the days and nights, years and years of wanting and wondering, and now he finally was where he'd longed to be, standing with Hannah in his arms, kissing her.

He'd longed to kiss Hannah Taylor since the first time he'd laid eyes on her at school when he and his family had moved to town.

He'd been eleven at the time.

Back then, just as he'd been working up his nerve to talk to her—he'd been working at it for almost four years—she started going around with Charlie. It had broken Mark's fifteen-year-old heart, but he knew that Charlie was the better man. Charlie was handsome and charming and one of the nicest guys Mark knew.

Then Charlie died.

Mark had left Hannah alone to grieve.

Then he'd left her alone because her ma was ailing.

Then he'd left her alone because her ma had died.

Then he'd left her alone because she was busy with her little brothers.

345

Then he'd seen her quiet, hurt expression when she'd been as good as thrown out of her own home to live in the tiny room over the diner, and he'd left her alone to get over that.

He'd been hauling the school's firewood. He lurked by the bank window like a cowering hound and watched her leave school so he could stumble outside and have a two-minute walk with her every day. He greeted her after church each week. Once he'd offered to carry her groceries.

He admitted his attempts had been pathetic, just like everything about him was pathetic.

Then today, at his ma's prodding, even though he was in the middle of the bank audit late on a Saturday afternoon, working in the safe and filling cash bags, which took time to close up, he'd rushed out to lend her a hand hauling furniture. He'd offered earlier, but Mark suspected that if it hadn't been for his ma fussing at him to go help, Hannah would have handled the furniture herself and he would have let her.

And now . . . now he was kissing her, and not only had she not slapped him but she was kissing him back!

Her arms settled around his neck, and Mark almost lost his mind from the sweetness of it. He wanted to break off the kiss and beg her to marry him, but that would require talking, and somehow when he was around Hannah something jammed up in his chest and words were close to impossible.

So instead, since it was going well, he kept kissing her. He wrapped his arms around her waist and pulled her closer and she came to him. She willingly, even eagerly maybe, tightened her arms on his neck.

He slid one hand into her hair and tilted her head to slant his mouth over hers and deepened the kiss. She stayed right with him.

The whole world seemed to go away as Marcus poured all his years of longing into one endless, perfect kiss.

Marcus never wanted this moment to end.

A sharp rap at the door made Hannah jump out of his arms.

"Hannah Taylor, have you got a man in there?"

Rosella Bindle's nasal north-Texas twang made both of them whirl toward the door as if they'd been caught doing something wrong, which they most certainly had.

Mark felt his cheeks heat up in the blush he so despised. Going to Hannah's room and shutting the door, a single man and woman—it was scandalous.

He glanced sideways at Hannah just as she looked frantically at him. He saw more than guilt on Hannah's face, though. He saw shock, as if she'd just now realized she'd been kissing worthless Mark Whitfield.

Mark couldn't stand to be alone with that expression another second. He hurried to the door and turned the knob. It was locked.

Mark looked at Hannah. "Did you lock the door?"

"No!" She grabbed a key hanging from a nail and reached for the lock. In her rush to escape him, she dropped the key with a loud *ping*, which was as good as a confession that they'd locked themselves in the room on purpose.

Mark swooped to pick it up at the same time she did, and they almost cracked heads.

Mrs. Bindle hammered louder. "You make yourselves decent and get this door open."

Hannah looked at Mark and said, horrified, "Make yourselves decent?"

Mark's face felt so hot it would likely ignite any second. He jammed the key into the lock and quickly got the door open. Mrs. Bindle marched in.

Essie was right behind her, looking upset. Mark's mother stood one step behind Essie with the look of a woman whose son had just been sentenced to hanging. In fact, Mark thought his ma, a very calm woman, looked a bit overly—perhaps even theatrically—upset.

Short and brusque, Rosella stormed straight into the middle of the room, all of three steps, as if she were charging to the rescue. "Now see here, Hannah, I made the rules absolutely clear when you moved in."

"Mrs. Bindle—" Hannah started politely.

"There were to be no gentleman callers of any kind."

"It's not like it seems," Hannah argued.

"It seems," Rosella said, "like you and Mark were alone together in your bedroom with the door locked."

"Well, then it's exactly like it seems, but I can explain—"

"I run a respectable business downstairs," Rosella said, cutting Hannah off.

Mark thought *respectable* was a little much. She ran the only diner in town, so it kept fairly busy serving tough beef and overcooked beans, with biscuits that veered erratically between doughy and rock hard, never finding a middle ground. It wasn't overly clean, and Rosella was known to keep the boisterous crowd of customers in gales of laughter with her insults. Her customers were mainly single cowboys, because anyone with a wife ate at home.

"Mark, what is the meaning of this?" his mother demanded. She sounded distraught.

"He was helping me carry," Hannah tried to explain.

Rosella narrowed her eyes. "Helping you carry on, it seems to me."

"You've been up here quite a while actually," Mrs. Whitfield said.

For one awkward moment Mark wondered how long he and Hannah had spent kissing. True, it had only seemed like a minute, but Mark had lost track of time.

"Essie," Hannah said, turning to her stepmother, "you know I only left the store a few minutes ago."

Mrs. Claasen chose that moment to yell up from the street below. "Are you coming back, Hannah? We'd like to lock up the store now."

Mark knew he should jump in and defend Hannah's honor, but he was still stunned from the kiss and how Hannah had responded to him. And talking never came easily to him at any time, but especially not under duress.

"As the only teacher in Dry Gulch, you have an obligation to uphold the very highest moral standards." Rosella sounded lofty for a woman who slung hash for a living. "You think the minute my back is turned you can ride the whirlwind?"

Mark almost smiled at that image. It *had* been a little bit of a whirlwind. Mrs. Bindle was hitting the whole situation just about exactly right. Except how in the world had the door gotten locked?

"Mrs. Bindle, except for a few brief visits from my family, I've never had so much as a visitor. How can you think so poorly of—"

Mark finally found his tongue. "If you were watching us, you saw us come up those stairs only minutes ago."

"Now, Mark," his ma said, "it was more like—"

"Let me finish!" He'd never spoken to his mother like that before.

She arched a brow at him that threatened reprisal later, yet Mark went on talking. "I carried that chair. I set it down and then moved the other out of the way. Neither of us swung the door shut and neither of us locked it. It must've jammed somehow when it closed."

"By itself?" Essie asked with quiet skepticism. "Closed and locked by itself?"

Mark ignored the interruption. "We're on our way right now to collect the other pieces of furniture that Hannah purchased at Claasen's. Now, would we stay in here when we know Mrs. Claasen is waiting to close?"

"I really do need to hurry, Hannah," Mrs. Claasen sang out from below.

Mark soldiered on in the face of some of the more formidable women he'd ever seen, most especially his ma. "Would we leave that furniture while we—as you so rudely put it— carried on? If you don't trust Hannah and me to do this chore, then I suggest you all come along and grab a piece of furniture." He looked at Essie, then his ma. "I will not hear a word against Hannah. Do you understand me?"

His mother narrowed her eyes a bit. Essie looked more amused than chastised.

Rosella said, "I'll be watching you, and I want this door left open even if you have to prop it!" With an indignant huff she stalked out of the room.

Mark met his ma's eyes next. "We'll talk about this later, Ma."

"I'll go in just a moment," she said, every inch the wealthy banker's wife. She turned to address Hannah. "You, young lady, might want to straighten your hair. It seems to be quite a bit messier than when you were buying furniture a *half hour ago.*"

Mark winced. *A half hour?* Had they really been up here for a half hour?

Hannah reached for her hair, and only then did Mark realize it was hanging free. He was shocked at how much he wished he remembered doing that.

Ma plucked a long blond hair off Mark's collar, and with a quick rub of her thumb and two fingers she opened her hand to let the hair float gently to the floor. "Your hair could stand straightening, too, son."

He wondered what it looked like. He seemed to remember Hannah's fingers there.

"You can be sure we *will* talk about this later." Ma jerked her head with the attitude of a woman who was not easy to fool, then turned and stomped with unnecessary firmness down the stairs.

This was not the first time Mark was glad he had his own home.

That left Essie, the closest thing Hannah had to a ma. "Essie, I respect Hannah too much to ever hurt her or harm her reputation. And you know Hannah well enough to know she's completely honorable. Please, head on down now."

With a smirk Essie said, "Her pa's gonna hear about this."

Silently, exchanging not so much as a glance, Hannah hurried out after Essie. Mark made a halfhearted attempt to stop her, but Hannah dodged his outstretched hand and scurried along after her stepmother. Mark could do nothing but follow.

They finished toting the furniture, getting separated as Hannah practically ran back and forth between Claasen's and her room. Mark hustled to keep up so she wouldn't do it all herself. Rosella watched them from the bottom of the steps the whole time.

Hannah got so far ahead of him that they were meeting on the street, and each time they did she'd give him an insincere smile. It was more than their getting caught "whirlwinding" by Rosella. Mark could tell she'd had time to think things over and was horrified that she'd let him kiss her. Hannah had always been perfectly polite to him, but she had sent out clear signals that she wasn't interested. Now she'd had a weak moment and was shamed by her behavior. Mark hurt for her discomfort at the same time he felt like his heart was breaking.

It was worse than all the years of not knowing. It was worse than all the frustrating dreams he held in his heart. At least he'd been able to lie to himself and think somehow, someday, God would open her eyes. Well, now her eyes were wide open, and she was horrified at what she saw.

His steps slowed as he carried the table to the bottom of her steps. He didn't want the job to be over because he was sorely afraid it was the first and last time he'd ever do anything with Hannah. He got to the alley door of the diner just as Hannah came down the stairs dragging the ugly chair that had been in the room when Mark had first entered.

He said in a voice that sounded pitiful to himself, "I'll bring the old bed down and haul it and the chair for you."

She nodded without looking up and passed by him wordlessly. He hefted the table upstairs. He lingered a moment, hoping she would follow him up and he could say something, anything, to put her at ease. *Forget what happened between us, Hannah. It'll never happen again. I know you think I'm a poor excuse for a man. Please, can't you love me anyway, like I love you? Marry me . . .*

But she didn't come, which was probably just as well. He finally left and found her standing on the landing near the alley door—along with Rosella, who was standing like a watchdog at her side.

Mark walked down the steps and faced her. There was no possible way he could have even the briefest private word with Hannah.

"Thank you for your help, Marcus," Hannah said primly, staring at her feet.

"I was glad to be of service," he replied.

Hannah looked up and their eyes locked for a moment. Mark searched for some indication she wanted to spend more time with him. He only saw that she'd risked her respectability and her livelihood for a kiss she regretted with all of her heart. It was too much. He walked past her without another word.

* Chapter 8 *

There were only a few folks gathered for church. It was early but Mark hadn't been able to sleep after the disaster with Hannah, so he'd been up and ready for services early. Rudy was there. He was a good friend. Clayton Weber had arrived, too. He'd married Grace, who used to teach with Hannah, before Grace lost her vision. Grace now stood talking with Nelda, her belly round with a baby. The two women stood close to the church door, chatting while the men gathered by the hitching post.

Somehow Clayton and Grace were making their marriage work in tough circumstances, while Mark couldn't even find the nerve to ask Hannah to spend some time with him.

Mark walked toward his friends, wondering how he was going to live without even the hope of Hannah ever loving him. He'd never been able to work up the nerve to talk to her before. And now, after yesterday's humiliation, talking to her had passed into the realm of the unthinkable.

He felt the air stir as he caught the sweet floral scent that moved with her. Or he was just so fiercely attuned to her that there was some kind of connection between them—

apparently a connection that went only one way. He wasn't sure how he knew, because he hadn't seen her yet, but Hannah had just arrived.

How come every other man had the nerve to go after the woman he wanted? He pondered that until he wanted to punch himself in the head.

Hannah would pass them and say hello politely, and Clayton and her brother-in-law would say hello back, while Mark's throat would clamp shut so he could only nod or touch his hat or make some vague noise that she probably wouldn't hear. Then she'd go off to huddle with the women until the church bell called them inside.

Except she didn't do that this morning. When Mark spotted Hannah, she wasn't anywhere near. She stayed well away from him to get to Nelda and Grace. Mark took her avoidance as a direct blow and was still reeling from the implications of how unhappy she was about his oafish kiss. He didn't hear what Rudy said.

Rudy shook Mark's shoulder. "So, did she?"

Mark shook his head to try and clear it. He stuttered as he forced the words out, "Did she w-what?"

Rudy laughed loudly, a trait Mark had always thought was crude, but then Clayton joined in only slightly less raucously, which wasn't like him.

Finally Clayton said, "He asked you about Hannah. I heard the two of you were caught . . . uh, canoodling." Clayton tried to look serious, but he couldn't quite stop chuckling.

"*Canoodling?*" Mark shook his head.

Rudy said, "High time."

Mark gripped Rudy's shoulders. "What did you hear?"

"In her room," Rudy added.

"I . . . I helped her carry a chair," Mark sputtered. "We didn't—"

"With the door closed." Clayton raised his eyebrows and grinned.

"The door swung shut by itself," Mark protested.

"Late at night," Rudy said.

"It wasn't even dark yet. We hadn't—"

"You were in there with the door locked for hours," Clayton said.

"Hours!" Mark realized he was yelling and dropped his voice to a whisper. "We weren't in there for *hours*. More like two minutes. Who said—?"

"Now, Mark," Clayton said, dismissing Mark's anger with a wave of his hand, "nobody believes Hannah would have a man in her room. Even the gossips who are embellishing the story know it can't be true. It's just so fun."

"Fun?" Mark felt his stupid head start to heat up with a blush. It was like a curse!

"We've been waiting for her to show up, to see if she'd come and throw her arms around you for all the world to see," Rudy said with a laugh.

"She didn't," Clayton pointed out. "As a matter of fact, she seems to be avoiding you. That's going to be a problem."

"A problem? What . . . how . . . why is that a problem?" Mark was still trying to believe what he'd just learned.

"It's a problem because it'll be hard being married to a woman who won't come near you," Rudy said.

"Married!" Mark felt a thrill of joy race through his body, heavily spiced with panic.

"C'mon, you've been in love with her for years. She needs

a husband. It makes perfect sense." Rudy said it so confidently that it made Mark's stomach twist. He'd never told anyone how he felt about Hannah. Well, his father and mother knew, but how did Rudy know?

"But she doesn't . . . I can't . . ." Mark didn't know what to say. All he could think about was Hannah's reaction to kissing him. She'd been disgusted. It would kill him to see her look at him that way for the rest of her life. Still, Mark knew how it worked. Rudy and Clayton were right. Hannah's reputation would be in shreds by day's end if they didn't announce an engagement. Her job would most certainly be taken away. Even if they got the school board to see the story had been blown way out of proportion, they could never allow her to teach again in their town.

A hard hand clamped on his shoulder and wheeled him around.

Hannah's father.

It was too bad Mark's instinctive reaction to Hannah's presence hadn't warned him about Jerome Taylor.

Jerome jabbed one of his fat fingers right in Mark's face. "There'll be a wedding this very day, Whitfield."

Mark shook his head, again trying to clear it. He saw Hannah look up from her little circle of women friends. She had the same frantic expression he must have had on his face. She was learning the same gossip he was. Their gazes locked for a split second before Hannah looked away.

Mark turned back to Jerome Taylor. "Mr. Taylor, sir, nothing inappropriate happened between Hannah and me." Well, a little inappropriate maybe. "She bought some furniture. I helped her carry it home. The door to her room swung shut. That is all—"

"Shut your mouth, boy!" Jerome was a full head shorter than Mark, but his belligerent attitude didn't give an inch.

He'd said it so loudly that Mark glanced up. They were still alone, though more parishioners would begin arriving soon.

"Now, Jerry, Mark didn't do anything to deserve . . ." Rudy began in a conciliatory tone to his father-in-law.

Jerome wheeled around to face Rudy with a glare so hostile that Rudy, who was a stagecoach driver and a mighty tough man, backed up a step and fell silent.

Turning back, Jerome jammed his finger so close to Mark's face he almost poked him in the nose. "I know nothin' happened because I know my girl. She's a decent woman. All I want to hear about is when you're plannin' to have the wedding. If I thought anything like what you're talking about happened, I'd be coming for you with a shotgun! The fact is you were in that room alone with my Hannie, the door shut and locked, and now you'll do right by her or . . . or . . ." Hannah's pa stumbled over his threats, but he didn't need to go on. Mark was getting the message loud and clear.

"Mr. Taylor, please. Of course I'll do right by Hannah, but nothing happened and . . ." Mark glanced around again. Rudy and Clayton were listening with rapt attention, big grins on their faces.

Mark took Jerome's arm and pulled him aside. Jerome Taylor had been banking at Whitfield Bank for years. Mark knew him well and considered him a friendly acquaintance, if not a friend. Mark had always thought Jerome Taylor was a self-centered old coot. His treatment of Hannah was insensitive and at times outright cruel. His desire for male children had brought about his late wife's untimely death as far as Mark was concerned, and now his next wife was continuing the tradition. Standing there being lectured by the ornery old codger didn't sit well at all.

Mark's voice dropped to a whisper. "Mr. Taylor, it's not a question of me wanting to marry her, sir. I have admired Hannah for some time now. But she doesn't share my feelings. And I don't want to be responsible for forcing her into a marriage she doesn't want."

Because he was off-center from leaning down to whisper to Mr. Taylor, Mark was knocked sideways a few steps by a blow to his shoulder. He turned to see that Hannah had been pushed up beside him. Mark swallowed hard when he saw who had a firm grip on her arm.

His father had joined the fray.

"There'll be a wedding after church today." Loyal Whitfield was given to making pronouncements during the best of times, which this wasn't. He looked from his son to Hannah's pa, and the two of them nodded in satisfaction.

"Agreed," Mr. Taylor said.

"Parson, there you are," Mark's father said. "Mark and Hannah are getting married. Today. We'd like you to perform the ceremony."

The pastor's gentle smile spread wide. "This is wonderful news, and it comes as no surprise to any of us."

"Some of us are a little surprised," Hannah mumbled.

"I'll be ready to officiate the ceremony immediately following church. Right now it's time for services, folks. Let's all go on in."

Mark looked around and saw the whole congregation had arrived while he'd been having his little meeting.

Mother came up at that moment and said, "Welcome

to the family, Hannah." Mark looked at his mother and thought she looked far too cheerful for a woman whose son was involved in a scandal.

Mark had a notion to ask her why she was taking this so well, but before he could do so, he was pulled one way by his father while Hannah was pulled another way by hers.

There would be no moment alone. There would be no quiet talk between Mark and Hannah. Mother was poking him in the back, forcing him to move. He hoped Hannah didn't adopt that habit.

"Hannah!" Mark cried.

She turned back as she was towed along.

"I'm sorry," he said, "but I guess there's no other way."

"We're stuck with it." She threw her arm—the one not in her father's grip—wide as he dragged her toward the church.

As far as proposals went, it left a lot to be desired.

✶ Chapter 9 ✶

Hannah watched in amazement as her wedding turned into a celebration. She suspected everything to do with the Whitfields was done on a grand scale. Tables were dragged outside of homes and carted over to the church to line the walls.

With the slightest of nudges from Prudence Whitfield, every woman in town went home and brought her Sunday dinner to the church. Hannah saw roasts and hams suddenly appear on the tables. She saw a mountain of fried chicken and bowl after bowl of vegetables and salads. There were several tables of cakes and pies. Coffee boiled happily on the church's heating stove, sending out its enticing aroma.

Adding to the party were Christmas treats. Everything that could be called a Christmas decoration or Christmas candy was purchased by the Whitfields from Claasen's General Store. The ladies hung up the decorations, and the children were lavished with candy, which made the day into a festival.

Someone even rode into the woods near town and cut down a Christmas tree. Greenery decorated the church inside and out and draped the borrowed tables.

The weather could be moody during a north-Texas winter, but it picked today to be lovely, as if the Whitfields could even command that.

After the couple had spoken their vows, Pastor Eldridge said, "You may kiss the bride."

Marcus leaned forward and clumsily bumped his lips against the corner of Hannah's mouth. He smelled nice, and for a second Hannah remembered that she'd enjoyed kissing him. Marcus pulled back instantly. The whole town applauded. Hannah noticed Rosella Bindle, Essie, and Mrs. Claasen clapping hardest of all while they whispered together.

She thought she saw a bit of a smug smile on Grace's face, and Hannah was reminded of her own meddling and Grace's whispered remark, "*I know you'll have your own happy event soon.*"

It was now more than clear that all the outrageous accusations had been part of a scheme to force this marriage. Hannah liked to think she'd been much more subtle in her meddling than any of these ladies.

Hannah and Marcus walked down the aisle after the applause died, and before they had a second of privacy, Prudence Whitfield took Hannah under her wing. Essie fussed over her as if she were the mother of the bride. Then all the church ladies bustled about serving food.

The whole town stayed, spilling out onto the churchyard and stretching the party into the evening. As dusk settled, lanterns came out, several fiddles and banjos were produced, and lively renditions of every Christmas carol Hannah had ever heard lilted on the early-evening air and raised everyone's spirits. A bonfire was built up as the setting sun lost its power to warm the crowd.

First planned for all of one hour, Hannah's wedding had turned into the biggest thing to ever happen in Dry Gulch, Texas.

Hannah went through it in a daze, unable to grasp all that had transpired in the course of a single day. She had to listen to Mack Danvers, just back in town from a visit with his grandson, brag up a storm about little Harrison toddling around and how he loved the pup his grandpa had brought him. Hannah found it a relief to listen to Mack's bragging about Neill and Clara having their own ranch now. It took her mind off the astonishing fact that she'd gotten married today.

She managed a fairly rational visit with Grace, who was excited about a book to help her read by touch, called a Monsieur Braille alphabet.

Dottie Brighton spent a few moments talking about a letter she'd received from Lucy and Andrew Simms. They lived in North Fork now. Andrew's business of selling and installing windmills was flourishing, and they had a bright future ahead of them. And Andrew's aunt Martha was on a world tour. Dottie even had postcards from Paris that Lucy had sent along with her last letter.

Hannah wasn't really in Marcus's company until Clayton appeared with the Whitfields' fine black buggy. Hannah and Marcus were unceremoniously tossed into it.

Clayton drove them home, all of three blocks. Hannah and Marcus sat silently side by side. Hannah was careful not to make eye contact with him for fear of what she'd see. Instead she kept her eyes firmly fixed out the window.

They came to a halt and Clayton climbed down, tilting the buggy. He opened the door and reached his hand out to Hannah. She had no choice but to let him help her alight.

She noticed she was at Marcus's house. She hadn't even considered where they were going, but of course they were going here. She knew he had his own home. She would need to abandon the room she'd spent yesterday making pretty. Her head started spinning—as it had a hundred times this day—to think of how drastically her life had been changed in twenty-four hours. In fact, it was probably almost exactly twenty-four hours since Marcus had set the chair down and pulled her into his arms. She heard the creaking of the buggy as Marcus climbed down behind her, and she took a few steps forward to make room for him. Then she heard Clayton call a cheery good-bye over the hoofbeats of the departing horses.

Marcus stood silently beside her. She was only distantly aware of the fact that he was staring at the house as intently as she was. Floating through the darkness came the beautiful refrain of "Silent Night," accompanied by the voices of the faithful of Dry Gulch.

"Well . . ." She didn't recognize her own voice. She cleared her throat and tried again. "Shall we go inside, Marcus?"

"It's Mark," he said quietly.

"What?" She turned slightly to look at him but without committing herself to facing him head-on.

"Mark. Everybody calls me Mark." The last few words faded until they were barely audible.

"They do?" Hannah thought it was funny that she'd never heard him called that. But then she thought about it and couldn't really remember his name ever coming up. Back in their school days he'd been called Marcus, she was sure of it.

He nodded silently.

"Well then, *Mark* it is." Hannah didn't know why she

was surprised that she didn't even know this much about her new husband. Husband! The very idea threatened to send her back into her daze, but she forced herself to head for the house.

She heard Marcus—Mark—trailing along behind her.

There was light gleaming out of every window of the wide house made of boards rather than log and stone like most of the buildings in town. Someone had come ahead of them to light the lanterns and make their homecoming more welcoming. She got to the front door and reached for the knob. It was locked. Marcus produced a key and opened it. She stepped inside.

It was beautiful.

The hallway was painted in a light shade of yellow, the exact shade of her favorite bonnet.

"There are two bedrooms on the left." Marcus cleared his throat as he pointed awkwardly. "On the right is a parlor." An open door on her right revealed finely made furniture and upholstered couches. There were rich, heavy drapes adorning the windows.

"Down this hallway," he continued, "the kitchen's on the right, with another bedroom on the left." She saw that the hallway stretched all the way to the back of the house. Hannah didn't know what to say. It was already more house than she'd ever seen.

She felt a hand rest on the small of her back.

"I hope you like it, Hannah. I know it needs a woman's touch. You can change anything you don't like."

She turned to face him at last. His concern for her happiness pierced the strange foggy world she'd been dwelling in all day. "Marcus . . ."

"Mark," he said.

She must have quirked her lips a little in a half smile, because she saw his eyes flicker to her lips and linger there a moment.

"Mark, I haven't seen it all yet of course, but it's *beautiful*. I don't think I'll want to change a thing."

Then, with no warning, much like yesterday, he kissed her. And just like yesterday, Hannah liked it.

✶ Chapter 10 ✶

He thought he might keel over from pure happiness.

Thinking of falling over in a heap made him think of the upholstered sofa in the parlor. He lifted Hannah clean off her feet and carried her in there. He lowered himself onto the sofa and pulled Hannah right along with him until he cradled her on his lap.

When they sat down, Hannah pulled back a little as if she was noticing where she was for the first time. He didn't think that was a good idea, because if she had a chance to think clearly she might never want to kiss him again, so he slid one hand into her hair and tilted her head back a little further until she was nearly lying across his lap, and he rushed back into his dreams that were coming true.

He lifted his head and stared into her beautiful blue eyes. He saw himself reflected in her pupils and wondered what she could possibly be thinking about.

Then Hannah said, "My furniture! I just bought all that new furniture!"

Mark said, "I have furniture."

Hannah pulled away just a bit. She looked at him with

her eyes wide as if he'd spoken words of great wisdom. "You do, don't you?"

He nodded.

Hannah said, "Let's bring my furniture here."

Mark almost laughed out loud to think Hannah wanted to bring her things over. That sounded like she intended to stay. He grinned at her, and she rested both of her hands on his face and kissed him with such aching sweetness that some of the words Mark wanted to say were jarred loose.

"You're beautiful."

She withdrew only slightly. "Oh, Marcus, thank you."

"I love you, Hannah. I . . . I didn't just decide because of the way we had to get married. I've admired you for a while—quite a while. A long, long, long while. But I . . . I didn't . . ."

"It's my fault, Marcus."

"Call me Mark," he reminded her. "Everybody does."

"Okay."

"It's not your fault," he said firmly. "Nothing's your fault. You're perfect."

She smiled sadly. "It is my fault that there's never been anything between us. I've spent so much time moping. I don't know if it was Ma dying or Pa marrying Essie. Or maybe watching my little sisters get married before me."

"Or Charlie," he said quietly.

Hannah nodded. "I just haven't been able to think about anything else. It's been so selfish, the way I've been wrapped up in myself for so long."

"You've been through a lot. You needed time."

"Six years?" Hannah asked incredulously.

"Apparently."

She smiled at him. "You're sweet."

Mark knew he was going to blush. He had a lot of things about himself that he didn't like but none so much as the baneful red that washed over his cheeks when he was embarrassed. And having Hannah give him a compliment was too much. He dropped his chin down, wishing that she wouldn't notice.

"You're blushing because I said you're sweet?" She lifted his chin and ran a finger over one cheek, then the other, taking her time, studying him.

He shrugged and prayed for the heat to leave his head before his hair caught fire.

"I like it, Marcus . . . Mark. I'm going to try and make you blush five times a day."

And that set his blushing off again, and he laughed just a little bit, something he'd never been able to do about his blushing in his life.

She kissed his face as if she were savoring the red, and Mark began to think of his wretched fair skin as something private and special between the two of them and that helped him to talk again. He thought he ought to confess the worst news he had for her first. "I'm not good at talking, Hannah, especially to someone as pretty as you. I don't mean to be difficult. Your life with me . . . well, I'll try and get better. I know you don't want a man who won't tell you what's in his heart."

He waited for her to nod and say, *Yes, I remember now what you're really like,* and then climb off his lap.

Instead she said, "You told me you loved me." She caressed his burning face again as his cheeks reddened with his confession of what an awkward fool he could be.

He said fiercely, "I do love you."

"Maybe a man can say what needs saying without it taking a lot of words."

"I'll try and say what's important, Hannah. I'll try to never go a day without letting you know I'm the luckiest man on earth."

He saw tears well up in Hannah's eyes and immediately began apologizing. "I didn't mean to hurt your feelings. If you—"

She wrapped her arms around his neck until he could hardly breathe, and he heard her first cry. It was a sob that tore out of her throat from so deep it shook her whole body.

"Hannah honey, what did I say? I'm sorry. I wouldn't hurt you for the—"

She pulled away from him so suddenly that he thought she was getting out of his lap, and he thought he might cry, too, as he braced himself for her to walk away.

"That is the nicest thing anyone has ever said to me, Mark Whitfield! Quit apologizing for it. Sometimes . . ." Her voice broke, but she steadied herself. "Sometimes a woman cries because she's happy. Did you know that?"

Mark shook his head helplessly. He said weakly, "I don't know anything about women. I'm not sure I know anything about anything."

Hannah smiled at him, then suddenly she was laughing. She threw her arms around his neck again and laughed so lightheartedly that Mark couldn't help but laugh himself.

✶ Chapter 11 ✶

But sitting there in Mark's lap seemed too idle for all that she had to do. Such as plan her whole life. She jumped up, and the reluctant way Mark looked when she stood made her heart warm toward him even more than the kiss had. When she realized how radically different her feelings were right now than they had been before he kissed her last night, she had her first bout of uncertainty.

What was true? A lifetime of not having any romantic notions about Mark or a day of being completely in love. Because, to be honest, she had to admit she'd been in love with him ever since he'd kissed her last night.

She said hesitantly, "There are things we should talk about."

Apprehension flooded across his face. "Okay."

She couldn't stop herself from smiling. There was something infinitely appealing about a man adoring you. And she wanted to climb straight back onto his lap and start kissing him again, but things needed to be said. "The thing is, Mark, up until last night I have always been under the impression that you didn't like me very much."

Mark gasped, "What?" and then he stood.

"Now, don't be upset, but I think we should clear the air, don't you?"

"Hannah, I have been trying to get you to notice me for, well, forever."

"But you never talked to me," Hannah protested. "You didn't even look at me. In fact, I thought you didn't like me, other than in a friendly way, because I would swear that you've been deliberately avoiding me for years."

"No I haven't," he insisted.

"I decided at Nelda's wedding that since we were the only two single people in town, at least the only two church-going single people in town, that we would be a likely match."

"At your sister's wedding? That was a long time ago."

"Yes. I mean, I wasn't exactly sure we were . . ." Hannah wondered if she should have started this. She would never admit to Mark that she had dreaded the idea of being stuck with him. Right now, looking at his entrancing blue eyes and his disheveled dark blond hair, all she saw was a man who was sweet and smart, and she couldn't remember what she'd found fault with. She couldn't think of anything about him she didn't like.

She was suddenly frightened of her emotions, not knowing whether to trust her old feelings or her new ones. And underlying her fear was such a strong desire to be married that her longing for that might make any man seem appealing. In short, was she in love or was she just desperate?

Hannah was practical enough to know it didn't matter. They were married and they'd strive to have a good life together. But she wanted everything started off on a good footing. She turned away from him and sat down in another chair. She looked up at Mark and said, "Sit down."

"You're coming to your senses, aren't you?" he said forlornly.

Hannah couldn't stop herself from smiling. "Please, sit."

"It's too late," he said firmly. "We're married, and I'm never letting you go."

Hannah smiled again. "If it helps any, I have no intention of coming to my senses."

That must have struck him as funny because he grinned.

She added, "However, I think if I did come to my senses, I'd still want to be married to you. How do you like that?"

He shoved a chair around so it faced her, then took his seat. "I like that fine."

"Now, you say you've liked me all along."

"I've loved you, not liked you. There's a difference and I don't want you to forget it."

"Well, in all honesty, I haven't loved you." She glanced at Mark and saw him flinch at her bluntness. "The idea of us being together had occurred to me because of the logic of it, but I wasn't harboring feelings for you until now. And now those feelings are so strong that they almost frighten me."

He looked crestfallen when she said she'd only begun to care for him this instant, but he was no less determined. "I think that's because you've been having such a hard time. You just haven't had room in your heart for a man."

Hannah nodded. "I have always liked you. I've always known you were an honorable, hardworking, kind man. Marriages have been built on less, I think."

He scooted his chair closer and grasped her hands in his. Their knees bumped together, and when Mark leaned forward they were almost nose to nose. He said, "I want the woman who has been prepared for me by God. I have believed for a long time that you were that woman. That doesn't mean we won't ever have hard times. I'm a quiet man. Like I told you, I struggle with . . . with my . . ."

Hannah slipped one of her hands free from his and ran her finger lightly over his face. He was blushing again.

He forced himself to go on. "I'm no good with words. I'll never be a poet. I'll never speak flowery words to you. I . . . I don't want you to be disgusted with me. You deserve the very best."

Hannah traced her finger over his cheek as she listened to this kind, shy man speak so eloquently from his heart. "That's flowery talk, Mark."

"It is?" he asked hopefully.

"Yes." Tears bit at her eyes, and she knew that Mark noticed them immediately because he began shaking his head in regret for them. She realized how sensitive he was to her feelings and thought that sounded like a wonderful trait in a husband. "What you said was beautiful. Just because the words come hard, it doesn't mean you won't say them."

"I'll try, Hannah. I promise I'll try."

"And, Mark?"

"What?" He was looking so deeply into her eyes that he seemed mesmerized.

"This love for you that has blossomed in my heart—it's wonderful. It seems like . . . like . . ." She smiled, feeling self-conscious all of a sudden. In truth, she wondered if she might not be blushing herself. "Now *I'm* trying to be a poet."

"I'll listen to anything you want to tell me."

"What I want you to know is, my affection for you is like frosting on a cake."

"Well, that's poetic, I suppose," he said rather dryly.

Hannah relaxed when Mark made that tiny stab at a joke. She realized then that he had a sense of humor, and that was something she wanted in her life. It made it easier for her to keep talking. "What I mean is, the cake was already there. I've thought of you as a man I admire and like. So, adding the frosting—romantic feelings, I mean—to my respect for you is easy. It seems right. If I had gone from thinking you were a low-down skunk . . ."

He chuckled softly.

". . . to loving you . . . well, I would be worried about that. I've watched my sisters marry men who wouldn't be my choice but who are perfect for them. When I was young I believed there was a man like that for me, too. But I had given up in recent years. And now here you are. Here you have always been. I feel like God has performed a miracle in my heart. He has opened my eyes to see what was right in front of me. And maybe I needed to go through all I have in the last few years in order to appreciate what a special man you are and how lucky I am to have you care for me."

He leaned forward and kissed her very gently.

"Can I say one more thing?" she asked breathlessly.

"You can say anything," he said, moving their hands until he cradled both of hers in his and held them like they were precious gifts.

"It's . . . it's hard to be Leah."

Mark shook his head. "Leah?"

"Leah, from the Bible. Remember how Jacob wanted to marry Rachel and he worked seven years to earn the right?"

"Yes, Leah was Rachel's older sister. But I've never thought of her story as being an important one. It was how much Jacob loved Rachel that was important."

"Well, Leah is important to me. Pa teased me after both my sisters got married that he should have put me in a heavy veil and passed me off as the bride because the oldest should be married first."

"Don't take this the wrong way, Hannah, but I don't think I like your pa very much."

She nodded, then shrugged and went on. "Anyway, when people think about Jacob, they think about Jacob and Rachel, and they think *poor Jacob*—tricked into marrying the older sister. His love was so strong he agreed to stay and work another seven years to earn Rachel. But what about Leah? No one thinks about how humiliated she must have been to have been married in such a fashion. Ugly and undesired, unmarriageable except through her father's lies."

"Hannah," he whispered fiercely, "you are not ugly and undesired. I won't let you say such things about the woman I love."

"Thank you, Mark. I didn't mean I was ugly, although sometimes it's hard not to feel that way. I just want to say that I think I know how it was for Leah. It's so hard to be that older sister. I had to keep smiling, and I truly was happy for my little sisters. But it hurt.

"I think underneath all my grief for Ma and Charlie, and the pain of losing my brothers to Essie, was the notion that there was something wrong with me. That made it hard for me to believe any man would want me. And it made it easy for me to mistake your shyness for dislike. Having you want me for your wife heals so many old hurts.

For that alone, even without your decent nature and your kisses . . ."

"The cake and the frosting?"

She smiled. "Yes, the cake and the frosting. Even without them, I'll always think of you as my knight in shining armor. You have saved me in so many ways. I love you and I consider it the highest honor to be your wife."

Mark stood up, pulling her with him, and kissed her until her head felt as if it were spinning. Then he said gruffly, "Let me give you a tour of the house."

"I'd like that."

As they left the room, Hannah thought of her ma dying with her seventh child. "Mark, do we have to have seven children?"

He staggered slightly and bumped his shoulder against the doorframe. "Seven children?" he repeated weakly.

"I don't think I want to have that many."

"Hannah, I'm an only child. Seven children, that's inconceivable to me. No, we most assuredly do not have to have that many children."

"What if the first six are girls? Won't you want to keep trying until we have a son?" she persisted.

"I like girls." Mark turned to her and drew her close. "I'd like a couple of little girls who look like you. Two children, regardless of whether they're girls or boys, sounds fine to me."

"Men want boys, Mark," she said matter-of-factly.

"Maybe ranchers want boys, to help them or to leave the holding to, but I'm a banker. I'm not going to mind if I don't have someone to take over when I retire. I'll just sell the bank to someone. Besides, the girls will probably get married, and their husbands can have the bank."

Hannah nodded with a serious expression on her face as he talked. She felt one last weight lifting off her shoulders and realized in a sense that Mark was rescuing her again. "Good, because it was real hard on my ma."

"We are *not* having that many children!"

"Well, I wouldn't mind four," Hannah suggested. The thought of two didn't seem quite right to her.

He grinned. "How about we have two and then decide about more, one at a time?"

"That sounds perfect."

He lifted himself away from the doorframe as if his knees were trustworthy again. "Now that that's settled, let me show you the house."

Mark started leading her to the left side of the house. Earlier he'd said there was nothing to the left except bedrooms.

But she was sure they were beautiful, so she went along.

Her thoughts still lingered on Leah, with her constant quest for Jacob's love, with her gift of one son after another, all to no avail. And Hannah, for the first time, took another view of that ancient Bible story.

Perhaps Leah wasn't as unwanted as it seemed. After all, she did have six sons and a daughter. Surely that meant Jacob paid her some attention. And her sons stood equal with Rachel's as patriarchs of the twelve tribes of Israel. God had named a child of Leah's line, Levi, to be the father of a tribe of priests. Leah's son Reuben saved Joseph's life. Judah's line was the one King David came from, as well as Solomon and Joseph, Jesus' earthly father. So it turned out that Leah had been a very significant member of a great nation—a nation that survived to this day. A nation that provided the world with a Savior.

Hannah decided she wasn't going to feel sorry for Leah anymore—or herself. She decided all of this as Mark took her on his tour, which proved to be very short.

Mark's room.

And she had no idea if it was pretty because they never got around to lighting a lantern. She and Mark discovered yet another part of love through the long winter night.

And Hannah—the quiet, lonely Texas meddler with a gift for helping other lonely people—knew she'd finally met her match.

Two-time RITA Award finalist and winner of the HOLT Medallion and Carol Award, bestselling author **Karen Witemeyer** writes historical romance to provide the world with more happily-ever-afters. She is an avid cross-stitcher and shower singer, and she bakes a mean apple cobbler. Karen makes her home in Abilene, Texas, with her husband and three children. Learn more at www.KarenWitemeyer.com.

Regina Jennings is a graduate of Oklahoma Baptist University with a degree in English and minor in history. She has worked at the *Mustang News* and the First Baptist Church of Mustang, along with time at the Oklahoma National Stockyards and various livestock shows. She lives outside of Oklahoma City with her husband and four children and can be found online at www.ReginaJennings.com.

Carol Cox is the author of over 30 novels and novellas. A third-generation Arizonan, she has held a lifelong fascination with the Old West and hopes to make it live again in the hearts of her readers. She makes her home with her husband and daughter in northern Arizona, where the deer and the antelope really do play—often within view of the family's front porch. Learn more at www.AuthorCarolCox.com.

Mary Connealy writes romantic comedy with cowboys. She is a Carol Award winner, and a RITA, Christy, and Inspirational Reader's Choice finalist. She is the author of *Swept Away* and *Fired Up*, books 1 and 2 in the TROUBLE IN TEXAS series, as well as the KINCAID BRIDE series, LASSOED IN TEXAS trilogy, MONTANA MARRIAGES trilogy, and SOPHIE'S DAUGHTERS trilogy. She is married to a Nebraska rancher and has four grown daughters, two sons-in-law, and two spectacular grandchildren. Get more details at www .MaryConnealy.com.

More Western Romance From Bethany House!

⬧ BETHANYHOUSE

More Western Romance from Bethany House!

BETHANYHOUSE

 Stay up-to-date on your favorite books and authors with our *free* e-newsletters. Sign up today at bethanyhouse.com.

 Find us on Facebook. facebook.com/bethanyhousepublishers

 Free exclusive resources for your book group! bethanyhouse.com/anopenbook

anopenbook